Thunder in the 🗹 S0-AFR-441
Passions
on the Ground...

SAM HOLT. The blue-eyed son of a Michigan auto worker, he was the only Top Gun who hadn't come out of the Air Force Academy—and every day he had to prove that he belonged.

x x x

JACK STANG. A blond, blue-eyed former football quarterback, he was the epitome of the Air Force Academy graduate. And with his scheming, knockout wife, he would do anything to destroy Sam Holt.

x x x

BECKY MERRILL. Her childhood in rural Arkansas had not prepared her for being an Air Force wife. While her husband was trying to climb to the top, she was slipping fast—into a danger zone of alcohol and drugs.

x x x

MEGAN ROBERTS. Only her flaming red hair gave a clue to the fire that burned her heart. A painful childhood had left her unwilling to trust—until a handsome test pilot named Sam Holt touched her for the first time.

x x x

"Enthralling!...Should appeal to anyone who appreciates quality reading."
—Rave Reviews on *Beginnings*

Also by Eileen Nauman

BEGINNINGS

Published by
POPULAR LIBRARY

Eileen Nauman

NIGHT FLIGHT

POPULAR LIBRARY

An Imprint of Warner Books, Inc.

A Warner Communications Company

POPULAR LIBRARY EDITION

Popular Library ® and the fanciful P design are registered trademarks
of Warner Books, Inc.

Cover art by Franco Acconero
Cover design by Anne Twomey

Popular Library books are published by
Warner Books, Inc.
666 Fifth Avenue
New York, N.Y. 10103

 A Warner Communications Company

Printed in the United States of America

First Printing: June, 1990

10 9 8 7 6 5 4 3 2 1

DEDICATION:

To the wives and children of military families everywhere, whose silent contribution is never mentioned, much less given ribbons or medals for sacrifice and grit—but certainly deserve them.

and

Doug Benefield, Air Force and civilian test pilot, deceased. A wonderful friend whom I think of often. You gave the ultimate sacrifice.

NIGHT FLIGHT

— 1 —

WHERE the hell was Captain Curt Merrill? Sam Holt stood there, anxiously searching the gathering crowd of thousands who anticipated the start of the balloon rally shortly. Twisting a look across his shoulder, Sam watched his seasoned crew preparing his rainbow-colored balloon for flight. If Curt didn't show up, he'd have to forfeit the race.

That was something he didn't want to do. Restlessly, his gaze moved across the bone-colored Mojave Desert that surrounded the small town of Lancaster, California. Thirty miles away was Edwards Air Force Base, his home. His life. Throwing his hands on his hips in a typical Air Force pilot gesture, Sam wondered if his friend of five years was having family problems—again, and if that was why he was running late.

The restive crowd reminded Sam of bright-hued birds. The rally was to raise money for an orphanage down in Los Angeles, but Sam ruefully admitted he'd fly on *any* excuse and in *anything* just to fly—whether it had wings or not. When he wasn't testing the latest in combat jets, he was drifting through the sky in his balloon. Coming back to earth was always a downer. Lifting his chin, he gazed up at the dawn sky, the sun having just edged over the horizon, sending a pale pink wash of color across the desert.

Nostrils flaring, he automatically picked up the dryness of the desert, the smell of propane used to power the balloons, and a hint of flowery perfume worn by someone in the crowd. Where was Curt? Looking at his watch, he searched for him with narrowed intensity. Perhaps Becky Merrill was feeling under the weather again was all he could surmise. Or maybe it was Curt's six-year-old daughter, Patty, who had fallen suddenly sick?

There were only five minutes left until the gun would sound to start the race. Sam *had* to have the mandatory passenger on board. He wasn't about to forfeit the race. No way. Swiveling to the left, Sam saw his target. Surrounding him were twenty hot air balloons being readied for flight. The constant, sporadic blasts of propane-fed flames shooting heat into the behemoths continued to shatter the silence.

All his focus centered on the red-haired woman with a camera in hand, as she moved unobtrusively among the crowd of nearly five thousand spectators who had come to view the race. A grin curved the corners of his mouth as he surveyed her. Behind him, his crew chief called to him, telling him they were ready for him to board. Sam lifted his hand in acknowledgement. First, he had to capture his unsuspecting passenger. He was going to abduct her, and take her skyward with him.

The thought was provocative, and Holt savored the idea. It was crazy, but, why not? Over at Edwards the pilots and enlisted crew chiefs had always accused him of being just that. Damn, but she was young and pretty. And alone. No man around her, no children in evidence, and no ring on her left hand. *Oustanding*.

"Hey, Clark," he called to the *Los Angeles Times* photographer who was there to record the race for the annual charity event, "you want something different for your paper on this race? A new angle?" No newspaper reporter or photographer could resist words like *new* and *different*.

Clark's eyes gleamed. He had three cameras hanging

around his neck. He grabbed a Yashica 35 mm, getting it ready. "Yeah."

"Follow me and stand by for action," and Holt spun on his heel, aiming himself through the crowd of onlookers.

This was working out just fine, he thought with a grin, and zeroed in on his red-haired target. She was slender, wearing an apricot sweater, a white silk scarf, and white slacks. *Couldn't be more than twenty-five.* As he drew closer, Sam liked the coverlet of freckles across her porcelain skin and flushed cheeks. It was her large, vivid green eyes that made his heart begin a hard, unrelenting beat. Her nose was thin, finely sculpted, but it was her parted lips, sensual and full, that made his pulse jag erratically.

Holt laughed at himself. Suddenly, he was nervous. Him! At twenty-nine, he knew how to get a lady's attention. But abduction of a stranger was going to be a little more tricky. He'd always been creative about chasing and capturing the woman he wanted. Her long, unruly red hair tumbled across her small shoulders, silky strands curved into thick crescents against her sweater. The bangs across her smooth, unmarred brow emphasized her thickly lashed eyes. *Part girl, part woman.* The freckles gave her a decided air of a young adventuress just waiting for the next quest to begin so she could take part in it.

Looking across his shoulder, he called to Clark. "Ready?"

Almost running to keep up, the photographer held on to his cameras, trying to keep them from bumping into one another. "Yeah. Hey, what are you up to now, Holt?"

Laughing, he said, "See that red-haired lady standing over there?"

"Yeah?"

"I'm going to sweep her off her feet and take her up in my balloon. My partner never arrived, and I'm not forfeiting the race. She'll be my teammate."

"But—do you know her?" he asked, digging frantically in his shirt pocket for a notebook and pen.

"No, but I will shortly. Stand by, you might get some great shots." *Of me getting decked*, Sam thought wryly, if she didn't have a sense of humor and go along with his abduction plans. The delicious curve of her lips, the shining excitement in her eyes told him instinctively that she *would* go along with his impromptu plan. His mind whirled with explanations that he could give to persuade her to go along with his crazy idea. Otherwise, she might take a swing at him, or try to squirm out of his arms as he carried her back to the gondola. Red-haired women could turn into screaming, shrieking harpies upon occasion. That was part of their allure, their unpredictability. They reminded him of the jets he flew to the edge of their flight envelopes, while testing their strengths and weaknesses, never knowing their unpredictability until pushed too far.

Megan Roberts sensed excitement, lifted her chin, and looked to the left. She saw a man, perhaps in his early thirties, dressed in a worn leather bombardier jacket, light-blue shirt with the collar open, and jeans, striding directly toward her. His dark-blue eyes were intent upon her, and her heart leaped unexpectedly. On his heels was a photographer, running to keep up with him. What was going on?

Vivid impressions struck Megan as he closed the distance between them. He had black hair, military short, a square face, straight nose; and his mouth was pulled into a careless smile of devilry. She looked back into his eyes, and she saw a mixture of amusement and interest. His stride was long and relaxed, his head up, his shoulders thrown back with pride. A tremor of expectation rushed through her. Only she seemed to be aware that Something was about to happen. The other people stood watching the balloons that looked like colorful Easter eggs on the ivory desert. She had come to take photos of them for her second grade class.

Megan took a step back as the man approached, watching the photographer anchor himself, raising the camera, getting ready to take pictures. The man gave her a wink, stepped up to her, slid his arms beneath her legs and back, and lifted her off the ground.

"Hey!" Megan gasped. She inhaled his clean, subtle masculine scent. "What are you doing?"

"The name's Sam Holt, Red. Now, don't struggle." He turned toward Clark, smiling triumphantly for the camera.

Flashbulbs popped in rapid succession. Her arms had automatically gone around his shoulders. At least she couldn't take a punch at him that way. "Hang on, I'm abducting you to my gondola." He grinned at her, thinking how beautiful her large green eyes were at close range. There were flecks of gold in them.

"I—what?" Megan started to struggle. "Put me down!"

"Now, take it easy, Red. You don't want to embarrass us, do you? That guy's from the *Los Angeles Times.* This is great news: BALLOONIST KIDNAPS DAMSEL AND TAKES HER TO HIS CASTLE IN THE CLOUDS" He grinned. "Great headlines, huh?" She was feather light, but warm and soft against him.

"Well—" Megan ceased struggling, feeling heat rush to her face. The photographer kept shooting film of them as he carried her. "Balloon? What are you talking about? Is this some kind of publicity stunt?"

"Sure," Sam lied glibly, approaching the basket. His men had hold of the lines; they were ready to take off. Any moment now, the gun would sound and the race would begin. "This is just a stunt to get the public's attention for the orphanage down in LA," he lied again. "More people will donate money as a result. You don't want those kids to go hungry, now do you?"

Nonplussed, Megan didn't know what to do. She saw the woven basket known as a gondola, coming up. Above them, rising high in the pale dawn sky, was a rainbow-colored balloon above it. "But—I've never been up in a balloon! I'm afraid of heights!" Her voice went off key. "Put me down!"

Laughing, Sam gently placed her in the gondola, leaping into the basket right behind her. "You bet." The gun went off, signaling the start of the race.

"Trail lines free," Holt shouted to the men, his hand on the handle to turn on the propane to create the flame and heat needed to lift the balloon off the desert.

Megan gripped the side of the gondola, feeling the balloon lift off beneath the ear-splitting roar of the propane flame. There was a lurch, and then a gentle forward swing.

Without thinking, because she feared heights, she dropped the camera to the wooden deck, gripping the sides of the gondola. Should she try and jump? People were watching, laughing and waving at her, delight written in their expressions. She braced herself, unaccustomed to the movement of the balloon. With a little cry, Megan tensed, afraid she was going to fall out.

"I want out of here!" Her voice was a mixture of anger and stridency.

Sam gave her a pained look. She had turned waxen, the flush to her cheeks gone. Contrite, he tried to soothe away her anger. "Hey, it's going to be okay. Trust me."

Fear nudged her anger aside. "Trust you? You had no right to do this," Megan stammered, shutting her eyes, and feeling suddenly dizzy.

The instant she swayed, Sam moved to her side. "Come here," he ordered, sliding his arm around her shoulders, bringing her against him. She was shaking. Dammit. He felt like a first-class heel, now. "I'm sorry," he apologized, "but I needed a partner or I had to forfeit this race. It was for charity..." Dividing his attention between Megan and the wind currents, he watched the other balloons maneuvering. The silk of her hair felt good against his jaw, and she smelled spicy and sweet. "Place your feet apart, it will help steady you." All around them, balloons were rising like a group of startled butterflies, moving ponderously, flowing in all directions on the invisible air currents. Beneath them, the crowd broke into a swell of cheers. "Wave to the people below," he told her, hoping to divert her fear. "You'll make their day."

"Can't you get this thing back on the ground?" she whispered, clutching at him, keeping her eyes closed.

"Too late," Sam said apologetically, feeling guilty because she was genuinely afraid. "Look, you aren't going to fall out. I've been flying balloons for almost ten years and never lost a passenger yet. It's fun. Slowly open your eyes."

Hesitantly, Megan pried open her eyes. "Oh, my God..." The ground was falling away, the people becoming mere dots of color on the desert. A light breeze moved around them. She was aware of Holt's strong, steadying body against hers. "I don't believe this . . ."

Laughing gently, Sam studied the other competitors and decided to level off at five hundred feet. Usually, there was a ribbon of air at that elevation. "You're a good sport," he praised her, delighted with her closeness. "Enjoy the view. You're stuck here with me for at least two hours."

Heart pounding in her throat, Megan barely looked down. The people were being left behind, the Joshua trees scattered across the Mojave looked tiny. "H-how high are we?"

Checking the altimeter, Sam said, "Five hundred and ten feet."

Shutting her eyes, Megan took several deep breaths. "This is crazy." And then she opened her eyes, giving him an accusing stare. "You're crazy." The crow's-feet around his eyes deepened as the balloon swung toward the sun rising in the east.

Sam guided her over to one wall of the gondola and instructed her to hold lightly to the railing. Her knuckles turned white immediately. Worried, he retrieved a thermos of coffee, removed the cup, and poured her some, hoping to divert her attention. "Yeah, I've been known to do crazy things every once in a while. Here, this will help steady your nerves."

Gratefully, Megan took the plastic cup between her trembling hands. She had a moment to study him. He'd said his name was Sam Holt. Indeed, he had a sense of humor, laugh lines bracketed his mouth and the corners lifted naturally. The amusement in his cobalt eyes helped lessen her dread to a degree. Lancaster sat thirty miles from Edwards. Was he an Air Force officer? He looked like it. Some of her shock was squelched by the fear of that thought. She wanted nothing to do with military men. Not ever again.

"Better?" Sam asked, keeping one hand on the handle and the other around his mug of coffee.

"I don't know yet."

"What's your name?"

"Megan Roberts."

"Pretty as your red hair."

She studied him, shaking her head. "Whatever led you to do this? I mean, why me?"

He shrugged, grinning. "Your hair stood out like a flaming banner in the crowd. The guy who was supposed to fly with me didn't show up, so I needed a partner in order to qualify for the race. You looked like you courted excitement, so I concocted the whole thing and took advantage of the P.R. angle for the orphanage kids."

Some of the tension drained from Megan, but not much. He couldn't be a pilot. They cared about no one but themselves. This man obviously cared about the orphans, or he wouldn't have brought his balloon to the race, or thought up this harebrained stunt. Judging from his clean, executive lines and trendy clothes, he was probably a local business-man from Lancaster. "That's some creative maneuvering, Mr. Holt."

"Call me Sam." He extended his hand, holding her smiling green eyes. "And thanks for going along with my idea. I was counting on that."

His hand was warm and firm. Megan hesitantly returned his devastating smile. "My friends call me Megan. Do you live in Lancaster?"

Sam nodded, pointing toward the northeast portion of the city. "Over in that area of town. Too high and far away to see it from here, though. Are you from around here, or are you from LA and like balloon rallies?"

Relaxation didn't come. Every time he turned the handle, she jumped, the blast of the flame made the entire gondola shiver. It felt as if the deck were going to fall out from beneath her feet. Megan tried frantically to focus on some-thing more positive, fighting to keep her fear cornered. The flight was beautiful and silent except for the occasional roar of the flame. All around them were other balloons at various elevations.

Sam cocked his head, watching her wrestle with and seemingly control her fear. There was a touch of color back in her cheeks. He repeated his question, understanding her need to focus on controlling her fear. "Are you from LA?"

"No. I'm a school teacher over at Edwards. I teach second graders. And I'm embarrassed to admit it, but this is the first balloon rally I've been to." Her voice was beginning to steady, the wobble gone. Talking helped to keep the fear at bay. "I read about the race Friday night in the newspaper and decided to come over this morning to get some photos for my kids. I know they'll love seeing the photographs of the balloons."

Raising his brows, Sam nodded. What a piece of luck! "So you teach school at the base. How long have you been there?" He knew every single woman on base, or so he thought, at least the ones who frequented the officers club in search of a good time with a handsome pilot like himself.

"Only a month. I arrived in August, rented an apartment in Lancaster, and signed a one-year contract with the base."

"Brand new, then." That's why he hadn't seen her; it was only September 21.

Megan nodded, trying to enjoy the ride—and Sam Holt. "Yes, it's my first job. I'm excited about teaching the children on the base." She managed a small laugh. "I'll have quite a story to tell them Monday morning." The charisma surrounding Sam was impossible to ignore. Discreetly, she noticed he wore no wedding ring. Although she wasn't looking for a man, she was relieved he wasn't married. Probably divorced. Someone as handsome and roguish as Holt couldn't remain single for long.

"You looked like you had a soft heart," Sam teased, "and I was right. Any kids of your own?"

She shook her head. "No."

"Husband?"

Megan smiled. "I'm single, if that's what you want to know."

"My lucky day. So am I."

Giddy from the exuberant way he attacked life, Megan asked, "What are you?"

"A guy who likes adventure, and red-haired women who aren't afraid of a little excitement."

"What else?" she pressed, curious.

Laughing, Sam held up his hand. "Now wait a minute. I abducted you, you didn't abduct me. As the abductor, I should be able to question you at length about yourself without having to answer your questions. Right?"

"You're impossible," Megan parried.

"And you're flexible under some incredible circumstances. How about if I tell you everything you want to know about me just after we cross the finish line? I'd like to win this race." He glanced around, and then grinned. "Right now, we're ahead. So, you tell me about yourself, I'll listen, and then when we're done, I'll take you to lunch. How's that sound?"

How did it sound? Wonderful! Megan nodded. "Okay, Sam, you've got a deal." She had come back to Edwards with trepidation, a lot of fear, and anxiety. That was a month ago, and thus far, she had made few friends or even acquaintances until school recently started.

Rallying beneath Holt's infectious smile, Megan leaned against the wall of the gondola, absorbed the newborn day, and Holt. Her fingers tightened momentarily on the woven basket. Was her plan to come back to Edwards a good one? After receiving her degree, she could have taught anywhere. All Edwards reminded her of was pain, sorrow, and grief. Right now, she didn't want to look at the answers to those questions too closely.

Holt noticed Megan's features growing thoughtful. He had to divide his time between the altimeter, adjusting the heat within the balloon, and reading the wind current speed and direction. Her green eyes were suddenly shadowed; a haunted expression in them. And that luscious lower lip of hers was tucked between her teeth as she stared down at the deck.

"Any regrets?" he asked.

Megan snapped up her head. "What? Oh, I'm sorry. No . . . no regrets, Sam."

"You nose-dived."

With a shrug, Megan whispered, "Just thinking . . ."

He picked up the camera and handed it to her. Maybe if

she had something to do, she wouldn't remain uncomfortable. I'll bet your kids will like the pictures you shoot from here."

Touched by his thoughtfulness, Megan accepted the camera. If she shot some photos, it would continue to keep the fear in some very small corner of herself. "You're right. Thanks."

Enjoying her gracefulness, Sam saw her shoulders drop, indicating she was truly relaxing for the first time. The wind played with her red hair, moving it restlessly across her shoulders. The sun glinted through the strands, setting them on fire as she took her first photograph of the nearby mountains.

"Up here," Sam confided to her, "you can think," he said. "That's why I like ballooning: it's quiet, and you're away from the things down below that create the problems in your life. In the sky, things just seem to become more black and white, you get more objectivity."

She liked his sensitivity. There was a lot to like about Sam Holt. "Have you always ballooned?"

"Yeah, since I was twenty. I'm twenty-nine, now."

She forced herself to look upward into the balloon that was many stories high. "This is a beautiful one. I like her rainbow colors."

Sam looked up, studying the inside of the balloon that swirled with a multitude of colors. Then he looked back at her. "You remind me of a rainbow: red hair, green eyes, pink cheeks."

Lowering her lashes, Megan absorbed his husky compliment. "Thank you, Sam."

"It's not blarney, although there is a drop of Irish blood in my background."

"Irishmen are always good with a line."

He adjusted the flame, sending more hot air into the balloon. "Yeah, but we're poets of the heart when a woman captures our attention."

Heat suffused Megan's cheeks. Sam had certainly captured her heart this day. She tried to look at him objectively.

There was nothing to dislike about him. He seemed at ease in the sky, a bird without wings but able to fly anyway.

"So, you're a school teacher. I imagine that keeps you pretty busy on weeknights with grading papers and such." Below them was nothing but Joshua trees sticking out their prickly arms across the desert. The Mojave was a merciless mistress: over a hundred degrees during the day, dropping to shivering temperatures at night. It was too bad Megan couldn't enjoy the contrasts between the sky and earth, or the myriad colors and the gentle sway of the balloon.

"I'm busier than I'd thought I'd be. I work over at the day-care center three evenings a week."

"Two jobs?"

She shrugged. "I'm a workaholic by nature." Since graduating with her teaching degree, there were plenty of bills and loans to pay off. Megan had found a small one-bedroom apartment in Lancaster that could help her remain within her meager budget.

"Not me. One job's plenty. I like my time off to pursue things like this."

"You appear competitive, not driven."

Sam liked her insight. "Bingo. That's me all right." He wondered why she was driven. "So, you've just moved out here. From where?"

"Columbus, Ohio. I went to Ohio State for my degree." Megan wrinkled her nose. "I miss the green grass, trees, and flowers."

"I know what you mean." She was honestly beginning to relax, and it made him feel better. Megan's body language wasn't as stiff, her knuckles no longer white. He grinned. "We're arch enemies, you know."

"Oh?"

"Yeah, I graduated from Michigan, Ohio's arch football rival."

Laughing, Megan clapped her hands. "So, you're from Michigan?" He stood easily, feet spread far enough apart to compensate for the sway of the balloon. The wind ruffled his hair, several strands dipping to his brow. She enjoyed watching him brush them back into place with his long, large-knuckled fingers.

"Born and raised there."

"What made you come out here to this godforsaken desert?"

"I promised to answer all your questions after we win," he teased. "Tell me more about yourself."

There wasn't that much to tell in Megan's opinion. "I was born in Oakland, California, moved around a lot with my family, and loved Ohio so much that I wanted to go back there for my degree."

"Then what drew you back out here?" Sam asked, watching that same darkness come back to haunt her green eyes.

The question hit her squarely, and inwardly she flinched. Nervously, Megan moved around in the gondola and took more photos. "I'm kind of hungry. Do you have any food on board this thing?"

Having the good grace to not pressure Megan, Sam nodded. Leaning down, he dragged out a small picnic basket. "Believe it or not, I have two McDonald Egg McMuffins in there, two cherry tortes, and orange juice. Help yourself."

Relieved that Sam wasn't going to pursue her past too closely, Megan set to work getting them their breakfast. Sam's questions had opened up old wounds, old hurts that Megan didn't want to address right now. She had given herself a year to resolve those painful issues. As she stood there eating the food she didn't taste, Megan wished the race was over so that she could shift the focus on Sam. He was, by far, more interesting than her agonizing past.

"Well," Sam said dryly, "second place isn't bad." Even now, after they had crossed the finish line, another crowd of thousands stood waiting to watch them land. He was elated with the finish. The race had been good, the company even better. Within the next fifteen minutes, they would be earthbound again. And then, he'd take this luscious red-headed woman to a long, enjoyable lunch. Megan intrigued him. She hid from him, he sensed. Not in a defensive way, but she was shy and introverted considering her blazing red hair. Megan wasn't like most women her age. No, there was a refreshing vulnerability to her.

"I think second place is great, considering you had a passenger who doesn't know a thing about ballooning," Megan pointed out. Slowly, they were beginning to descend toward an open area away from the million onlookers. "Now, it's your turn. Tell me about yourself."

"Born and raised in Michigan." Sam deliberately left out the fact his father had been a struggling blue-collar union worker for the auto industry. Most pilots, especially test pilots, came from white-collar, upwardly mobile families. He was a black sheep at best among his professional friends. And it was something he kept to himself.

"Single?"

"Yes. And ladies with red hair have always interested me."

"Oh?"

"They're complex." He motioned to her hair, the thick strands a copper frame around her features. "Your hair is a combination of gold, copper, and burgundy colors. Not one color, but many. That indicates a lot of facets to you."

Her laugh was free, and she was delighted with how he saw her. "Complex isn't a word I'd use on myself, Sam."

"Oh? What words would you use to describe yourself?" He was interested in how Megan saw herself.

"Shy, responsible, a workaholic . . ." Megan hesitated. "I guess that says it all."

He had to divide his attention between Megan and the forthcoming landing. Below, he spotted his team at the outskirts of the crowd. Releasing the risers to allow ample amounts of hot air to escape would help them descend more rapidly.

"What about you?" Megan challenged. "Are you in a business here in Lancaster?"

Sam swung his attention back to her. There was pride in his voice. "I'm a captain in the Air Force and in the business of being a test pilot over at Edwards."

A gasp escaped Megan.

"Hey, you look like you've seen a ghost," Holt joked, watching all the color drain from her cheeks. He had to pay attention to the landing since the ground was coming up rapidly. Working the handle, sending more heat into the balloon, their descent was slowed dramatically, and they hovered ten feet above the desert. Below, his crew of three men had gathered, reaching out for the trail lines.

No longer worried about the landing, Megan gripped the side of the gondola. She stared at his intent features as he steered the balloon closer and closer to the awaiting crew who were reaching up to grab the ropes hanging over the side of the gondola. Her mind whirled with shock and then despair. Closing her eyes, Megan tried to draw in a breath, but couldn't.

"Prepare for landing," Sam called. He knew Megan was afraid of heights. Figuring her reaction was due to that, he worked the handle, wanting to make the landing smooth and uneventful for her. Briefly, he saw his friend Curt Merrill at the edge of the crowd, an unhappy look on his face. Beside him were his wife Becky, and their daughter Patty. He managed a wave in their direction, feeling the gondola lightly scrape the desert floor. The crew ran outward, using their weight to anchor the balloon into the place. Holt threw them a thumbs up, meaning: okay!

Turning, Sam moved over to Megan, his hand resting on her shoulder. "Megan? You all right?" Her knuckles were white, fingers dug into the woven side of the gondola. Giving her a small shake to make her relax, Sam said, "It's over. We're down. You can open your eyes now."

It was agony to open them and stare up into Holt's handsome face. She saw concern in his eyes. Pulling away from him, Megan moved to the opposite side of the gondola. The space was too small, and she felt confined and suffocated, needing to escape.

Megan looked out across the crowd which remained at a respectful distance. Her heart was pounding unrelentingly in her breast, and she felt nothing but pain and betrayal. "I have to go," she croaked, gripping her camera. "How do I get out of this thing?"

Sam scowled and lightly leaped out of the basket. Before Megan could protest, he placed his hands around her waist, lifting her up and out of the gondola. "There, you're grounded again," he teased, his hands lingering around her. "Hey, talk to me."

Swallowing back a lump, Megan stepped out of his dangerous embrace. Holt was too charismatic, too overwhelming to her senses as a woman. Somehow, he'd slipped inside her walls she swore would never come down if she ever met a man in the military, especially a pilot. "I—I have to go, Captain Holt. Please, excuse me . . ."

Sam stood nonplussed, watching Megan turn and walk quickly toward the crowd. He saw Becky and Curt Merrill moving toward him from the opposite direction. "Megan!" he shouted. "Wait!" To his chagrin, he saw her quickly disappear among the hundreds of people pressing forward to watch the balloon deflate.

"Damn," he muttered under his breath. He couldn't just take off and chase her down. What had he said to make her run off? Mulling over their conversation, Sam couldn't find anything. Reluctantly, he turned toward his approaching friends. It didn't matter; he knew where she worked, and that was enough. Megan Roberts was fair game, and he was intrigued by her. One way or another, he was going to see her again.

"Hi, Curt and Becky." Holt leaned down, watching little blond-haired Patty race toward him, her tiny, thin arms outstretched. "Come here, squirt!"

"Uncle Sammy! Uncle Sammy!" and Patty threw herself into his arms.

Chuckling, Sam swung Patty upward, hearing her peal of laughter. Settling her into his arms, she hugged him fiercely. Sam pressed a kiss to her hair and gave a welcoming smile to her parents. Some of his happiness dissolved when he realized Becky had been crying. Curt looked grim.

"Sorry you couldn't make the race," he told Curt.

"Yeah . . . well, Becky didn't want me to go up."

Sam suppressed his reaction. "I see." Curt was the number-three slotted test pilot. His light-brown hair was cut short, his azure eyes intense and restless looking. Like most pilots, he possessed a deep chest and broad shoulders. He flew test flights a couple of times a week. A balloon was tame and safe in comparison.

Sam gave her a game smile. "Becky, how are you?" She was a petite woman who reminded him of a bird. She had Patty's thin blond hair and wore a simple but colorful cotton dress that emphasized her slender build.

"Just fine," she answered, forcing a smile, her voice barely above a whisper. Clasping her hands nervously in front of her, she glanced up at her husband. "I'm sorry, Sam, I just got the jitters about Curt going up in a balloon."

He liked Becky's soft Arkansas drawl. Since they'd come to the base three months ago, he'd reestablished a close relationship with the family. Off and on throughout the last six years, he'd flown with Curt in different fighter squadrons. Sam knew about Becky's fear of Curt crashing. It was a common problem among some of the wives and girlfriends of pilots. "I understand, Becky."

"I tried to explain it to her," Curt said in an aggravated tone. "It's just a stupid balloon, Becky! Look at it! Does it look dangerous to you now?"

The woman bowed her head, remaining silent.

"Don't pick on her," Sam said, slipping his arm around Becky's thin, slumped shoulders. "Not all people are birds, Merrill." He wanted to defuse the tension around the family. Sucking her thumb, Patty happily rested her head on his shoulder. "Come on, gang. What do you say we go back over to my house and have a barbecue? My crew will be coming along as soon as they get the balloon stowed. I can tell you all about the race. We took second, did you know that? And did you see that gorgeous redhead that was with me?"

"That was Miss Roberts," Becky said in awe. "I didn't know you knew her."

Chuckling, Sam squeezed Becky, trying to give her some confidence. "We just met." Becky was from the hills of

Arkansas and had been married to Curt for eight years. In Sam's opinion, she had never left the hills in some ways, always afraid of planes and respectful of most of the twentieth-century machinery. Becky was simple, but that didn't take away from her warm, generous heart. Because she knew Sam was single, she had Curt invite him over for a delicious home-cooked meal at least twice a week. No, Becky had her priorities straight: things at home, family and children were important to her.

Merrill stood there and grimaced, watching the balloon begin to fold and flow across the desert floor as the rest of the hot air escaped form the side vents. "Miss Roberts called Becky yesterday."

"Oh?" Sam raised his brows, quickly putting together the pieces. "About you-know-who," he said, meaning Patty. The seven-year-old girl was precocious and Sam had seen her throw tantrums upon occasion.

Unhappily, Curt nodded. "Yeah. She called Becky in for a parents' conference this coming Monday. I can't make it because I'm flying that day, so she's going over by herself."

"Good news?"

"No. I'll tell you later, when you-know-who is out of earshot," Curt told his friend.

"Roger," Sam nodded.

Becky looked up at Holt. "Monday Curt flies."

Sam tensed inwardly. "Yes, that's right, Becky."

She cast a nervous look up at her husband. "Every time gets harder. I worry so much about him. What could happen—"

"Honey," Curt ground out under his breath, "Sam doesn't want to hear about your silly fears." Curt placed his hand on his wife's elbow and lead her toward the balloon to inspect it.

"They're not silly fears!" Becky cried softly, holding her husband's light-blue eyes. "It's worry! What if you died? How would we survive? How could I make ends meet? What of Patty's future and the schooling we have planned for her?"

"You have nightmares," Curt remonstrated. "And you

worry too much. Every time I'm going to fly, you can't sleep the night before. God, Becky, you'd think after eight years, you'd stop this and get used to the fact that's what I do for a living."

Miserably, Becky looked back at Sam holding her daughter. Patty liked the pilot fiercely and was always well behaved when he was around. Miss Roberts had tried on the phone to diplomatically tell her that Patty was creating scenes in her first grade class. What could she do? What? Becky hung her head and followed her husband meekly. She was afraid of the forthcoming meeting with the teacher on Monday. So many problems were mounting up on her, she didn't know how to deal with all of them. So many.

— 2 —

"**B**ECKY, something has to be done about Patty." Curt turned on his heel and rested against the drainboard. It was 11 P.M., and their seven-year-old daughter was in bed, asleep. "Miss Roberts said she was being disruptive. What did she mean by that?"

Becky sat at the kitchen table, her thin fingers wrapped around a mug of black coffee. They had both taken a bath earlier, and she was wrapped in a cotton robe. He stood in his blue-striped pajamas. "She said Patty would have spells."

"Spells of *what*?" Curt folded his arms against his chest, glaring at his wife. Becky's vagueness was maddening at times.

With a shrug, Becky sipped the coffee and refused to look up at Curt. "Ya'll know how she'll be silent and then suddenly start talking and shouting."

Inwardly, Curt cringed. When Becky dropped into her soft Arkansas twang, he knew she was feeling pressure. Coming from an upwardly mobile Boston family, Curt had been drilled on proper pronunciation of words and the correct use of the English language. Becky's high school background from the mountains of Arkansas needed drastic remodeling if she was to fit into the mold of an ideal Air Force wife. She had courageously thrown herself into the diction lessons and had made both of them proud. He tried to take the demanding tone out of his voice. "And she starts screaming in class?"

"I'm afraid so. Miss Roberts said the class would be quietly working on a project, and she'd suddenly start talking out in a loud voice without raising her hand or anything." Becky chewed on her lower lip, feeling guilty. Somehow, she hadn't raised her daughter properly. It had been a shaming experience to be asked to come in and talk to Miss Roberts about her daughter. Not that Miss Roberts had been nasty about it. On the contrary, she'd been extremely sympathetic.

"How long would she do it?"

"Ten or fifteen minutes at a time until . . ."

"Until what?" Curt held on to his anger.

"Sometimes, Miss Roberts would have to take Patty out of the class and take her to the nurse's room until she agreed to raise her hand before she needed to speak."

With a groan, Curt shoved away from the drainboard. "Do you know how this is going to look if General Dalton or Colonel Yale gets a hold of this information, Becky?"

Snapping her head up, she studied her husband's darkly clouded features. "I'm *very* aware of it, Curt. And ya'll don't have to raise your voice to me about it."

"Dammit, in the first grade, she was fine. What happened over one summer? Patty's been in school three weeks and now this is suddenly happening."

Nervously, Becky ran her fingers across the smooth surface of the pink ceramic mug. "This last summer we moved to Edwards," she said, her voice barely above a whisper. "We moved from the F-15 squadron in Florida to here. You went from flying fighters to testing planes—" She bit down on her lower lip, avoiding the anger in his eyes. She'd said too much.

"You're blaming *me* for Patty's behavior?"

"I didn't say that, Curt."

"What the hell difference is there between flying a fighter and testing a plane?"

"Ya'll keep your voice down or you'll wake Patty."

Nostrils flared, Curt jerked out a chair opposite of where

she sat. "Just where," he demanded tautly, sitting down, "did Patty pick up your fear of me testing jets? Ever since we moved here, you've been on pins and needles, Becky. You're going to have to get over it. You're going to have to stop this insane worrying about me every time I take the *Eagle* up for a test flight."

Squeezing her eyes shut, Becky whispered, "Miss Roberts thinks my fear of you flying is being transferred somehow to Patty."

"Do you tell Patty you're afraid?"

"Of course not!"

Glowering around the kitchen, Curt shook his head. "Kids are like an antenna: they pick up on everything whether it's spoken about or not." And his daughter was exceptionally intelligent and sensitive for her age.

"Miss Roberts thinks that part of the problem might be the fact you don't see Patty very often," Becky ventured softly. She forced herself to meet her husband's gaze. "She feels Patty is reaching out for attention because she isn't getting enough at home."

"I don't believe it! Where does Miss Roberts get off saying that?" In his own family, his father owned a thriving brokerage house and was a workaholic. Most of the time, he wasn't around for Curt or his younger brother, Jim. He hadn't misbehaved in school just because his father hadn't had the time to spend with him. Why should Patty?

"She was an Air Force brat herself, Curt. Miss Roberts was raised in a military family and went to schools just like Patty's going to. She knows what she's talking about."

"Maybe." Curt compressed his mouth. "How can I give Patty more attention, Sparrow?" It was his nickname for Becky because she reminded him of a sweet, harmless little bird. Sparrows had no defenses, no huge curved beak or talons like a hawk or eagle with which to protect themselves. Becky was vulnerable in many ways, and he tried to shield her from so much that could disrupt the ultrasensitive world she lived in. How could he shield her from his flying? Ever since he'd started testing, their marriage had been in a flat spin that he couldn't seem to get a handle on.

With a shrug, Becky ventured, "Instead of coming home, eating, and going to study, you might take an hour and play with Patty. Miss Roberts said we need to pay attention to the school work she brings home, praise her, and be interested in what she has to say."

"Great!" Curt rose, the chair nearly tipping over. "I don't *have* an hour to spare in the evenings! Do you think I *like* going into that office and studying until midnight every night? Don't you think I'd like to spend time with you and Patty? Testing's different, Sparrow. It demands everything I've got to stay up with Stang and Holt. I'm number three in the standings. I've got to make it to number two in flight ratings to stay and be considered for other testing projects coming down the line later on. I *can't* spend that hour with Patty." And then, more softly, "Or you."

Becky blinked back the tears and lowered her head so Curt couldn't see them. "I know ya'll's back is against the wall. Being a test pilot means everything to you."

"Believe me," Curt whispered with feeling, "I don't like the hours either. When I was a part of a fighter squadron, we had more time in the evenings to spend together. I'm sorry, Sparrow, but Patty is just going to have to roll with the punches like we are. She's going to have to somehow adjust."

"There's one ray of hope."

Curt came around the table and placed his hands on Becky's small shoulders, feeling the tension in them. He began to massage her tense muscles. "What's that?"

Leaning back, Becky rested her head against her husband's strong, lean body. "Miss Roberts recognized there's special strains and demands put on Air Force children. Even though it's her first year here since graduating, she's going to fight hard for a new way of teaching the kids. It's called *outdoor education.*" She placed her hand on his and absorbed his warmth, his love for her.

"Outdoor education? What will that mean?"

"Miss Roberts wants the children outdoors more often.

She feels to pen them up in a room for six or seven hours a day isn't the best thing for them. You know how Patty loves to get up and move around.''

Leaning down, Curt kissed her temple. "Yeah, that little pipsqueak of ours is a real adventuress.''

"Well, she's put in a request to the school principal to have her idea approved. If it is, Curt, it means the children in her class will be the test model for it. If it works, then the other grades would be allowed to use it, too. I think if the children went on field trips, on hikes, and got outside, it might help.''

"Patty would be too interested in what was going on around her to create trouble,'' Curt agreed. He coaxed Becky out of the chair and drew her into his embrace. The worry in her eyes haunted him. No longer was she the laughing, airy sprite he'd married eight years ago. Coming to Edwards had made her eyes go dark with fear, her once flushed face almost waxen appearing. There was strain around her eyes and soft mouth. Kissing her hair, he held her tightly.

"Let's hope,'' he murmured, "that Miss Roberts gets her way. It would be an easy out on Patty's problem, I think.'' He loved Becky fiercely. Eight years earlier, he'd flown into Blytheville AFB in Arkansas on a training mission when his plane was grounded for two days in order to get a new engine. He'd met Becky over at the O Club where she'd recently gotten her first job as a waitress.

Curt smiled, rocking his wife in his arms, the memory still warm within him. Becky had spilled a plate of spaghetti all over him in her nervousness to be a good waitress. The O Club manager was appalled and had apologized profusely to him for Becky's act. Becky stood nearby, crying. It was when the manager turned and fired her on the spot that Curt had taken action. He couldn't resist her tears or the cute Arkansas twang she had. He had defended her, but the manager refused to take her back.

Leaving the O Club, Curt had walked with her for a couple hours afterward. Becky was one of the few members of her large family to venture down from the mountains and try to make it in what she termed the "real world." Her vulnerability, her honesty, struck him hard.

He kissed her temple. "Remember when you spilled that spaghetti all over me, Sparrow?"

Becky moaned. "Oh, Lordy, do I ever."

With a chuckle, Curt added, "I finally got you to quit crying enough to convince you I was going to live—spaghetti stains or not."

Laughing softly, Becky nestled her head in the hollow of his shoulder. "I fell in love with you then. You cared about me, about me getting fired. I was so lost. I didn't know what to do."

"We went to your apartment you leased with two other girls and you washed my shirt."

With a sigh, she looked up, drowning in his dancing blue eyes. "You were so kind, Curt. You still are, even to this day."

"And you were like a small bird with a broken wing: fragile, pretty, and completely unable to fend for yourself out in the world. I fell hard for you."

"I remember." Resting her head against his chest, a quiver passed through Becky. "I remember how afraid I was because you were a pilot. Planes scared me even then."

"You were just raised in a different world was all," he murmured, pressing another kiss to her hair. It had taken him nearly a year to convince Becky to marry him because she was fearful he'd die in a fiery crash. Finally, she gave in to his need for her. His family wasn't happy about Becky or her lineage, but Curt didn't care. He loved her, and that's all that mattered. A year later, Patty was born, and his family was grudgingly accepting of Becky—finally.

"You're shaking," he whispered, holding her a little more tightly..

"I'm still scared of those planes, Curt."

"I know." If only Miss Roberts could find a way to deal with Patty, their lives wouldn't continue to be on the edge of a razor blade. Neither his wife or child had been happy since his transfer to Edwards. Curt wanted to place blame for his daughter's behavior on the recent move. It had to be that and only that. Not the fact he was now a coveted test pilot. Leading her from the kitchen, he shut off the light.

Brad Jamison, assistant principal, hesitated at the door to Megan Roberts's classroom. The late September heat moved through the quiet halls of the now empty school. The children were gone for the day, and so were most of the teachers. He held her request for a change of curriculum in his hand. Easing open the door, he spotted Megan at the board. She was drawing a huge hot air balloon on the board in colored chalk.

There was nothing not to like about her, Jamison had decided. He walked quietly into the room. She had been hired while he was away on vacation. Normally, he did the hiring. But, to his surprise, this red-haired vixen was here when he'd come back from summer vacation three weeks ago. The principal, Jake Hamilton, had hired her.

Hamilton didn't have bad taste, Jamison thought. Being divorced, Brad was always interested in pretty, young and single women. Even another teacher. Halting midway into the room, Brad watched her. The cascade of unruly red hair across her shoulders was like a crimson cape. Or was it a red flag? In the teachers' conferences with the administration, she'd been absent, which was unusual. He really didn't know this woman, but if her slender shape was any indication, it was going to be a real pleasure working with her. Besides, she was new and would be on probation for three years. Megan Roberts would be a pliable, willing creature and would realize that her job could be pulled from her at any time if she didn't go along with what he wanted.

"Megan?"

Megan turned, startled by a male voice so close behind her. Eraser poised in hand, she saw a short, bulldog-shaped man in a gray suit standing in the center of her room. He had thick blond hair and a neatly trimmed mustache, his eyes were a dark brown color. Perhaps it was his short, squat appearance that made her go on internal guard; Megan wasn't sure. His face was round, and he appeared to be in his early forties. It was the light in his small eyes that bothered her.

"Yes?" *Who was he?* Her gaze fell to the folder in his grasp, and she recognized it as her outdoor education curriculum plan.

Holding out his hand, he came forward. "We haven't met yet. I'm Brad Jamison, assistant principal."

His fingers were strong, holding her hand far longer than necessary. Megan pulled her hand from his grasp and set the eraser down. "Mr. Jamison, it's nice to meet you."

He grinned. "I hope you mean that, Megan. You're certainly a bright spot here at school. Beautiful young teachers aren't the norm, and if your credentials from Ohio State University are any indication, I'd say Mr. Hamilton has hired a very special lady."

Scowling, Megan went to her desk and kept some distance between them. She didn't know what to expect from the administration because this was her first job at a school. Linda Yarnell, a motherly woman who had taught at bases for eighteen years, had warned her that the teachers' union and this particular school administration weren't on good footing with one another right now.

"I would hope that Mr. Hamilton hired me because I was a good teacher, not necessarily a 'special lady.' "

Brad's smile broadened. He liked her spirit and spunk, her chin raised at an imperious angle, her green eyes flashing with a hint of anger. "Do I hear feminism talking?" he teased, walking over to her desk.

Megan sized him up. "I'm sure you do. But that shouldn't come as any surprise. It's 1990, and feminism started in 1970. Everyone's had twenty years to adjust to the fact that a woman is an equal." She smiled slightly. "I see you have my curriculum suggestion in hand. Is that what you've come to talk about?"

"Ah, yes. Your suggestions." Brad made himself comfortable on the corner of her desk, no more than a foot separating them. Megan was dressed in a bright kelly-green shirtdress, the brass buttons and belt showing off her figure and complexion.

"I wasn't sure who should receive my proposal," Megan said, holding her breath. *Would admin go for it? Would they allow her to change the education model to help the children?*

"I'm the curriculum coordinator, Megan. I know you're new here, so all's forgiven."

"And what did you think?"

He held the file in both hands, tapping it lazily against his knee. "I think it's rather radical—"

"Wait a minute, Mr. Jamison—"

"Call me Brad."

Megan frowned. Was he making a pass at her? He couldn't be. Still, her instincts warned her that Jamison wanted something from her. "All right . . . Brad. If you've read my file, you know I'm an Air Force brat. I grew up on bases, and as a matter of fact, I graduated from this very high school five years ago. I feel that my insider's knowledge of what these children need is worthy of attention."

Brad smiled. Like any new teacher, Megan was enthusiastic and out to change the world. She'd find out very quickly that admin and the union didn't operate that way. "You are in the position to know more than most of our teachers about the children of military parents."

"It's more than that, Brad." Megan walked around and faced him. "My second grade class has a couple of disruptive children, and I feel my education model will help them integrate so that I can get on with the job of teaching *all* the children in the class."

"Who are they?"

Taken aback by his unexpected and almost wolfish interest, Megan hesitated. And then, she reasoned that he *was* the assistant principal. Jamison would know sooner or later about her reports on the children, anyway. "Patty Merrill and Scotty Stang. Both are children of test pilots."

"I hope you've been sensitive enough not to report this, Megan."

She stared at him. "What?"

"Reporting their behavior to the front office will make it look bad for the fathers. You know how officers' fitness reports will make or break them careerwise. Even school reports on their children can adversely affect their careers.''

Placing her hands on her hips, Megan shook her head. ''I would think, Mr. Jamison, that your first priority, indeed, your only one, would be the children of the schools. Patty and Scotty are borderline dysfunctional. Patty's problems are different from Scotty's, but they need attention and quick action.''

Placing the folder on the desk, Brad stood up. ''You know, with that red hair, I figured you'd be a fighter, Megan.'' He reached out, brushing her scarlet cheek. She gasped, her eyes going wide with shock, and she quickly stepped out of his reach.

''What do you think you're doing?'' Megan rattled.

''You're a very beautiful lady. I think,'' Brad went on softly, ''that we ought to discuss this over dinner tonight in Lancaster. What do you say?''

Trying to steady her breathing, Megan stared over at Jamison. ''I don't like what you're suggesting. And even more, you had no right to touch me.''

''First-year teachers have a lot to learn.'' He pointed to her folder. ''Stay friendly with me, Megan, and maybe I'll seriously consider your outdoor education proposal.''

Anger vibrated through her. Jamison had no right to do this. ''In other words, if I don't play along with what you want, or give you what you want, you'll ignore my proposal?''

''I always said redheads were particularly astute and canny. Yes, that's the deal, Megan.''

''Don't call me Megan. I'm Miss Roberts to you. And I'll take my proposal to my union and get backing for it.''

With a laugh, Brad turned and walked away. ''You're going to find out the hard way that if you don't deal with me, your proposal isn't going to take off.''

Megan stood there shaking with anger after Jamison had left. The bastard! Who did he think he was? He was parading around like king of the jungle, inspecting her, making a pass at her, and then expecting her to fall into his arms. With shaking hands, she put the rest of her lesson plan into her briefcase.

"Are you still here?"

Megan heard Linda Yarnell's friendly voice. She looked up and snapped the briefcase shut. "The perils of being a first-year teacher," she joked. Linda was a bit overweight, but at forty, she looked much younger than her age. Her square face was almost free of wrinkles, and Megan wondered how she did it while working with Jamison around.

"I just saw Jamison coming like a steam engine down the hall. Was he in here?" Linda placed her worn cowhide briefcase on a desk.

With a grimace, Megan told her what had transpired. Her heart sank when she saw Linda's brow furrow. "What does that scowl mean?"

"Tread lightly, Megan. Your status as a teacher isn't firmed up, yet."

"Does Jamison go around fondling all the other teachers?"

"He's never tried it on me." She laughed. "I'm too old for him. Seriously, I haven't heard anything from the other teachers."

"Can't the union do something about it?"

"Do you have a witness so that you could slap him with a sexual harassment charge?"

With a groan, Megan muttered, "No."

"He's smart, so watch it."

"He's stupid if he thinks he can stalk me."

"You rebuffed him. I doubt he'll try again. More than likely, you've made an enemy."

Setting her jaw, Megan glanced down at Linda. "I know you have eighteen years as a base teacher, and I'd like to sit down sometime with you and have you fill me in on what the union can do to help me get this proposal before the school board."

"Why not have dinner with us tonight? You're new in Lancaster, and I'm sure going back to a lonely apartment isn't a whole lot of fun."

It wasn't. Megan managed a tentative smile. She knew Linda's husband was a lieutenant colonel and flew the space shuttle plane to and from Florida. It was a dangerous job in her opinion, but Linda's kindly face didn't show the effects of it as her mother's had. "Yes, I'd like that. Thanks."

Linda pointed to the balloon she'd drawn on the board. "How was the balloon rally?"

Sam Holt's image wavered before Megan. An incredible feeling momentarily overwhelmed her. He was more than likable, but she had to fight his effect upon her. "Uh . . . it was okay. I'm going to have the children make and color their own balloons tomorrow. I got the photos developed today." She patted her briefcase. "I'll pass them around to the children so they can get some ideas of colors and designs."

"I like what you're doing," Linda said, walking out with her. "Hands-on teaching is something we're in dire need of, Megan. I'm glad you're here. You've just got to be careful how you butt heads with admin and still keep your job."

Megan agreed. More than anything, she didn't want to lose her job, but changes *had* to come about. These children had special pressures and demands made on them that civilian children did not. She knew from her own experience. And somehow, she was going to make it better for them. "You know," she told Linda softly as she locked the door to her room, "I had some wonderful teachers in the third, fourth, and fifth grades. If I hadn't, I don't think I'd be whole today." And then she laughed, embarrassed. "They gave me direction, love, and care when I wasn't getting any at home. I want to be there for these children, Linda. But I want to improve their world at school. I know it can be done. And I know I can do it."

"Just be aware of *how* you do it, Megan. Getting any changes in this school system is like pulling teeth."

"Then, I'll become a dentist. I'm not taking no for an answer. These children's lives are too important not to fight for."

— 3 —

S AM was more careful the second time around making conversation with Megan Roberts. He'd wrangled some time off so that he could meet her at the school. Still dressed in his one-piece, green flight suit, he took off his garrison hat as he walked through the opened door of her classroom. The secretary at the principal's office had given him directions. Megan was at her desk, working. Behind her, on the chalkboard, was a colorful balloon. And on three other walls were large, multicolored balloons obviously made and cut out by her children. It looked like a flower garden in her room, a place where creativity abounded and was encouraged. He grinned and gave a light knock at the door so as not to startle her.

Megan lifted her head. Her lips parted. "You . . ." The word escaped softly, underscored with disbelief. She was unhappy with her response: her heart thudded powerfully in her breast as if to underscore his unexpected presence.

"Hi. I thought I'd drop by and try a different introduction so you wouldn't run away from me again." He eased into the room, acutely aware of the distrust in her glorious green eyes. Megan wore a loose cotton blouse of pink, a colorful scarf, and white cotton skirt. Her small feet were encased in a pair of sensible sandals.

Megan leaned back in her chair, trying to assemble her

32

scattered thoughts. Holt was more than handsome, but the flight suit brought back terrible, searing memories. She put her pen down.

"Why are you here?"

Ignoring her defensiveness and the tenor of her tone, he dug into one of the large pockets of his flight suit. "Remember those pictures I'd shot from the balloon?"

"Yes," she answered warily.

Sam wanted to defuse the brittle tension he heard in Megan's voice.

"I thought you might like to share these with your kids," he said, handing her the pictures he'd shot from the balloon.

Surprised that any pilot would be so unselfish, Megan hesitantly took the photos and looked through them. "They're beautiful . . ." She looked up at him, noticing that lazy grin on his face, and managed a smile. "My children will love them. That was thoughtful of you, Captain Holt. Thank you."

"Can't we make it Sam and Megan?"

Just the way he asked melted Megan's initial distrust of why he was here. Still, she couldn't afford to encourage him, even though a part of her liked him.

"No, I'm afraid not, Captain."

Hard to catch, Sam decided, not at all deterred. Pointing to her knapsack on her desk he asked, "Going somewhere?"

"I was about to go out and scout out a route to take my children on a hike later this week."

"Great. Mind if I tag along?"

She glanced at him. "Since when is a test pilot interested in anything earthbound like rocks or plants?" The bitterness had leaked through in her voice, and she was sorry, not meaning to take her past out on Sam. His eyes sparkled with devilry, and Megan realized he hadn't taken her reaction personally.

"When I got assigned to Edwards six months ago, I didn't like the desert very much. Being raised in Michigan, I was used to water, trees, and green lawns. There were six kids in the family, and we were raised near a lake." He glanced at her to see what kind of effect his conversation had on her. Maybe, if he shifted the focus to him, she wouldn't withdraw as much.

Megan gave a short, derisive laugh. "You're way out of your element, then."

Good, at least she was talking with him. He grinned, noticing that her lashes had lifted enough to reveal those heart-stopping emerald eyes. "I'm letting the Mojave grow on me."

"The desert reminds me of a skeleton," Megan said more to herself than him, and looked out the window. "It's a bleached-bone color, and nothing much survives out here." *Not even the test pilots.*

Sam digested her statement. "I never thought of the desert as a skeleton."

"The Mojave takes lives, Captain."

"That's a pretty macabre way of looking at it," Sam said, seeing her point. A number of test planes and pilots had augered into the unforgiving floor of the white desert.

Megan closed her eyes. "I don't see much that's positive about any military base."

"Except the children?"

"Yes, the wives and children are the casualties. They're worth being here for, fighting for..."

Megan had plenty of nice qualities, Sam decided early on. There was just this one streak in her about the military that was like a raw, seeping wound that hadn't healed yet. He could forgive her for that. God knew, he had some open and bleeding wounds himself, and remembered the death of his best friend, Russ Davis. Five months ago, Russ flew a night test with him, and everything went wrong. Sam broke out in a light sweat over those hellish memories, and he wiped his brow. He'd walked away from the crash, but Russ had died with the plane. Megan was right: the Mojave held a lot of skeletons.

Quirking his mouth, Sam realized Megan had picked up her jeans and hiking boots and was heading for the door. As if sensing his unasked question, she turned.

"I'm going to change and be back in a minute."

"I'll wait."

Her heart sank. "I'd rather you didn't."

"I need the exercise."

"I've never met a pilot who liked to hike."

"Until I came along, Red. Maybe I can be of help. Who knows?"

With a shake of her head, Megan disappeared. In the teachers' lounge, which was empty, she changed clothes, unhappy. Whether she liked it or not, his endearment touched her deeply. No one had called her "Red." Maybe "Carrot Top" when she was a kid, but not Red.

Returning to the room, Megan picked up her knapsack, notebook, and pen. Sam stood expectantly, giving her a smile that sent her heart skittering.

Megan felt heat crawling up her neck and into her face. Sam Holt was entirely too confident about himself as a man and realized his effect on her. Mouth dry, she croaked, "Follow me."

Sam fell in at Megan's side and noticed the easy way she walked. They left the school and headed out back toward the desert, which wasn't far from the asphalt parking lot. The sun was low on the horizon, the sky a light blue above and a dark gold ribbon of color along the horizon. As usual, it was a cloudless day. Edwards offered some of the finest flying conditions in the world because of the dry desert environment.

"So what kind of hike is this going to be for your kids?"

"A rock hunting trip." Megan took several samples of different stones and put them in her knapsack. "I'm interested in creating a classroom where their five senses are stimulated. Nowadays, kids are glued to their classroom computers. They lose so much that way."

Sam nodded thoughtfully. "Less boring if you get them outside, too. It gets them involved."

"Yes." Megan tried to ignore Holt's closeness. He picked up a few other pebbles and handed them to her. His fingers barely brushed her palm, but it sent a delightful sensation up through her arm.

Sam studied her. He saw her subtle, feminine response to

his touch in her lustrous eyes. "I don't have any kids, but is that kind of teaching done here at Edwards?"

"No, and I'm going to fight to get outdoor education included as part of the curriculum." Hesitating, Megan wondered if she should talk to Sam about her problems with Jamison. Just the interest he displayed coupled with the care exuding from him made her add, "I'm already meeting resistance over my proposal."

Sam responded to her contralto voice lined with conviction. When she sat down in the sand and crossed her legs, the notebook balanced on her knee, he smiled openly. There was an incredible naturalness to Megan. One he applauded. He couldn't imagine Melody Stang, the wife of chief test pilot Jack Stang, out here, much less sitting in the sand. Melody remained well dressed and spotless no matter what the occasion. He crouched down opposite Megan. "You're bucking the system." In the military, that wasn't a wise thing to do. There was chain of command, and no one in his right mind ever challenged it. Not if they wanted a continued career in the service.

"I know, I'm biting off a lot, but I don't care. The children are worth defending, Sam. They need time out of the classroom. They need to touch, feel, taste, and smell the world around them, not just have their noses buried in a book or riveted to a computer screen."

"Could this fight to get the proposal accepted affect your job?"

"Maybe."

"What's that mean?" Sam didn't want to lose her now that he'd found her. If Megan got fired for pushing too hard, he had a personal interest in this battle of hers. If she got fired, she'd move away, and that was the last thing he wanted her to do.

Glancing up from studying some rocks, Megan held his serious gaze. "It means I've got to be careful. I didn't come back here for nothing . . ." and then she bit back the rest of what she was going to say.

"A lady with a mission," Sam posed softly. He waited for her to respond to his baited statement, but she refused to add anything else. Sam noted there was no ring on her left finger. Risking everything, he asked, "Are you married?"

"No." Megan panicked. "You're hunting me, Captain, and I'm not interested."

Sam shrugged. "Naw, I'm not hunting you. I like you, though. You're different." *And pretty.*

Megan halted and turned to him. She challenged his blue eyes that were dark with undeniable warmth toward her. "I'm not interested, Captain."

"Sam."

"I'm not interested in a relationship with a man right now. This is my first year of teaching, and I have other, more important priorities." That wasn't quite true. It just couldn't be a man in the military, and especially not a pilot. The pain from the past was too much for Megan to overcome. She would never date a pilot.

"At least I'm not in competition with another man," he joked, realizing she was serious. Megan almost seemed afraid of his uniform. At his age, Sam knew not to push her too far. Giving her a mock salute, he said, "I'll let you get on with your rock collecting. Maybe we'll run into one another some time."

Megan stood there watching him turn and leave. Disgruntled, she forced herself to concentrate on the rocks. Holt was chasing her, and she knew it. Right now, all she wanted to do was get home, take a bath, and then do her weekly shopping. Anything to take her mind and heart off Sam Holt.

The forty minute trip to Lancaster from Edwards put Megan in touch with just how tired she really was. Once at her second-story apartment, the air conditioning was cooling and welcoming.

Megan looked around the quiet, peaceful apartment, badly needing what it offered her tattered emotions after the run-in with Holt. In one corner, near the ivory drapes, was a floor-to-ceiling dark-green bamboo plant. Anything green did well under her coaxing hands. There was a huge peace lily in a brass container spreading its many leafy arms out from the opposite corner near the door. A green and white spider plant hung from a ceiling fixture above the color television hidden in the intricately carved mahogany cabinet.

The light scent of lavender came from the potpourri in her bedroom. Megan inhaled deeply and pushed the flats off her feet, digging her nylon-clad toes into the thick, plush carpet. The tiny pink roses in the ivory wallpaper gave her a sense of being in another era, another time. A gentler one, that was for sure, than the one she lived in presently.

Her Friday night shopping had to be done. With a groan, Megan prepared the bath and sprinkled orange-scented crystals into the water. Padding to the adjoining bedroom, Megan undressed and took the white chenille robe from the French-door closet. She gave her Victorian canopied bed a look of longing. The pale-blue canopy had thin chiffon veils that could be drawn about the bed, making it look highly romantic and ethereal.

Sam Holt unexpectedly came to mind as she stepped into the fragrant bath water. He was a man of many facets, too. Most of the time, he was his jet jockey side. But when he displayed an interest in children by bringing over the photos, she felt surprise and then, longing. The look in Sam's eyes when he spoke briefly about his family made her want to know him better even if he was a pilot.

The humidity in the bath made her hair curl. Anchoring her abundant hair on top of her head with bobby pins, she slid into the water. Why on earth would she want Sam's attention at all? It was a foolish, romantic thought that had no grounding in reality, Megan decided. None at all.

Sam Holt's shock turned to utter delight as he wheeled his cart into the vegetable section of Basha's Market. There, standing over the corn, carefully choosing cobs, was Megan Roberts! He halted, absorbing her beauty. She was dressed in a pair of burnt sienna slacks, comfortable shoes, and an extra long pale pink shirt, the panels hiding her nicely shaped rear and curved thighs. It was her riot of red hair around her shoulders that glinted with copper, burgundy, and wine highlights that mesmerized him.

What were the odds of both of them shopping at the same market at the same time? Fate had intervened, and happily, he intended to take advantage of the situation, wheeling his cart down in her direction. He savored her forthcoming reaction.

"Well," Sam drawled, leaning lazily against his cart, "I said I'd be seeing you again. I just didn't realize it would be this soon."

Megan's head snapped up. Sam Holt stood only a foot away from her, brazenly male and completely confident. He wore a blue plaid cowboy shirt, the sleeves rolled up to his elbows. The jeans were faded, but perfectly molded to his narrow hips and long, powerful legs. His cowboy boots were old although highly polished. Her lips parted and she dropped the ear that was in her hand. It thunked to the tile floor.

Both crouched down to pick it up at the same time. Their heads slammed together.

"Ouch!" Megan sat back on her heels.

"Roger that," Sam said ruefully, and gently rubbed his brow. He gave her an embarrassed look. "Great minds run in the same direction. We have great timing, too."

Miffed, Megan stared at him. She touched her forehead. "You've got a hard head, Captain!"

"I thought *you* did."

Grabbing the fallen corn on the floor between them, she straightened. "You followed me here!"

Sam got up. "No . . . I didn't. Honest."

Jerking a plastic bag off the roll above the counter, Megan muttered, "Do you know the odds of us meeting at the same market at the same time, Captain? Come on!" She stuffed the errant ear into the bag and tried to concentrate on choosing several more. Her hand trembled imperceptibly as she randomly selected the corn.

"They are rather phenomenal," Sam admitted, going back to his cart and enjoying watching her. "But I believe in fate."

"I don't! Especially with pushy pilots. You planned this." She gave him her best glare, hoping to make him leave her alone once and for all. "Now stop following me!" She turned the cart around, heading off for another aisle— any aisle other than the one Holt was in.

"Feisty. I like that." Holt went in hot pursuit.

Thinking she'd lost him by zooming up and down several aisles, Megan stopped in front of the spaghetti section. Looking over her shoulder, she saw no one coming. Leaning down, she looked over the canned tomato section. A squeaky sound alerted her a cart was coming from the opposite direction. Scowling, Megan looked up.

"Hey, is it a crime to shop for spaghetti?" Holt asked, holding up both his hands in a sign of peace.

"You followed me!"

"Nah, I wouldn't do that, Red." It was a lie, but Sam didn't care. She looked positively beautiful when she was angry, her green eyes narrowed with flecks of emerald fire.

Mollified when Holt called her Red, Megan backed off. "I just don't believe you. You followed me to this store."

"I don't even know where you live. How could I?"

"You could have followed me from the base earlier."

"I drive a black Corvette. Did you see it in your rear-view mirror at any time?"

"No," Megan grudgingly admitted. Maybe Holt was right. Maybe this was a chance encounter. It had better be. She wouldn't put up with any man's pursuit of her.

Leaning down, Sam picked up a box of spaghetti. "I go over to Captain Curt Merrill's house once a week. He's a fellow test pilot. We've been friends for over seven years. It's my turn to bring a casserole," he said conversationally, "so I figured spaghetti would be a good meal for all of us. Their daughter Patty is my godchild. She calls me Uncle Sammy." He smiled fondly, putting the item in his basket, noticing Megan's sudden interest. "I'm not really, but I like being part of a family even if I'm single."

Another generalization about pilots was blown. Megan stood there and watched as Holt put his hands on his hips. "You must be an Academy graduate. They teach you guys to never quit once you've got a goal in mind." In this case,

Holt's goal was *her*. Sam gave her that lopsided, boyish smile and it sent her heart pounding again.

"Nah, not this guy." He held up his hand. There was no ring on his hand to identify him as a graduate. "I'm not a member of the brotherhood of ring knockers. I came up the hard way. The *real* way—on my own."

Interesting. Megan kept that thought to herself this time. "Then it's obvious you have a sponsor," she flung back, the anger draining out of her voice.

Sponsors. The magic word that could make or break a career, and Holt knew it. He had the good grace to blush and look sheepishly down at his scuffed cowboy boots. "I wouldn't know about that. I'd like to think I got here on my hard work, my flying skills, and savvy." Looking up, he held her gaze. "I don't like the idea some general saw me a few years back, liked the stuff I was made out of, and decided to help me along by being at the right place and time to juggle my career for me."

Megan quirked her lips. Most officers would die to have a sponsor in the upper echelons of rank. "Sort of independent, aren't you?"

Grinning, Sam said, "I don't know about that. Patty loves me just the way I am."

"That's pretty unusual for a pilot to be interested in children."

"Why?"

"It just is," Megan repeated stubbornly.

He cocked his head, assimilating the feelings behind her answer. "We do other things besides fly planes."

"Most of you don't."

Sam reached down, choosing two cans of tomatoes and placing them in his cart. "I like kids. Patty likes the horsey-back rides I give her when I come over. That little gal is bright."

If only her father had the same kind of philosophy that Sam had. Trying to stuff all those feelings back down deep where she kept them, Megan mustered a partial smile.

"I just hope Patty realizes what she's found in you."

Sam raised his eyebrows, a careless smile breaking the

planes of his face. Megan was so serious, and her eyes were dark with some unidentifiable pain. Wanting to make her smile, he teased, "How could *any* woman, even a seven-year-old little girl, resist my considerable charms? I mean, I'm single, no present lady friend, twenty-nine years old, handsome as hell, intelligent—"

Megan stared at him. "You're impossible, Captain! Impossible!" She quickly wheeled on by him.

"Maybe," Sam muttered under his breath, watching Megan hurry on down the aisle at almost a gallop. "Go ahead, Red, run away," he called after her, his voice carrying strongly. "It won't do you any good."

Megan disappeared around the corner and Sam chuckled indulgently. Let her go—this time. There would be other times. Damn, she was beautiful. And bullheaded about dating a man in uniform. *I've got my gun sights on you, sweetheart, and you're mine. You just don't know it yet. But you will . . .*

— 4 —

"TIME for our nightly Tac and Strat session!" Melody called from the living room. Every night they got together about 2200 to compare notes of what went on for each of them during the day at the base, or in Lancaster. Jack had christened it their Tactics and Strategy sessions, or Tac and Strat. Their son, Scotty, who rarely went to bed before 11 P.M., was in his room at the end of the hall playing with computer games. Melody wore a colorful silk caftan of rose, plum, and pink that outlined her curved body to perfection. She sat down on the intricately carved Queen Ann chair, placing her steno pad on the polished maple table.

"Jack?" she called again.

"Coming . . ."

Smiling, she watched her husband come from the side room where he had his study and office. At twenty-nine, he still looked like the college football quarterback she'd married eight years earlier. Whipcord lean, Jack had always reminded her of a wolf. His eyes were hazel colored, sometimes almost an amber tone when he made hot, hungry love with her. When he was going to fly a test flight, they were narrowed and green looking, reminding her of a hawk intent upon his prey. Now, as he swaggered toward her in his red shirt, dark brown slacks, and loafers, she saw his eyes were a blue green. That was a sign he was happy.

She smiled and tilted her head up to receive his kiss. "Mmmm, this is almost my favorite time of night," she said, returning his swift, hard kiss with equal fervor.

Jack grinned, sat to her left, and opened up his notebook. "I like a woman with long, thick black hair. Reminds me of a river moving quietly through the darkness. Never can tell how deep it is, or the currents that run under it."

"That's why you married me, Captain Stang."

"Roger that, pretty one. You're mysterious, elegant, and no one but me knows what lurks below your surface." He smiled and flipped open the notebook, ballpoint pen ready. "Okay, let's get down to brass tacks here, and then I'll court you properly in the bedroom later."

"Promise?" Melody liked the challenging smile on his long face. Jack wasn't pretty-boy handsome, but he had other assets. His eyes were large and intelligent. His aquiline nose had been broken two times during his four years at the Air Force Academy when he was their star quarterback. The thin, white scar across his left cheek only emphasized his bold, hawklike features. Jack's chin warned everyone he was a warrior. It was square and strong. He took after his attorney father in looks a great deal, but his genetic scientist mother had given him her facile intelligence and remarkable eyes. A good combination, in Melody's opinion.

"Have I ever broken a promise to you, yet?" Jack reminded her archly.

"Never. Okay, you go first." She took a third piece of paper, a chart graph, and placed it between them.

"Okay, today Merrill and Porter flew the F-15."

"How'd it go?" Melody was hoping Merrill screwed up in some way, to keep him pinned down in the number three slot.

Grinning, Jack said, "Porter's having to reschedule the test for tomorrow."

Melody clapped her hands. "Excellent! What happened?"

"Roger that. Merrill couldn't hit the landing spot with the bird because we had stiff crosswinds."

"Better him than you," Melody said with genuine feeling. Bad weather was a fickle and unaccounted for variable in testing. If it had to strike, Melody always hoped it was when one of the other test pilots was flying, so it would drag down their percentile rating, and not Jack's. "So far, so good."

"Right. I fly tomorrow."

"And Holt?" She didn't like the upstart bastard, and had no respect for anyone who wasn't a graduate of the Academy.

"He flies the second test with Porter."

"Who's your flight engineer?" She hoped it was Pete Johnson. He was a fellow ring knocker. Lauren Porter was too, but Jack hated her with a passion.

"Pete. I lucked out. Holt get's sourpuss Porter, and I get my buddy."

Melody checked off several items, and made a red line on the graph which charted all three test pilots concerned with the short-landing F-15 *Eagle* assignment. "I *wish* you would get on Porter's good side. She's a major, you know. One rank above you, and the boss of that project. Really, Jack, if you could just overlook her feminist attitude and get in good with her, she might boost your percentile rating." Flight engineers had input on rating the test pilot's flying skills; Melody sensed strongly that Porter deliberately lowered Jack's scores to get even with him for constantly challenging her because she was one of the few women in a man's world.

Rearing back in the chair, Jack gave her an irritated look. "That bitch and I aren't ever going to have a cease fire, Melody. Every damn time I get around her, she jumps on me for something I said or did."

Sympathetically, Melody said, "You can't help it if you're a football hero, the number-one slotted golden arm heading for the next assignment: testing the B-2 bomber. Women like Porter want it all. They don't want someone like you around to remind them of what they aren't or can't ever be. There's no such thing as a woman star quarterback, so Porter is going to have to work hard to be recognized in other ways. She's competitive, just like you.''

''It'd be my luck she'll get assigned to the B-2 project, too. Damn.'' Jack brought the legs of the chair back down on the carpet, scowling. ''Isn't there anything you can do from your end? She's engaged to Major Ryan Malone who's assigned to NASA on the base. What do your contacts have on him?''

''Unfortunately, nothing. Judy, who works over at the NASA cafeteria, tells me he's never made a pass at another woman over there. I'm afraid he's true-blue to Porter.''

''There isn't a jet jock alive that's single who wouldn't respond to a pass from a good-looking body.''

Melody tapped the pencil on the table in thought. ''Well . . .''

''Uh oh, you've come up with a plan.'' Jack was delighted, always intrigued with the way Melody thought.

''What about Liza? She's new, and according to my source over there, a blond bombshell who hangs around at the O Club every Friday night in a leather miniskirt and tube top. If I'm right, Malone likes the model type. Look at Porter: She's thin as a toothpick.'' Melody gestured to her full breasts.

Jack grinned. ''I like my woman with some flesh on her bones.''

''Don't I know it.'' Melody was five feet, nine inches tall, weighing one hundred and thirty pounds. Jack had always liked her full figure, and so had she.

''I've heard on the grapevine this Liza is new and hot.''

''Yes, she showed up at the O Club about a month ago. So far, she lays the jocks, but hasn't got tangled up with one on a steady basis yet. She likes to play the crowd.''

''Maybe you ought to send Judy over to talk to Liza about making a few passes at Malone. Have Judy slip her a twenty or fifty to do it.''

Melody arched one eyebrow. ''And Liza may do it for free because she thinks it's a challenge, or fun. You know how those groupies are. And even if Malone doesn't take the bait, everyone in the cafeteria will see Liza and him sitting together. She's an outrageous flirt.''

Rubbing his hands together, Jack grinned. "Yeah, I like that. Let me know when you set it up. I'll make *sure* Lauren hears about it pronto. I'd like to see something knock her on her arrogant ass. Maybe stirring up some gossip and innuendos in her personal life will make her screw up on the software programming or testing."

"Just make sure it's not a test you're flying," Melody warned darkly.

"Don't worry, I'll make sure Holt or Merrill is scheduled to fly with the bitch. I'll just drop the bomb and then sit back and watch it explode." Jack leaned forward. "Now, what have you heard today? Anything juicy or gossipy I can spread over at Ops tomorrow morning?"

"Hmmm, I don't know. I had lunch with the NASA wives today. Of course, Sandy Yale, the wife of your boss, Colonel Bob Yale, was there. I made sure I sat with her."

"I'll bet you out-aced all the rest of the captains' wives who wanted to sit with her, too."

"Of course. I'm not a banker's daughter for nothing, sweetheart," Melody laughed.

"Add to that a master's degree in psychology," Jack congratulated her, proud of her accomplishments. "Between the two, honey, you maneuver very well."

"In and out of bed," she reminded him, laughing.

Jack slid his hand over hers, giving it a squeeze. He liked her maneuvers in bed. Never had he met a woman who matched his sexual appetite like Melody did. "So, what new gossip did you pick up today? Anything?"

Melody consulted her notes she always kept on a steno pad. She carried it in her briefcase wherever she went on base. At luncheons, club meetings, or dinners, she would memorize names with places and gossip, later writing it down in the car where she wouldn't be seen.

"Well, Becky Merrill was supposed to be there, and wasn't. It's not like her not to be present. You know how Merrill pushes her on us. That Arkansas hillbilly will never make it as an Air Force wife."

"True," Stang returned, thoughtful. "She wasn't there?"

"No."

"I wonder why?"

"I asked Scotty if Patty was in school with him, and he said yes. So, it couldn't be because Patty was ill and Becky had to stay home and take care of her today."

"Hmmm. Unusual."

"Yes, but we don't have anything concrete to make a pro or con assessment on it."

"I think I'll hit Merrill with it tomorrow morning and see how he reacts."

"Good idea. As my corporate father would say: keep the enemy off balance—attack."

"That's another reason why I love you: your very successful family."

"*Rich* and successful family," Melody corrected.

"That doesn't hurt either."

"Yours is just as well off as mine."

"True. You can't say that for the rest of these guys, though."

"No, they're not as astute or business oriented as we are," Melody pointed out. "Or, they don't cultivate those skills."

"Good thing they don't," Jack muttered, "or it would make my goal to become a major the first time around, harder." Very few officers made their next rank the first time around when they came up for promotion. Usually, it was on the second, third, or even fourth try, that they managed to get the next rank. To make it the first time was spectacular, alerting everyone that the officer had a hell of a powerful sponsor behind him. Jack prayed that if he had a sponsor, he'd come through for him this February, when he was up for major the first time around.

"You've got a sponsor," Melody cut in, "so don't worry. As long as you remain number one in the testing phase, no one will deny you your major's leaves in February, darling." She reached out and placed an inviting kiss on the grim line of his mouth. In moments, his mouth softened, became hungry, and she languished in the fire that always simmered so close to the surface of his needs.

Reluctantly, Jack eased from her delicious, welcoming

lips. He held her dark-green eyes that mirrored longing that matched his own. Smiling, he tunneled his long, slender fingers through her thick ebony hair. "You're a very beautiful woman, in a very beautiful body."

"And you love me that way," she added huskily.

"We've got one more thing to discuss, and then we can get to pleasure," Jack told her, and withdrew his hand from her hair. He could taste the lingering sweetness of her on his mouth.

Disappointed, but understanding, Melody straightened. "It has to be about Holt."

"Yes." Jack tipped back in the chair and stared up at the light-blue ceiling. They lived on base like just about everyone else did. With their combined incomes, they were able to afford a sumptuous house in Lancaster, but decided against it because he wanted to be close to the action and politics of the base. "I had number-one slot sewn up before that bastard was assigned here six months ago."

Melody gave an unladylike snort. "You'd think that the crash one month after his arrival that killed Russ Davis would have washed him up, but it didn't."

Jack rubbed his jaw in thought. "Yeah, when that happened, I knew he had a pretty powerful sponsor. No, some general upstairs put the word out to keep his ass here and flying. And look at him: in six months, we're half a percentile apart in test ratings. Damn." He glanced over at Melody. "How can a nongraduate worm his way into the brotherhood like that? Those jokers that graduated from flight school can't compare to a ring knocker."

"He's hungry," Melody put in quietly. She got up, walking around the oblong table covered with an expensive damask tablecloth. "I've been piecing a profile together on him, Jack. Holt isn't all he seems to be."

"I wish to hell you could get friendly with someone over at Personnel so I could take a look at his personnel records. Holt never talks about his past, or where he's been or what he's done."

"That's my point, darling: he's got a past he's hiding or running from. Or both."

"He's got a smart mouth on him, too." Jack didn't like Holt's ability to land on his feet. "He reminds me of a junkyard dog: lousy breeding, aggressive, and wants it all."

"Don't we?" Melody laughed, and placed her arms around her husband's broad shoulders. She pressed a kiss to his military short dark-brown hair. "We were luckier than Holt. We had parents who recognized our natural abilities and gave us opportunities to capitalize on them. Plus we have better bloodlines."

Jack slid his hands along her arms, scowling. "All I can get out of Holt is that he graduated from Michigan State with a degree in aeronautical engineering. From there, he joined the Air Force and went to flight school."

"I overheard Porter say one day that his whole life is flying. He doesn't have a girlfriend."

"He's over partying it up every Friday and Saturday night at the O Club along with the rest of the studs. He's got his pick of women. Why should he want a steady significant other?"

Wanting to soothe Jack because she felt the tension gathering in his shoulders, Melody began to gently knead his scalp. He groaned, tipping his head back against her body and closing his eyes.

"My source at the O Club says he flirts a lot, drinks a little, dances a lot, but rarely takes one of the groupies to his house in Lancaster. He's not the party animal we both wished he was."

"He's careful," Stang muttered, enjoying her fingers massaging his tight scalp.

"Holt's not stupid enough to drink heavily. He knows alcohol and flying don't mix. No, the man's savvy as a wild animal." Indeed, Melody thought, there was something primal about Sam Holt. Because she was a psychologist, she was trained to watch and record. Holt walked quietly, his eyes constantly perusing, missing little, if anything. "He's a lone wolf type," she told her husband. "And he doesn't trust anyone enough to let down his barrier about his past to them. What we need to find is a woman who can get past those walls. Armed with his past, you might be able to get him upset and maybe, lose some of that cool behind the stick of a jet.''

"Right now I needle him about the crash. That gets a hell of a response out of him.''

"Yes, he's guilt ridden over Russ Davis's death. You should keep reminding him of that when it's prudent.''

Chuckling, Jack slowly opened his eyes and looked up at her. "Don't worry, I do. Tomorrow, I'm going to start on Porter's case about it.''

"Oh, Jack, don't! She's just as strong and bullheaded as you are. The whole thing will backfire on you.''

He smiled. "Don't get upset, Melody. You're not the only one that took psychology. I want to put Porter and Holt at odds. I want to break up their buddy system they've established between one another. If I can put doubt in Porter's mind that she'll be dead flying with Holt, then she may start grading him lower.''

"I see . . .''

Jack patted her arm and stood up, coming around the chair and pinning Melody against him. She felt good in his arms, and he felt that familiar, burning feeling in his lower body, wanting her, needing her. "Yeah, tomorrow ought to be a banner day. I can bug Merrill about his no-show wife, and get Porter thinking about Holt in a different light. I can hardly wait.''

Melody nodded and rested her head against his shoulder. "There's one more thing we need to discuss, darling.''

"What's that?''

Hesitating fractionally, Melody said, "Scotty. I got a call from Miss Roberts today.''

Groaning, Jack pulled away from her. "What now?''

"Jack, Scotty won't or can't sit still in class. He's being totally disruptive. You know how he is around here: in constant motion. Ever since he was born, he's been on the move.''

"Well, dammit, there's nothing wrong with it. Scotty will be a star athlete when he grows a little more. He's in Little League this year. That ought to take the edge off him.''

Risking his temper, Melody added, "Jack, our son had

this problem last year, and it seems to be worse this year, from what I can tell. Miss Roberts apparently hasn't looked at his personnel file at school yet.''

"There had better not be anything incriminating in Scotty's file. We paid plenty of money last year to have those reports destroyed. If she files a report, Melody, it won't look good for my fitness report if it gets out and around base. If Colonel Yale or General Dalton get ahold of that kind of damaging information, I'm in big trouble. The kid has *got* to straighten out!''

Upset, Melody moved away from her husband and went to sit down. Automatically, she checked down the hall to make sure Scotty's door was closed. It was. "Jack, keep your voice down. This is our problem and we've got to solve it.''

"Who'd you talk to last year when that damn teacher, Linda Yarnell, blew the whistle on Scotty?''

"I talked to Brad Jamison, the assistant principal.''

"What did he want to destroy those reports?''

"Money, of course.''

"Get him on the horn. Tell him to get to Roberts and tell her to knock it off.''

"He'll want more this time, Jack.''

"So, give it to him! Money is something we don't have to worry about. But money can't buy my test pilot career. You give Jamison what he wants.''

"Jack,'' Melody protested, "I really think we ought to get Scotty to a doctor in Los Angeles and have him tested.''

He resisted the plea. "Dammit, Melody, you've been on me about this for over a year.''

"Yes, because Scotty isn't normal for his age.'' She saw his eyes narrow with fury. "And don't go getting angry with me, Jack. It's not my fault.''

"Scotty was born premature. Could that be it?''

"Possibly.'' She rubbed her brow in thought. "Part of my degree in psychology was with dysfunctional and behavioral problems involving children, Jack. I really think Scotty is hyperactive.''

He snorted. "We've been over this before: I'm not going

to have my son on some drug that dulls him to the point of behaving like a mental retard! Dammit, Scotty is bright and intelligent, Melody! There's nothing wrong with him! It's these lazy-assed teachers who don't want to baby-sit them like they should who are at fault."

Rising, she said nothing. Jack followed her down the hall toward their bedroom.

"You'll call Jamison in the morning?" he demanded tightly.

"Yes, I'll call him."

— 5 —

THE first voice Holt heard when he swung in the doors of Operations Tuesday morning, was that of Jack Stang.

"Hey, Merrill, my wife said Becky wasn't at the NASA luncheon yesterday. How come?"

Frowning, Holt took off his garrison cap and tucked it in one of the pockets of his dark-green flight suit. He saw Curt at the weather desk, Stang standing next to him.

"She had the flu," Curt lied.

"Flu? In late September? That's kind of early for it to be going around, isn't it? Scotty hasn't said anything about it at school, either."

Uncomfortable beneath Stang's needling scrutiny, Curt took the weather information and turned away. Becky hated the luncheons, always uncomfortable in large groups of people. She had called General Dalton's wife and begged off with a case of flu. If she missed too many luncheons, it wouldn't look good on his fitness report, which was issued every six months, but Curt didn't have the heart to get angry about it. Becky was still under strain from this last move. He nearly ran into Holt.

"Morning, Sam."

"Morning, Curt."

Stang turned, sizing up his competition. "How'd the balloon rally go, Holt? Did you come in dead last?"

"You're just a sunny spot in my morning, you know that, Jack?"

He grinned. "Is my pessimism showing?"

"No, your ignorance. I came in second out of twenty entries." Sam turned, walking down the highly polished white tile hall, Curt at his shoulder. Merrill was chuckling under his breath.

"Holt one, Stang nothing. Damn good thing you're bright eyed and bushy tailed this early in the morning," Curt said, flashing him a grin, "because I never am."

"Stang doesn't know when to ease off the throttles. How's Becky doing?"

Lowering his voice, Curt told Sam the truth.

"Smart idea about the flu angle," Sam congratulated.

"Yeah, with Stang snooping around, looking to heap any kind of gossip and trouble on my head, I had to think of something to cover for Becky," Curt growled.

"Hang in there, buddy, don't let him get to you. Once he does, it's all over," Sam warned. He worried about Curt, who didn't have a thick skin like he did. Stang was one of those people, who, if he didn't stir up the pot on a daily basis, creating chaos and roller-coaster feelings among his compatriots, wasn't happy. Of course, everyone else was unhappy when Stang did it, not totally immune to his sometimes lethal comments. Still, Sam felt as long as he dished it back at Stang just as strongly, he'd keep the pilot somewhat in check. Somewhat...

They halted at the door that said Design, and entered. Sam spotted Major Lauren Porter at one desk, leaning over a bunch of blueprints, cup of coffee in hand. She was dressed, as usual, in her olive-green flight suit and highly polished black flight boots. However, that didn't detract from her femininity in Sam's opinion. Lauren was elegant, like a thoroughbred with good breeding. She was tall, thin, and refined. Unlike a lot of other women flight officers, she wore makeup when she wasn't flying. Today, she didn't, because she'd be in the cockpit with him later.

They found out a long time ago that air would leak out between the oxygen mask on a woman's face if she wore makeup. Already, his day was getting better. Sam raised a hand in her direction.

"Morning, Port." The last five months of working with the flight engineer had been pure joy in Sam's opinion. She was their boss and headed up the *Agile Eagle* project. Chestnut hair, intelligent brown eyes, and a computerlike brain plus Lauren's good looks was an excellent combination. It didn't hurt matters that Lauren preferred to fly with him, and gave him higher percentile marks for flight skills.

"Hi, Sam, Curt."

Holt headed to the thirty-cup coffee maker near her desk. It was only 0700, but everyone in testing was hard at work. It was one of the few professions he could think of where the people involved hated to leave work at night and could hardly wait to get back to work *early* the next morning.

"Well," Lauren said, continuing to study the blueprints on the F-15 *Eagle*, "did you get lucky and run into Stang out at the weather desk?"

"Yeah."

"He's in a particularly virulent mood this morning."

Chuckling, Sam handed a cup of coffee to Curt, took one for himself, and then ambled over to her desk. "That's nothing out of the ordinary."

"That's all right," Merrill said, sitting down at his desk. "Holt nailed Stang's tail to the ground."

Lauren's thin brows rose. She glanced over at Holt, who leaned over her shoulder and studied the prints. "Oh?"

"Yeah, so far the score's in my favor."

"Let's tally it up at the end of the day," Lauren warned dryly. "Stang's usually ahead by that time."

A careless grin crossed Holt's face as he studied the proposed new landing gear assembly on the F-15. "*If* he stays out of your gun sights, Port. Only then does he win. Otherwise, you shoot him down."

"Well," Lauren muttered, pulling her computer keyboard closer, punching in some numbers and studying the monitor intently, "I'm in a bad mood today, so he'd better watch his mouth or he'll crash and burn so fast it will make even his seasoned head spin."

"Ohhh," Merrill hooted with delight. "I hope Stang is stupid enough to walk through the door. When Lauren is 'on,' she's ready to go Mach 3 with her hair on fire."

Laughing, Lauren shook her head. "You're both crazy."

"But you love us anyway," Sam said, sipping the scaldingly hot coffee.

"I'd never admit it." Frowning, she put some more numbers in the computer, unhappy with the readout. "Darn . . ."

Sam studied the numbers on the monitor, and then the blueprint under her elbows. "Problems?"

"Yes . . . and no. I'm working with the McDonnell design engineers over at Palmdale to reinforce the landing gear assembly on number 71290. After Stang cracked the frame on the left gear two weeks ago, we're trying to figure how it occurred and then ensure it doesn't happen again."

Sam nodded. The F-15 was the hottest fighter the Air Force owned. It was a single seater, although two had been specifically rigged with a second seat for the flight engineer during the ongoing test flights. There were three Air Force flight engineers working on the *Agile Eagle* project, and he considered Lauren the best. So did General Dalton, the head of testing. "That gear assembly cracked because Stang dropped the bird to the deck in order to make that fifteen-hundred-foot landing limit."

Hell, Stang had stalled the bird. The F-15 had literally fell from an altitude of thirty feet, like a rock dropping out of the sky, and slammed into the end of the runway. During the inspection, Lauren, who rode with Stang on that test, was the first to discover the crack. Stang had bitched that she had it in for him; an immature response, but Holt didn't expect much else from the golden boy here at Ops. Stang knew he was number one, and it was obvious to him. He had one hell of a powerful sponsor—no matter whether he flew good one day and lousy the next, he could do no wrong.

Tapping the monitor, Lauren remarked, "Holt, you took your test pilot training with the Navy."

"That's right." Sometimes, the services swapped pilots and put them through the other's test pilot school. Holt had been fortunate enough to be chosen to go to Patuxent River, Maryland, and take the U.S. Navy equivalent to the Air Force test pilot school. Only there, Holt had to learn how to land and take off from the heaving deck of a carrier; something no other Air Force pilot had experience doing. That was one of the reasons he'd been chosen for the *Agile Eagle* project; creating a bird capable of short takeoffs and landings, just like a naval aircraft. The Air Force chief of staff had decided that during a wartime situation, most runways would be bombed, making the F-15 incapable of taking off because of the craters. So now, they were redesigning the bird for a much shorter takeoff so it could get into the air and fight.

"Tell me, did Stang land it properly? When he dropped in, I thought he'd come in too high. And when he hit," Lauren ruefully rubbed the back of her neck, "I felt like I'd been in an auto accident. I think I got whiplash out of the deal."

Sam nodded sympathetically. "I watched the landing. He brought the nose up too high and stalled it. When you come in for a carrier landing, it's a controlled crash situation. You have full flaps and slats down and locked, the nose is up, but just this side of stall position. Stang went over the stall limit, and the bird fell."

Using his hands, Holt showed her what he meant. "If the nose is pitched up at the correct angle, you get a last moment cushion of air that helps to take the brunt of the landing jolt."

"And the gear assembly doesn't take half the punishment as a result. Right?"

"You got it." And then he smiled. "It's all in the attitude of the nose, Port."

Grumbling, Lauren went back to study the figures on the monitor. "That chauvinist bastard crashed my bird and crippled it. Probably handles his women the same way: he figures a little abuse is good for them.''

Chuckling, Sam watched Lauren work for several minutes. Flight engineers frequently adopted the plane they worked with as their own; their baby, so to speak. Lauren's chestnut hair gleamed with a few red highlights, reminding him of Megan Roberts. By military regs, her hair barely brushed the back of her collar. There was nothing for him to do until 0800, when the second F-15, tail number 71291, would be prepared for the flight. He'd take the jet up and run it through a series of landing tests and try to hit the magic fifteen-hundred-foot limit—without cracking the landing gear. So far, no one had been able to because of a number of reasons. It was the flight and design engineers' headache to figure out why, and then fix the situation so they could.

"Met a gorgeous redheaded lady Saturday out at the balloon rally,'' Holt confided. He saw Lauren's mouth curve into a doubtful smile. She was a feminist of the first order, and Sam respected her for it. "Now, don't go getting that look, Port. It's not what you think.''

"Usually you tell me about the gorgeous blond, brunette, or raven-haired beauty you've met over at the O Club on the weekend.''

"Well . . .''

"Red's your favorite color.''

He brightened. "Yeah. And she's got the spirit of a redhead.''

"I know: you like your women hot, like the jets you fly.''

"Now, Port.''

Lauren gave him a one-eyebrow-raised look. "Sam, what you do in your free time's your business. I just don't like hearing about you guys chasing down these poor teenage groupies who don't know any better. That's like letting a fox into the chicken coop, and you guys aren't the chickens.''

Smiling, Holt nodded. "Touché, Major. No, this lady's different.''

"Sure.''

"Honest, Port, she is. Listen to this . . .'' and he filled her in on Megan Roberts from beginning to end. Sam saw interest in Lauren's eyes when he was done with his story.

"A school teacher? That's really blasé compared to what you normally like. I mean, a month ago, it was that black-haired sprint car driver from LA. Two months ago, it was a blond-haired mountain climber from Europe. Isn't Megan a bit pedestrian for your tastes?"

Raising his hands, Holt protested, "No way! She's a fighter, and I like that."

"It doesn't sound like she's too crazy about you."

"Give her time. I rub off on people."

"Don't I know it."

With a smile, Sam straightened, going for his second cup of coffee for the day. "Port, I'm your favorite pilot, and I know it."

With a chuckle, Lauren wrote down a set of figures on her test flight form. "I know, Holt: nobody needs to tell test pilots how great they are. They'll tell you themselves."

The door opened. Holt barely turned his head and saw that it was Stang. He had a bunch of weather maps in hand.

"Hey, boys and girls, we've got excellent winds today," Jack announced. He threw the data down on his desk and ambled over to the coffee pot.

"That your second or third cup, Holt?"

"Second."

Jack reached for his ceramic mug that had SUPER STAR written on the side of it. "Coffee makes the nerves jittery, Holt. And you're flying in less than one hour."

Watching the tall, lanky pilot, Sam leaned against the wall and sipped his coffee. "I'll take my chances," he returned dryly.

"Shaky hands," Jack added, "are a bad start to your day. You could blow the test this morning."

"I don't think you'd mind," Sam offered.

With a shrug, Stang wandered over to Lauren's desk, looking over her shoulder. She ignored him. "Can't say I'd cry over it, Holt. I need to put more distance between you and I in the percentile ratings. And I don't have to worry about Merrill."

Sam saw Merrill scowl, hard at work on some test flight reports that needed to be brought up to date in time for the Friday meeting of all concerned parties on the project. Curt was a good five percentage points behind and had had three weeks of bad luck on test flights. The winds had made the flights Curt flew tricky. As a result, many of the tests were blown and had to be rescheduled. It wasn't Curt's fault; he was a damn good pilot. It was just the luck of the draw.

"Well, maybe the winds will be with me this morning," Holt said. He had to get down to the lockers, put on his G-suit chaps, pick up his helmet, and get out to the apron where the crew was preparing the *Agile Eagle* for his test flight. "Port, you coming?"

"Yes, I'll meet you down at the lockers in about five," she called, concentrating on the numbers before her.

"Hey," Jack said, trying to get Lauren's attention, "how're you and that fiancé of yours doing?"

Quirking her lips, Lauren refused to look up at Stang. "That's none of your business, Jack."

"Oh . . ." He smiled slightly. "Set a date for the wedding yet? My wife wanted to know. She likes to buy gifts ahead of time."

Sam slowed his walk toward the door, keying in on Stang's latest needling. He had a habit of picking on the two individuals who had to fly a test. Did he do it consciously or unconsciously? Stang's competitiveness didn't have any honorable borders or lines. Anyone who didn't fly with him was against him. And since Port wasn't going to fly the test with him, Stang saw her as the enemy.

With a dramatic sigh, Lauren buttonholed Stang. "I keep my private life private, Captain. If and when we get married, you'll probably be the last to know."

Holt winced. Lauren's voice was cold contempt. She hated Stang because he was a male chauvinist, while she was the ultimate feminist. "See you at the locker, Port," he called merrily, disappearing out the door.

Jack ambled over to his desk. He didn't have to fly today. Instead, he'd watch how Holt and Porter flew the test this morning. Hopefully, Holt would screw it up. Worried, he sat down, pulling over a manual on the F-15. Last week, he'd been responsible for putting a fracture in the gear assembly. They were still repairing the bird over at Palmdale as a result. Only one bird was still available for testing, slowing down the projected curve. That wasn't good. It put pressure on everyone to make up for lost time.

Looking up from the open manual, Jack studied Merrill. The pilot was buried in a pile of meteorological data on his desk. "Hey, according to Scotty, Patty really throws some temper tantrums in Miss Roberts's class. What's going on with that kid of yours, Merrill?"

"What?" Curt scowled, jerking a look in Stang's direction.

"Patty. Your kid's causing havoc in Scotty's class. He came home Friday and said she threw her pencil across the room and started screaming—for no reason at all." He grinned. "Maybe she needs a little discipline."

"Maybe," Merrill said, anger vibrating in his voice, "you need to mind your own business."

Jack sat back, rocking in his chair. "Can't do that, Curt. Scotty's education is getting interrupted with Patty's antics. Maybe Miss Roberts needs to invoke the spanking paddle rule. That always quiets them down."

Lauren glared at Stang and stood up. The pilot smiled easily, watching her pick up her briefcase and walk to the door.

Good, Jack thought, they were alone. Now was the time to really put the screws to Merrill. If he could keep the pilot agitated, he would continue to fly poorly. Getting up, he sauntered over to Curt's desk.

"Hey, look, I'm concerned about Patty. And I'm sure you are, too."

Merrill's hand curled into a fist, and he stared up at Stang's narrow, intent features. "Patty's fine," he ground out.

"This isn't the first time Scotty came home from school telling us about her."

"Look, Patty's just going through a stage."

With a shrug, Jack muttered, "Some stage. Maybe that

wife of your needs to show her a belt or switch instead of sweet-talking her.''

With a snort, Merrill forced himself to look down at the data, not really seeing it. ''Stang, it's well known you don't believe in sparing the rod to spoil the child.''

''That's right, buddy. My dad used to beat the hell out of me with a belt when I screwed up. But,'' he grinned, ''look at the results. I'm the chief test pilot, and number one in the ratings. A little punishment goes a long way. Maybe you ought to think of using a little on Patty so she doesn't keep disrupting Scotty's class.''

Taking a deep breath, Merrill gritted, ''I'm busy, Jack.''

''Roger.'' Sauntering back to his desk, Jack smiled, satisfied. Merrill was thoroughly agitated. He was overly sensitive about his wife and kid and responded like a porcupine to Stang's comments. *Excellent*. His mind swung back to Holt. Only one thing seemed to get to that bastard: the crash five months ago. Yes, it was time to start reminding Holt about it again. Maybe it would shake his confidence.

Megan sat at her desk in the classroom and looked over her teaching guide for tomorrow's activities. A week had gone by since she had run into Sam Holt in the market. The windows were open, providing some relief from the sweltering temperature, but it wasn't enough. Three P.M. was the worst heat of the day, and she wiped a thin film of perspiration off her brow. Why couldn't she concentrate? Why?

Looking up, Megan stared unseeingly across the quiet room. Since meeting Sam Holt, her concentration had been anywhere but on teaching. His smiling face with the deep crow's feet at the corners of his eyes haunted her. How could it? He was a captain in the Air Force. A pilot was dangerous to any woman, to her heart, and the very survival of her soul.

''Damn,'' she whispered, putting down the pen and staring at the lesson plan on the desk. Rubbing her eyes, her mind revolved back to her proposal on outdoor education. Under Linda Yarnell's guidance, she had handed it over to her. She was president of their union. What was going on with it? Why hadn't she heard anything yet?

Brad Jamison jerked open the door to her room and strode toward her, his round face screwed up in fury. Megan got to her feet, fingertips resting lightly on her desk.

"What do you think you're doing?" Jamison rasped. He halted at her desk and glared at her. "If you think you're going to issue a weekly report on Scotty Stang for my office to handle, you're mistaken."

Megan's mouth dropped open. She had expected Jamison to attack her on the union rep pushing her proposal. Taken aback, it took precious seconds to gather her thoughts. "Scotty Stang has been completely unmanageable the last week, Mr. Jamison."

Savoring her discomfort, Brad jabbed a finger toward her. "There is *nothing* wrong with the boy, Miss Roberts."

Anger flared through Megan. "Really? Well, why don't you spend just an hour in my classroom and watch him. He's hyperactive!"

"Now you're a doctor and diagnosing."

Her fingers curled into her palms. "No, I'm not a doctor, but when I see a child who can't sit still for more than two minutes, who can't retain focus, and has to move around continually, I can recognize the symptoms of hyperactivity."

"Until the parents decide to get their son to a doctor, you have no business writing down such diagnosis, Miss Roberts." He threw her report on her desk. "Now, I suggest you forget this little fiasco."

Megan stood there, digesting Jamison's hate for her. His brown eyes were a muddy color, narrowed with fury. "I know why you're doing this, Mr. Jamison, and you're not getting away with it."

One corner of his mouth jerked upward. "You're new, Miss Roberts. And you don't know the system . . . or how to play the game yet." He pointed to her report. "You'd better get with your union rep and get filled in on how to make out a report."

"I'll do that." Jamison swung away and Megan called out strongly, "But this isn't going to be swept under the rug. Scotty has real problems. You can expect another report on your desk next week.''

Halting at the opened door, Jamison gritted out, ''There's nothing wrong with the boy. That's my assessment, and it carries weight, Miss Roberts. You'd better think twice before writing up another report on the boy. It makes *you* look like an incompetent teacher.''

Megan was about to retort when Sam Holt appeared. She blinked, shocked by his presence. Jamison looked him over, glared, and then shouldered on by him. Holt frowned and watched him for a moment before returning his attention to her.

''Hi. Did I walk in on World War Three? I heard you two all the way down the hall.'' Sam ambled into the room, concerned for Megan. She stood stiffly behind the desk, her green eyes filled with fury.

Megan's eyes widened. Sam was wearing his olive-green flight suit, the dark-blue garrison cap with silver piping at a cocky angle on his head. Holt removed his cap and walked across the room. He was darkly tanned, his blue eyes dancing with amusement and undisguised interest. Megan fumbled with the lesson plan, shutting it. ''I thought it was World War Three, too,'' she muttered. Trying to gather her strewn emotions, Megan added, ''I didn't expect to see you again.'' Her voice sounded shaky and low. Dying inside because Holt affected her powerfully, Megan tried to cover up her response to him.

Sam smiled, stopping at the front of her desk. ''Now, Red, did you really expect me to disappear from your life? How can I? I go to sleep thinking about you, I wake up thinking about you.''

''Lines, Captain. All lines.'' Or were they? That disturbing, intense look in his eyes made her feel unsure, and thoroughly feminine. Holt was *very* good at getting a woman's attention and response.

Sitting on the corner of the desk, Sam shrugged. ''Not a line with you.'' Megan looked nervous, so he added, ''Really, I came over for a reason.''

Sitting back in her chair, Megan heard the sarcasm in her

voice. "This had better be good, Captain, because I've heard every line in the book that you jet jocks wrote."

Running his fingers along the silver piping on his garrison cap, he glanced over at her. "I heard Captain Stang say that Patty's causing some disruption in her class. His son is Scotty Stang."

Megan didn't know whether to be relieved or disappointed. Holt had come about Patty. He wasn't really stalking her. "I know you're close to Patty, Captain, but I don't think I ought to be discussing her family problems with you."

"Yeah, I know the policy, but . . ." Holt pursed his lips for a moment. "I was just over at Curt and Becky's house, and frankly, I'm worried about Becky, Patty's mother."

"She's such a frail, sensitive thing." Megan said more to herself than him.

"Becky's just plain old hill folk. I've always felt this kind of life was rough on her," Sam agreed, holding her gaze.

"This kind of life is tough on every woman and child of a pilot," Megan said with feeling.

"I know it is."

She gave him a nonplussed look. "You mean, a pilot is actually going to admit that?"

"Kind of obvious, isn't it?" Sam parried. "I know pilots are supposed to be egotistical with no sensitivity or awareness of anyone but themselves, but Becky's a hard-luck case. She just hasn't adjusted to the demands the Air Force puts on its people."

Megan had to shake herself. Her father never had that insight about herself or her mother. "I feel like I'm hearing things." She got up, wanting to get away from Holt, from the feelings he was stirring to life within her on strictly a personal and feminine level.

Sam studied her as she walked over to the chalkboard, cleaning it with an eraser. Megan looked pretty in the flowery summer dress with dolman sleeves and a simple, lacy white collar. It brought out the highlights in her mass of red hair that was drawn behind her ears and captured with a pink ribbon. She was wearing that same wonderful spicy scent that made him want to nuzzle into her hair and kiss her until she was breathless. Sam got up, sauntering over to the board.

"Look, I feel like there's a wedge between us, Megan." He groped for the right words and watched her green eyes widen. "Ever since you found out I was a pilot in the Air Force, you've been taking shots at me. I've tried to figure out what I did or said to deserve it, but I haven't come up with anything."

She felt heat rush to her cheeks, and she turned away, continuing to erase the board. "Captain, I just don't care for pilots."

"Yeah, I kind of got the feeling you didn't." He opened his hands. "But I came here today to discuss Patty with you, one adult to another. Can you look past my uniform and maybe give me some hints on how to help the kid and her family? Curt's like a brother to me, and frankly, he's not flying well because he's worried about his wife and daughter."

Stung by his honesty, Megan stopped her activity. She stared down at the dusty eraser. "Forgetting you wear a uniform isn't the problem, Sam. I simply won't discuss a child with someone other than the parents. I hope you understand."

He nodded. "I like your morals and values."

Oddly, Megan was relieved by his understanding that she couldn't speak in confidence about teaching matters.

Changing the topic, Sam said, "Who was that guy that just left? Or is that another confidential matter you can't speak about?" he teased.

Megan finished cleaning the board. "That's Brad Jamison, the assistant principal. I can't tell you what it was about, but I can say personally, between you and I, he doesn't like me."

"Why?" How could anyone dislike Megan?

Wiping off her hands on a cloth she kept in the drawer of her desk, Megan offered, "I'm bucking the system and it's obvious Jamison doesn't like a strong-willed woman who insists upon fighting for what she feels is right."

"Oh, your outdoor education proposal?"

"That's behind this latest episode with Jamison," Megan guessed.

"Look, maybe you ought to be more careful around this guy. He wasn't very happy looking when I came in. He's got the authority to hire and fire. I'd hate to lose you now that I've just found you."

Warmth fled through Megan, and she tried to make light of his serious comment. "I'm not going to cower or quit just because Jamison has the ability to get me fired. I believe I can keep pushing and still get my way without losing my job."

Admiration for her spirit made him smile. "My money's on you, Red. I can't believe any man would turn down anything you asked for."

"I hope you're right, Sam..." Then Megan caught herself. It was so easy to talk to him, and she groaned inwardly. He was a pilot! There was nothing they could share. Nothing!

Heartened because she'd trusted him just a little bit, Sam tendered her a slight smile. "There's something else we need to discuss, Megan."

"What?"

"I've been putting some pieces of our conversation together. You don't like men in uniform, especially pilots. I don't mind getting turned down by a lady because she doesn't like me personally, but to get shot down because I wear a uniform is something else."

Nervously, Megan moved away from the desk. Sam followed her.

He placed a hand on her shoulder and gently swung her around. "Red, tell me what happened. Were you married to a pilot and he augered in? I'd like to know."

Pain reared up through her and yet, Sam's hand on her shoulder muted some of it. His touch was one of comfort, not sexual in its overtones. Sam was inches away, and she could feel the heat, the strength of him. His fingers tightened imperceptibly.

"I need to know, Megan. Please. It's important to me."

He wanted to add, *you're important to me*, but he sensed Megan would run from him if he admitted that.

Megan bowed her head, fighting back unexpected tears. Holt's voice was low and filled with compassion. "My father was Colonel Steve Roberts, a test pilot here at Edwards," she whispered.

Holt's hand slipped off her shoulder. His eyes went wide as he assimilated the anguish behind her words. Suddenly, it all made sense. No wonder she was wary of pilots, she was still grieving for his loss. Roberts had been a very famous Air Force test pilot who had augered into the Mojave a year ago. "Damn . . . I'm sorry . . ."

Megan couldn't stand his pity and moved away. "Don't be."

Her tone was hard. Unforgiving. "You must have still been at school when you got the news?"

She fumbled with her papers and jammed them into her briefcase. Megan said, "Yes, I was in my junior year at Ohio State. This young Air Force lieutenant was at the door of my dorm at 5 A.M. in the morning, and he looked awful. He'd been assigned from the Columbus, Ohio recruiting office to come and tell me my father was dead." She snapped the briefcase closed with finality. "I don't know who was whiter: him or me."

Silence filtered into the room. Sam watched the shadows move across her face. "That's why you're afraid of a man in uniform."

Barely turning her head, she met and held his sad blue eyes. "I'm not afraid of you."

Something wasn't making sense. "Fear of the uniform, fear of losing someone you love to a plane? Isn't that it?"

"You'd never understand."

"Try me."

Stubbornly, Megan shook her head. "Sam, I don't hold anything against you as a man. But I can't—won't *ever* have a relationship with a man in the military. The Air Force has taken everything I ever loved away from me."

"Your father, yes, but what about your mother?"

Tears burned in Megan's eyes, but she refused to allow

them to fall. "The Air Force killed her too." She defiantly stared across the room at him. "What no one really ever knew was my mother turned to alcoholism to numb her fear of losing my father when he started testing jets. As she got worse, my father started running around on her. He didn't care if my mother knew he was partying over at the O Club and going home with the groupies. Seven years ago, she committed suicide because he refused to give up flying. She just couldn't take it anymore."

"Jesus," he stumbled, "I didn't know . . ."

Megan tore her gaze from Sam, unable to stand the agony mirrored in his eyes.

It hurt to breathe for a moment. Sam gently held her accusing glare. Everything made sense now. "You ran away on Saturday after I told you I was in the Air Force."

"Yes." Megan didn't understand why she felt so much pain in her chest. Holt was Air Force. He was a thirty-year man. There was nothing between them. Or was there? His face was readable. None of the arrogance that he'd walked in with was there now. She couldn't handle the compassion reflected in his features.

"Hell of a note, isn't it?"

Crossing her arm against her chest, Megan asked, "What is?"

"Us."

"What do you mean?"

Sam held her mutinous look. "I can't help it, lady, I like the hell out of you, and I'm not giving up because I wear a uniform." He took a couple of steps toward her and watched the panic mount in her eyes as he closed the distance between them. Lowering his voice, Sam admitted, "The moment I saw you, something happened to me, Red. I'm sorry about your past. Maybe with time, that can be overcome."

"Give it up, Captain," she quavered, backing away from him. Megan allowed her arms to drop to her side. "This is no chase and I'm not the quarry! You can play those games over at the O Club every night after you fly, not with me. So forget it!"

"I'm not going to give up," he informed her softly. "And I don't see myself as a hunter or you as the bait."

Megan shook her head. "You forget: I grew up on bases. I saw what you guys do to the girls, the women, the families."

There was such deep, vibrating anger coming from her that Sam knew he'd pushed her enough. Holding up his hand in a sign of peace, he managed a strained smile. "You're hurting, Megan, and you've got reason. I'd like to try and be a friend to you, an ear to listen, if you want. You're new here to Edwards, and probably don't have very many friends."

Holt's unexpected departure from the routine the jocks played threw her. All her anger over her father's callousness toward her and her mother's suicide seethed just beneath the surface. Yet, Megan didn't want to unleash it at him. And it was true: she was lonely, the process of making friends took time. Groping for words, she uttered, "Friend?"

"Sure." The crow's-feet at the corners of his eyes deepened. "I have four kid sisters and"—he patted his broad shoulder— "I've got lots of practice holding them, listening to them, and letting them cry."

Defensively, Megan said, "I've never seen a jet jock be a friend to *any* female."

"Yeah?"

"Yes!"

"Try me."

"What?"

"I said: try me. Test me out."

Warily, she sized him up. Holt was up to something, running a new game on her. "What do you mean?"

"Let me be your friend. I'm not such a bad guy, Megan. My friends will tell you I'm eccentric as hell, but I'm not a jerk. I don't have too many bad habits . . . well, I do have a tendency to drop my clothes where I undress and not put them in the clothes hamper."

Sam was impossible! The terrible tension between them suddenly dissolved when she laughed. It felt wonderful to take a deep breath because the past was hurting her so badly. The laughter absorbed her pain and neutralized it.

Grinning, Holt threw his hands on his hips. "See? I'm good for you."

The laughter died on her lips. There was such panic within her that it made her feel shaky. "No, Sam."

"No to what?

"No jet jock can be a friend to me."

"Why not?"

"Because . . ."

"Because you've never tried it before, that's why."

She turned away, wanting more distance between them because if she didn't, Megan knew she'd run into his arms just to be held. No one had held her at two of the most terrible times in her life, and with Sam standing there, strong and capable when she presently was not, it was too much for her to deal with.

"Megan?"

Whirling around, she said, "I'm too scared, don't you understand that? Please, leave me alone, Sam! I—I'm still too hurt, too . . ." She pressed the palm of her hand against her aching brow. "Don't do this to me. Just let me alone! I've got enough to work through here at Edwards without you adding to it!"

Her cry serrated him and made him visibly wince. More than anything in that moment, Sam wanted to take her into his arms. It was obvious that she carried pain around with her daily by being here at this base. Colonel Roberts had augered in a year ago at Edwards. Megan had come back. Why? To rectify her past? Work through her grief and loss of her father? Mother? Holt had a lot of questions and few answers.

"Take it easy," he coaxed huskily. "I'll leave." He didn't want to address the other issues. Megan was in enough pain. A large part of him was extremely protective of her, but something cautioned him to leave her alone. *Give her room.* Throwing her a mock salute, he said, "I'll be seeing you around, Red."

Megan stared after him. Holt's walk was cocky, brazen.

She liked the way he squared his broad shoulders. So why did she feel disappointed when he left? Hadn't she expected Holt to ask her out, or give her another line? Jet jockeys never quit once they had drawn a bead on their target. Wearily, she called it a day. Right now, her small Victorian apartment was all she wanted. There, she could hide and lick her oozing wounds that Holt had torn open by asking questions.

Her hands shook as she locked the desk drawer. So why had she leveled with Sam? What was so different about him that her heart trusted him, even if her wary head didn't? With a mutter of disgust, Megan put the keys in her purse and headed to the door. There were more important issues to address than that of Sam Holt muddying up her life.

— 6 —

CURT took off his sunglasses as he entered his home. The bright October sunlight poured in through the screen door when he opened. it. It was 1700, and he expected to find Becky in the kitchen cooking their dinner. Sniffing, there was no hint of food in the air like there usually was. Frowning, he hooked the sunglasses into the breast pocket of his green flight uniform.

In the past month since Patty's problems began in school, something had gone wrong, and he couldn't identify what it was. Becky was withdrawing from him, and it left him worrying constantly about her. About them. He found Patty playing in the kitchen, pots and pans scattered around her on the floor. Scowling, he looked around.

"Where's Mommy!" he asked her, crouching down.

Patty shrugged. "Don't know."

What the hell was going on? "Put those away, Patty. You know you're not supposed to play with them. The floor's dirty."

"Daddy . . ."

"Do it!" He straightened, glaring at his daughter, and watched as she stuck her lower lip out in a pout.

"Becky!" he called loudly, his voice carrying. "Becky!"

No answer. She would never leave Patty alone like this. Was she taking a bath? Agitated, Curt strode through the living room and down the hall. As he neared the master bedroom, the distinct smell of whiskey assailed his nostrils. Heart starting a hard pound, Merrill froze, stymied.

The door was locked. Cursing, he pounded on it. "Becky! Dammit, open up this door!" His voice carried down the hall. Breathing hard, Curt tried to capture his escaping feelings. "*Becky!*" Doubling his fist, he beat heavily on the wood.

Patty came running, poised at the end of the hall, her eyes large. Curt snapped his head to the right. "Get back in the kitchen!" he roared at her.

Tears formed and fell from Patty's huge brown eyes, and she turned with a sob, disappearing.

Anxiety paralleled his anger. No answer. What had Becky done? Drank whiskey because he'd flown today? Fear avalanched over him. He put his shoulder to the door and slammed all his weight into it.

The door gave way after the third try. Wood splintered. Merrill fell into the room and reclaimed his balance. The place was dark, reeking of whiskey.

"Becky?" His voice was wobbly. Squinting, Curt could barely make out her still form on the tangled covers of the unmade bed. Turning, he flipped on the switch, the sudden light hurting his eyes.

"Jesus . . ." Curt choked, hurrying to the bed. Becky lay in her bathrobe, unmoving. Beside her on the dresser was a bottle of half-consumed whiskey. Anxiously, Curt leaned over his wife and gripped her by the shoulders.

"Becky? Becky? Wake up!" Frantically, Merrill realized she had either passed out or had fainted. Sitting down, he brought his limp wife into his arms, her head lolling against his shoulder. Placing his hand near her small, fine nostrils, he waited. There! He could feel the moisture of her breath.

"Sparrow?" Oh, God, why was she doing this to him? He gently shook her and started to rub her cheek. "Wake up!"

With a moan, Becky raised her hand, and then it fell

limply back to her side. Barely lifting her lashes, she saw Curt's frozen features. "H-honey?"

Relief cascaded through him. He held her tightly against him. "Jesus Christ, Becky, you scared the hell out of me . . ." Curt buried his face in her hair. She felt so small and helpless in his arms. He kissed her hair, damp brow, and cheek that was now flushed with returning color. Looking into her half-closed eyes, he realized she was drunker than hell. Swallowing his anger, grateful that she had only passed out from the liquor, Curt simply held and rocked her.

"What a scare," he muttered. "I came home and Patty had all your pots and pans on the kitchen floor. I didn't know where you were . . ." Shakily, he threaded her uncombed hair through his fingers. The strands were so incredibly fine, almost gossamer, once again reminding him of her frailness.

"Why—I don't even recall Patty coming home. Oh, dear . . ."

"Sshhh, it's okay," Curt murmured, kissing her.

Struggling, Becky sat up. Her head ached intolerably, and she rested it between her hands. "Ohh, dear . . ."

Afraid to lose contact with her for fear she would disappear like fog before sunlight, Curt kept his hand on her small shoulder and rubbed it absently. "Don't try and talk, Sparrow. You've got to have an awful hangover. Let me fix you a bath, and you can start sweating it out. I'll make you some coffee later."

"Y-yes, that would be nice," she whispered faintly, keeping her eyes closed because every time she opened them, the room started spinning. "Patty?"

Merrill lifted his head and looked toward the entrance to the bedroom. For the first time, he saw the condition of the door. It was hanging by one hinge, the wood splintered and broken near the doorknob. "She's out in the kitchen."

Sliding her hand to his, Becky gripped it. "I—I don't want her to see me like this, Curt. P-please keep her out of here until I can get cleaned up."

That was why Becky had locked the door. Curt compressed his lips, but said nothing. "Okay, Sparrow. Just sit there until I get your bath water ready. I'll take care of Patty."

Miserably, Becky whispered, "Okay . . ." The small, functioning part of her mind felt nothing but relief over his reaction. Curt was home. He was safe. Knowing he had a flight scheduled for late this afternoon, she'd started drinking early this morning. Whiskey was the only thing that dulled her pain and worry over the fact that he might crash and be killed. Before, she had drank, being careful not to let Curt know about it. Today, her fear had been overwhelming, and she had drank far too much. Becky barely raised her head and watched Curt move to the bathroom attached to the master bedroom. She shivered, a chill racking her. The presence of the flight suit he wore made her nauseous. If only . . . no, he'd never do that. Later, after she got sober, she'd talk to Curt. She had to.

Patty watched television, her tiny chin resting in her small hands. Merrill had changed into civilian attire, a pair of dark-green slacks, and a white short-sleeved shirt. He'd opened a couple cans of pork and beans, thrown in some hot dogs, and heated them in the microwave for himself and Patty. Worry haunted him. Ever since he'd yelled at her, Patty had withdrawn. She hadn't eaten much of her dinner, either.

Rubbing his face, Curt realized he ought to be studying the flight manual for the next test he'd fly two days from now. But who the hell could study? Becky was slowly coming out of her drunk, and Patty had retreated into a shell of hurt silence. What should he do?

"Come here, Punkin." He scooped his daughter up. Pulling her arms tightly against her body as he positioned her in his lap, Patty shut her eyes. Curt embraced her and kissed her wrinkled brow. "I'm sorry I yelled at you earlier," he whispered. "But Mommy was sick, and I got scared."

Patty tensed, stubbornly refusing to open her eyes.

Merrill sighed, leaned back on the couch, and stroked her pigtailed hair. "Sometimes Daddy doesn't have time for you, does he? I wish I did, but I don't." He kissed her again, feeling her beginning to finally relax in his arms. That pout of hers was disappearing too. Smiling gently, Curt squeezed her. "Daddy loves you, Punkin."

"Mommy doesn't."

Frowning, Curt studied his daughter. Her huge brown eyes opened, staring up at him mutinously. "Of course she does."

"Uh uh."

Cupping her chin, he forced Patty to look at him. "Mommy hasn't been feeling well lately. But that doesn't mean she doesn't love you."

"Door was locked. Why'd she lock it, Daddy?"

Forcing a partial smile, Curt whispered, "Mommy didn't mean to. It was an accident. Next time you come home from school, she'll meet you at the gate." He looked up. Becky stood in the hall, bedraggled looking in her blue jeans and pink tank top. Her hair had been washed and combed, hanging limply around her shoulders.

Becky moved slowly to the couch, all her attention on her daughter. She sat down and slid her arm around Curt's shoulders. Gently, she stroked Patty's head.

"Mommy's sorry she didn't meet you this afternoon."

"You locked the door, Mommy."

"I know, honey. I didn't mean to. It was an accident." She leaned over, kissing her daughter. "I love you."

Curt watched his daughter blossom beneath Becky's care. In moments, Patty wiggled out of his arms and into hers. Relief surrounded him. The crisis was past. Just the way Becky cuddled Patty, and loved her with unabashed affection, brought tears to his eyes. That was one of the many things he loved about Becky: her openness, her ability to love fiercely.

"When do you fly again?" Becky asked in a hushed voice, holding Patty in her arms.

"Friday."

"More landing tests?"

"Yes." And then he added when he saw darkness in Becky's eyes. "Same old thing as before. It's not dangerous, it's simple."

Mouth quirking, Becky stared sadly at the television. "Nothing about testing or flying is safe, Curt."

Running his fingers through his hair, he got up. "Don't start," he warned her tightly.

"Where are you going?" She needed time with him, to heal herself.

"To the office. I've got to study."

"But—"

Curt turned. "Listen, I've got to put in a couple hours every night or I'll fall behind, Becky! You know that." When he saw her face become sad, he added, "Will you be okay now? Can I fix some pork and beans for you before I go study?"

"No . . . ya'll go ahead, go." She closed her eyes and rested her brow against Patty's hair. She heard the door shut quietly down at the end of the hall. Pain jagged through her, and Becky drew in a deep, uneven breath. When would all this anguish she carried daily in her heart go away? When? Did the other Air Force wives go through this kind of hell?

Becky had been afraid to talk about her fears to anyone because it might get around. And she knew gossip could ruin Curt's career. Desperately needing to talk to someone, her sluggish mind ranged over whom she could confide in. Curt didn't want to hear about her fears. He'd heard about them for seven years. Who to call? Who would understand? She stared at the phone, chewing on her lower lip. Of all the officers' wives, Becky had always admired beautiful, poised Melody Stang. Curt had warned her never to get chummy with her, but hadn't said why.

Transferring Patty to her other arm, she picked up the phone, punching in the numbers that would connect her with Melody, who lived three doors down on Sharon Drive.

"Captain Stang's residence," Melody answered.

"Hi . . . Melody, this is Becky. Becky Merrill."

Melody raised her eyebrows and sat down. "Yes, Becky." This was the first time she'd ever called. Something was up because Melody sensed the hesitancy in the woman's voice. Sweetly, she said, "How wonderful to hear from you."

"T-thank you, Melody. I—uh, called to ask you something."

Melody watched as her husband sauntered into the living room, test manuals in hand. Jack gave her an interested look, as if asking her who was on the phone. "Of course, Becky. How may I be of help?"

"I know this sounds silly, but I had to ask someone this question. A wife, I mean. Your husband flies. Do you ever get afraid before he goes up? I mean, bad dreams or a terrible fear that stalks you, and it won't go away 'til ya'll know he's safe?"

"Is that how you feel?" Melody probed gently, delighted with this new-found information. Becky had always kept to herself, and rarely could be drawn out to make even polite, social conversation at the fetes and club meetings.

"Oh, yes, ma'am, I do. I—I just needed a friendly ear, Melody. Every time Curt goes up, it gets worse for me."

"It's like that for all of us," Melody put in sympathetically. Of course, it wasn't, but she wanted Becky to trust her enough to tell her everything. She had ultimate confidence in Jack's flight skills and never worried about him flying or testing jets.

"I'm so glad to hear that," she sighed, a quiver in her voice.

Leaning back on the couch, Melody smiled triumphantly at Jack and gave him a thumbs up sign. "Listen, I have all the time in the world, Becky. Why don't you tell me everything, dear. After all, we're Air Force wives. If we don't stick together and help each other, who will?"

Curt stopped studying at midnight, too torn up about Becky's drinking. He left the office, shutting the door quietly. Patty was already in bed, asleep. He walked to the master bedroom. Becky was in bed, but she wasn't asleep. Girding himself, he went and sat down, his arm across her.

"How are you feeling, Sparrow?"

"Better," she murmured, absorbing his touch as he caressed her hair. "Did you get your studying done?"

With a grimace, Curt shrugged. "What I could of it, I did." He leaned over, pressing a kiss to her waxen cheek. "We have to talk, honey. What you did tonight scared the hell out of me."

Becky avoided his gaze. She held his hand against her stomach, needing his continued touch. "I didn't mean to, Curt."

"How long has this been going on?" he asked hoarsely.

"N-not long."

"What's that mean?"

She squirmed. "It means I take a drink or two when I know ya'll are going to test fly. That's all."

A heavy sigh came from Curt. He cupped her face. Becky's eyes were so huge and dark with fear. "You can't do that. You can't use alcohol to escape into, Becky."

"Well," she whispered, choking on a sob, "it's easy for you to say! You're not the one left behind. You don't have to worry if you're coming back. I do!" She sat up, moved away from him, and pulled the blankets about herself. "Don't you know how scared I get? Every time a jet flies overhead, I get this tightness in my belly. And Lordy, when that Klaxon goes off that means there's been a crash. I die inside until you can call me."

Curt hung his head. "Sparrow, I'm sorry, I truly am. But you've got to get ahold of yourself. You can't drink this way. It's bad for you. For us." He reached out, gripping her hand and gently pulling her into his arms. "Dammit," he said against her thin blond hair, "I love you. I don't know what I'd do without you and Patty. You're my life, Sparrow. My life."

Miserably, she shook her head, her fingers digging into his shirt front. Tears soaked her tightly shut lashes. "No," she sobbed, "flying's your first love, Curt Merrill. I've always known that. You love your flying more than you do Patty and I."

"That's not true!" he rasped, gripping her by the shoulders.

"It is!" she cried out.

Breathing hard, Curt stared at her contorted face, her cheeks wet with spilled tears. "No," he said, his voice quavering, "nothing could be further from the truth, Becky. My God, the last eight years of my life have been the happiest I've ever had. Haven't they been for you?" He was afraid of her answer, wondering if she loved him less than he had always loved her.

Wiping her face with a trembling hand, Becky said, "I—I've always been happy with ya'll. It's the Air Force, the pressure they put on me and Patty that's bad, Curt."

Dragging her into his arms, holding her tightly, Curt rocked her. "You've just got to get ahold of this problem, Becky. Whatever you do, don't tell anyone about it. If word gets out, my career could be sandbagged. We'll work this out together, okay?"

It hurt to breathe, to feel. Becky mutely nodded her head against his chest. Curt's arms were strong and secure around her. "I'll try..."

"Other pilot's wives don't have this problem," he went on. "They're not afraid like you are."

"Who can I talk to about this, then?" Becky asked in a small voice.

Curt thought for a long moment. "Sam Holt's a good ear. You've known him for the last seven years, Becky."

Sniffing, she mustered a slight smile. "He's like my big brother Alvin. Those two have so much in common. Sam cares for everyone."

"Yes, yes he does. Talk to him, Sparrow. Maybe he can give you some pointers. I'm subjective about this, and he'll be objective. Plus, he's someone safe to discuss this with. Sam won't spread it around base and hurt my career."

"Noooooo . . ." Sam Holt's scream caromed off the walls

of the bedroom. The covers slipped away, revealing his naked chest. Trying to reorient himself back to the present, Holt savagely rubbed his face. Russ Davis's image hung in his memory.

"Dammit," he whispered hoarsely. Throwing back the covers, he swung his legs across the bed. The hardwood floor was cool in comparison to his hot, sweaty body. It felt good, it brought him back into the present. Wiping his cheek with the back of his hand, Holt realized he'd been crying.

Shoving himself to his feet, he stood there, the moonlight pooling around him. His upper body gleamed with a heavy film of sweat. The drawstring pajamas clung damply to his lower body. When were these nightmares going to stop? When? Holt could smell himself and winced. It was fear sweat, not the normal kind of perspiration odor.

"Need a shower . . ." He walked unsteadily toward the bathroom. Holt didn't turn on the electricity, the moon providing enough light to see the handles to the shower. He wanted the water cold, to snap him out of the past and bring him back to the present. His mind revolved out of control, the sequence of events leading up to the crash still hovering over him.

Angry at himself, Sam jerked off the pajamas and moved into the cold, steady spray. With a gasp, he faced the cascade of water. In moments, the worst of the nightmare was pummeled away beneath the pulsating streams. Ducking his head under the shower, he scrubbed his hair and face with renewed savagery, wanting to erase the last of the memory.

When Holt stepped out twenty minutes later, he was shivering. Wrapping a yellow towel around his waist, he walked back into the bedroom, his feet making puddle prints across the walnut hardwood floor. With trembling hands, he groped for and found his blue terry cloth robe in the tangle of blankets at the bottom of the bed. Pulling it on, he let the towel drop to his feet.

He needed some coffee. Glancing at his watch, he saw it was 0300. The nightmare always came at that time. Padding through the large, silent house, Holt made his way to the kitchen. He fumbled for the percolator and coffee. Trying to forget the remnants of the nightmare, Sam focused on Megan Roberts. His hands steadied.

"Megan Roberts," he whispered, his brow wrinkling. Two weeks ago after speaking with her at the school, he'd sent her a dozen yellow roses and one red rose. And he hadn't heard a thing back from her. Well, what did he expect? She had been honest with him: she didn't like men in uniform. "Correction," he muttered, plugging in the coffee maker and then moving to the back door, "she doesn't like pilots." He liked her, civilian or not. Could he help it if her beautiful green eyes filled him with a peace he'd never known? Or that burnished red hair reminded him of a vivid, breath-stealing desert sunset? Looking out the window, Sam saw that his neighbor's house was dark and silent.

At least some people were able to sleep at night, Holt groused to himself. Rubbing his face, feeling the bristly growth of beard beneath his fingers, he wondered if the replay of the crash would ever end. With renewed feeling, Sam refocused on Megan. Damn, but he liked her. She was a woman who knew herself, who utilized her fiery spirit to achieve her goals. There was so much he saw going on in those eyes of hers. If only she'd give him a chance. If only. . .

Moving to the table, Sam sat down, staring tiredly at the coffee maker as it gurgled away. Normally, if he sent a woman flowers, she'd respond with a phone call, thanking him. He'd heard nothing from Megan, and she knew where he worked. Megan couldn't send a card, because she didn't have his address. It was easy to concentrate on her, and Holt pictured her face in the front of his mind, erasing Russ's features.

The delicious odor of fresh coffee began to filter through the kitchen, and Holt felt the tension start to gradually ease from his shoulders. Rubbing the back of his neck, Sam knew it was because of Megan. She had an interesting face, the kind he could look at forever and always find something new and pretty about it. No, she wasn't a raving beauty, but she was indeed arresting. Besides, he didn't like perfect-looking women. Melody Stang fell into that category.

Holt wouldn't be surprised if she hadn't had plastic surgery done to her nose, eyes, and chin to create the Grecian symmetry in that face of hers. She was a vain person in comparison to attractive Megan Roberts. No face was perfect. His test pilot observations had confirmed that a long time ago. Every face was made up of two halves, neither quite resembling the other. One eye would be slightly smaller or larger than the other. One side of the mouth was thinner or thicker, or perhaps, one corner curved up or down more than the other. Little things, important things about the face, entranced Holt. And Megan's slightly asymmetrical face was positively fascinating. He wanted the chance to simply stare at her, absorb her features, and tell her how unique and attractive she was to him.

"Contrasts," he muttered, slowly getting up. Life was nothing but contrasts of gray, not black or white. It was the grays that made life interesting in his opinion. Retrieving a cup, he poured himself some coffee and sat back down at the table.

For once there was relief from the nightmare because he had Megan Roberts to concentrate on. She was like sunlight in his life right now. "Hard to catch, too." Sam grinned slightly, sipping the coffee. "How do you catch a red-haired sunbeam who hates pilots? Good question, Holt. You're so good at solving crossword puzzles, complex flight tests, and flying finicky jets, why don't you solve her?"

The challenge hung provocatively in front of him as he slowly turned the mug of coffee around in his hands. Okay, Friday he'd drop over unannounced at her school and ask her out as a friend, not as a date. Maybe have a Perrier, or something nonalcoholic. That was harmless enough, and aboveboard. Give Megan a chance to know him. Of course, he wouldn't make the mistake of showing up at the school in his flight suit. No, he'd bring along some civilian clothes and change before going over to see her. God, how he hated dressing up in a suit with a chokingly tight tie at his throat. He much preferred the open collar of his one-piece, comfortable flight suit. But, to get Megan, to begin earning her trust in him, he'd even go that far for her. It was the ultimate sacrifice for a pilot to struggle into a suit and tie.

A slight smile shadowed Holt's mouth as he savored the plan. He'd never met a woman yet who wouldn't say yes to his idea after sending her flowers. He relied on guilt to make them agree to go with him. The plan was a good one. After finishing off the coffee, Holt went back to bed. Tomorrow was Thursday, and Stang was scheduled to fly the test. All he had to do was observe the test, record what he saw in a report, and hand it to Lauren and designers. An easy day with no complications—no contrasts.

Jack waited in the Design room at his desk, eyes on the door. Merrill and the three flight engineers were already at work. Where the hell was Holt? Looking at his watch, Holt was ten minutes late. A thrill arced through Jack. Melody's astute observations were correct: Holt must not be getting a good night's sleep. How else could he explain his lateness?

The door opened. Jack leaned forward, intent. Holt entered. His flight uniform was wrinkled and unpressed, and to his delight, there were dark circles visible under Holt's eyes. In his right hand was a suit, shirt, and tie on hangers. He watched as Holt hung up the civilian clothes on a hook behind his desk.

"A little late this morning, aren't you?" Jack drawled.

"Had some things to do," Sam answered.

"I've been noticing," Jack said, leaning back in his chair, "that you've been looking peaked lately."

Sam grinned. "Stang, you're letting your imagination run away with you." He looked at his watch. "Usually you aren't up to firing speed until 0730. What happened? You're early."

Returning the grin, Jack shrugged. "Nothing." He motioned toward Holt. "You've got dark shadows under your eyes. You been sleeping well lately?"

Sam's mouth quirked, and he turned, going to his desk. His mind was spongy this morning because of sleep loss, and Stang was sharper than usual with his observations. He needed a cup of coffee—fast. "I know your mother's a scientist, but I didn't know she was into sleep therapy," he tossed back, going to the coffee maker. He raised his hand to the three flight engineers who were huddled, heads together, over some last-minute decisions before Stang's flight.

Jack studied his manicured fingernails. "My mother's a genetic scientist, Holt, and I've got her powers of observation. You look whipped, as if you've been having bad dreams or something the last couple of nights."

Holt scowled, but with his back to Stang, he couldn't see his reaction. Needled because the pilot was on target, he said, "I think you're jealous, Jack." Sam grinned at him and ambled back to his desk, coffee in hand.

"Of what?" Jack scoffed.

"I'm single, good-looking as hell, and have my pick of any lady over at the O Club I want." He pointed to his eyes. "You're right, buddy: long nights with some luscious-looking ladies. Eat your heart out."

With a sharp laugh, Jack put his boots up on the desk and watched Holt. "Word's out you don't take any of those ladies home with you. No, I think something else is bothering you . . ."

Irritated, Sam sat down, pretending to be busy. "You've got an overactive imagination. Instead of testing, maybe you ought to change your vocation and go into writing fiction books."

Grinning, Jack watched him closely. A flush had crawled up on Holt's face. Good, he was on to something! His excitement soared, because this was the first time he'd shaken Holt up. There was a scowl on his face, too, his lips pursed. Bingo! His sixth sense told him the crash was still bothering him. And if that was so, Holt was in for it. That way, sooner or later, his flight confidence would have to start to erode, and then, he'd maintain a clear-cut lead for the number-one slot.

Friday's were always tense around Ops. The week's worth of testing had to be cleaned up, analyzed, absorbed, and then the next week's tests laid out. Not only that, but Holt was scheduled to fly next Monday. Rubbing his hands together, Jack leaned back. *Monday* . . .

— 7 —

"**H**EY," Sam called, "where are you going in such a hurry?" He saw Megan hurrying toward her car, her arms filled with books and homework. Surprised, Megan whirled around toward the voice. Her pulse quickened. Sam Holt was dressed in a gray suit, light-blue shirt, and dark-blue tie. Nonplussed, she watched him approach. The change in him was startling. Without the flight suit, the image of the pilot disappeared. His smile went straight to her heart, and she drowned in the warmth mirrored in his cobalt eyes.

"I almost didn't get here in time," Sam said congenially in way of a greeting, and halted in front of Megan. She looked pretty in the peach shirtdress, her red hair a lovely complement against the color of the silky fabric. He saw gold flecks in her green eyes and hoped that it meant she was happy to see him.

"Hello, Captain," Megan said uncertainly. How devastatingly handsome he looked in a suit. Any corporation would scoop him up in a second, she thought disjointedly.

Sam touched the lapel of his jacket, giving her a distressed look. "Captain? How can you even suggest that when I'm in civilian clothes?"

She grinned, watching his mouth curve into a self-deprecating angle. "If it walks like an Air Force captain,

89

talks like an Air Force captain, it must be an Air Force captain.''

Sam laughed fully. ''Shot down! Here, let me help you.''

Before Megan could speak, he took the armful of papers from her. ''Thank you.''

''Which car is yours?''

''The red Toyota over there,'' she said, pointing down at the end of the huge parking lot.

''Red hair, red car. I knew your fiery spirit would show up in other places. You're a crusader at school, and hell on wheels in the vegetable department of a grocery store. I'll bet you drive like Parnelli Jones, too.''

Megan walked at his side, pleased that he checked his long, lanky stride for her benefit. ''I do, but you don't have any room to talk. You drive a Corvette as I recall . . .'' The least she could do after receiving the lovely yellow roses from Sam was to be civil with him, she told herself. Megan wanted to rationalize why she wanted to be friendly and on a first name basis with him. She looked up to see the happiness in Holt's eyes, feeling joy tumble unexpectedly through her.

With a laugh, Sam said, ''Driving a 'Vette was the closest thing I could find to flying a jet.''

''No truer words were ever spoken by a test pilot.'' The wind was playful, lifting strands of her hair across her shoulders. Overhead, the Friday afternoon sunlight was bright and blinding in the pale-blue desert sky. Megan unlocked the rear door of her car so that Sam could put all the papers on the seat.

''Thank you,'' she murmured. He was so tall and proud looking that Megan couldn't tear her gaze from Holt. There was some undefinable aura about him that she'd not seen in another test pilot. And whatever it was, she wasn't immune to it, and she realized Sam knew that. He closed the door and faced her.

''Did you get the flowers I sent?''

''Yes . . . they're lovely, Sam. I'm sorry I didn't let you know I'd received them.'' She shrugged. ''I really expected you to show up the next day at school, and I was going to thank you then.''

''But I didn't.''

''No.''

''You figured I'd capitalize on the situation: wooing you with flowers, and then show up to take advantage of your lowered guard?''

Megan felt heat rise in her cheek, and she avoided his smiling eyes. ''You ought to get paid for reading my mind.''

''I like what's in your heart, Megan Roberts,'' Sam said in a low tone, and held her widening eyes. ''I'll be honest though: When I first met you, I was going to chase you down until you said yes to me. But, I've changed my mind. The flowers were my way of saying: let's start over and be friends.''

''I don't think friendship is possible between any pilot and a woman,'' Megan admitted, feeling guilty.

''Why?''

Uncomfortable, she crossed her arms against her breasts. ''I—''

''No lines, remember?'' Holt reached out and barely touched her hair, caressing the clean, curled strands. ''I want a relationship with you, Megan, and I think friendship is a good place to start.''

Panicky, she stepped away, her arms dropping to her side. ''Sam, you're asking for the impossible!''

''Nothing's impossible.'' Pursing his lips, Sam steeled himself and gathered up the courage to ask her out. All day he'd sweated out this moment, rehearsing what he was going to say over and over again. All the words fled. ''Look . . . it's Thursday night. I'd like to take you out for some dinner, maybe some dancing. We've both got to drive to Lancaster where we live. There's the Antelope Valley Inn. They've got good food, and it's quiet.''

Shaken, Megan fumbled for the keys and jerked open the door. ''No!''

''Hey, hold it.'' Sam gently gripped her by the shoulder and forced her to turn toward him. ''Talk to me, Megan.'' Her face was pale, her eyes containing the hunted look of a rabbit cornered by a predator. But dammit, he wasn't a predator intent on hurting her! Megan didn't know that, though. His fingers lightened on her shoulder. "Don't run."

"Please," she whispered tautly, "let go of me, Sam. I have to be over at the day-care center in half an hour."

"Day care?"

"Yes, I work over there Monday, Wednesday, and Thursday evenings."

"I didn't know."

Heart pounding hard in her breast, she gave Holt a pleading look. "It's not going to work between us! It can't."

"It can if you want. I'm willing. And, I like you."

"Pilots are always willing."

"You like me? Maybe just a little bit?" he coaxed huskily.

"Sam—"

"Hold it. How about something harmless? Maybe another meeting at the grocery store? We can shop together."

Megan uttered a sigh and studied him. Sam's face was guileless albeit shadowed with a touch of anxiety in his eyes that she would say no. "I don't shop until Friday night."

"Sounds good to me. How about if I meet you at the same market, by the corn, say . . . at 1900—I mean, 7 P.M.?"

With a little laugh, Megan shook her head. His tactics were endearing, if nothing else. "No."

"Tell me the truth. Do you like me, Megan?"

"It doesn't matter if I like you or not!" she quavered and climbed into the Toyota.

Megan's words didn't match what he saw in her eyes. If he was any judge of her reaction, she liked him just as much as he did her. *Fair enough.* Leaning over, Holt said, "I'm not giving up on you, lady." He gave her a slight smile. "I'll be seeing you around," and then with an irrepressible grin, "maybe even in the veggie department." He gently shut the door to her car, stepped away, and allowed her to escape.

Standing there, watching her car disappear down the road, Sam turned and walked back to his Corvette. Progress had been made. He'd established a beachhead with Megan, even if she was going to fight him all the way. That was all right, and he smiled, his walk growing lighter. Redheads were expected to make situations complex—and interesting. A plan was forming in his head. Next Friday, he'd drop over to the school and ask her out. Then, she couldn't say no to him. Looking up at the sky, he saw the clouds were coming in from the west. He had to fly Monday morning. Was it going to rain? God, he hoped not.

Jack waited impatiently for Holt to show up at Design on Monday morning. Lauren Porter was already at work, rechecking the test to take place shortly. Merrill was looking haggard and drawn at his desk, in a foul mood. Jack drummed his fingers on the desk and smiled to himself. Last Friday, he'd noted that Holt was looking worse, the shadows under his eyes darker. Mentioning Davis's death to him on both days last week seemed to be pushing Holt's buttons. *Good.*

The door swung open. Holt appeared, his flight suit splotched and darkened with rain. He pushed his long, lean fingers through his hair and smoothed it back into place on his head.

"Hey!" Jack called out in a rolling voice. "Wasn't it raining that night when you augered in with Davis?"

An incredible surge of anguish overcame Sam. He jerked to a halt. It had been raining hard that evening. The test had been postponed until the shower had moved by the base. The pain Sam felt turned into white-hot fury as he drilled Stang with a glare.

"Yeah, it was raining, Stang." He forced himself to move, cursing himself for falling prey to the bastard's premeditated attack. Stang was dangerous in a cunning, manipulative way. Sam saw Lauren's head snap up, her eyes filled with understanding and sadness for him. He managed a nod in her direction, muttered, "Morning," and dropped his briefcase and garrison cap on his desk.

Curt didn't look any better than Sam felt. Holt nodded to the test pilot and then walked over to the coffee maker. His hands visibly shook when he poured the coffee, and he wondered if anyone saw it. He'd had repeated nightmares about Russ's death on Saturday and Sunday. Night was becoming his enemy, a time of day when he no longer felt comfortable—or safe. Turning, he saw Stang watching him like a cougar ready to pounce on its victim.

"You know, Major," Jack drawled in Porter's direction, "you've got to go up and fly with Holt in this weather. Aren't you a little worried about it?"

Lauren refused to even look in Stang's direction. She copied some figures from her calculator to the flight test form for Holt's flight. "I'd be a hell of a lot more worried if *you* were in the front seat, Captain."

Merrill snickered.

Jack twisted his head and glared over at Curt. He saw Holt saunter by, grinning. "I still say with this kind of weather, it makes landing with the *Eagle* tricky."

"Holt has good hands," Porter replied confidently. The best set in the business, in her personal opinion.

"I question his judgment."

"You would," Holt said, keeping his voice free of anger and sitting down at his desk. "In fact, Jack, you'd like to see me screw up this flight, wouldn't you? Your percentile rating would move out of the danger zone, buddy." He jabbed a finger at him. "Right now, I'm on your six, and only a half a percent of a point away from being even with you for the number-one slot. I intend to keep it that way."

Stang shrugged eloquently. "On your six" was a combat fighter pilot's terminology meaning his jet was directly behind the other's plane and could shoot it down. "It's raining, Holt. Just like it did when Davis was in the rear seat. The only difference is it's day, not night. If I were you, Major, I'd be a little concerned about hitching a ride with Holt today. You notice the dark circles under his eyes? Ever wonder why he has them? He didn't have them when he first arrived at Edwards." Jack grinned, watching Porter's angry features. "No, he got them after he let Davis die."

Holt launched out of his chair. He grabbed Stang by the shoulder and shoved him around in the chair so that he faced him. "You're way out of line," Holt breathed savagely. "I didn't *let* Russ die!"

"Sam!" Porter sprang to her feet and moved toward the two men. "Ease off. He's just trying to shake you up, don't you see that?"

Longing to wipe that smile off Stang's narrow face, Sam released the captain's shoulder. "Someday," he grated, "that mouth of yours is going to get you into real trouble," and he stepped away.

"Come on, Sam, we've got to get ready for the test," Lauren said tautly, glaring down at Stang.

Jack relaxed. "Go for it, boys and girls. I'll be watching you at the end of the runway, along with the fire trucks." Jack knew the fire trucks were always positioned along the runway whenever a test flight was flown. He just wanted to place one more needle into Holt's already shaken demeanor.

Porter gripped Holt's arm, literally dragging him toward the door. "Come on, Sam . . ." she pleaded tightly.

Walking down the hall toward the lockers where their G-suits, helmets, and oxygen masks were stored, Lauren glanced over at him. "You okay?"

"Yes."

"Doesn't sound like it."

Holt glared at her. "I said I'm fine, Port."

"Okay."

His hands shook badly as he zipped his G-suit on. The chaps hugged his lower body, hips, and waist. When under a stressful climb or using evasive flight maneuvers, the chaps would inflate, forcing blood into the upper body so the pilot wouldn't faint and lose consciousness, possibly losing control of his plane as a result.

"Stang is a real bastard," Lauren muttered, straightening after donning her G-suit. She pulled the duffle bag containing her helmet and mask down from her locker.

"Among other things," Holt added. He tried to shake off the anger and concentrate on the forthcoming test. The rain was letting up outside the windows of the locker room, but a cold chill racked him. The test. He had to concentrate on the test. Without warning, he saw Russ Davis's young face hovering before him. Holt scrubbed his eyes.

"Sam?" Lauren asked sympathetically, waiting for him at the door that would lead out to the tarmac where the bus was waiting to take them to the hangar where the *Eagle* was parked.

He jerked the duffle bag out of his locker and swung around. "Let's get this show on the road." Now Lauren was looking at him doubtfully. Was she questioning his ability to fly? He couldn't accurately gauge the emotions in her eyes. She was far less readable than Megan.

Megan. Sam clung to her name and allowed her attractive, smiling features to replace Davis's face. A drenching calm filtered through the shakiness he felt in his gut. Within moments, Holt felt steadier, some of the fear subsiding. But not all of it.

They swung out the doors, the pall of rain steady once again. The sky was crying for the loss of Russ as far as Holt was concerned. Hitching a ride in the bus, they drove over to a hangar housing the *Agile Eagle*. Automatically, Holt forced himself to focus on the forthcoming test.

The restricted area lay at the western end of Edwards, a long row of huge hangars capable of keeping several jets hidden within their aluminum-skinned sides. The bone color of the desert was darker today, the scant sagebrush and many-armed Joshuas looking greener because of the life-giving rain. The concrete apron was shiny with water, a rarity at Edwards. Within fifteen minutes they were rolling out of the hangar and into the pall. The *Eagle's* twin engines mounted at the rear of the fuselage whined, and she trembled beneath Holt's boots and guiding hand. A small board with the test runs was strapped to his left thigh, the pages plastic coated for ease of flipping over and reading. Flexing his Nomex-gloved fingers, Sam pointed the bird toward the end of the long, ten-thousand-foot runway.

"Sam?"

"Yeah, Port?" He scowled, pulling down the clear plastic visor that came to rest across the top of his oxygen mask. The day was gray, and they'd be flying below the cloud cover, so the dark visor to reflect the brightness of the sun wouldn't be needed.

"That was a lousy shot Stang took at you earlier. I'm sorry."

Taking a deep breath, Holt shook his head. "Forget it, Port. I have." *Liar.* Stang was right: the same conditions were present when he lost Russ. He felt silly, wanting to tell Port that if something happened, she was to eject and not wait like Russ did. But of course, she was familiar with egress procedure: the rear cockpit always ejected first. She would think he was questioning his own flight confidence if he voiced his concern. It was better to say nothing and not let her know how he was really feeling.

"Are you sure?"

"Positive."

"Well . . . if you ever want to talk about it to someone, I'm here, Sam."

His eyes crinkled. "Too bad you're engaged, Port. I'd marry you in a second." Her laughter drifted over the intercom, and Holt relaxed slightly.

"You know what?"

"What?"

"I really believe you mean that."

With a chuckle, he swung the bird around with the aid of the rudders, the nose pointing down the long, black runway slick with rain. "I do, I do. But that big bruiser of a fiancé of yours would bend me into a pretzel if he found out I was sweet on you. Besides, he's a major, and I'm only a lowly captain."

Lauren laughed, giving her cockpit straps a final tug, tightening them as much as possible. "Well, what about this redhead you keep mooning over?"

"Megan?" More of the tension was easing. He knew Lauren was trying to get him to relax, sensing his discomfort.

"The one and only? Any progress with her?"

"A little."

"You mean there's one woman who has withstood the storm of your mesmerizing personality and turned you down?"

He ran up each engine and checked it out before they took off. His hands moved swiftly, with ease of knowing, across the dials and switches. "Right now I've got her saying 'maybe.'"

"That's a good sign."

"I think so. Okay, you ready back there? All preflight checks completed."

"Roger. Complete."

Holt called the tower and got clearance. The F-15 quivered as he eased the throttles forward. Instead of excitement taking over, which was the normal feeling he experienced, dread set in. Scowling, Holt realized fear was stalking him. Trying to shake it, he released the rudders. The *Eagle* bolted forward, screaming down the runway.

In moments they were airborne. The rain struck the clear plexiglass canopy and disappeared. They would make the standard ninety-degree right turn, climb to fifteen hundred feet, make the dogleg turn paralleling the strip, and then one last ninety-degree turn which would line them up with the end of the runway.

Down below, as Holt executed the dogleg turn, he saw the dark-blue Air Force truck positioned at the end of the fifteen-hundred-foot marker. Stang and Merrill were both in the truck, and acted as observers. On the other side of the runway was an airman videotaping the entire landing sequence. Both the observations by the test pilots, plus the videotape, would be minutely analyzed back at Design once the series of tests were completed.

"Okay," Lauren said, "drop slats and flaps one hundred percent, Sam.'"

On the last landing tests, they had been dropped to ninety percent. "Roger, slats and flaps down and locked at one hundred percent." Their entire conversation was being taped, so they kept to procedures only.

"Landing gear down."

He pulled the lever and felt the bird quiver as the gear unfolded from beneath her fuselage. A green light popped on. "Roger. Gear down and locked." Sweat suddenly bathed him, cold and icy in its grip. Blinking his eyes, Holt tried to steady his breathing. He wrenched his attention to the altimeter and the speed gauge. Russ's faced danced before him. It was the same kind of approach, the same kind of weather, and the same runway.

Holt's heart started a rapid staccato beat in his chest. His breathing became ragged, and he was sucking in oxygen like an air-starved person on the verge of suffocating. Sweat dripped into his eyes, making them sting, blurring his vision. The bird dropped toward the deck. His hand tightened painfully around the stick. The runway raced up to meet them. Russ's screams filled Holt's ears. Frantically, he shook his head and tried to get rid of Russ's cries.

"Trapped, trapped. Jesus, I'm trapped! Sam, eject! Eject!"

The *Eagle's* tires bit into the concrete, puffs of blue smoke rising off the wet, glistening surface. Breathing hard, Sam tried to concentrate. The fifteen-hundred-foot marker raced by. Too late! Too much speed! Dammit, he hadn't landed at the lip of the runway where he'd intended. He was giving more attention to the crash than to the present. The red marker flashed by. In disgust, Holt jammed the throttles forward, lifting the bird off in a touch and go.

"It's okay, Sam," Lauren soothed from her rear seat. "Just take it easy. This is the first time we've done it in the rain."

Pulling up slats, flaps, and landing gear, Holt couldn't get rid of the tension. It hung around him like a lead cloak, and he felt as if some invisible hand were jamming his neck down between his shoulder blades. Lauren's voice was soothing, but it didn't help his frantic feelings. He hauled the responsive *Eagle* around in the same pattern. This time he had to hit the landing mark. Holt was sure Stang was clapping his hands with glee over his screw-up. Damn, he had to concentrate!

More sweat popped out on Holt's wrinkled brow and slipped down his taut features. Blinking his eyes, his breath coming in gulps, Sam lined up the bird and forced her to hit the lip of the runway. He had to make the fifteen-hundred-foot mark. He just had to!

A gust of wind struck. The *Eagle* bobbled beneath his

hands. He corrected swiftly, hand and feet performing a calibrated ballet. But his hand moved a quarter of an inch too far. The earth raced up to meet them. Holt heard Lauren gasp. *Too fast! Too fast!* The *Eagle*'s tires slammed into the runway surface. Instantly, Holt dropped the nose, and worked the rudders hard to stop. The red flag was coming up. *Stop! Stop!* Steam shot in all directions around the wheels. Rubber from the wheels was torn off by the concrete. A shriek vibrated through the air.

A fire light indicator popped on, glaring bright red in the cockpit. Sam's eyes bulged. *Where? Where was the fire?* He could smell it.

"Sam," Lauren rasped, her voice husky with tension, "we've got a fire somewhere."

"Roger." Quickly, he brought the bird to a halt, only twenty feet past the red flag. *Dammit!* His mind spun with options, with terrible choices. He rapidly scanned the gauges. *A fire where?* The engines sounded fine, but he stopcocked the throttles, instantly shutting them down. Twisting around, he saw the lime-green fire trucks racing down both sides of the runway toward them.

"Wolf One, this is Mobile One." Stang's voice tensely came over his earphones. "You've got a fire in the port wheel well of the brake. Stay put, the fire trucks are on their way. Advise you sit tight."

"Roger, Mobile One." Holt took his thumb off the button located on the stick and whispered, "Jesus," falling against the seat, suddenly so weak he couldn't even hold up his head. Thank God, it was only a landing gear fire. A nightmare of possibilities fled through his mind. If it were an engine fire, the *Eagle* could have exploded right there on the runway. Or, they would have had to either leave the cockpit and try to make a run for it, or eject. None of the possibilities were good or safe.

"Sam?"

"It's okay, Port. It's okay. We're safe . . . safe."

Lauren's voice was shaky. "Yeah, what a scare . . ."

He saw the trucks halt on either side of them, silver-clothed and hooded, firefighters racing toward them with hoses. In seconds they had doused the fire with foam. Shakily, he shoved up the visor and wiped his sweaty face.

"Hell of a landing," Lauren's laugh was strained. "I almost thought you were going to make that fifteen-hundred-foot marker."

Holt looked to his left: they were twenty feet outside the marker. "I gave it one hell of a try."

"Brother, did you."

Sam grimaced. "Got whiplash, Port?"

Ruefully, she chuckled. "No worse than what Stang gave me a month ago."

"I'm sorry."

"Don't be. If it hadn't been raining, you'd have made it! The bird was sliding."

"Not if it causes a fire in the landing gear every time," Sam muttered. His insides were quivering as if a hand were violently shaking his guts. Automatically, Sam massaged his belly and watched the firefighters move the hoses out of the way. There was nothing to do but wait until they were clear, and then, he could take the bird back to the hangar and they could inspect for damage.

Enthusiastically, Lauren added, "Tires can be redesigned to take this kind of a landing, and brakes with their sealants can be changed to prevent a fire, Sam. You did it! Well, almost. Did you log how you came in for that last landing?"

He snorted softly, throwing a thumbs up to the fire captain stationed in the truck. Mobile One, which contained Stang and Merrill, came into view. "Let's talk about my flight antics back at debriefing, shall we?" His flying had been nearly out of control. He'd been so scared, caught up in the previous crash sequence, that a goodly portion of what he'd done to almost accomplish the fifteen-hundred-foot landing had been on instinct alone, and lost. Honestly, Sam couldn't remember what the degree of flight attitude the bird had, or worse, the landing speed. He'd totally forgotten to look at the speed indicator. Jesus, he was a screw-up.

"Mobile One to Wolf One, you may proceed back to the hangar. Fire Unit One will accompany you—just in case."

"Roger, Mobile One. Wolf, out." Holt flicked off the radio, getting back to the business of taking the wounded bird to the hangar. He moved the F-15 very slowly because when he had to make the turn to go into the hangar, he didn't want to have to use the brakes very much and cause them to overheat, or possibly, catch fire again. What a lousy day. He hated Mondays; it was a constant reminder of Russ dying.

Holt noticed Stang standing impatiently on the concrete floor of the hangar as he climbed out of the cockpit of the F-15. Once on the ground, Sam removed his helmet and placed it beneath the crook of his arm. It was then that he smelled himself—the sweat of fear. The odor was strong, and he had no doubt everyone else, including the enlisted crew who worked with quiet efficiency around them, could smell it, too. Desperately, he longed for a hot, scalding shower to wash the sweat and the memory off him.

Lauren gave him a sympathetic look as she placed her helmet in her duffle bag. Stang was already beneath the landing assembly inspecting the damage the brake fire had caused. Needled, Holt put his duffle bag on the seat of Mobile One and then walked back to the *Eagle*.

"Hell of a landing both times," Jack told him as he drew up to the port wheel.

Sam ignored the comment. Both landings had been lousy, the kind a green rookie would make before graduating from flight school. Lauren approached from the opposite direction, her notebook and pen poised, ready to take notes on the burned brake lining.

"Hey, Major, you got whiplash?" Jack taunted.

"No more than what you gave me when you cracked the landing gear, Captain."

"Looks like you're both in the doghouse," Curt said, mustering a smile, trying to lighten the growing tension between Stang and Holt.

"At least Sam has come the closest to making that fifteen-hundred-foot mark," Lauren reminded Stang testily.

Undeterred, Jack walked around the brake and continued

to examine it closely. He was hoping Holt had cracked the strut, but it appeared intact. Lifting his head, he stared at Holt. "Just what kind of landings were those anyway?"

Compressing his lips, Holt said, "Carrier landings."

"Looked like rookie landings to me."

Anger shattered Holt, but he held on to it, his eyes narrowing on the other pilot. "Until you've graduated from the Navy test pilot facility, I don't think you'd recognize a carrier landing from a rookie one, Jack."

Shrugging, Stang smiled easily. "No wonder the Navy has such a high budget. They must burn the hell out of the brakes on all their aircraft if they land it like you just did."

Hanging on to his shredded composure, Holt disregarded him. It was the only thing to do. If he kept responding to Stang, it would only escalate the tension felt by everyone, and right now, his nerves were raw. Sam needed to get away from here, away from the memories. As he walked back to Mobile One to write down preliminary notes on the flight, he felt scared. Never had he wanted to be away from testing before.

Wiping his brow with the back of his hand, Sam made himself comfortable on the front seat. The knot in his stomach was twisting, hurting even more, if that were possible. The fear wouldn't go away! Was it going to continue to screw up his flight responses? Closing his eyes, Sam dragged in a deep, shaky breath and released it. He had to get a handle on this! Russ's death was encroaching on, and eating away his confidence.

Lauren came over a few minutes later, and she drove. Glancing over at him, she said, "You know, when I need someone to talk to, my fiancé is my best ear."

Holt tried to ignore Lauren's suggestion.

"Sam, you're talking to me, not someone out to cut your throat."

He glanced over at her. "Talking is dangerous to anyone in this business."

"Usually, yes." Lauren gave him a small smile. "Still, everyone needs someone special when things get rough for us, Sam. Do me a favor, and go talk, okay?"

Without warning, Megan's features swam before his closed eyes. Holt clung to the image and wanted to erase the memory of Davis, and of the last hour of testing. God, he *had* to see her! He had to talk to someone. Instinctively, Sam knew she would be a good listener. There was no way he could talk to anyone here. No, better a civilian. Megan understood about jets and flying, even if she didn't like them. As soon as the day was done, he was going to drive over to the school and see her. He needed her.

Lauren broke the silence in the pickup as she drove toward Ops in the downpour. "I can use your help the rest of the day on a software program I'm developing for next week's test. It might mean you won't get away from Ops until about 2100 tonight."

"Yeah . . . sure, no problem." The last thing Holt wanted to do was hang around Ops any longer than necessary. The shattering need to see Megan was like a scream needing to be released from deep within him. Somehow, Sam knew he'd have to hang on until he could see Megan. God, but it was going to be tough to do that.

— 8 —

THE knock on Megan's apartment door at 10 P.M. startled her. Frowning, she left her work clothes on the bed. She had just changed into a pale-green, cotton short-sleeved sweater and white cotton pants that were baggy but terribly comfortable. Who could it be?

Opening the door, her lips parted. "Sam." His name came out in a whisper of disbelief. He looked incredibly tired, darkness in his eyes, his hair damp from the rain.

"Hi," he began awkwardly. Just the sight of Megan, her red hair loose and tumbling free across her shoulders, lifted some of the strain he'd felt all day. "I—uh, need a friend to talk to. I know it's late, but . . . I was hoping you were available."

Their conversation last week about him being a friend to her tugged at her heart. Sam was dressed in a pair of well-worn jeans, scuffed cowboy boots, and western shirt with the sleeves rolled up to his elbows. As her gaze met and held his weary blue eyes, all her defenses melted.

"Sure . . . come in," and Megan stepped aside to allow him entrance. Intuitively, she realized something was terribly wrong. What jet jock *ever* confided in anyone? Much less a woman. She could never recall her father talking over with his family what happened to him on any given day at the base. Quietly closing the door, she watched Sam halt in the middle of the living room.

"This place," he said, awe in his tone, "is like walking back into Victorian England. It's beautiful." And so was Megan. He'd seen the denial to his request in her features when he'd asked to come in and talk. Then, her lovely green eyes had softened, become understanding, and Sam had to stop himself from dragging her into his arms and kissing her. Right now, Megan represented a serenity and stability that he desperately needed.

She moved hesitantly to his shoulder, managed a slight smile, and tried to hide her nervousness. "Thank you. I refer to it as my castle: someplace I can come and hide when the world gets too ugly."

Self-consciously, Holt put his hands in the pockets of his jeans and studied his well-worn boots. "That's what I need right now, a safe place."

"And a safe person?"

"Yeah." He lifted his head and drowned in her emerald eyes. "You were the only one I could think of—wanted to talk to," he began quietly. "You're an Air Force brat. You grew up in my world, so you know the pressures, the problems." The change in Holt was startling. His shoulders were slumped, head bowed. There was none of the arrogance of before. Megan knew Sam was leveling with her. It was on the tip of her tongue to say: I wish my father had had the insight you do, to know when to let down and talk. But she didn't. "It's not often a pilot wants to talk about his problems," she agreed gently. Reaching out, she slid her fingers around his arm and lead him toward the blue velvet couch. "Come on, sit down. How about some herb tea?"

"Yeah . . . that sounds good. No more coffee. I'm strung tighter than a—" Sam flushed, the rest of the saying something no woman should hear. "Well, no more coffee," he apologized. He sat down, grateful that she understood his needs. It was just one more reason to like Megan. When the chips were down, she let go of her defenses and came to the other person's aid.

Sam sat there, his hands clasped loosely between his legs.

The dark splotches of rain had made the light-blue shirt material cling to his upper body. Megan had the wild urge to sit down, place her arms around his shoulders, and hold him. The urge was ridiculous, warming. "I'll make us tea," she said, "and be right back."

Watching Megan turn and leave, Sam became aware of a throbbing heat centered in his lower body. She was small and graceful, that mass of red hair glinting with auburn highlights beneath the soothing lamplight of the living room. Forcing himself to put his hunger aside, because this wasn't the place or time, Holt looked around, absorbing the abundant peace that surrounded him.

The fact that Megan Roberts was a pure romantic made him feel even more relaxed. There were fresh carnations on a Queen Ann walnut lowboy in front of the couch. He inhaled the flowers' subtle fragrance. Another scent caught his attention. It was roses, if he wasn't mistaken. On top of a Victorian, walnut, pedestaled writing desk was a wicker basket filled with dried yellow rose petals. Megan must have taken the bouquet he'd sent her after they had bloomed, and kept them.

Sam liked her old-fashioned ways; he approved of them. The greenery in the room spoke of someone who embraced solitude and nature. Twisting around, he saw several pots of blooming African violets on the windowsill behind him. Yes, everything Megan touched was better off for it.

Megan returned ten minutes later. On a mahogany tray were delicate china cups painted with floral designs. The teapot, a Victorian spherical silver antique with leafy flutes, released the subtle scent of almonds, and it smelled inviting. Everything was pristine, delicate, and feminine—a direct dichotomy to Sam's masculine world of metal, instruments, and computers.

"It smells great," he said, meaning it, as she set the tray down on the lowboy.

Some of her nervousness melted away beneath his fervent comment. "Thanks. It's almond flavored, my favorite. When I've had a tough day at school, I come home, take a hot bath, and then make myself some tea and just sit out here in the dark and let down.''

''Sounds like a good thing to do.'' Sam cradled the thin china cup between his hands, thinking that Megan was like the porcelain. Despite her fragility where her parents were concerned, and the obvious agony Air Force life had caused her, he sensed a special kind of strength about her. And he needed that strength now.

The slender brass lamp in the corner cast very little light about the room. ''Do you want more light?''

''No. I like it the way it is.'' The sterling-silver spoon in the sugar bowl was fluted, dainty against his large, masculine hand. Again, Holt was struck by the utter femininity of Megan and her surroundings. ''I like your home.'' *I like you*. He managed a smile, lifting the teacup in toast to her. ''And thanks for letting me in. I know it's late, and we both have to work tomorrow.''

Curling up on the couch, legs tucked beneath her, Megan held the cup between her hands. The shadows accentuated the exhaustion she saw in Sam's face and eyes. ''I really didn't think you were serious about a friendship,'' she admitted in a hushed voice. ''Seeing how you look tonight, I think you could use one.''

With an abrupt laugh, Holt held her eyes. He saw unsureness in them. ''I told you I was different than most jet jocks.'' With a shrug, he turned, staring down at the golden-colored tea. ''I had no idea this would happen, though.''

''What?'' Megan waited, wondering what would drive Holt here late at night during a rainstorm. ''The only way I knew my father had had a bad day at Ops was when he would find fault with the dinner I cooked, or the way I cleaned the house, or if I didn't wash the dishes up soon enough after we got done eating.'' Megan stared off into the shadows, her voice lowering. ''I came to sense the feelings he never showed us. Father really only had one mood: distant, unreachable, and no emotions. But he wasn't in the minority. All the jet jocks I met were like him. He just got more demanding and critical when a day went bad.''

Holt's hands closed over the teacup. It felt breakable, and he held it gently. He acknowledged the rage welling up through him over Megan's plight as a youngster. No child should have to walk on eggshells around a parent. "It sounds like you were chief cook and bottle washer growing up."

"My mother couldn't handle my father's flying, so when I turned nine, she went to bed to become an invalid of sorts. I was responsible for cooking and cleaning from that point on." Megan saw the compassion in Holt's face. For an instant, she wanted to continue, having never told anyone about it before. "Look, you didn't come over here to listen about my childhood. I just wanted to let you know I'm no stranger to jet jocks who have bad days. What happened over there that has you looking so exhausted?"

He remained silent, wrestling with very real anger toward her father. No wonder Megan hated the military establishment. What kind of parents did she have? Over at testing, Colonel Roberts had been idolized for his abilities. Even after his death, he was a hero to be looked up to, every test pilot aspiring to follow his hallowed footsteps.

Yet, looking at Megan, Colonel Roberts's image tarnished before him—forever. To force a nine-year-old girl who wore her heart on her sleeve into the duties that should have been her mother's was wrong. Holt tucked all the thoughts away, wanting time to digest them. It would help to understand Megan's reactions to him, and now, she'd given him plenty of information to absorb.

"Over at Ops where we test, nobody really tells anyone else how they feel," Sam began wryly, holding her gaze. The shadows caressed her cheekbones, emphasized her eyes and parted lips. Lips that he desperately wanted to feel and taste beneath his—not out of lust, but out of care and sharing. "If I told anyone else about this, those guys would take it and use it against me. Right now I'm in a tight two-way race with Captain Jack Stang, the chief test pilot, for first place on the B-2 project coming down the line. If Stang knew this, he'd use it like a weapon and bludgeon me with it."

"I understand. There's always infighting in the ranks, jostling for position, for the next brass ring." Megan said it without rancor or accusation. The world of test piloting was the most competitive job she'd ever seen.

"Right." Holt slowly turned the cup around in his hands. The words came haltingly, filled with pain. "I, uh, never talked to anyone after Russ Davis died. I mean, he was my best friend. He was a flight engineer," Sam explained.

Megan grew very still inside as she saw Holt struggle to speak on a highly emotional topic. Her father never had. He knew how to give orders and became super critical when in a nasty mood, but she'd never seen him lower his guard and become a human being with human needs like those Sam displayed without apology. "What happened?" she urged softly.

Holt stared off into the distance. "Russ was riding the back seat with me on a test flight six months ago when the bird crashed. It was a night flight." His throat constricted, the words strained. "I told him to eject. Three times. It was a mad race between us and the ground. The back seat always ejects first because if the front goes before it, the explosion from the eject could injure the other guy. So, I hung in there, yelling at him to bail out."

The terrible feeling that Holt could have been killed overwhelmed Megan. Her fingers tightened on the cup and saucer. The suffering in Sam's face brought tears to her eyes, but she quickly forced them back. Her father had always been disgusted by her tears, so she learned not to cry. "Was there a problem with Russ's seat?"

"Yeah," Sam croaked finally. "After the crash, the team found that the seat, or what was left of it, was inoperative." He shut his eyes, feeling the sting of tears behind his lids. "Dammit, Megan, he died. I screamed at him to bail out, but it was too late. The ground was too close. I had to eject . . ."

Reaching over, she placed her hand on his arm and felt the tautness of his muscles beneath her fingertips. "Sam, you did what you could." Her fingers tightened as she saw tears appear and bead on his short, spiky lashes. The realization that he trusted her enough to show his tears shook her deeply. "Russ knew the only other option he had was to physically try and climb out. It sounds as if he panicked and didn't try."

Forcing back the tears, Holt blinked his eyes several times, wildly aware of Megan's hand on his arm. Her touch was electric and dredged up more feelings from the crash. He wanted to turn and find his way into her arms and be held. Containing himself, Sam looked over at her. Tears were trailing down her cheeks, silvery paths telling him of the pain she felt for him. The discovery was like a blow to his bruised heart.

"You're something else, you know that?" he said. Placing the tea on the lowboy, he captured her hand and held it between his. She fed him strength, a sense that it was all right to show his emotions. With Megan, he was safe, and he knew it.

Sniffing, Megan put the teacup aside and reached up to brush the tears from her cheeks. "I'm sorry, I didn't mean to cry . . ."

"No." Holt captured her other hand, stopping her from wiping the tears away. "Tears . . . crying, is okay. . . ."

"For women, but not for men?" Megan asked him gently. She looked down at their hands. Holt had darkly tanned ones, his fingers long and capable. Hers were small and glaringly white against his. Another reminder of their differences.

Bowing his head, Holt nodded. "For a second, I thought I was going to cry."

"It would have helped."

"Maybe."

"Is this rule number 22: Test pilots never show any emotions and never cry?" she teased.

With a weak laugh, Holt said, "I guess it is. You've got all those rules down pat, don't you?"

"I lived with those rules for eighteen years."

The pain in his chest widened. Not for Russ or for himself, but for Megan. Stroking her hand, Sam felt the firm softness of her flesh beneath his. "Sometime," he murmured, holding her eyes that were awash with tears, "I'd like to talk to you more about your early life."

Megan laughed, but it wasn't filled with humor. "Sam, you don't want to hear it."

"Yes, I do." His voice grew husky with undisguised emotion. "I want to know the woman who lives in this beautiful apartment. The one who dries rose petals and has a magic touch with African violets."

A *frisson* of panic shot through her. How easy it was to fall into Sam's dark-blue eyes and drown in the care he was extending to her. How easy it would be to seek and find his arms, kiss him, and touch the fire that smoldered in his eyes like banked coals. Megan pulled her hands from his. "You're scaring me," she whispered.

"I didn't come over here tonight to do that. I just needed a civilian ear, a trustworthy one, to let me get this off my chest." Holt rubbed his furrowed brow. "Stang is needling the hell out of me. This morning, on a test flight, it was raining just like the day of the crash. Stang kept reminding me of it, and I fell for his trap. By the time I got in the cockpit, I wasn't on top of things. I blew the test, Megan."

"How?"

"The exact flight conditions existed as on the day of the crash, except, it wasn't at night. And it was a Monday on top of everything else. Stang knew it and kept mentioning it. By the time I got out to the bird, I was angry and upset. Port . . . Major Lauren Porter, the chief flight test engineer, knew it, too. She tried to calm me down, but it didn't work." Holt gave her a wry look. "The only thing that helped me was to picture your face in my mind. My nerves stopped jangling, and I was able to focus to a degree on the test."

Shaken, Megan looked away. "That's quite a compliment."

"The highest," Sam agreed quietly. "You've always had the ability to tame the beast in me since I met you."

Megan wrestled with her next statement. Sam's honesty allowed her to say it. "When things get out of control at school, I think about you."

Holt smiled, warmth flooding him. "Yeah?"

"Yes."

"We're good for one another, Red."

She liked the nickname he'd given her. "Sometimes . . ."

Sam held on to his other comments. He wanted to say, *No, all the time, Megan. All I need you to do is recognize it and not run away from it.* He remained silent, trying to give her that comfortable space she needed with him. "Well, whatever the percentages," he added drolly, "you helped me out there today."

"What happened on the flight?"

"Blips of the crash kept hitting me, and I blew both tests. I don't even remember the landing speed or the attitude of the bird, Megan." Holt shrugged. "I heard Russ screaming in my head, and I broke out in a sweat. The next thing I knew, we'd slammed onto the runway. A brake fire developed, so the rest of the testing was delayed."

"A fire?" Megan's heart started a slow, dreaded pound. "A fire?"

"Hey, take it easy. It was just a fire in the wheel well was all." He reached over, grasping her hand. But the fear in her eyes spoke volumes. Slowly, Sam realized that she was terrified for him. That meant that she liked him—a lot. The discovery made him soar, but the down side made him wince. "The fire trucks had it out in seconds. It was no big deal."

Yes, it is! Megan withdrew deep within herself. She had told herself from the beginning that Sam meant nothing to her. Nothing! But that wasn't true because her feelings were screaming out in sheer terror over the brake fire incident. Needing something to help steady her emotions, she picked up the cup, hands trembling. Worse, the realization that this must have been how her mother felt every time her father flew, nearly paralyzed Megan.

"What's wrong?" Sam asked, watching the darkness stalk her telltale eyes. "Megan? Talk to me."

"I—oh, God, I didn't realize there was a fire aboard the bird. You could have been killed."

"No, now listen to me, it wasn't anything. A lousy wheel well fire is nothing."

Sam was too vital, too alive, to die in a fire. Megan drew in a ragged breath. "I'm sorry, it's none of my business, not my—"

"Sure it is," and he smiled gently. "We like each other, so we're naturally concerned about one another."

The words, barely whispered, soothed some of her internal panic. Sam had spoken for both of them. And Megan was too tired, too torn up by his other admissions to deny the truth any longer.

He patted her hand. "Listen, I'd better go. It's eleven-thirty, and we've both got to get some sleep." The need to lean over and kiss her was real, and Sam barely resisted. More than anything, he wanted Megan's trust in him. If he pushed too soon, took selfishly, she'd run just as she had run that morning of the balloon rally. Getting up, he took her cup and saucer from her lap. "Will you be okay?"

Megan saw the genuine concern in his features. His hand was warm and comforting on her cool, damp one. "Yes, I'll be fine." She stood and took the cups to the kitchen and set them on the drainboard. Sam halted at the entrance. When she turned around, a few feet separating them, she heard him speak in a low tone.

"Promise?"

"Promise." Megan saw the intensity in his eyes change, and for the first time she yearned to lean upward and feel the strength of his mouth. She saw he wanted to kiss her. His eyes narrowed, and her breath caught in her throat. A cry, a sound of need, issued from her as she felt his arms go around her. Contact with his body was electric, galvanizing. Automatically, her lashes swept downward as she felt Sam draw her against him. The moment was fragile and exquisite. She felt his moist breath caress her cheek as he leaned down to claim her. Lips parting in advance of him, Megan surrendered to his arms, her name a prayer coming from him seconds before he captured her mouth beneath his.

Megan had expected his kiss to be powerful, perhaps even hurting, from her own limited experience. Instead, the scrape of his beard against her cheek sent a delightful arc of prickles through her. The brush of his mouth was tentative and questing. She felt the inherent strength of it, yet the incredible gentleness with which he molded her lips to his. A bonelessness flowed through her as he ran his tongue fleetingly across her lower lip, and Megan moaned. But it was a moan of pure pleasure because he was sharing with her, not taking selfishly as most men did.

Sliding her arms around his neck, Megan stretched upward, wanting more contact with him, wanting to relish him as a man who savored her as if she were some fragile, breakable being. Megan wasn't disappointed, tasting the salt of him, the hungry fire of his returning, claiming kiss. Nostrils flaring, she caught his masculine scent and threaded her fingers through his thick, silky hair.

Gradually, Sam broke contact with Megan. Their breath mingled in a ragged symphony as they stood, brows pressed against one another. His arms tightened around her, and he felt her willowy suppleness and the firmness of her small breasts against his chest. Nuzzling her hair, inhaling the sweet, spicy scent of her, he smiled.

"God, I've dreamed of this for so long," Sam admitted in an unsteady voice. Her lips were as soft as he'd imagined. Her response to him was bold, and he applauded her courage, her ability to be a woman sure of her own needs with him.

Heart still pounding erratically in her breast, Megan lifted her chin and drowned in the brilliant blue of his hooded gaze. Never had she felt more a woman, never more aware of the beauty that a man could share with her. Words wouldn't come, and she saw him give her a very male smile; one filled with tenderness. Sam caressed her hair and placed a chaste kiss on her cheek.

"I like what I see in your eyes," he told her huskily. "They're a deep green, with gold fire in them." Stopping himself from touching her more intimately, Sam directed her attention to the desk.

"I see you took the roses I sent to you and used the petals even after they bloomed." Sam smiled, memorizing her lovely face, and wide, trusting eyes. "I like your old-fashioned ways."

He'd seen the basket of rose petals, Megan thought disjointedly, reeling from his tender kiss. Of course, Sam was a test pilot, and he was trained to notice nuances. Still, the observation made her feel good, and she smiled slightly. "Old-fashioned in all ways."

Reluctantly, Sam released her. "Fair enough," he said. "Forewarned is forearmed." He smiled fully, teasing her. "Good night, Red. I owe you one."

"Good night . . ." Megan stood there, a cry lodging in her throat. She wanted to ask Sam to stay. Stay and do what? Confused, feeling so many rich emotions brought about by Sam's kiss, Megan decided to say nothing. Right now, she was feeling, not thinking. It wasn't the right time to make coherent decisions.

Sam left quietly without a backward glance. How long she stood there in the quiet of the kitchen, lost in the world of his hot, hungry kiss, Megan didn't know. When the clock struck midnight, she realized she had to get a bath and some sleep. Work came early and was demanding.

Once in bed, she tossed and turned, their entire conversation running through her head and heart. How easy it was for Sam to trust her, when she didn't trust any pilot. Or did she? With a sigh, Megan shut her eyes. Tomorrow she had her own war to wage at school. Brad Jamison was continuing to block her proposal. The union was putting more pressure on him, but it wasn't doing any good. Not only that, but Scotty Stang was becoming an increasing problem. Perhaps Linda could help her thread through the delicate situation and she wouldn't get fired.

"As president of the union," Linda Yarnell said, "Jamison told me he's turning down your proposal because he says the entire military school curriculum would have to be changed."

Megan frowned, sitting with Linda in the teachers' lounge. They had half an hour between the morning and afternoon classes for lunch. Most of the teachers were outside eating their lunches at the picnic tables beneath the shade of the trees. It gave them a modicum of privacy to talk.

"He knows as well as I do that we could use my second

grade class as a test model. Nothing has to be changed for that.''

Megan looked around the lounge. The plastic chairs were empty, cups and paper bags scattered on the three long wooden tables. "He's blocking it because I turned down his advance.''

"You can't prove it, so we have to think of something else.''

"I'm not above using my father's considerable influence here at Edwards to get someone other than Jamison to look at the idea, Linda.''

"Such as?''

"My father was good friends with George Dalton, the commanding general of the base. Maybe I could wrangle a dinner invitation out of him and make a pitch for it.''

With a shrug, Linda said, "In this man's Air Force, it's who you know that counts, not what you know.''

"Then, you don't mind if I try it?''

"No.'' Linda smiled. "It would be a pleasure to see a woman use the system, for once.''

"Great.''

"What about your other problem with Scotty Stang?''

"I've put in another report on him. This time, with the correct wording.''

Linda's dark-blue shirtdress matched the color of her eyes. Megan had purposefully worn a bright-green blouse, beige slacks and a bright fall scarf to buoy her flagging spirits. "Something's going on in admin. I filed four reports on Scotty Stang last year when he was in my class. They've disappeared.''

"That's why I didn't have an inkling as to his behavior,'' Megan said. "Well, this year will be different. I'm not going to forsake twenty-three other children just to baby-sit Scotty. He needs professional help. If I don't get any action on it shortly, I'm going to the parents for help.''

Linda sighed. "Captain Stang will hit the roof like he did last year when I confronted him about it.''

"I'm not going to lose on this issue, Linda. Scotty's

well-being is at stake too, even if his father doesn't realize it.''

"Not to change the subject, but you know there's a cookies and punch Halloween party for the children of the officers and their families at the O Club tomorrow. That includes kindergarten through the third grade classes.''

Wrinkling her nose, Megan said, "Don't remind me.''

"Try and keep Scotty Stang and Patty Merrill apart, or I'm afraid their fighting with one another will cause you embarrassment.''

"I know. You'll be there, won't you?''

"You bet. Gotta run! See you after school.''

Going over to the sink, Megan rinsed her hands and dried them on a towel. Absorbing Linda's advice, she centered her attention on her heart and instincts. Surprisingly, she felt calmer. Her plan to contact General Dalton was sound. Yes, she was making inroads here at Edwards and wrestling with the past. Sam Holt wasn't supposed to be a part of that equation, but he was.

— 9 —

OLD, disturbing memories hit Megan as soon as she entered the officers club with her class. It was 1600, and time for the Halloween party. Her father always dragged her over here for every activity involving the children of officers. He wouldn't think of missing any event, even if she was terribly shy and uncomfortable at them. Megan herded her twenty-five charges, all dressed in various costumes, into a side room far removed from the bar and dancing area. Her sensitive nose caught the stale smell of alcohol and cigarettes from the bar area at the other end of the hall. The interior of the O Club was prestigious, with dark-stained oak paneling and thick beams overhead. The walls were plastered with photo memorabilia of its world-famous test pilots and the planes they'd tamed.

She avoided looking at the photographs, not wanting to see her father's picture she knew was there. Scotty Stang, dressed in his silver astronaut costume, helmet cocked on his head, lead the group proudly through the doors. Megan kept her hand on Patty's shoulder. The Merrill girl was dressed in a gossamer fairy-tale outfit, replete with a pointed hat and veil. Megan thought Patty looked like a beautiful little princess. It was obvious that the costume had taken many hours to make, painstakingly hand sewn. Becky Merrill was quite a seamstress in Megan's opinion.

Unfortunately, Patty wasn't behaving like a well-heeled royal.

Inside, Megan saw a number of O Club waitresses and waiters acting as supervisors to get the children seated by grade groups at specially assigned tables. Along the walls were groups of proud, expectant parents. Her heart fell when she saw Sam Holt standing with Curt and Becky Merrill at the far end of the long, rectangular room. Why was he here?

Whether she wanted to or not, Megan quickly searched Holt's face. Their talk must have helped him. He didn't look as tired, the shadows beneath his eyes were fainter. Dressed in his dark-blue uniform, she grudgingly admitted he looked devastatingly handsome in it. His gaze moved to her, and she quickly averted her eyes and focused on the task of getting her class served the orange-frosted cupcakes and red punch.

"Look," Becky whispered eagerly to Curt, and gripped his arm, "doesn't our Patty look cute?"

Curt grinned, watching his thin, gangly daughter lift the pale-pink skirt with both hands in order to walk. "She does look cute," he agreed, his heart swelling with pride. Becky had spent two weeks sewing late at night to make her costume. It had been a labor of love, the work worth it. His daughter was so careful in sitting down, arranging the transparent folds of her dress around her long, thin legs, in such a ladylike fashion.

Lifting the camera, Becky took several photos. "These will look so good in our album, Curt. My daddy and mama will be tickled to get these. Why, they'll dote on Patty's pictures. Mama will be proud of me for the sewing job I done."

Worriedly, Curt looked down at his wife and gave her a reassuring smile. "Your parents will like the photos, Sparrow. I think you did a good job on the costume." Becky was flighty today, dropping regularly into her hill accent. Tomorrow he'd fly a test, and that was why. Gently, Curt put his arm around her waist and tried to give her the unspoken support she needed. Official gatherings like this always made her nervous because she felt so terribly insecure among all the other well-groomed wives of officers.

Holt leaned over, whispering, "Take a gander, Curt." To their left, Sam watched Jack Stang and his wife Melody make their entrance. All the rest of the parents stood in small groups, chatting. He was sure the Stangs had timed their arrival to be the last couple through the doors. The entire room seemed to shift and focus on them. Stang, as always, looked impeccable in his blue uniform, every crease in place, every ribbon straight and flush to the next one on his chest, and not a speck of lint on his clothing. Melody was stunning, as always. Her black hair was coiffed into a feminine style, emphasizing the Grecian planes of her face.

Holt leaned lazily against the wall and made a comparison between Megan, who wore a breezy, sleeveless gold sun dress that complemented her red hair, and Melody. There was nothing but an air of business about the Stangs. Melody wore a carefully tailored designer suit of dark-blue and white houndstooth made of light wool. The braid trim and frog closings complemented her husband's uniform. Sam preferred to watch Megan. Her cheeks were flushed as she moved from one student to another, getting them settled down, ending squabbles, and keeping them quiet for at least five minutes.

Holt watched Megan caress a boy's hair here, place her hand on the shoulder of a little girl crying there, and then crouch down to kiss her brow to stop the tears. Megan had done as much for him last night, their kiss hovering hotly in his memory. Watching her lips move and form words, that smile haunting him, her eyes expressive with each feeling as she coaxed the little girl past the crisis, made him ache to make love with her.

"She's really something," Becky said in a whisper to Sam, "isn't she?"

Sam nodded, thinking Becky looked awfully pale today. "Ms. Roberts has a nice touch with the kids," he agreed. *And a nice touch with me.* Sam wanted her open and vulnerable to him in the same way she was with the children. Would that ever happen? God, he hoped so. Never had he wanted anything more in his life.

"Patty just adores her," Becky gushed. "She's doing better at school since the teacher's conference, too."

"Honey, Sam doesn't want to hear about that."

Frowning, Becky looked up at her husband.

"No, it's okay," Sam quickly assured him, giving Becky a smile. "After all, I'm her 'uncle.' I'm interested in how Patty's doing at school, too."

Moving restively, Curt grimaced. "Thanks for coming. You didn't have to."

"Becky invited me. How could I turn her—or Patty, down?" Sam had been surprised when Becky had called him over at Ops and begged him to be there at the party for the children. She was worried that Scotty and Patty would fight, and wasn't sure she could control Patty. Realizing it would be another chance to meet with Megan, Holt enthusiastically accepted her invitation.

Although Megan had given him a jaded, wary look when she saw him in the room, Sam felt being here was the right decision for Becky's sake. *Megan probably thinks I'm stalking her.* He excused himself and went to retrieve Becky and Curt some red punch. Wasn't he stalking Megan? Holt didn't really want to answer his own question. There was such a driving need to be with her, explore her, know her, that it warred daily with his concentration on testing activities. As he poured the punch into the delicate cut-crystal glasses, he smiled to himself. At least he thought less about Russ since meeting Megan, and that was a good sign for his own peace of mind.

Megan got a breather when the waitresses served the cupcakes and punch. The children immediately settled down to the task of eating. Nervously, she knew she must greet each set of parents, make small talk, and say something nice about their child to them. They hadn't taught this phase of interpersonal relationships in college, either. Perhaps, if she'd been an extrovert, it would have come easier, but she wasn't. Linda Yarnell, who was across the large room, gave her a game smile. Rallying, Megan went about her expected duties.

Holt waited patiently, watching Megan make the rounds. The Stangs glowed like proud parents when she talked to them. He watched Melody maneuver shortly thereafter, moving through the crowd to make small talk with each officer's family. Probably collecting grist for her mill, Holt ruminated.

Megan grew nervous as she approached the Merrills. Sam stood next to Curt, a cup of punch in each hand, as if waiting for her. Mouth dry, she shook Becky's hand, shocked at how cool it was, and how limp her handshake.

"Mrs. Merrill, are you all right?" Megan searched her face, saw darkness in her eyes, and a light film of sweat on her face. Memories of her mother looking exactly that way slammed into her. It took everything Megan had to stand there and pretend to be unaffected and calm.

"Oh, I'm fine, fine, Miss Roberts. Don't our Patty look cute in her little princess costume?"

"Honey..." Curt begged, and gave Megan a look of apology, his arm going around his wife's shoulders.

Cupping Becky's hand between both of hers, Megan forced a smile. "She looks positively beautiful, Mrs. Merrill. I've never seen a prettier princess." The scent of chocolate on Becky's breath triggered another reaction in Megan. Many alcoholics ate chocolate or mint to cover the smell of liquor on their breath. And Becky had that same haunted look in her eyes her mother had had so often. Was Becky drinking? Was that part of Patty's problem?

"I think," Sam said, stepping in to rescue Megan from Becky's planned barrage, "that Ms. Roberts needs a recess. Here, have a glass of punch. Come over here and stand next to me." Holt didn't wait for Megan to protest. In fact, he saw relief in her eyes, a silent thank you going to him for his insight. It made him feel good. Damn good.

Taking the punch, Megan sipped it gratefully. Sam stood there, looking around, hovering protectively close, but not close enough to make her feel uncomfortable. The din of noise in the room was high, the children's excited voices mingling with that of the parents talking to one another in cloistered groups. The captains flirted with the majors. The lieutenants all hung together, at the bottom rung of the officers' ladder. A few brave ones worked their way over to speak with the captains, having the good sense to make their points with someone more powerful than themselves.

"You have a nice touch with those kids," Sam complimented her, meaning it. He inhaled her spicy perfume that was made warm and fragrant by her skin. He wanted to drown in her large green eyes. "And you're prettier than any lady here."

Megan felt protection emanating from Holt. She heard the tremor in his husky voice, allowed it to cascade over her and stabilize her nerves. "Thanks, Sam." She tried to make light of his sincere compliment. "But I'm afraid Melody Stang looks as if she walked straight out of *Vogue* magazine. She's breathtakingly beautiful."

Holt shrugged. "I guess."

Megan stared up at him. "You guess? Don't you think she's pretty?"

"If you like perfect women, I suppose she is." Sam wanted to thread his fingers through that fiery mass of unruly red hair of hers like he'd done the night he'd kissed her. "I like a woman who doesn't wear a lot of makeup and isn't afraid if her hair is out of place, or if there's a stain of red punch on her dress." He had the good grace not to point out the stain, but it was on her skirt.

"Oh dear . . ." Megan laughed softly, giving him a wry look. "All part of being a second grade teacher, I'm afraid."

"Don't apologize. On you, it looks becoming as hell."

His voice vibrated through her, lifted her, and put her in touch with a new and vital part of herself. At a loss for words, Megan discreetly cleaned off the stain as best she could and then sipped her punch.

"You're far more beautiful than Mrs. Stang."

"Now you're patronizing me, Sam."

He held up his hand. "No, honest, I'm not."

"She's the most stunning woman here in this room." Megan said it almost wistfully, wishing that she would look that elegant, but she knew she wasn't, and never could be. Melody's fingernails were polished a deep red. She looked down at hers: two nails had been broken, two others needed attention, and the last one was long and perfect thus far. It would probably be broken before the day was over.

"I like a woman who isn't afraid to dress in a pair of jeans and forget that *Vogue* image," Sam confided conspiratorially. His eyes glimmered with mirth. "You're not afraid to wear your hair down, or get it blown by the wind. I lay you odds that Melody Stang has a ton of hair spray in hers to keep it looking like that."

Laughing, Megan relaxed. "You're right."

"Not only that, you don't see her over there with her son. She doesn't want to get orange frosting on her suit, or," Sam looked significantly down at the stain on Megan's dress, "punch all over her. It would ruin her image."

"You're impossible, Holt."

"But you like me anyway?"

The smile died on her lips, and Megan looked away from him. She felt his hand on her arm briefly.

"Just a little bit? Come on, it's not going to kill you to admit it. I'm not the village idiot, I can see you like me."

His touch was fleeting, evocative. For an instant, Megan wondered what it would be like to be loved by Sam Holt. She was powerfully drawn to his tender, sensitive side he always displayed shamelessly and without apology with her. Swallowing hard, she croaked, "You are likable, Captain."

Sam snorted, watching the red flush sweep across her freckled cheeks. She was chewing nervously on her full lower lip, and he wanted to lean over, capture that luscious mouth, and soothe her with a slow, thorough kiss. "But do *you* like me, Ms. Roberts?"

Squirming, Megan said, "Excuse me, but I've got to get back to my children."

"Minx," Holt said under his breath as she left his side. He grinned and watched her walk away. No one moved like Megan. There was such a refined grace to her, such fluidity. With a sigh, he leaned back against the wall and knew he was in heaven.

Before Megan could reach her class, she heard Patty let out a shriek, get up, and race down to where Scotty Stang was sitting. The girl raised her arm, hitting the boy on top of the helmet. Scotty immediately put up a wail that careened around the room. She heard Becky Merrill yell at Patty, and saw Captain Jack Stang form a soundless curse with his lips.

"Patty. . ." Megan breathed softly, gripped the girl by her arm, and hauled her off Scotty, "no, you can't hit him!" Megan wanted to die of embarrassment. All the other teachers had their charges under control. Hers was the only table where problems had erupted.

"He said I couldn't fly!" Patty wailed, tears forming and falling down her cheeks. "And I can! I can!"

Scotty's small square face screwed up with renewed fury as he launched off his chair, struck out, and hit Patty on the shoulder in a glancing blow. "I did not! I'm the astronaut! I'll fly! Your stupid fairy wings won't get you to the moon!"

Megan crouched down, separating the children, but Scotty was big for his age, and he tore loose, trying to hit Patty again. The girl dodged his fist, lifted her skirts, and kicked him in his shin. With a howl, Scotty hopped around on one foot. Desperate, needing help but afraid to ask, Megan tried to keep the children apart.

Becky appeared out of nowhere, gently taking Patty out of her grasp. "Ya'll grab Scotty," she ordered her quietly, lifting the girl into her arms.

"Settle down, Scotty," Megan told him firmly, guiding him back to his chair. "You don't hit girls. It's not nice."

"I don't care!" Scotty yelled. "She said I wouldn't make it to the moon!" He punched his chest with his small thumb. "My father says I'll be a test pilot just like him. I'll fly to the moon, maybe Mars! Patty doesn't know what she's talking about! Dumb girl!"

Megan saw Jack Stang and his wife coming around the table. They looked like a pair of eagles poised and ready to rip her throat out with their combined claws. She groaned to herself. Grateful that Becky had Patty soothed, Megan stood and tried to fix a smile that would tell the overprotective

Stangs that everything was under control once again. But one look at the captain's livid face, and she died inside.

"Hey, Merrill," Jack snapped, "why don't you keep that wild animal of yours caged? Scotty wasn't doing anything, and she deliberately got up and struck him." He glared down at Megan. "We saw the whole thing, Ms. Roberts," he ground out. "Scotty is innocent. She had no right to hit him."

"That's right," Melody put in smoothly, coming up behind Jack and wrapping her hand around his arm. "Ms. Roberts, I hope you weren't scolding Scotty. He was sitting there eating his cupcake and minding his own business, when Patty got up and hit him."

Becky held Patty in her arms and stood next to Megan. "Captain Stang, this isn't World War Three we have here. Just a little tussle between kids. Ya'll don't need to blow it out of proportion."

Stang seethed, glaring from Becky to her husband. "Captain, if I wasn't among women and children, I'd tell you what I really felt."

"Tell me tomorrow morning," Curt whispered tightly. He saw the redness creep into Stang's face and enjoyed the pilot's discomfort. "Now, why don't you put your heavy artillery away and back off? Ms. Roberts has everything under control. She doesn't need sidewalk superintendents."

"Please, everyone relax," Megan begged. "The children are fine. Let's get them back to their seats."

Becky took Curt's handkerchief, gently wiping the tears off Patty's face. "It's all right, squirt. Let's get you back to your chair. Miss Roberts wants ya'll to sit down."

"I'm gonna get to the moon first!" Patty shouted, gesturing down at Scotty. "Girls can be astronauts too!"

"You can be anything you want to be," Becky confirmed to Patty.

"Girls can't fly!" Scotty shouted. "They're too stupid!"

Megan drilled Stang with a cool look as she put Scotty back down and in his chair. "Is that what you teach your son? That women are stupid? That they're second-class citizens compared to men?"

Jack stiffened. He knew better than to create a scene. Melody's hand tightened on his arm in warning to remain silent. The colonel's wife, an ardent feminist type, was very much interested in their conversation.

"Listen, Patty sweetheart," Becky said, crouching down beside her daughter, "a girl can do anything a boy can. She may not be as physically strong, but she's got just as much brains, and maybe more, than a man. So don't let anyone tell you that you can't go to the moon if that's what you want to do."

"I'll go," Patty muttered defiantly, glaring down at Scotty. "And I'll get there before he does!"

"Crisis ended," Megan told everyone with a forced laugh, easing the tension. She gave the two children an extra cupcake. Megan breathed a huge sigh of relief. She watched as Sam eased the Stangs back and toward a group of majors, wanting to thank him for his divine interference. At that moment, she wanted to throw her arms around him and give him a kiss as a reward for his help.

Both sets of parents left the scene and went back to their respective walls to resume their desultory conversations within their chosen groups. Watching Megan closely, Holt decided to rejoin her. The situation had her rattled.

"You did good," he praised her.

"I'm not so sure," she managed softly.

"Coming from a family of six, I was always the one who had to settle the squabbles among the younger kids."

"Maybe you ought to be a teacher instead," Megan said with feeling. "You handled Stang and his wife well there at the end."

"Second nature." Sam wanted to make Megan feel as if she hadn't blown the situation, because she hadn't. "You did fine."

"If I was a person who drank, I'd want one now. That was so embarrassing . . ."

He cocked his head and held her unsure gaze. "There's a real nice picnic area at the other end of the base. It's private and quiet. How about if I grab us a couple of bottles of Perrier, some sandwiches, and drive you over there after the kids get on the bus?'' He looked at his watch. ''You've only got ten more minutes before the party's over.''

The invitation sounded heavenly. Megan needed to talk, to discuss how she might have handled the crisis differently, and Sam obviously had ways she could incorporate into her teaching agenda. ''As a friend?'' she asked, vividly recalling their kiss.

He grinned. ''Remember? I owe you one for last night?''

''You paid it back just now. You don't owe me a thing, Sam.''

''Chin up, Red.'' He saw she was terribly defeated by what had occurred, probably thinking that everyone was looking at her as if she were an ineffective teacher. Nothing could be further from the truth, and Sam wanted the time to make her believe differently. ''We'll have a picnic, sit, and talk. As friends. Deal?''

She closed her eyes for a moment. ''Deal,'' she said.

The picnic spot, known as Shady Place because of the grove of cottonwoods surrounding the five wooden tables, was ideal in Sam's estimation. He'd put together sandwiches from the restaurant, found a cardboard box to put them in, along with the promised Perrier. The evening air was still hot and dry, the sun hanging low in the sky. Nevertheless, the shade beneath the cottonwoods was considerably cooler.

Spreading their meal out before them, Sam invited Megan to sit opposite him at the green-painted table. He'd gotten rid of his blouse, taken off his tie, and opened the collar of his uniform. If someone saw him, they could write him up for being out of uniform, but he didn't care. No one would, however, because Shady Place was known as the lover's spot. The only people who came here wanted privacy, to be alone. Sam wondered if Megan knew that, and decided she didn't. He wasn't going to mention the spot's infamous record, either.

''Turkey sandwiches, slices of cheddar cheese, sweet pickles, and Perrier with lemon. Not a bad dinner,'' he congratulated himself.

Megan smiled and sat down. ''It's so peaceful here,'' she

murmured, looking around. The six cottonwoods with their highly polished three-pointed leaves moved in the constant breeze across the Mojave. Much farther to the west, Megan could see the restricted area, the many hangars, and Ops, where Sam worked. Indeed, the quiet was healing, except for the occasional jet taking off from the runway. Plane activity at the base went on twenty-four hours a day, seven days a week.

"I find peace when I look at you," Sam said, pouring the Perrier into two plastic cups filled with ice and lemon wedges.

Taking the cup from his hand, Megan held his sincere gaze. "That's a beautiful compliment," she admitted softly. "I only wish I could say the same."

Sam nodded. "I know: I'm a military pilot, and you don't like them." He raised his cup. "To a lady who knows how to successfully fight trench warfare with children and parents."

She grimaced, sipping the tart, lemony Perrier. "You're far too generous with the accolades."

Sam opened his sandwich and ate it slowly. Megan's hands shook as she peeled back the plastic wrapper on her meal. He allowed the quiet to filter between them, aware that her shoulders finally dropped, the tension beginning to flow out of her. Finally, he asked, "How do you think the parents saw you handle that mini-crisis?"

Rolling her eyes, Megan said, "Poorly. I'm sure I looked like a young ingenue fresh out of college, unable to handle the situation hardly at all."

"No," Sam parried, "that's not how they saw it at all."

Her eyes narrowed. "How do you know?"

"Because after you left, I hung around and eavesdropped here and there on a group of captains and majors for a few minutes. There was admiration for you, Megan. One woman said you had the patience of Job. A major complimented your quick handling of the situation."

"Oh . . ."

"Feel better now?"

"I'm sure the Stangs are upset."

He grinned. "They live to be upset. It's their number-one priority. You have a perverse attitude about looking at the negative, don't you? Out of eighty sets of parents, who praised your efforts, you want to zero in on the one set who didn't."

Staring down at her half-eaten sandwich, Megan mulled over his observation. Holt hadn't said it accusingly. Instead, it was a gently put statement designed for her to look at, mull over, and use as an observation. She set the sandwich aside, holding his gaze. "You're right."

"I didn't say it to be right, Megan. I noted it because I don't want you to become self-critical of what you did. You need someone around to build your confidence, not tear it down." He frowned. "Maybe this is none of my business, but what the hell happened to you when you were a kid?" Even though Megan appeared strong and sure of herself, there was a touching vulnerability she tried to hide from him. He wanted to know why.

"I've never really told anyone about my life with my parents," she began hesitantly.

"No one?" Sam found that hard to believe. "Why?"

"Easy. My father was a famous test pilot. If I dared breathe a word of what was going on at home, it could have affected his military record, his goal to get his colonel's rank, you know that."

Frowning, Sam asked, "Then you couldn't confide in your friends at school, either."

"No. Kids always talk to their parents. The parents, the officers specifically, would spread it around the base, and my father's career would have been affected by it."

"What a lousy situation," he muttered angrily, looking off into the distance, watching a T-38 Talon jet take off.

"It didn't hurt me."

"Yes, it did." Sam gestured to her. "Friends talk. They share the personal side of themselves, their good times, their bad ones. Most people have that outlet, but you didn't."

Megan tried to lighten the intensity of his words. "Are

you telling me that it's like pulling teeth to get to know me?''

''Yeah, I guess I am.'' Sam studied Megan. The tension around her eyes and mouth had disappeared. ''How about now? Do you have a woman friend you can confide in? Talk to?''

''Yes. Linda Yarnell. She's the wife of Major Yarnell over at NASA.''

''Doug Yarnell. Yeah, I know him. He's fair and aboveboard.''

''Unlike Captain Jack Stang?'' Megan baited.

''Him.'' Sam said the word with obvious rancor.

''It was obvious you two hated each other's guts.''

''Nah, I don't hate anyone, Red. I think it's in Stang's genes to hate the competition though.''

''It doesn't bother you he does?''

''No. Should it?''

''It would me.''

''Why?''

With a shrug, Megan said, ''I'd feel uncomfortable if someone didn't like me.''

''I'm not spending my life groveling at that bastard's feet getting him to try and like me. Besides, Red, not everyone in the world *is* going to like me. That's reality.'' And then Sam smiled. ''Of course, I don't see how everyone couldn't help but like you. You're sweet, kind, loving, and trusting. Nice traits.''

With a laugh, Megan felt her appetite returning. She nibbled on the sandwich. ''I think, Captain Holt, you're a tad prejudiced.''

''Maybe,'' Sam hedged, enjoying her husky laughter. Damn, but she was pretty in his eyes. The wind played with her hair, the sunlight lancing through the leaves brought out the gold and auburn highlights of it. And there was warmth in her green eyes, a warmth he wanted to bury himself within forever. ''Your kids idolize you. I see it in their eyes. They've got good taste, too.''

She allowed his compliments to sink in, lift her depression, and make her feel better. "I love the kids," Megan offered.

"Why a second grade teacher? I'm sure you could have taught older kids. This is almost like being more a mother than a teacher at this grade level."

With a hint of a smile, she said, "In a way, I missed my own growing-up years. Now, I can recapture them, live them daily through the eyes of the children in the class. Someday, I want a family, maybe three kids or so. . . . The children are my teachers, too. I like the trade-off."

"It's a positive way of looking at things," Sam agreed. He finished off the sandwich and mulled over the questions he wanted to ask her. This time, Megan wasn't tense or on the defensive. If anything, she was trusting, and it made his heart soar unaccountably. Their kiss, he was sure, had something to do with it. And Sam didn't want to do anything to mess up the good vibes shared between them, so he stepped on eggshells when trying to find out more about her life.

"Your mother, what kind of a woman was she?"

Megan hesitated, then said quietly, "She had a degree in accounting, but you'd never know it. Her career was being an alcoholic."

With a grimace, Sam asked, "Did she ever get help?"

"No. Looking back on it, I don't think she wanted help."

"Why?"

"I think my mother used her disease as a way to get even with my father for refusing to quit the Air Force and stop flying or having affairs on the side. If she went to Alcoholics Anonymous and got well, it wouldn't change anything, so she had no reason to get well."

"When did this all start, Megan?"

Rubbing her brow, she looked past where he sat, the bluish mountains partly hidden by the yellow dust raised from the winds that always swept across the Mojave. "I remember her having terrible fights with my father when I was three. She drank off and on until I was nine. One day, she called me into her room after I got home from school. Mother told me that from now on, I was going to have to make meals, clean the house, and do the chores she normally did. If Father wanted something ironed or washed, I was to do it.'' She shrugged. ''From that day on, she drank continuously.''

Eyes narrowing, Sam studied Megan for a long minute, digesting the information, the terrible impact it must have had on her innocent heart. ''Your mother went to bed because she was angry and going to get even with your father? That was her way of handling the situation?''

''Classic passive/aggressive tactics, Sam. I learned that in college when I started taking psychology courses. Becoming a teacher helped me see myself. It was a good thing.'' Megan moved her gaze back to him. ''At the time, I didn't realize what she was doing. I do now.''

''Jesus,'' Holt whispered, wanting to crush the plastic cup between his hands, ''didn't she ever think what her decision was going to cost *you*?''

''Don't blame just her,'' Megan said. ''My father went along with it. To him, I was a shadow in his life. His real love, his real wife, if you will, were the planes he flew. He pretended nothing was wrong and gave me a list of things to do each day when I got home from school. As long as I got those tasks completed, he ignored me.''

''And if you didn't?'' Sam held his breath, wondering if Colonel Roberts had abused her physically. Some military men believed that physical punishment was good for the children.

''Don't look so upset. My father never had to lift his hand in threat to me. I was too scared, wanting to please him too much, not to get that list done every day.''

Roberts was a total jerk in Holt's opinion, but he remained silent. That explained so much about Megan, and her distrust of military pilots. Rubbing his jaw, he said, ''You were so starved for affection, for any kind of a positive stroke, that you worked hard to get that list done in hopes your father would praise you, right?''

Sadly, she nodded. ''Exactly. My dysfunctional family life became abundantly clear to me in college. That's why . . .'' Megan hesitated, unsure whether to confide more in Sam. But the compassion in his dark-blue eyes made her go on. "I came back to Edwards to put the ghosts from the past to rest. My past. I came here with a mission, and with priorities. I have to settle my own accounts, and I want to make the children's lives better at the school. Better than what it was for me. I know I can do both."

"That took a lot of courage. Most of your growing-up years were spent here, weren't they?" Roberts had been a test pilot at Edwards for fourteen years before he augered in.

Toying with the glass, Megan poured herself more Perrier, feeling some of the load she'd carried so long by herself slip off her shoulders. "Yes. My mother committed suicide when I was eighteen, a month before I was to graduate from high school here on base." She didn't taste the Perrier. "My parents are buried over in Lancaster, at the cemetery. Since coming back here, I've been afraid to go over and visit their graves. I guess I'm not ready to face them. I hope I will be, someday."

Holt hurt for her. He couldn't help himself, getting up and coming around the table. Sitting down, he took Megan's hands and held her eyes that mirrored the pain she carried. "Look, promise me one thing?"

His hands were warm and strong feeling on hers. "What?" The enormity of what Sam had done didn't make her feel panic, only cared for, and hope sprang strongly in her heart for the first time since coming back to Edwards.

"When and if you decide to go visit them, take me along?"

Holt was serious. Megan searched his somber-looking features. This was no line, and he wasn't playing a game with her. "Well—"

"Megan, you could use a friend right now. How you *ever* had the guts to come back here, set up your life with no friends, no support, took more courage than you realize." Holt shook his head and reached out, caressing her cheek. Her flesh was warm and damp from the hot afternoon. "I don't think you know how much courage you already have in place. And you're looking at what you think you're not doing right, zeroing in on handling a few squabbles among the kids.'' He wanted to gently shake her, to get her to see what he saw, but Sam realized that she was still mired in her past. Weren't they both? But his past was different than hers. His was much happier growing up. Megan had lived in a cloistered hell, had her childhood stolen, and been forced to act like an adult. She was made to help keep a broken marriage together. ''Well?'' he goaded, squeezing her hands gently. ''Ask me along when you decide to face them down?''

With a nervous laugh, Megan tried to withdraw her hands, but he wouldn't allow it. Holt was too close, too masculine and tender for her vulnerable emotions. ''If and when I do, I'll let you know. Okay?''

With a slight smile meant to buoy her spirits, he said, ''Okay, Red.''

It would be wonderful to simply lean forward, kiss Sam, and find herself in his embrace once again. Megan realized Sam could help her salvage those scattered bits of her soul she was trying to find by coming back to Edwards. Still, he was a pilot, and her father's brusque, cold treatment of her and her mother warred strongly within her. She wanted to trust Sam, to allow herself the privilege of admitting how much she liked him. How could she?

Sam read the desire in her eyes, and he gave her a slight smile, sliding his hand against her cheek. ''Come here,'' he whispered, and drew her forward.

Panic made Megan freeze momentarily, but his fingers caressed the nape of her neck, neither forcing or demanding to meet him halfway, to convince her that they should share another kiss. Megan found herself pulled into the smoky hue of his eyes, transfixed, the stroke of his fingers banishing her fear, and shutting off her mind that screamed out a warning to run away.

Instead, Megan surrendered to the promise in his tender gaze . . . a promise that simmered just beneath the surface and belonged to them alone. Her lashes swept downward, and automatically, Megan's lips parted, yearning for contact with his strong, eliciting mouth upon hers once again.

This time, his mouth was masterful as he captured her. There was nothing tentative or searching about his quest. Hungrily, Megan met and matched his heated assault, lost in a series of molten, liquid explosions that blossomed throughout her. His hands moved through her hair, and she tilted her head back a little more, feeling his lips trail a scalding path of kisses down the length of her throat. All she was aware of was the warmth of his hands, the soft fire of his mouth retracing the slender line of her jaw, finding and claiming her wet, waiting lips once again. His tongue traced the lower curve of her lip, inciting a blaze deep within her. Slowly, he lavished each corner of her mouth, and scalding fire erupted down through the center of her body.

A small sound, a breathless sigh, escaped Megan. Her fingers alternately opened and closed against his chest, the pounding of his heart beneath her palms, racing along in time with hers. His breath washed across her cheek and nose, moist velvet heightening her senses of him, of his tender assault. Unaccustomed to the whirling vortex of heat spiraling through her, dizzied and burning with a fire that raged hotly between her thighs, Megan tried to stop herself from falling down through it, and losing her last shred of coherency.

Slowly, Sam drew away from her wonderfully pliant, sweet lips that filled him with the ache of need. Her face was flushed, her lashes opening, revealing drowsy emerald eyes saturated with desire and a need that matched his own. "You're heady stuff," he whispered thickly, unable to stop himself from tunneling his fingers through her beautiful red hair. His breathing was ragged, but so was hers. Managing a self-deprecating smile, Sam eased his hands away from her hair, holding her gently by the shoulders because she looked disoriented.

"You look deliciously exotic," he said huskily. "Red hair and fire. What a combination you are, sweetheart . . ." Indeed, Megan's hair was mussed, her mouth glistening and parted, giving her the appearance of a woman who had been well loved by her man. The urgent throb of his flesh ripened, demanded satiation, but he controlled his need for her. They had been so close to losing what little control had been left that Sam was shaken in the aftermath of their torrid kiss.

"I . . ." Megan's voice was contralto, heavy with passion. It was so easy to fall into Sam's hooded gaze and feel the returning fire leap along every nerve ending in her body. Just his look made her vibrate with a longing that left her aching to be fulfilled by him.

"Don't talk," Sam urged, keeping his hands on her shoulders. Megan was honestly disoriented.

Feeling cherished, as if she were some priceless, beautiful gift to Sam, Megan barely nodded her head. His hands moved from her shoulders, downward, gently caressing her arms and hands, as if to ground her in the present. She closed her eyes, allowing his ministrations to do just that. The call of the birds, the hot wind against her face, and the frantic beat of her heart were all that permeated her spinning senses for at least the next five minutes.

Finally, Megan opened her eyes. Sam's hands remained around hers, as it to keep her stabilized. She studied those hands, remembering the wonderful feeling of them threading through her hair, gently kneading her scalp. Shakily, she released a breath of air. "Every time we kiss," Megan confided huskily, "is like a new world for me."

"What do you mean?" he asked her quietly.

With a small smile, Megan admitted, "I've never been kissed like that before."

Sam wondered how many serious relationships Megan had had, and concluded not many. Her innocence shimmered through her honest response to him. It hadn't been tainted by too many lovers who had "trained" her to respond. "Well, I've never experienced what I share with you, Red." He watched surprise and then pleasure come to her lustrous eyes. "We're kind of good together." *And good for one another.*

Reality was settling around her shoulders once more, and Megan regretfully allowed the euphoria that had exploded and then built heatedly between them to dissipate. This was the second time she'd kissed Sam. This time, it had become even more dangerous, and Megan had come so close to throwing away all her caution just to be one with him. No, that couldn't happen. She couldn't commit to him. He was a pilot—nothing but misery and unhappiness would occur even if they shared sexual compatibility. Sex was only one small ingredient of a good relationship, and that was something Megan had learned in college. Yes, she and Sam shared a molten chemistry between them.

But there was more than a bed to be shared, and Megan knew that. For her to sleep with someone signaled a total commitment to the partner, not just a one-night stand or a flip affair. Somehow, she had to control herself, control the urge to make love to Sam. God, but it was so easy, so natural between them. Megan got up, moving away from Sam.

"I—I think I should get home. Thanks for a lovely picnic, Sam. I enjoyed it."

Back on automatic. He sat there, watching her draw up those walls to protect herself again. *Okay, just stay patient.* "You're right." Gathering up the articles and repacking them in the cardboard box, he walked over to the trash barrel and threw them away. Turning, he saw Megan standing uncertainly, her hands clasped in front of her, the wind ruffling her sun dress, outlining her slender form. In that moment, Megan reminded him of a deer: defenseless, nervous, and ready to take flight and run.

Picking up his jacket, he guided her back to his Corvette. "You know there's a mandatory Christmas dance over at the O Club coming up. Colonel Yale told me I'd better show up or else. I don't have a date, and I'd like to escort you to it." He knew if he told her the *real* reason why he wanted her with him, she'd bolt. So, Sam lied, reasoning that it was a white lie—one that wouldn't hurt anyone and help his cause. "My fitness report comes up for review in late December. I figure if I show up, play the game, make the small talk, that the colonel will give me favorable marks. How about it? As a friend, will you help me out?"

Megan slid into the black leather seat, strapped on the seat belt, and thought about Sam's request. When he got in, starting the growling 'Vette,' she said, "I don't know. I hate going over to the O Club. Father used to practically live over there. Every time he had a fight with Mother, that's where he'd go until it closed. And then, he'd go home with a groupie and come home early the next morning."

Guiding the Corvette out from beneath the shade, Sam said, "A lot of guys spend time over there." He reached over, briefly touching her hand. "It won't be like that this time, I promise you." Grinning, he added, "Hell, it'll give you a chance to dress up and show off that gorgeous body of yours. I'm not such a bad dancer, and judging from the way you carry yourself, I'll bet you're pretty good on the dance floor, too."

With a laugh, Megan couldn't resist his teasing. "You're right on both accounts. I do love to dress up, and there's nothing more in this world I love to do than dance. And," she added thoughtfully, "it's part of facing my past, isn't it?"

"It could be," Sam hedged.

The idea felt good to Megan. Sooner or later, she had to revisit these old haunts, reacquaint herself with the painful memories once again, so that she could face them, walk through them, and finally release them. "I might not be a very good date, Sam. All the old emotions it will drag up might make me moody. . . ."

With a grin, he said, "I'll take my chances, Red."

Megan matched his smile. "Okay, I'll go with you—as a friend, all right?"

"You've got a deal," Sam agreed fervently.

Megan settled into the cockpitlike seat, thinking that the Corvette looked exactly like the instrumentation found in a fighter jet. "Thanks for being there, Sam."

Sam felt a twinge of pain again in his heart for her. Megan had grown up so alone, a shy little introvert who never reached out to ask for help or support for herself. He'd provided her an unexpected opportunity to face her past, and he felt good about being there to support her. Gripping her hand, pressing a quick kiss to the top of it, he promised, "I'll be there for you, good mood or bad. Friends help one another out."

A wonderful warmth flowed through Megan. The tenor of Sam's voice gave her the first real hope she'd had since arriving at Edwards. "It's nice to have a friend . . ." she admitted softly.

Tension flowed out of Sam. "I wouldn't want it any other way." As long as he emphasized their friendship, Megan was trusting him—just a little bit. With time, perhaps the career pilot image would disappear from her eyes, and she'd relate to him, Sam Holt. Never had he wanted anything more.

— 10 —

WHERE was that bastard, Holt? Jack almost bit out the words in Design where everyone was gathered for the daily 0700 meeting. Holt was late. Why? He sat at his desk and pretended to study a manual while his mind clicked off possibilities. Last night, Melody swore that there was something between him and that little redheaded school teacher, Megan Roberts. That was confirmed this morning by a crew chief who mentioned seeing Holt with her at Shady Lane yesterday evening.

Good, he had more shit on his arch rival. That explained why Holt sided with the teacher when Scotty was attacked by that little brat, Patty Merrill. Jack lifted his head and zeroed in on Merrill, who was in a conference with Major Porter. They'd be flying shortly. He was about to begin needling Merrill when the door opened.

"Hey, boys and girls," Holt announced, swinging through the entrance and lifting up two bakery boxes, "it's doughnut time!"

Stang heard the fifteen people, both civilian and military, cheer and then break into applause. Dammit, Holt was late because he'd stopped at a bakery in Lancaster. Every once in a while, Holt would spring for danish and doughnuts for those in Design. Reluctantly, Jack admitted he'd been upstaged—again. Why hadn't he thought of this nice little touch? Melody was going to have to help him remember this kind of gesture to put him in good stead with these people. Maybe he ought to make a note on his event calendar so he wouldn't forget.

Sam grinned over at Curt and Port and murmured good morning to them as he opened the boxes. Immediately, everyone converged on him and the table where he'd spread out the offerings.

"Come on, pig-out time!" Holt called, laughing. Last night he'd slept for the first time without any nightmares. And Sam knew it was because of his growing closeness to Megan. This morning he'd awakened happier than he could ever recall. Wanting to share his happiness, Sam decided that danish and doughnuts were always in vogue with the crew at Design. He saw Port give him a rolled-eyeballs look.

"Ahh, come on Port, you can have one."

"Holt, those are *fat city* for my hips! No way."

Sam picked up a cheese-filled danish, took it over to her desk, and held it provocatively under her nose. "Here, this is for you. I asked for a low-cal danish, Port. The guy finally found one." He held it out in her direction. "Honest, it's fewer calories. It's filled with soybean meal disguised with an almond flavoring added. Come on, be a good sport."

"Better watch it," Jack interrupted, standing in line to get his doughnut, "the hand that feeds you might bite you, Major."

Lauren frowned. "Captain, as usual, you're wrong," and she claimed the danish from Holt. "Sam, this better be low-cal or I'm going to get even with you."

Grinning, Sam stepped aside, watching Stang. The officer was taut this morning. Yes, something was up. Sam could sense it around Stang. "I'll live in dire straits until you weigh yourself tomorrow morning on your scale and see you haven't gained an ounce on that dynamite frame of yours."

Laughter bubbled up from Lauren, and she tasted the

danish. "Ohhh, God, this is good, Holt. I hate you, but I love you. Thanks..."

"Hey," Jack whispered over at Holt, "I thought you'd like to know Melody's lodging a complaint with the assistant principal over Ms. Roberts's poor conduct yesterday afternoon."

Holt's jaw snapped shut. He glared up at Stang. A warning went off deep inside him. Jamison was gunning for Megan anyway. This could get her fired. Jack was watching him closely for any kind of reaction, trying to gauge just how much Megan meant to him. If he let on, she could be in worse trouble, because Melody would make it tougher on her over at the school. Sam knew from experience that the Stangs, once they decided upon a sacrificial victim, wouldn't let up until that person was effectively destroyed. And he didn't want Megan run off Edwards because of constant, unrelieved pressure put on by the couple. Dammit, anyway!

"That's her problem," he lied smoothly, "not mine."

"Yeah?" Jack gloated, watching for a possible flare of anger from the pilot. Holt's eyes were opaque, unreadable.

"Yeah. Hey, listen, we've got a flight coming up in forty minutes. I've got paperwork to do before that."

Rising, Stang smiled. "Roger." He walked back to his desk and filed away Holt's reactions. He made a few notes on the pad he kept under lock and key in his desk drawer which he'd share with Melody tonight at their usual Tac and Strat session. Sitting down, he glanced at his watch. In exactly ten minutes, Melody would make her grand entrance to Brad Jamison's office and put the final nails in Megan Roberts's coffin. If she refused to stop making out reports on Scotty, then there were other ways to get her fired.

Melody made sure her Albert Nippon lavender suit was perfectly arranged over her hips before entering the school. She wore amethyst earrings and a simple, but elegant, Cartier gold watch on her right wrist. The children were already in class, the tile halls quiet as she made her way toward the principal's office.

Smiling to herself, she wanted to be a fly on the wall

when Megan Roberts was hauled in on the carpet and fired. The woman was really a poor excuse for a teacher in her estimation. She held the lavender leather purse a little more tightly, the matching leather heels complementing her expensive six-hundred-dollar suit.

Brad Jamison, dressed in a dark-blue pin-stripe suit was consulting with his secretaries when she entered. She watched his eyes widen considerably when she stepped into the office. Good, her image had the desired effect on him. Melody completely disregarded the three women staring at her.

"Good morning, Mr. Jamison." She held out her hand.

"Good morning, Mrs. Stang. I'm glad you could come. Step into my office?"

Smiling warmly, she came around the end of the counter. "Of course."

Flushing, he gestured toward the open door to his office. "Of course! Come in. And might I say, you're stunning looking in that suit."

Smiling demurely, Melody nodded. "Thank you, Mr. Jamison," and she followed him into the spacious office. He shut the door and came around to his side of the desk.

Melody dropped all pretense once she knew they were out of sight and earshot of the secretaries. "We want Megan Roberts fired, Brad. That ridiculous scene at the O Club yesterday afternoon involving Scotty is the last straw."

With a nod, Brad pulled a file from his drawer. "To make it worse, she's filed another report on your son, Melody." He handed her the file, watching her eyes narrow as she read it.

She threw it on his desk. "I thought the last check would cover problems like this," she said tightly. "I'm sure you're aware that Jack is chief test pilot on the *Agile Eagle* project over at Ops. If Roberts talks about this to other teachers, it could get around. We can't afford to have General Dalton or Colonel Yale get ahold of this information. It would hurt Jack's chance for an early promotion to major."

Brad nodded. "I've warned her, even threatened her, but she won't back off."

"What does it boil down to? What has to be done to get rid of her?"

"I have to prove she's inept." Making a frustrated sound, he got up. "I have to lodge a protest with the union, which I've done. We have to have reason to fire her, Melody."

"You've got plenty of them! She's picking on Scotty, singling him out! The poor boy is a nervous wreck when he gets home. Both Jack and I will swear to that. He spends half his day in the nursing room instead of the classroom. What kind of an education is he getting?" Melody gripped the purse, emotion leaking through her carefully modulated voice. "I won't have that, Brad. I simply won't tolerate it."

Scratching his head, Brad gave her an oblique look. "I'm doing what I can."

"Jack wants her gone. The sooner, the better."

"Are you aware that Megan is the daughter of Colonel Steven Roberts, the famous test pilot?"

Melody was unable to stifle her reaction. "What?" *Oh, my God!* The implications were there: Megan Roberts had a lot more clout than she'd suspected. In fact, Melody had completely underestimated Megan's power base.

Clearing his throat, Brad went on. "Firing her is going to be a ticklish matter. She has power on this base if she wants to use it. Frankly, I don't want a call from General Dalton over this. I'll need at least twice as much as the last check to ramrod this through."

Melody understood. "You'll get it. I'll put it into the mail today." Inwardly she seethed, angry at her lack of investigation on Megan. She was a far more dangerous adversary than Melody first thought. Megan Roberts was the *daughter* of Colonel Roberts, one of the most famous test pilots since Edwards had come into existence! Taking a deep breath, Melody hurried out to her Mercedes Benz, barely able to wait and speak with Jack tonight.

Megan sat very still as Brad Jamison shut the door with an ominous finality. The plastic chair made her back sweaty, and she longed for a cooling shower. The shirtdress she wore was damp beneath the armpits. She prayed Jamison didn't notice. Her school day was over when she received a call to come up to the head office. What was up? Was Jamison going to chew her out for the way she handled the Halloween fight between Patty and Scotty?

Jamison sat down and steepled his hands. "I think it's only fair to tell you that I've notified your union that I want you fired."

Megan sat up, her eyes going wide. "Fired?"

Working hard to curb a smile of satisfaction, he snapped out, "That's right."

Trying to control her breathing, Megan gritted out, "Why?" It had to be the outdoor education proposal.

"Your inability to control the children in your class. Putting out weekly reports on Scotty Stang has gone too far. You're singling out the child, making him an example. The parents are very upset, and I happen to agree with them: the problem isn't with Scotty, it's with the ability, or lack of it, of the teacher."

Megan glared at him. "That child is hyperactive! And I'm not making him an example. I refuse to have him disrupt the rest of my class."

With a shrug, Jamison muttered, "So, take it up with your union. I've filed for your firing."

Inwardly, Megan quivered in fury. "I'll fight you, Jamison. I'll do whatever necessary to vindicate myself in this matter."

"Go for it, Ms. Roberts. It won't do you any good."

She left quickly, clutching her briefcase, her fingers aching on the handle. Her mind clicked off a triage of things that would have to be done. First, she'd have to call Linda Yarnell to get a copy of the request to have her fired. She had no experience in union matters. Could Jamison get his way? Or would the union be able to save her job? Suddenly, the need to speak to Sam was overwhelming. Would he still be at Ops? It was 1600. Turning, she went to the empty teachers' lounge and picked up a phone. First, a call to Linda, and then, to Sam.

"Design, Major Porter," Lauren said, answering the phone.

"Yes . . . is Captain Holt still there?"

"Sure is. May I ask who's calling?"

"Megan. Megan Roberts."

"One moment." Lauren smiled and put the call on hold. She and Sam were the only ones left in the office. Everyone else had gone home for the day. "Hey, Holt, your lady's on the line."

Lifting his head from the report he was writing, Sam scowled. Port was grinning like she was sitting in the catbird seat. "What?"

"Megan Roberts is on the phone, dummy. Don't you want to talk to her? She wants to speak to you. Line one."

Shocked but pleased, Sam reached for his phone. "Thanks, Port."

"I promise to plug my ears," she answered dryly, returning her attention to her computer terminal.

Sam smiled. "I trust you Port. Eavesdrop all you want." He knew she wouldn't tell anyone of the conversation. He hit the button. "Megan?"

"Hi . . . I'm sorry to call you at work—"

"No, that's okay. You don't sound very good. What's wrong?"

"C-could I see you after work? I need to talk. Friend to friend."

His scowl deepened. "Sure. How about if I meet you over at the O Club?" As soon as he said it, he regretted it. "No, forget that." His mind whirled with options. He couldn't invite Megan down here because it was restricted and off-limits without clearance. "How about at your school?"

"No, I'd rather not."

Instantly, Holt knew that Melody Stang had something to do with it. "Okay, how about if I pick you up, in say"—he looked at his watch—"fifteen minutes? I'll take you out to a nice little Italian restaurant in Lancaster, we'll sit, talk, and enjoy a good meal."

"My car, though . . ."

"Leave it here on base for tonight. I'll take you into work tomorrow morning."

"Oh, Sam, that's asking too much. I get up early."

"So do I."

"Five A.M.?"

"Yes. Fifteen minutes, Red, and I'll be there."

"Okay. Thanks."

Sam hung up the phone, disliking the tone he heard in Megan's voice. She was upset. It had to be because of the Stangs.

"You look like a pit bull ready to bite someone," Lauren noted.

With a snort, Holt got up. He jerked open a drawer, tossing the report inside it, and then slammed it shut. "Yeah, I'd like to bite somebody."

"Megan has a nice voice. Rich and husky."

"Diverting me won't do any good, Port. I'm madder than hell at Stang."

"Oh, that little incident over at the O Club yesterday with his precious son?"

Holt felt his anger abate to a degree under Lauren's insightful comment. "Roger that." He hunted for his garrison cap and located it in one of the drawers of his desk.

"I don't know what Stang thinks he's going to gain by all of this," Lauren muttered. "I'm sure not impressed with him or his methods."

"Some four star is upstairs. It would be my luck it's the Joint Chiefs of Staff general," Sam said, putting on his garrison cap. He noticed Merrill's messy desk. Papers were strewn across the top of it. Of late, Curt had been less than organized. The old saying that if your desk was a mess, so was your flying, was an axiom around Design. Holt hoped for Merrill's sake the axiom wasn't true.

"I've never seen you like this," Lauren said seriously, leaning back in her chair and watching him. "Sam?"

He halted at the door. "Yeah?"

"You really are serious about this lady, aren't you? I mean, you're upset."

"I'm not going to lie to you, Port. I wake up thinking about Megan, I go to sleep and dream about her. Yeah, she's important to me."

She smiled gently. "It becomes you. Good night, Sam."

"See you tomorrow, Port." He disappeared out the door.

The urgency to see Megan, to find out what was causing her the kind of distress that she'd actually call him at work, gnawed at his patience as he drove to the school. Megan was waiting for him out front, briefcase in hand.

Sam liked the kelly-green shirtdress she wore. The small gold earrings and gold choker at her throat emphasized the verdant color of her lovely eyes. He leaned over, opening the door for her so she could climb in. Anxiously, he searched her features and realized she was pale.

As he drove off toward the main gate, he glanced over at her. "Hell of a day?" he guessed.

"Was it ever." Megan hungrily absorbed his profile, his eaglelike nose, his chin solid and strong. She instinctively knew Sam would be angry and upset if she told him her job was on the line. Earlier, Linda had said she'd just received the firing notice. There would be a union meeting tomorrow morning to get her side of the situation, and then action would be taken to protect her job. Rubbing her temple where a headache lapped, Megan uttered tiredly, "I've just had a really rough day, Sam." Skirting the whole reason, Megan added, "I feel like I'm sitting on a keg of dynamite concerning a child in my class."

Sam scowled, hearing the anguish in her voice. "I'd ask what it's all about, but I know how you feel about talking confidentially about the children. Jack Stang told me this morning that his wife was going to raise hell with the principal over that stupid fight that took place between Patty and Scotty."

Megan ran her fingers through her red hair and rubbed her scalp to try and ease the pain of the headache. "It does involve that fight to a degree," Megan admitted. "Thanks for understanding, Sam. I—I just need to be with a good friend for a few hours." Some things were hard to face alone. Megan wanted to tell Sam everything. But it would be one more pitched battle she'd have to fight because she knew how upset he'd become over the situation.

Panic shot through Sam when he heard her voice wobble. He slowed the Corvette at the front gate, the Air Police sentry saluting sharply, motioning him through. Outside the gate, he nudged the Corvette to sixty-five MPH, Lake Rosamond, one of the two dry lake beds surrounding Edwards, on their left.

"Coming back to Edwards was a hard thing to do," he told her softly. He appraised her taut, washed-out features. "It sounds like it's one of those days when you're questioning the wisdom of that decision."

"Believe me, it is. I just wish I was stronger because I don't feel that way right now."

"Aww, it's just a tempest in a teapot, Red," he teased, wishing he knew what had Megan so upset. Hooking his thumb in his direction he jested, "I'm your real problem, remember? You hate pilots, and I'm one. I happen to like you, and vice versa. That's the *big* problem you have to surmount," and he grinned, watching a soft smile touch her lips. Right now, all Holt wanted to do was stop the car, put his arms around Megan, and hold her. She had that need written all over her. To hell with it. He braked the Corvette and pulled it over to the berm.

"Sam, what's wrong?"

"Nothing," he muttered, placing his arms around her and drawing her against him. "Everything's right."

Stunned, Megan didn't resist. She found herself pressed against his light-blue shirt, his chest a pillow for her to rest her head against. As he ran his fingers gently through her hair, a little sigh escaped from her, all the tension exiting through his caresses. Sam felt so good, so strong and confident. Acquiescing, Megan moved her head against his shoulder, inhaling his masculine scent laced with a hint of woodsy cologne.

"That's better," Sam murmured against her ear. The need to kiss her again was excruciating, but he held himself in tight check. Resting his jaw against her glorious, silky hair, he went on in a low, coaxing voice. "Now, listen to me, Megan. You've come too far to quit now. Don't let the situation get to you." He inhaled her fragrance, feeling heat shaft nakedly through him. Megan was soft, vulnerable, and trusting—if only for a few precious seconds. Giving her a small shake, he reluctantly created a separation between them. Sam looked into her wide green eyes. "I believe in you."

As Megan eased away from him, her hand unconsciously moved across his chest. She felt his muscles tense and grow taut wherever she had grazed him. Shaky, she hadn't counted on her own heated reaction to Sam. His mouth, firm and commanding, was inches away. Megan dragged her gaze from it and forced herself to look up into his eyes, smoky blue with desire. "Sam . . ." His name came out like a breathless prayer. Megan rested her hand against his chest, feeling the urgent beat of his heart beneath her palm.

Holt felt her quiver, and he saw panic start to eat away at the desire in her eyes. Gently, he released her back to her own seat. "Just hang in there," was all he could say, watching a pink flush stain her freckled cheeks.

"It feels good to have support," Megan admitted. "This is a new one to me: somebody in my corner, cheering me on."

Controlling his urge to reach out and lightly caress her wonderfully thick, fragrant hair, Sam sat there. "It's about time, don't you think? You don't have to stay silent anymore, Megan. You can talk to me, tell me what's bothering you, and," he sighed, smiling at her, "what makes you laugh."

Touched beyond words, she couldn't tear her gaze from his face. There was an incredible tenderness in Sam's features, something she'd never encountered in another man—ever. "You make me laugh," she said softly, avoiding his gaze. "When I'm down, you pick me up."

Settling back into his seat, Sam knew he'd better start driving or he'd do something both would regret later. "And vice versa, believe me. You ready for that nice little Italian restaurant?"

Her appetite was nonexistent. "I'm pretty upset, but I'll try and eat."

"Good, I like a woman who has a healthy appetite. Can't stand these ladies who always order a salad and drink a glass of water when they're taken out to dinner."

Megan relaxed, feeling the power of the Corvette pin her

momentarily against the black leather seat. She needed Sam's unwavering support. They rode in silence, taking a back road to Lancaster and avoiding the interstate that always crawled with police willing to hand out speeding tickets. Pilots on the ground tended to think their car was a plane without wings and pushed them at high speeds as a result. Speeding tickets were handed out with great regularity around Lancaster. Near the city limits Sam turned to her and broke the companionable silence.

"I'd like to stop over at my home for a minute and change clothes before we go eat." He motioned to his uniform. "I don't like going out in public with this on."

"I understand."

"Yeah?" He smiled, thinking Megan had never looked younger. A gold reflection reminding him of sunlight danced in her green eyes. "You mean you don't think that's a line to lure you into my home, and then into my bedroom?"

She gave him a narrowed look. "It better not be."

"What if it were, Red?" Holt could picture her flaming red hair spread out like a halo around her head on the pristine white sheets of his bed. The image was hot, intoxicating.

"No, I trust you."

Sam groaned eloquently. "Putting the old guilt trip routine on me so I have to behave myself, huh?"

"Exactly."

The homes of Lancaster were nearly all one-story, long, rambling ranch styles with abode exteriors of white, yellow, or light brown to deflect the desert sun and heat. He pulled in the driveway of his white adobe three-bedroom ranch-style home. A lawn struggled to remain green. Several small palms along the border of the sidewalk and oleander bushes blooming with pink flowers partially hid the front of the house. It gave him a sense of privacy he liked.

"Come on, I'd like to show you my home," Holt said, getting out. Moving around the sports car, he opened the door for Megan.

Smoothing out her dress, Megan followed him up the red brick walk lined with yellow-topped and red-topped marigolds. "Do you take care of the landscaping, or hire someone to do it for you?"

Fishing the key out of his pocket, Sam stepped up to the door and opened the screen. "No, I do it myself."

Impressed, Megan noticed every bush and tree was neatly trimmed, and there was no sign of weeds present in the marigolds. "A pilot who likes earthbound things. I have a hard time believing it."

Opening the door, the central air conditioning surrounded them. "Just another little wonderful surprise about me to impress you with," Sam teased, gesturing for her to come in. He was glad he'd cleaned the house two days ago. Usually, dishes got washed once a week in the dishwasher. Until then, they remained stacked in the sink and all over the counter. Not a pretty sight, Sam thought, thanking his lucky stars they were washed and put away. He closed the door.

Interested in her reaction, Sam remained silent for a moment. Megan slowly turned around, pleasure written in her features. The foyer opened directly into the living room on the right. Down the hall and to the left was the kitchen. When she spotted his antique Victorian furniture, she gasped, turning to him.

"Why didn't you tell me you collected Victorian furniture like I did?"

With a shrug, he walked over to where she stood. "When I came over the other night, it didn't seem like the right time or place to discuss our mutual passion."

Enthralled, Megan admired his impeccable taste. "You're right, but, this is thrilling! May I snoop?"

With a chuckle, Sam gestured toward the living room. "Sure, go ahead. I'll go get changed."

Megan took another look at Sam, and then shook her head. "You really are full of surprises."

"Is that test pilot image finally starting to fade off me?" he teased drolly. Megan blushed beautifully.

"I had that coming, didn't I?"

"No," Holt responded huskily, "not really. I just need

you to see me as a man who happens to fly for a living, and not the other way around.''

She stood there, watching him walk down the beige-carpeted hall and disappear into another room. Mulling over Holt's entreaty, Megan knew he was right. She went to admire the Victorian furniture. There were four walnut spoon-back armchairs with matching nursing chairs. Each had serpentine seats and sat on bariole legs. They were exquisite pieces.

A long time ago, Megan had learned to stand quietly and simply feel a home. She did so now, finding an indescribable peace filtering through her. Sam's home was quiet, but not deathly silent. The fireplace had a mid-eighteenth-century Georgian brass and iron fire grate with a chinoiserie frieze. On the mantel was a Dutch pewter oval tobacco box and a Swiss pewter *bauchkanne* with a chain handle. Both pieces were rare finds and in perfect condition.

Turning, Megan wandered into the formal dining room, the walls painted a dusky rose color. A huge Victorian burr-walnut Sutherland table with shaped feet made her halt. The walnut surface showed a great deal of loving attention despite its venerable age. Six early Victorian yew-wood Windsor chairs sat around the oval table. In awe, she lightly ran her fingertips across the burr walnut and felt the satin finish.

The kitchen had a lot of open space, and all the modern and expected necessities. What Megan like most were the pots of small herbs that Sam had growing on the many windowsills. She leaned over, inhaling the scent of the sage and dill, and pinched off a bit of parsley and ate it. From the kitchen, she discovered his office. An impossible amount of shelf space hid all the walls, hundreds of book on technical topics across the shelves.

Curious, she looked at several photos that hung in front of his neatly kept desk. They were all family pictures. One was obviously with his brother and four sisters. The second was of his parents. Megan studied the smiling couple. Sam's mother was petite, with graying hair perched atop her head in a bun, her smile toothy and warm. His father, a tall, handsome man, wore coveralls. There was grease or mud on his hands. The photo was obviously impromptu, taken without giving them a chance to clean up first. She smiled gently, liking their worn, friendly faces.

There was a great deal of Sam's mother in him, she discovered. Somehow, that made her feel good. A woman's influence, she had found, always softened a man, and took away his hard, insensitive edges. The last photo was a graduation picture from the Air Force flight school, with Sam surrounded by his friends. He looked much younger then, his face unlined as yet, untouched by life.

The door at the rear of the office was ajar, and she walked through it.

Megan jerked to a stop. She was in the master bedroom, and Sam was in the process of finding a white T-shirt to put on over his dark-haired chest. He'd taken a quick shower, his skin gleaming beneath the low lighting. The dark-brown slacks he wore emphasized his maleness, and Megan took a hasty step back toward the office.

"Stay put," he said, pulling the T-shirt over his head. "I'll be decent in a second. What do you think of my bed?"

Megan admired the bold lines of Sam's upper body. His shoulders were proud, thrown back naturally, his chest deep, and his belly hard and flat. "Coming from any other guy, that would be a line, Holt."

He laughed with her, pulling a pale-pink shirt off a hanger from the walk-in closet. "Yeah, it would. Being the antique hound you are, you know it's not a line. I hunted the world for that bed."

"I believe it," Megan said, looking up at the incredible George III mahogany four-poster bedstead of Hepplewhite design. "How old is it?"

"Sotheby's put it at 1780." He quickly buttoned the shirt, stuffing in the tails and rolling up the sleeves to his elbows. "She's a beauty, isn't she?"

The paisley-print cotton material formed a canopy over the bed, the mahogany posts beautifully carved and highly polished. It was definitely of masculine cast, but the graceful, slender lines of the carved wood made it beautiful, not bulky or heavy looking. "Yes, it is."

Sam joined her, hands on his hips as they viewed the bed. "Want to sit on it?"

Megan stepped away, finding him irresistible in civilian attire. "Now you're back to your lines." Hair still dark from the shower and recently combed, he had a five o'clock beard shadowing his features, making him look slightly dangerous in her mind. Sam was more than a little dangerous if Megan dared acknowledge the pound of her heart, or the fact she felt giddy around him.

Picking up his tan camel-hair sports coat, he laughed. "But they're honest lines, Red. Come on, I'm hungry too." *For you. Only for you.*

— 11 —

"I took the privilege of looking at your family pictures in your office," Megan began, sipping the Perrier with a twist of lime. The small, intimate Italian restaurant was quiet and dark, suiting her needs. Sam sat at her elbow, and they were surrounded by a crescent-shaped black leather booth. It made her feel as if they were in protective arms, and intensified the sense of privacy.

Sam leaned back, idly running his fingers around the sweaty glass of iced tea. Giving her a grin, he said in a conspiratorial tone, "You know, I don't discuss my past with anyone."

"Why?" It was on the tip of her tongue to ask him what he had to hide. Certainly, nothing.

"Well," Holt hedged, "you being an Air Force brat and all, would understand what I'm going to say. Officers like Stang would take my ethnic background and shove it down my throat for his own good. Most pilots come from the upper middle class of society."

"And you didn't?" Megan guessed.

"Roger that one. Not that I'm ashamed of my folks, or my dad's job."

"Which is?"

"Was. He's retired now."

"But," Megan teased, watching him balk.

Squirming, Holt muttered, "Dad was a union auto worker in Detroit for thirty years." He glanced up quickly to see Megan's reaction.

"So nothing was handed to you on a silver platter?" Megan felt good about that. Sam had worked hard, struggled, and made something of himself. It said a lot about his belief in himself, his goals.

"Not a thing. I worked a paper route when I was nine until I graduated from high school. Dad also ran a small engine repair shop on the side, out in his garage, so I always helped him out there when I wasn't studying or tossing papers into people's yards."

"What about your mother?"

"A Polish emigré. She sought political asylum in this country and could speak very little English when she came over here as a teenager. Mom worked as a janitor at General Motors, where Dad was employed. They met and fell in love."

She smiled gently. "I like your mother's face. She looks very kind and forgiving."

Sam allowed the internal tension he was holding to dissolve. Megan honestly didn't seem to care that he came from a less than privileged background. "You're right," he said softly, remembering some poignant moments with his mother. "She came from sturdy farm people near Warsaw, but she'd always had this dream of coming to the States." With a shake of his head, he murmured, "Mom is still a dreamer to this day."

"I like that," Megan said. "I think she gave you the ability to dream, too."

"She did. When I was only three, I used to tell her and anyone else who would listen, that I was a bird and going to fly. As I got older, Mom supported my dream, telling me I was capable of doing anything I wanted to do. Plastic model airplanes became my passion as a kid. I devoured any book on flight I could find. When I was twelve, my mother proudly announced to our entire neighborhood that I was going to be a famous Air Force test pilot, because that's what I'd told her I wanted to be."

Megan felt her heart expand with joy. "You're so lucky to have a mother like that," she whispered, deeply touched that Sam would share such wonderful and private moments in his life with her.

With a grin, he said, "Well, it wasn't all a bed of roses. One time I used Mom's clotheslines, which were made out of thin cotton rope, as an imaginary landing place for my plastic airplanes. I painted the lines with black paint and pretended they were my four runway airstrips. And then, I rigged four of my models on wire so that if I pushed one down the clothesline, it would 'fly' *and* land. It was in hog heaven playing out there for hours with them. Everything came to a roaring halt when she came out with a load of wash to hang. Mom dropped the basket to the ground and screeched when she realized what I'd done."

Laughter pealed from Megan, and without thinking, she reached out, placing her hand over Sam's. The gesture spoke volumes. She saw his eyes narrow briefly, hope flaring in their dark-blue depths. Discreetly, Megan removed her hand. Trying to recover from her gaffe, she murmured, "I'll bet all those lines had to be replaced."

"So did my rear when she got done with me," Sam answered ruefully. "I was only ten, and with six kids in the family, things were tight financially. Mom didn't have the money to buy new clothesline, but I didn't understand that at the time."

"What did she do?"

"Being the practical Pole she'd always been, she went to a farmer friend and wrangled hay bale twine off him for something like a dollar. She came back, and soon, there were four lines of bailing twine in place of the painted clothesline. Mom hung the clothes and acted as if nothing had ever happened." He smiled fondly. "I like to think I have her common sense genes."

"A great gift," Megan agreed softly. A waitress in a black outfit and white apron approached with their meals. "I don't know about you, but I'm ready to eat," she said, indicating their meals had arrived.

Sam nodded. The oregano and garlic wafted by him as

the waitress placed the heaping platter of spaghetti and meatballs in front of him. Megan had ordered something far less messy: lasagna. He thanked the waitress, hungrily digging into the plate of food.

Megan ate little. All her precautions were wasted, however, because a splotch of sauce dropped on her dress anyway. Groaning, Megan tried to clean it off. She looked up to see Sam grinning.

"It isn't funny," she grumbled.

"Sure it is. Nobody should eat at an Italian restaurant if they don't want to get a little messy in the process."

"My father taught me to always be neat and clean." Megan's hand stopped in midair with the napkin. Now where did *that* come from? Frowning, she managed to get the worst of the sauce off her orange dress.

Holt wrapped the spaghetti between a large tablespoon and his fork. "So your father wanted a perfect little girl, eh?" He watched her reaction beneath his lashes.

"Father had an image to uphold. Perfect pilot. Perfect wife. Perfect home. And perfect child."

Sam placed his silverware back on the plate. He leaned over, taking his thumb and brushing a small speck of sauce from the corner of her mouth. She was soft, and he yearned to trace her beautiful lips, and then kiss her again. Heated memory of her mouth, her willingness, haunted him and almost goaded him into leaning over to claim her. The startled look in Megan's eyes cautioned him to do nothing further. "I kinda like the imperfect woman sitting here with me," he whispered. "That makes you approachable, not someone who looks so perfect that no one could attain her."

Holt's touch sent a *frisson* of sweet fire twisting down through her. Megan struggled to recover from his spontaneous gesture, but it was impossible. She tried to stop staring at his mouth and recalled his strength, his cajoling that had made her want to keep kissing him forever. Blotting her mouth with her napkin, she muttered, "I feel like Pig Pen from the *Peanuts* comic strip tonight."

Laughing, Sam pointed to his face. "Come on, Red, lighten up. I'm *positive* I've got some sauce splattered somewhere on this mug." He looked archly down at his shirt and examined himself closely. "Yup, see here? Three splatters. I've got you beat two to one."

"You're impossible," Megan giggled, the sudden urge to throw her arms around his neck and kiss him almost tangible. She wanted to feel that strong, smiling mouth beneath hers again. An ache centered in her lower body, and Megan had her answer of how she truly felt toward Sam.

"But likable?" Sam asked, holding her dancing eyes. He saw Megan sober slightly.

"Yes, you're very likable, Captain."

"Ouch. I thought what I did for a living was forgotten for now."

Sadly, Megan picked at her lasagna, her appetite gone. "I wish it could be," she admitted, her voice barely audible.

Sam put the plate of half-eaten spaghetti aside. He reached out, capturing her small hand. "Let's go for a walk. There's a nice children's playground down a block, with some trees and grass. I'd like to talk to you some more about your family."

Years of being silent, of not being able to share, rose within her at the husky entreaty in his voice. Megan lifted her lashes and probed Holt's reasons for the terribly personal request. The tender blue flame in his eyes told her everything. Without a word, she placed the napkin on the red-and-white checked tablecloth and stood.

Holt wouldn't allow Megan to reclaim her hand once they left the restaurant. Lancaster was lazy at this time of day, he thought, most people home for dinner right now. The traffic was sparse, and so was the foot traffic. That suited him fine.

Once they got to the playground, a city block of lawn, trees, and several picnic tables, Sam led her onto the grass. "Your father had one hell of a reputation over at Ops, you know."

"No, I didn't know that. As a child, I remember him as a quiet man, always seeming to be thinking or somewhere else." Sam's hand around hers felt comforting. "Father only spoke to me when it was necessary."

"Never did things like read books to you?"

"No."

"How about your mother?"

"She had her career. You know the rest: by the time I was nine, she decided to go to bed permanently."

"I can't believe your father let it happen."

"He accepted it." Bitterness leaked into Megan's voice. "As long as things ran smoothly at home, Father didn't care what went on, I guess. He used to tell me I had to get *A*'s in school, and be as good as him, or it would look bad for his career."

"Christ," Holt muttered. Placing his hands on her small shoulders, he saw the hurt in Megan's eyes, and wanted somehow to replace it with laughter and joy instead. She didn't have much of that growing up, he realized. "Plus, you assumed the duties of wife and mother to him, too."

"What do you mean?" Holding his stormy gaze, Megan tilted her head. A slight breeze ruffled his hair, a few strands dipping onto his brow.

"I gave our last conversation a lot of thought. Your mother abandoned you at nine. Also, she gave up on being a wife to your father. So, you had to carry demands on you no youngster should have had to haul around in an emotional sense."

"Well . . . yes." And then Megan shrugged. "It wasn't that bad, Sam. I was able to do it."

"That's not the point, sweetheart. Did you have time to play with other kids? To do crazy things like paint clotheslines with black paint?"

Megan looked away, avoiding his intense gaze. "When you put it like that, no, I didn't." And then, more defensively, "But I didn't miss it, either, Sam. It wasn't a big deal."

"You didn't miss it because you never knew that possibility existed. You can't miss what you don't have."

"You make it sound like they stole something from me." She wanted to escape from his hands. His fingers grew firm on her arms, as if he'd anticipated her flight reaction.

"They did," Sam said softly. Catching her moody gaze, he added, "You never smile, Megan. You don't joke around. When I do either of these things, I watch life come to your eyes, and I see a longing in yours to do the same thing. There's a little girl in there that's never been allowed to come out and express herself. Your father molded you into an overresponsible, guilt-ridden child who grew up trying to be perfect in order to stay out of trouble with him. And of course, you never were perfect, no matter how hard you tried, and that hurt your confidence, your self esteem.''

Megan stood very quietly, digesting his fervent, emotion-laden words. She felt Sam's hands move in a caressing motion across her shoulders, as if he felt her pain, her discovery that what he was saying was true. She stared down at his feet for a long time, not knowing what to say.

"Well, I came back here to find out about myself," Megan said. "Nobody said it was going to be pain free, did they?''

The urge to take Megan into his arms and tell her that she was an achingly desirable woman tremored through Holt. He saw her lower lip tremble, and he leaned down, pressing a chaste kiss to her hair.

"I'm sorry," he whispered, "maybe I said too much too soon. I haven't been able to get our talks out of my head since we had them. Mom always accused me of spilling the beans. I never was able to keep my mouth shut.''

With a shy, one-cornered smile, Megan forced herself to look up at him. What she found in Sam's eyes was a gift she had never received from anyone in her life. There was such care and warmth emanating from him that it broke the last barrier she'd hidden behind for so many years.

"Sometimes, when I was going through college," she admitted in a low voice, "I'd wonder why I was so driven, why I was afraid to slow down and take it easy.''

"Your father never did—you emulated him perfectly," Sam said with a grimace. "He drove himself. He drove others. Trust me when I tell you, he was one royal sonofabitch over at testing. He had one hell of a reputation for pushing others as hard as he pushed himself.''

"I—I never realized that.''

Lifting his hand, Sam removed several copper strands from her cheek. "It doesn't matter. What does, is you.''

"No, I want to know more about him, Sam.''

With a sigh, Holt added, "Your father never had any friends. He was a true loner. According to some of the older men in Design, the civilians who worked with him, he never smiled or joked, either."

"Just like me . . ."

With a laugh, he gave her a gentle shake. "I know there's hope for you. You've got flaming red hair. I've seen that devilish look come to your eyes and been on the receiving end of some of your spirited displays."

Megan smiled, feeling as if Holt was the sun and she was bathed in the rays of his love. Love? Startled, Megan quickly dodged the word and filed it away for a time when she could examine it more closely. "I've always lived up to my red hair."

"Stick around me, and I'm liable to bring out that side of you even more," Sam promised thickly, wanting so badly to kiss her, to tell her how much he liked her, believed in her.

Gently, Megan pulled out of his hands and stood a few feet away from him. Holt was a powerful, lulling aphrodisiac to her awakening senses, and she was on terribly dangerous ground with him.

"No you don't," he whispered, stepping up to her. To hell with it. She needed to be kissed, to be told in a beautiful, silent way that she was worthy of his affection, his trust and care. He didn't mind if she was perfect or not, because he certainly wasn't. Sam watched her eyes closely as he brought Megan into his arms. He saw panic coupled with desire in them. Leaning down, he was aware of her special, feminine fragrance.

This time, as he molded his mouth to hers, claiming her with fire, he felt her heated response. Megan's hands slid up the front of his chest. A groan started deep within him as her mouth opened to his and allowed their hungry fire to mingle and be absorbed by one another. His world anchored to a halt, the past forgotten, the future only a dream of the present as he focused on her texture, her slick, molten response to him. Hope soared within Sam as she kissed him in return. Each step was a step in trust, and he was grateful.

Controlling his explosive need for her, Sam gently broke

contact with her and opened his eyes, drowning in her verdant ones. There was awe and desire in them now, and he managed a shaky smile. He ran his hands gently across her unruly red hair that framed her face. "Every time we kiss," he told her thickly, "is like heaven."

Megan was breathing raggedly, and she needed Sam's hands on her shoulders to stop her from swaying unsteadily. Never had she been kissed with such tenderness, such love. "I—"

"Don't talk, just feel," he coaxed huskily.

And she did. They stood looking at one another, inches apart, the evening flowing silently around them. For Megan, it was so right. And if she were honest with herself, ever since she'd met Sam, it had felt that way. The smoky-blue color of his eyes spoke of his need for her in a way that sent an intense heat through her she'd never experienced before. *If only he wasn't a pilot* . . . The thought was there, but Megan allowed the feelings for Sam to blot it out of her mind for now. Just once, she wanted to enjoy him as a man, a person. It was a dream, her mind screamed at her. A dream that would disappear in the forthcoming moments.

Megan studied Sam with new intensity, not wanting to discuss the kiss, or what they might possibly mean to one another. Scrambling, she found another topic, a safer topic to talk about. "Just how did you figure all this out about me? Do you have a minor in psychology?"

Holt saw the panic returning to her eyes and assumed the kiss had unstrung her because it allowed her to relate to him as a man, not that God-awful pilot image. He wanted to give her time to adjust to the idea that he was a man who liked her more than he'd ever liked any other woman in his life. Bowing to her need, he said, "I've always been an observer of people, Red. You can't be raised with five other siblings and not get one hell of an education in human psychology. My family taught me a lot. Especially my mother. She used to tell us kids stories at night about the animals on her farm in Poland. Mom used to point out to us each animal was unique, just like people. She only had a high school education, but her perceptions about people, what motivates them and makes them the way they are, were passed on to us.''

Megan's fear was beginning to recede. Sam had lifted his hands from her shoulders. Although she ached for his continued touch, Megan stepped away. ''I know Ph.D.'s who are much less sensitive about people than you are.'' And then she added, ''Somehow, Sam Holt, I think you got the most out of your mom's stories and examples.''

With a shrug, Sam said, ''I don't know. Maybe I did. What's important is what I've seen it do to you. You're a race horse in a plow horse harness.'' He grinned, reaching out, gently ruffling her hair. The evening sunlight bathed the strands and set them ablaze. ''You can't have red hair and *not* be a hellion.''

''I'm a hellion.'' Jamison would find that out tomorrow, first thing. Megan had no intention of being fired without a fight.

''No argument out of me.''

''You're gloating, Holt.''

''Yeah, I know.''

Laughing, Megan crossed her arms against her chest. She saw Sam's mouth compress as he took those few steps forward.

''You never have to be defensive around me,'' he told her quietly, allowing her arms to fall back to her sides. ''I'm not going to take advantage of the trust you just gave to me.''

Rolling her eyes, Megan muttered, ''It's dangerous being around you! Not only are you an amateur psychologist, but you read body language as well.''

''Now you're getting flighty,'' Holt teased, wanting to place his arms around her. Right now, Megan needed protection. And he was the one who could give it to her.

Nervously, Megan turned, beginning to walk once again. ''With my red hair,'' she shot back across her shoulder, ''I'm allowed to get flighty.''

With a laugh, Sam easily caught up with her and captured her hand once again. ''That's my lady,'' he praised, ''get spunky and rebellious. It becomes you.''

An incredible ribbon of joy feathered through Megan, and

she laughed uninhibitedly. Sam was magic. This moment was magic. And then, reality settled on her shoulders once again. That was all it was: a magic moment out of time. Away from the real world, Megan thought sadly. He was a test pilot. The military was his real wife—his entire life. She was but an addendum to it, of secondary importance. Had her mother had moments like this with her father? Surely, they must have, she hoped. Love had brought them together, but somewhere along the way it had been destroyed by both of them and their inability to compromise. And somewhere in the middle, she had been growing up.

Frowning, Megan looked toward the sky. A robin sailed noisily across the playground. Sam was accurate about what had happened to her. She wanted to know more of how he saw her. He seemed to know her much better than she knew herself.

"I've got a busy week of testing ahead of me," Sam said, interrupting her far-off look. "How about you?"

Guilt needled her. "My week is going to be crazy." At least that wasn't a lie, because she never wanted to lie to him. She couldn't help herself when she asked, "When are you flying the *Eagle*?"

"Monday and Friday."

Both days, she would live in fear of the crash siren going off. When a plane went down, that siren could be heard everywhere on Edwards, even over at the schools. And it was always broadcast on every Lancaster radio station to alert military families who lived in town instead of on the base. Hands damp, she curled her fingers into her palms. Was this how Becky Merrill felt? Her mother? There was dread mixed with vague anxiety, and a terrible sensation of fear dominating her. Sam was wrong: her mother's fear *was* her fear.

"What's on your schedule after that?"

Uncomfortable with his interest, and realizing he wanted to see her again, Megan halted. The setting sun's rays bathed everything in a golden wash, Sam's face radiant. "Why?"

"Well," he hedged, "I'd like to ask you out to dinner. Tonight was kind of unexpected, and not a real date."

She tensed at the word *date*. "Sam, please . . . I like you as my friend . . . nothing more." Megan cringed inwardly over the lie. Sam was much more than a friend to her. Much more. She didn't want to hurt him, but couldn't help herself. She took a deep breath. "If-if you were a civilian, in any other kind of job, I would really think about it. But—"

"I'm a pilot," he finished, a terrible sadness filling him. He saw Megan hesitantly nod, and then lift her chin to shyly meet his eyes. Frustration blotted out his grief. "Dammit, Megan, I'm Sam Holt, the human being! Test piloting gives me a paycheck every two weeks, that's all."

"It's more than that," she accused, her voice growing strong with conviction. "I've never met a pilot yet who flew just because of the money offered for doing it. It's not that kind of career."

Grimacing, Sam stepped back, throwing his hands on his hips. "Look, what we've got between us is good and solid, Megan. I can feel it here," he said, pointing at his chest. "My heart doesn't lie to me, and yours doesn't either." He probed her features mercilessly. "Hasn't the last month or so proven to you that I'm more than just a pilot? Don't you like me as a man, and not because I wear a damn uniform and a set of wings?"

Fear drenched her happiness that had been there moments before. "Sam, I *can't* separate the man from the uniform and pilot's wings! I've *never* lied to you about this. I've always been up front with you about my fears."

Holt wanted to shake some sense into her. "Your fears are your mother's fears, not necessarily yours!"

"That's not true! And don't shout at me!"

"I'm not shouting. I'm just trying to make a point. Megan, you don't have to live your life *exactly* like your mother did. You are your own person. Don't you realize that? Your mother's fear became yours. What I'm trying to say is: you don't have to own them. They aren't yours. If you'd give us just half a chance, you'd find out that you wouldn't get scared if I went up and tested a jet.''

Hurt, Megan whispered, ''It's not going to ever get that far, Sam.'' She crossed her arms against her chest. ''It doesn't matter whether I have my mother's fear or not. I *saw* the end result of her marrying my father. The Air Force killed her as much as he did! How can I forget that? How can I ignore that? It's part of my experience, Sam, and dammit, that's valid!'' Megan whirled around. Her small apartment sat only six blocks from the playground, an easy walk home. She had to get away from Sam. He was making her hurt too much, look at herself and her life too closely.

''Hold it,'' Sam ordered. He gripped her by the arm and pulled her to a stop. ''Where do you think you're going?''

''Let go of me!''

Nostrils flaring, Sam held her furious green eyes as she tried to pull out of his grasp. ''Running?'' he taunted. Her eyes widened, and he saw his question strike home. Instantly, Megan stopped fighting him.

''You have no right to stand there and accuse me of running or not running,'' she gritted out, jerking her arm out of his grip.

''Oh, yes I do. I happen to like you one hell of a lot, Megan. *That* gives me the right.''

''Well,'' she rattled, ''I'm taking that right away from you! Just stay away from me, Sam! Leave me alone!'' She spun around on her heel and ran across the playground.

''Dammit,'' Holt cursed savagely, watching her run away from him because he was a pilot. Scuffing the grass with the toe of his shoe, Sam was angry at himself, not her. And then, a grin leaked through his serious demeanor. ''Little hellion made a command decision and carried through with it. Good for her.''

He didn't mind that she expressed her independence and acted on it. Sam applauded that in Megan. Within a minute, Megan had disappeared from view. Holt stood there, watching the sky gradually darken after the sun had set. Mulling over their searching conversation with one another today, he felt hope. Strong, vibrant hope. With a rolling laugh that filled the air, Holt turned around and headed back toward the Italian restaurant where his Corvette was parked. Yes, positive headway had been made with Megan today. Slowly, but inexorably, she was beginning to accept him as a man, not a pilot. Her reaction at the latter was simply old fear raising its head.

Rubbing his hands together, he silently congratulated himself. If he continued to be patient and understanding, Megan would gradually accept him as a man and forget he was a pilot. And when that happened—not if—they were both going to be the happiest people in the world. "Red," he murmured, "you're mine. You just don't know it yet, but you're getting used to the idea . . ."

Megan wore a suit the next morning. After an hour-long conference with Linda on her union options regarding the school wanting to fire her, they both went to Jamison's office.

Jamison motioned them in. Megan shut the door, standing. Linda Yarnell sat down, handing Jamison several papers.

"We're contesting the administration's proposed firing of Megan," she told Jamison quietly.

Jerking the papers toward him, Brad frowned. "You can't be serious! You want Scotty Stang to be tested for hyperactivity?"

"That's right," Megan said tautly, coming forward, glaring down at him. "By union rights, I can request it to be done to *prove* my reports have validation so I can't be accused of incompetence in teaching."

Dammit! Jamison pursed his thin lips, studying the request. He was caught. And he hadn't expected Megan to fight back.

"All right," he muttered irritably, "I'll contact the Stangs and request their cooperation."

"And if they don't?" Megan demanded.

"Then, I'll withdraw my request for your firing."

Linda nodded. "Until we know what the parents' decision is, Megan is reinstated into her class?"

The word ground out. "Yes." This morning, Brad had

called in a substitute for Megan's class. Now, he'd send her home.

A flutter of relief fled through Megan, and she managed a smile at Linda as she stood up. "If you'll excuse me," she said, "I've got a class to teach." But first, she was going to call Grace Dalton, the general's influential wife. It was time to use some of the leverage her father had built here at Edwards. Could she get Grace to agree on a dinner that would include Principal Jake Hamilton and herself? She wanted to alert General Dalton to her outdoor education proposal, knowing full well that Hamilton wasn't even aware of it, thanks to Jamison. There was more than one way to play this game, and Megan was going to use the system.

Jamison sat there for a long time, seething. Finally, he picked up the phone and called Melody Stang. If they wanted Megan fired, they would have to go for the test. Would they?

When Megan arrived home that night, she found a huge bouquet of springtime flowers in a pot next to the door. Frowning, she wondered if Sam had given them to her, but that was impossible. Leaning down, she picked up the card and opened it. Inside was a hand-written note.

Dear Megan,
    I must speak to you soon about Scotty and his problem. Let's get together for lunch next Saturday. I'll meet you at the Antelope Valley Inn at noon. Melody Stang.

Wrinkling her nose, Megan tucked the note away in her pocket and unlocked the door to her apartment. A major part of herself wanted to throw the flowers out, but they were so fresh and beautiful, she didn't have the heart to do it.

Going to her small office, Megan had to get her lesson plans done. As she sat down at her desk, her mind moved ahead to this coming week. Sam flew Monday and Friday.

Oh, God, those days would crawl by for her. Rubbing her brow, Megan closed her eyes and experienced a sense of helplessness she never knew existed. Right now, she wished her mother was alive, so that she could ask her if this is what she felt before her father would go up to test fly. How was she going to handle her worry? How?

Megan's mind refused to stay centered on the lesson plans. Inevitably, it swung back to Sam, to their kiss, their searching, poignant conversation with one another. With a stubborn shake of her head, Megan forced him out of her thoughts. But she had no way to remove him from her heart. She wondered how Becky was handling her husband's flying, aware that she worried a great deal, too.

Curt tossed his garrison cap on the couch in disgust. Becky looked out from the kitchen.

"Ya'll look tired."

He picked up Patty, giving her a kiss and then set her down. Entering the kitchen, he kissed Becky. "It was a bad day, Sparrow." Curt poured himself coffee and sat down at the table.

Becky watched him covertly, putting the finishing touches on the nightly salad. "What's wrong?"

"I'm just not getting the breaks I should over at Ops," he said, rubbing his face tiredly. "Stang and Holt are in solid. Promotion for early major is coming up. I need those oak leaves." And then, he leaned back in the chair and tipped it back, staring blankly up at the ceiling. "I wish to hell my sponsor would kick in. Right now, I need his help. I'm not getting as much flying in as the other two pilots. If only he could schedule me in for more testing, I could raise my percentile and get out of third place."

Risking Curt's anger, Becky said, "Maybe ya'll don't have a sponsor like you thought . . ." Right now, she'd do anything to get Curt away from Edwards. If he couldn't make the cut as a test pilot, he would be put back into a fighter squadron. That was something she could deal with better than his testing planes.

"I'd better have. How could I have gotten this far without one?"

She shrugged, pretending innocence. "Other officers have gone a long way without a sponsor, Curt."

"Christ, what would I do if I didn't have one? I'm dead in the water."

Becky sat at the table. After a few minutes she asked, "There's no shame in being a pilot in a fighter squadron," she said softly.

The chair thunked down on the floor. Curt grimaced. "My father expects great things from me. He brags to everybody I'm a test pilot, now. How can I let him down?"

Wincing inwardly, Becky turned and said nothing, going to the silver drawer. Didn't Curt ever think that he was letting her and Patty down by fighting so hard to remain a test pilot?

"Did you know that the Stangs got an invitation to eat with General Dalton this Friday night? We didn't get one. Why them and not me?"

"Because Jack has a sponsor, that's why," Becky boldly offered. Perhaps, if she could pick away at Curt's belief that he had a sponsor, he might seriously think of transferring back to a fighter squadron.

— 12 —

MEGAN dressed carefully for the dinner with the Daltons and Jake Hamilton. She arrived at the general's sprawling residence on Edwards at exactly 7 P.M., Friday night. She wore a stylish lavender silk shirt and a long skirt of the same color. The sash was hot pink, her white silk scarf simple but elegant. A pair of low-heeled shoes rounded out her wardrobe. Megan wanted to be casual appearing and relaxed. With her possible firing from the school still hanging over her head, she felt unsure of the dinner, or of Hamilton's reception to her presence, much less making a pitch for her proposal.

The single-story home was a yellow stucco color with a red tile roof, and many well-manicured bushes surrounded the residence. Pushing the doorbell, Megan tried to calm her hammering heart. This was one time when Sam's presence would be wonderful, but this was something she had to do on her own. Guilt niggled at her because she had withheld so much information from Sam despite his concern for her welfare the past week. When it was all over—one way or another, she'd tell him everything.

A black man dressed in a starched white jacket and black pants opened the door. Megan smiled and handed him the invitation.

"Right this way, Ms. Roberts," he invited.

Megan had been in this home a number of times before as a teenager when her father had been invited over for dinner by other commanding generals. The rich interior was distinctively Persian, with rare and expensive rugs covering the highly polished oak floors. However, a military veneer still pervaded, the antique swords on the wall reminding everyone a warrior lived here. She heard voices, snapping her attention back to the reason why she'd come.

In the dining room, Megan halted. Her mouth nearly dropped opened. There, standing next to George Dalton, were Jack and Melody Stang. Swallowing hard, Megan saw Melody's eyes widen enormously. Captain Stang was in his dark-blue uniform, and Melody was dressed in a black cocktail gown that emphasized her Raphael-like figure. She was stunning looking. Megan felt underdressed, but shoved away the feeling.

"My dear," Grace said, coming over to her, "how long it's been since we last saw you. Come in, come in."

Megan gave Grace a quick hug, liking the trim fifty-year-old woman with steel-gray hair. She wore a bright-yellow silk dress that spoke of her station on the base; understated, and yet expensive. "Thanks for having me, Mrs. Dalton."

"Oh, pooh! You always called me Gracie when you were a teenager. Why change now, Megan?" She smiled and gripped her shoulders. "My, you've turned into a lovely young lady. George, come and meet Megan!"

Megan watched the Stangs' as well as Hamilton's reactions to the general's enthusiastic welcome for her. She knew Hamilton was ex-Air Force, so her warm reception by the most powerful man on base wasn't wasted on him, either. Normally, a general shook hands with his guests, but George gave Megan a huge bearhug.

Smiling at the short, squat general, Megan returned the hug. "Thanks for having me, General."

"It's an honor to have you dine with us, Megan," he assured her heartily, and he turned to his other guests. "You know that Megan is the daughter of Colonel Steven Roberts?"

He frowned. "Damn, I miss him, Megan. I'm sure you do, too."

She forced a smile she didn't feel. "Yes, I do." If her father had only lived after her graduation. Megan had planned to have many long, serious talks with him once she arrived back at Edwards. Now, it was too late.

When the general introduced her to the Stangs, Megan pretended nothing was wrong, greeting them warmly. The panic in Melody's eyes coupled with Jack's anxious look, told her they were just as shocked that she was here with them. It was obvious the Daltons, and perhaps Hamilton, knew nothing of what was going on with Scotty or her job. The Stangs probably were worried that she'd tell Dalton about the infighting going on over their son. Were they stupid enough to bring it up in dinner conversation? Megan prayed they were going to be as discreet about the topic as she was, and say nothing. She had larger fish to fry tonight.

The dinner bell rang, and Megan found herself seated to the left of Dalton, a place of honor. Hamilton was on his right. Grace sat at the other end of the Queen Anne cherry table with the Stangs. Through the first course of broccoli-and-cheese soup, Megan kept a low profile. Hamilton appeared to be in good graces with Dalton, the two men exchanging old Air Force stories. The salad arrived, and Megan watched as Melody adroitly entered the decidedly male conversation, turning it instead to banking and her father's massive holdings in California. Megan admired Melody's assertiveness and confidence. There weren't many captain's wives who would interrupt and deftly manipulate the situation as she had. Dalton appeared suitably impressed with Melody's wit, charm, and intelligence. So was Megan.

When the beef Wellington arrived, Dalton turned his attention to Megan.

"So, what have you been up to, young lady? I know Steve was terribly proud of your grades at Ohio State."

"What kind of grades did you get?" Melody inquired sweetly with a smile that didn't quite reach her eyes.

"I graduated with a 4.0, Mrs. Stang."

"Oh . . . I see."

Chuckling, Dalton cut into his thick, juicy portion of beef Wellington with relish. "Melody, this little red-haired gal is a spitting image of her father. She's feisty, goal oriented, and knows what she wants out of life. Don't let those freckles she wears fool you."

Jack smiled sickly, losing his appetite. Melody meekly pushed the meat around on the china plate trimmed in gold.

"Speaking of goals, General," Megan said, waiting for just the right opening, "I do have one in mind that I'd like to share with you and Mr. Hamilton. I'd like your feedback on it."

Dalton's thick gray brows rose. "Oh? I know how devoted you are to teaching, so this must be something special, Megan."

"It is, sir." Megan glanced across at Hamilton's round face. At sixty-five, he was plump and flaccid, but that didn't take away from his alert dark eyes. "I want you to know that teaching is more than just a job to me. It's a mission."

Dalton grinned. "I hear Steve Roberts talking."

"And like him, I crusade for what I believe in." Megan took a deep breath, her hands still over her plate of barely eaten food. For the next five minutes, she outlined her plan to the two men. Internally, she held her breath, and watched their faces carefully for reaction after the explanation.

"I like the idea, don't you, Jake?"

Hamilton nodded. "It sounds refreshing. How long ago was this proposal submitted, Megan?"

"Over a month ago, Mr. Hamilton." Megan wondered if he was aware that Jamison was trying to get her fired. He certainly didn't act as if he knew. Some principals let the running of school be handled by their assistant, while they handled more political matters. She wasn't going to bring it up.

"You know how antsy those children get at that age, Jake," Grace put in, enthused. "Why, I think Megan's plan has merit, don't you?"

Jake nodded. "Yes, yes I do. I'll see that Brad has a copy of it on my desk tomorrow morning."

Megan smiled. "Wonderful, Mr. Hamilton."

"Now, I can't promise you anything."

"I understand that."

Dalton snorted. "With Megan's credentials and her father's name behind her, I'm sure the people in the Pentagon won't disapprove of her idea. At least, for a trial run."

Inwardly, Megan wanted to jump up and down for joy. She knew Dalton was going to back her, and that Hamilton wasn't going to dispute his decision. "Well," she said breathlessly, "we could use my class for a model this year. I'm sure we'd get enough data to see if it warranted further exploration."

"Not only is Megan bright," George told Hamilton conspiratorially, "but she's reasonable. A good combination. You're just like your father, Megan. Damn, but he'd be proud of you . . . And I am, too. I think your influence here at Edwards will reap nothing but positive benefits for our men."

"I'm doing it for the children," Megan said quietly.

On the way out the door later that night, Melody caught up with Megan and gripped her arm. She managed a slight smile.

"Are we still on for next Saturday's luncheon, Megan?"

Megan saw the worry in the woman's eyes. "Yes, of course."

Melody released her. "Good . . ."

Hamilton came up along side of Megan. "I was impressed with your presentation on the outdoor education idea, Megan. You have my promise that it will take priority."

"Thanks," she said, suddenly wanting to get away from all of them. Power games were something she didn't enjoy participating in. Her father had drilled it into her early on, that it was a way of life in the Air Force. She was now seeing it firsthand. As she got in her Toyota MR2, her hand shook as she placed the key in the ignition. Her stomach was knotted like a huge fist, but more than anything else, she wanted to talk to Sam.

No, it was more than just talking with him. She'd run the gauntlet this evening by herself. If Sam had been here, his silent support, his belief in her, would have helped her feel more secure about her actions. Pulling away from the house, Megan glanced up at the starry night.

"Eject, Eject, Eject!" The words were torn from Holt as he jerked upright in his bed. With a groan, he realized the same nightmare had stalked him again. Rubbing his sweaty face, he glanced over at the luminous dials of the clock on the bed stand: 3 A.M. Same time, same dream. The crash had occurred at that time.

Trembling, he sat on the edge of the bed, fingers dug into the mattress, and stared at the darkened wall. Bits and pieces of the killing crash that took Russ's life fled before his eyes. On purpose, Holt centered on Megan, and his breathing began to steady. It was Monday morning, and he'd be flying the *Eagle* at 0800. Less than five hours away. At least, it wasn't raining.

"Dammit," Holt muttered, getting to his feet. He needed the cooling effect of a shower to bring him back into the present. The fear sitting in his belly was real, and he rubbed his hand across that area, trying to erase it. The fear remained. Ever since he'd blown the test with Lauren during the rain, Sam had felt that knot of fear growing larger each time he flew. Nothing got rid of it except to focus entirely on Megan, her face, her soft, willing lips, and his need for her in all ways.

Turning on the bathroom light, Holt winced, cursing because it hurt his eyes. Turning on the shower, he remembered the fear he'd seen in Megan's eyes when he told her he'd be flying today and Friday. Maybe she'd picked up on his fear. Unsure, Sam stripped out of the drawstring pajamas and stepped into the icy cold water. As he savagely rubbed his face, Holt hoped that Stang wasn't going to needle him this morning. He wasn't up for it.

Jack lay in wait for Holt, idly drumming his fingers on his desk. Melody did the same thing when she was getting ready to launch an offensive at someone, he mused. Originally, it had been her habit, but over the years he'd picked it up from her by osmosis. Funny how in a good marriage, both partners traded little idiosyncrasies with one another, each becoming more like the other.

Design was quiet and intense this morning. At 0600, everyone was here, civilian and military alike, except for Sam. He was late—again. A good sign. The flight today had the new brake system installed on the F-15. Dammit, he should have gotten this test today, not Holt. Anything new ought to be flown by the chief test pilot first, not by a rookie back-up. Stang contained his frustration and anger and waited for Holt to enter the room. Today, he'd brought doughnuts for everyone. Jack wasn't about to be upstaged by him again.

Merrill looked grouchy, speaking in monosyllables to those who dared go over to his desk to consult him on the upcoming test. Unusual for him, Jack thought, making a note to jot that observation down before the end of the day. Something was definitely going wrong at home for him. He was glad Becky had called Melody weeks before, letting the cat out of the bag about how she feared Curt flying. From then on, those weekly phone calls from Melody to Merrill's wife were keeping things on edge between husband and wife. Good. He didn't need Curt at a hundred percent, or he'd be just as good as Holt. And Holt posed enough of a problem in the ratings for him.

Major Porter was tenser than usual too. Stang smiled broadly to himself. Melody had gotten one of the cocktail waitresses at the O Club to spread word that her fiancé was having a hot and heavy affair with a groupie. Lauren had obviously gotten wind of it. Restless because Holt still hadn't shown up, Jack got to his feet, sauntering over to her desk where she was working at the computer terminal.

"Hey, I heard on the grapevine last night that your fiancé was making eyes at Liza Cooper," he baited, coming to a halt and leaning negligently against the desk. Stang grinned to himself when Lauren's head jerked up, her eyes blazing.

"Captain, I don't indulge in gossip. And, I'm busy. Now if you don't mind—"

"Easy, Major. It's just that this Liza is a blond bombshell. I heard she's got every jock in the place drooling over her hot, luscious body."

Lauren glared up at the pilot. "Stow it, Captain. You can't bait me."

"Aren't you worried about your boyfriend? Major Malone's a damn good-looking man. Way I heard it, Liza made a pass at him over at the NASA cafeteria yesterday afternoon."

Brows dipping, Lauren punched more figures into the computer. "I heard no such thing."

"Hmmm," Jack said, crossing his arms, "maybe you ought to check it out. Melody was over there yesterday for lunch and saw it happen."

"Sometimes," Lauren ground out, refusing to look up at Stang, and knowing exactly what he was trying to do to her, "your wife gets names, dates, faces, and locations mixed up, too."

Digging into the breast pocket of his light-blue shirt, Jack produced a polaroid, dropping it nonchalantly on her desk. "Want to bet?"

Lauren looked at the photo. In it was a modellike woman in a tight and very revealing leather miniskirt leaning over Ryan at the NASA cafeteria. He was smiling up at the blond, younger woman. She clenched her teeth. "Where did you get this?"

"My wife saw someone shooting the picture of Liza Cooper and your fiancé. She rushed over to retrieve it, to save you embarrassment. She thought you might want this. If someone else got hold of it, it might cause you some uncomfortable moments."

With a cocky salute, Jack gave Lauren his best sympathetic smile laced with understanding and pushed off from the desk. Chuckling to himself, he strolled back to his desk. Porter was going to wonder how in the hell the photo was taken. She'd realize Major Malone wouldn't pose for this kind of thing. So, she would treat the photo, the situation, as real. And then, all hell would break loose between her and Malone, making her less focused on her job here at Design.

Maybe, if she screwed up a few times in a row, General Dalton, who had a keen eye on the project, wouldn't worship the ground she walked on. Porter was capable of making mistakes. He was just going to help her commit a few. If he could get her removed as head flight engineer on this project, then Fred could be put in her place. And Fred was far more apt to give him higher flight rating scores than Porter.

Sitting back down, pretending to be busy with paperwork, Jack laughed heartily to himself and watched Porter across the way. Her jaw was tight and her face was pale. Good, she was in just the right mood and emotion he wanted her in for this flight. Unlocking a drawer in his desk, he pulled out his notebook, gleefully jotting down his observation.

Wait until Porter got ahold of Major Malone tonight after work. He wished like hell he could be a fly on the wall for *that* fight! Actually, Judy, the little waitress at the cafeteria, took the photo—for a twenty dollar bill slipped to her by Melody. And Judy promised never to divulge her part of the plan to anyone. A phone call the night before to the Cooper woman had cinched the deal. Melody considered the hundred dollars well-spent money that would give them tenfold dividends towards his career. An excellent business investment.

Of course, both had thought Liza would do it for nothing, but she was shrewder than they'd anticipated. No matter. It was worth it. Liza had come strutting into the cafeteria the next day, leaned over Malone, and asked for his autograph. He was the copilot who flew the space shuttle to Florida. She wanted the autograph for her small son. Would he give her one? Of course he would. What pilot could resist such a sweet, irresistible request from such a stunning, sexy-looking woman? None could. So, Judy got two great photos of him smiling up into Liza's comely face.

Melody had shown him the photos last night, beside herself with pride. Liza had purposefully leaned down, her breasts lightly brushing Malone's shoulder. What a hell of a photo! And it was going to stopcock the testing today, he was sure. If Porter wasn't up for the test, it still made Holt look bad. And that's all Jack wanted. Melody filed the other photo for later use. The wrong photo at the right time in someone's career could sandbag them. Never could tell when it might come in handy at some future date. At that instant, Holt swung through the door.

Stang pretended to be busy, covertly watching the pilot. Holt looked strained, the shadows worse beneath his eyes. Good, both of them were going to be bears in the cockpit this morning. Mentally rubbing his hands together and congratulating himself and Melody, Jack could hardly wait for the test flight to be flown. It was going to be a humdinger. His job was easy: He'd be one of the observers. The video crew was going to videotape the test, as usual. He couldn't think of two nicer people to screw up and get on videotape today.

"Hey, you look like hell," Stang sang out so that everyone in Design could hear it.

Sam ignored Stang. He was late because he'd overslept. *Dammit!* Jerking open a drawer in his desk, he pulled out the flight test program he was to fly with Lauren. Grabbing a cup of coffee, he went directly to her desk.

"Sorry I'm late Port," Sam said as he perched his hip on the corner of her desk. "You look terrible."

"Not today, Sam," she gritted out. "I'm not up for a lot of teasing."

Sipping the scalding coffee, he saw the tension around her mouth and eyes. Ordinarily, Lauren was gregarious and filled with laughter in the morning. "Fair enough," he muttered. "Looks like we're both in the hurt locker today." *Hurt locker* was a Navy term he'd picked up while going through Navy test pilot school. It meant the person was in deep trouble.

Glancing up at the pilot, she snapped, "Look, all I want is to get this flight over with as soon as possible. You do your job, I'll do mine."

What the hell was wrong with Lauren? Sam eased off the desk and took her warning as real. She was uptight. Was she angry because he was late? She was a perfectionist about being on time, about flying things right the first time around. Was Lauren worried that he was in the cockpit with her, never having forgotten the rain incident last week?

Edgy, Holt glanced over at Stang. His head was bent and he was working diligently on a report. Merrill looked unhappy and tense. This was working up to be a ball buster of a Monday. And then, Sam focused back on Megan. Was she worried about his flight this morning? After their fight last night, he wasn't sure when he should approach her again and try to mend fences.

As he went back to his desk after picking up Lauren's flight requirements on the test landings, Sam kept thinking about Megan. Should he call now and reassure her? Maybe she was in as foul a mood as everyone here at Design and would refuse to talk to him. And then he'd be in deeper hock with her. Maybe he should call her after the test. Sam sat down, pulling a pen from the sleeve pocket of his flight suit. More than anything, he didn't want to leave Megan anxious and worrying. Yes, he'd call her afterward. That way, he'd have the time to talk without having to hurry to complete the test.

Megan stood at the window of her classroom. It was 8 A.M., and she could see a few planes flying the pattern around the airstrip in the distance. She knew what an *Eagle* looked like, and she didn't see one in the pattern. Not yet. Gnawing on her lower lip, she forced herself to turn away from the window and devote her energies to her children.

Earlier, Jamison had called her into his office, his face flushed with anger. But he kept it out of his voice. In a clipped tone he'd told her Hamilton now had her proposal. Megan inquired about the Stangs and whether they were going to get Scotty tested. Jamison said he hadn't heard what they were going to do, but until they made a decision, she would teach. Why were the Stangs hesitating? It made the luncheon date with Melody Stang this coming Saturday that much more important. Something was up, but Megan couldn't get a sense of what.

She returned her attention to her class. They were busy coloring their paper dinosaurs. Moving to each desk, she would praise the child, touch their head or shoulder to reinforce her words, and watch their faces light up with pride as they showed her their effort. Most of the dinosaurs were poorly cut out, the crayon colors scribbled in all directions. Megan wryly reminded herself that the children were being creative, moving with the flow of how they felt with each color.

She stopped at Patty Merrill's desk. The dinosaur was cut out in huge lops, part of the tail and two legs missing, as if she didn't care if it was cut out properly or not. Black crayon in her fist, she bore down hard on the paper. Every other child was using bright, vibrant colors. Worried, Megan crouched down, her hand on Patty's small shoulder.

"Why just black, Patty?"

"It's how he feels today."

"Oh?"

"Bad day," she said, putting even more pressure on the crayon. It snapped in half.

Megan saw tears form in Patty's eyes. Quickly, she pulled a Kleenex from her pocket, gently dabbing her cheeks. "Was the dinosaur having a bad day, or are you having one, honey?"

Sniffing, Patty hung her head, stared at her dinosaur, and refused to speak.

"Maybe," Megan suggested softly, "if you color the rest of him with bright colors, your day will go better. Would you like to try it?" At that moment, she heard the throaty growl of an F-15 taking off in the distance. Was it Sam? Was the test beginning? Inwardly, Megan chastised herself. She'd been around bases too long, able to identify the type of plane that was flying by sound alone. Desperately, she forced herself to address Patty's problems.

"I don't want to! Mommy's black. Daddy's black. Everything's black," Patty said, her lower lip protruding.

Rubbing Patty's shoulder, she placed a red crayon in her

hand. "Sometimes, honey, parents do have bad days. The best way to help yourself is color your world differently." Megan wasn't going to infer that Patty had to make her parents happy, or that it was her fault. "Go, try some red, or maybe yellow, for sunshine. I'll bet if you do, your day will go better. Why not try it and see?"

Reluctantly, Patty made a long red line on the dinosaur. Her pout receded. She took the yellow crayon from Megan. "Yellow for sun?"

Rising, Megan smiled. "That's right. And green for grass and trees. You could even have a rainbow dinosaur, if you wanted. Think how happy your day would be, then."

Patty shrugged. "It'd get black when I got home."

Hiding her reaction, Megan said nothing and moved on to the next child. All her old feelings she thought were gone forever, came back. She remembered sitting in her fourth grade class and dreading the ringing of the bell telling all children that it was time to go home. The nausea in her stomach was nonstop from the moment that bell rang. It just got worse as the school bus approached her house. By the time she stepped off the bus, Megan was close to vomiting. Sometimes, when her mother's drinking was worse than usual, she would run to the bathroom and do exactly that.

With a shake of her head, Megan stood in the middle of her classroom. Coming back to Edwards to face old ghosts was much worse than she'd ever anticipated. Patty's problems had dug out her own childhood. And Sam . . . taking a breath, Megan tried to push his smiling face and easygoing nature away.

It was impossible. She heard the F-15 jet engines grow louder. That meant the fighter was parallel with the runway, barely a half a mile from the school complex. It took everything Megan possessed not to run to the window and look to verify what she already knew. Hands growing damp, she turned her back on the windows and tried to escape her fear. Sam was testing the brakes on the bird. The last time, they'd caught on fire. Megan knew what could happen if the wheel well fire spread and was not caught quickly by the fire crews. The aviation fuel in both wings could ignite, killing everyone on board.

"Another round of tests down the drain," Jack muttered, sitting at the Design table with fifteen other people. To his delight, the F-15 hadn't been able to make the fifteen-hundred-foot marker even with the reinforced brakes installed.

Lauren jerked her head toward him. She was sitting midway down the long, rectangular table littered with ashtrays, Styrofoam cups filled with coffee, calculators, and papers. "Captain, I didn't ask for your assessment of today's test!"

Stang heard the anger vibrating in her voice. He had to be careful. Adding a brilliant smile, he looked at everyone. "Hey, I'm just as disappointed as you are."

"Yeah, well if you're so disappointed," Holt snarled, "why don't you come up with a better idea on how to anchor that bird at fifteen hundred feet?" He was disappointed in his own flying performance. And he knew Port was too, but she hadn't said anything. Two out of the seven tests were blown by his lousy flying.

"Look," Bill Hodges, the civilian test pilot soothed, "it's just one of those days when nothing goes right. Let's chalk it up to that and put our heads together on how we can get this bird slowed down enough, without going into a stall situation, to nail it at fifteen hundred feet."

Running his fingers through his hair, Sam realized with a sinking feeling that the session wasn't going to end quickly. He wouldn't be able to call Megan and alleviate her fears or worry. Damn. That made him even more irritable, if possible. The knot of fear in his stomach was still with him. During the flight, it felt like he was carrying around a twenty-pound stone in his gut. His flying showed it. He was sure Lauren was going to grade his lackluster performance fairly. Last time, she hadn't, this time, she would have to.

"Well," Stang murmured, "I believe I've got the answer." All heads turned to him, expectant. He saw disbelief and anger in Porter's eyes. Holt grimaced. Jack's mouth lifted into a broad smile. "You flight engineers have overlooked one intrinsic factor."

"What?" ground out Lauren, taking the insult personally.

Jack picked up a plastic model of the F-15 sitting on the polished maple table. He pointed to the engines at the rear of the plane. "Simple. I suggest we redesign part of the engine *shape*. Right now, the afterburner exhaust nozzles are round. How about we make them square? That might create a flaplike surface that might slow the bird down enough for a short landing. A round nozzle doesn't add that much drag, a square one would."

"He might be right," Sam said, thinking out loud. Turning to his right, he saw Lauren pondering the suggestion. "Design could make a model with the redesigned exhaust nozzles and test it in the wind tunnel. The computers would tell us if it has possibilities."

Lauren nodded. It would be just like Stang to have sat on this idea for weeks, making her military and civilian team look bad, just so that he could time his suggestion to make himself look *very* good. Right now, they were behind schedule, and General Dalton wasn't happy. He had let it be known that she was instrumental in keeping this testing on time—or else. Hatred for Stang soared through her. Just looking into his eyes, Lauren knew he'd been sitting on this design change idea for quite some time.

General Dalton would read her report, single out Stang, and sing his praises. Yes, there was more than one way to get noticed *and* make points with the higher ups. Lauren grudgingly gave Stang his due. The bastard was the purest kind of political animal she'd ever had the misfortune to work with. He ought to run for president.

"Okay," Lauren said, buttonholing her civilian counterpart across the table, "let's do it—now. I want all test pilots to stay after this meeting. We need to discuss the nozzle shape in minute detail. Then, I want all flight test engineers in here after that, and we'll go over the particulars of redesigning, making up new software for the program, and getting a model into the wind tunnel as quickly as possible with the redesign. Questions?''

Holt sat back in the chair, disgusted. He knew Lauren well enough that when she locked onto an idea, everyone stayed until it was hammered out. It was going to be impossible to call Megan. Looking to the left, he saw that Curt Merrill wasn't very happy about it, either. A whole day locked away in a smoky room wasn't a test pilot's idea of joy.

''If we push on this''—Lauren punched numbers into the calculator between her hands—''we ought to have a test flight prepared three weeks from now.'' She turned to Stang. ''I'm sure General Dalton will schedule you to fly it.''

Sam said nothing, his Friday flight scrubbed. Because of his lousy performance today, Lauren was assigning Stang, not him, to the next flight. Stang was grinning.

''Fine by me,'' Jack said.

Lauren sat back, thinking for a moment. ''Sam, do me a favor?''

He sat up. ''What do you need?''

''Call Patuxent River and talk to their design people. If my memory serves me correctly, didn't they consider square nozzles on the enignes of one of their fighters? I know they didn't carry through with it, but I'd like you to get any test data you can, plus talk to the people in Design.''

''Okay.''

''Better yet,'' Jack volunteered, ''why don't you TDY him to the Navy test pilot school for a week or two and do an in-depth investigation? Phone calls aren't going to get what you want, Major.''

Holt saw Stang's deft maneuver: on temporary duty, TDY, he'd be out of sight, out of mind. Stang was afraid he'd protest the change of pilots. He was damned right he was going to. But one look back at Lauren, and his hopes sank. She was delighted with the suggestion.

''Great idea! Sam, I'll talk to Colonel Yale and get TDY orders cut for you. Fly down today, retrieve the information we need. I can give you up to seven days back there to get it." Lauren smiled at him. She trusted Holt's ability to get what she wanted, making her job easier.

"Will do," Sam said. Personally, he felt Porter was expecting too much, too soon. How could they possibly redesign in such a short period of time, even if the wind tunnel tests verified Stang's suggestion? But Lauren was responsible for keeping this project on schedule, and she didn't have a choice. And thanks to his screwing up two test flights in a row, that helped put them behind. He considered the TDY assignment just punishment, and said nothing further. Still, Sam wanted to try and get ahold of Megan, one way or another. He didn't want to suddenly drop out of her life—especially after their fight.

Trying to sit still, Sam's mind was elsewhere. If he could keep Megan informed, that might take the edge off her anxiety. Part of Curt's problem with Becky was that he never discussed any flight, and never would call her after he landed to neutralize her fears. Holt believed if Megan knew, her anxiety level would dissolve. Education and communication were the keys. Now, if only he could cut free of this meeting.

Curt Merrill looked positively harried, scribbling idly on a pad of paper in front of him. Lately, he hadn't been volunteering much of anything for the testing. Sam grimaced to himself. Was this whole project cursed?

Curt knew something was wrong the moment he entered their home at 1900. He'd called earlier to tell Becky that he was going to be late. Today had been a marathon session centering on redesigning the engine nozzles. Tossing his garrison cap on the sofa piled with clothes that needed to be washed, he waded through Patty's strewn toys in the living room and made it to the kitchen.

"Becky?" No answer. Normally, if he was late, his dinner was in the oven. He was starved. Opening the stove, there was nothing in there. Scowling, he shut it and went to the laundry room at the rear of the house.

Outside the screen door, he saw Patty playing in a small sandbox. Becky looked up from loading the washer.

"Hi, honey," she greeted. Lifting her arms, Becky placed them around his neck.

Curt kissed her gently, concerned at the paleness of her features. "What's wrong, Sparrow? You don't look good." He brushed a limp strand of blond hair off her damp brow. Her smile was halfhearted.

"Ohhh, nothing. I'm just in one of my moods."

He rocked her to and fro in his arms, enjoying her slight form against him. "I didn't fly today," he reminded her. The odor of liquor was on her breath, and he stilled his anger and fear.

"I know. But"—she eased out of his arms and returned to loading the washer—"it just seems every day is harder to get through even if you don't fly."

Merrill stood here, vacillating between reading a manual on the engine design of the F-15, or talking to Becky. Every time he tried to, they always ended up in a fight. He was too tired to do that tonight. "Well," he said, patting her awkwardly on the shoulder, "you're just going to have to hang in there for me, Sparrow. Things are bad over on the project right now."

Instantly, Curt was sorry he'd phrased it that way. Becky swung around, her eyes growing huge and shadowed. "I mean," he said, "we're having problems getting the bird to land within fifteen hundred feet."

"So," Becky quavered, "Melody was right. You really are in trouble."

"What does Melody Stang have to do with this?"

Wincing, Becky shut the lid on the washer. "She called me this afternoon and told me there were design changes on the *Eagle*. I got worried."

Gripping her shoulder, he turned his wife toward him. Her delicate face was pinched with worry. "And so you took a drink because of that?" he demanded in a lowered tone.

Becky nodded. "It soothed my nerves, Curt." She held out her hands. They shook perceptibly. "I had to do something! My nerves are shot!"

Groaning, Curt's voice rose a notch in frustration. "Becky,

I told you to *never* talk to that Stang woman! She's out for herself and her husband. Can't you get that through your thick head?''

"Don't yell at me!'' she cried, walking down the hallway toward the kitchen.

Merrill followed. "Dammit, I will! She called and deliberately upset you. I told you to stop hitting that bottle of whiskey. It isn't good for you, Becky!''

In the kitchen, she jerked open the refrigerator and pulled out a lasagna casserole. "Well just how am I supposed to get information, then?'' She slammed the door shut, opened the stove, and literally dropped the casserole into the oven.

Hands draped across his hips, Merrill growled, "Look, I don't tell you anything because most of it's classified top secret and you know that! What I can tell you, I do. Every time, I do, you nose-dive into one of those depressions of yours.'' His voice cracked. "Just what the hell am I supposed to do, Becky? I'm damned if I do, and damned if I don't. You don't want to hear anything because it upsets you. And if I do tell you something, it puts you on edge for days afterward, and you hit that goddamn bottle of yours.''

She stood there, hands clasped in front of her, barely able to look at him. "I'd rather know, Curt,'' she said in a small voice.

"I don't believe this,'' he shouted, throwing his arms up in frustration. "Years ago you told me *not* to say anything. So, I didn't.''

"I guess I've changed my mind . . .''

Breathing hard, Curt rasped, "Fine!''

Tentatively, her voice barely audible, Becky said, "Melody says that Jack always calls her before and after he flies. That way, she doesn't worry so much, and she knows he's safe.''

Lips thinning, Curt studied his wife, wrestling with real anger. How the *hell* had Stang been able to worm his way into their life? Melody wasn't to be trusted. "Look, the

Stangs are out for themselves, Becky. They set people up. Don't listen to her!''

Lifting her head, Becky's voice became strident with anger. ''Curt Merrill, you're acting like an ostrich with his head in the sand! Melody Stang has helped me. I have someone I can talk to now, when I'm feeling blue. She listens. She understands.''

Stalking around the kitchen, Merrill muttered, ''Better than I do? Is that what you're saying?''

''Well . . . you come home, eat, and then lock yourself in your office to study some stupid jet manual! I can't talk to Patty because she doesn't understand. What do you want me to do?''

Frustration ate at him. ''Look, I've got to study tonight, Becky. We're at a critical juncture with this damn project. I can't afford to screw it up now.'' He lifted his hand. ''I'll try and talk to you each night at bedtime, okay? Maybe we can steal a few minutes then. I don't want you talking to Melody Stang. She hasn't got your best interests at heart, believe me.''

Hope showed in her voice. ''We'll talk?''

Anger sloughed off him. ''Yes, we'll talk tonight, when we go to bed.'' Looking at his watch, Curt asked, ''Will you bring me my dinner in the office? I've got to get on those manuals or else.''

''Sure,'' she whispered, managing a crooked smile filled with hope.

Becky's eyelids began to droop. She lay in bed, fiddled idly with a loose thread on the blanket, and waited for Curt to get done with the manual. The novel she was reading had been tossed aside. It was 1:30 A.M. Nodding off, she awoke the instant her chin dropped downward. Where was Curt? All evening she'd looked forward to the quality time he'd promised.

Because she felt happier, Patty had responded too. She wasn't the little imp she usually was every evening. For that, Becky was grateful. Sliding down beneath the covers and nestling her head into the pillow, she centered on their daughter. Today, Patty had brought home a rainbow-colored dinosaur from school. The front half was black, but the other half was colorful. Becky had proudly pinned it up in Patty's room. For once, an evening had almost gone smoothly.

Almost . . . Patty had stood crying outside her father's office door because, as usual, it was locked and he didn't want to be disturbed. Becky had picked her up, kissed her, and taken her for her nightly walk down the block, and then had given her a bath.

With a sigh, Becky could no longer keep her eyes open. The day had been too stressful, and the argument with Curt had taken a further toll on her. In moments, she was asleep. And alone.

— 13 —

BECKY met the bus and smiled as her daughter came racing around the front of it, her pigtails flying. She opened the gate for her, picked Patty up, and kissed her cheek. Fridays were always special because Patty looked forward to the weekend, and perhaps, an hour or so with Curt. Time was something he couldn't give her during the week.

Walking up the steps, she carried Patty to the door and opened it. Curt had called earlier, saying that they had run into some problems over at Design, and that he'd be a couple hours late. As long as he wasn't flying, Becky didn't care. A part of her wondered if Curt was lying to her. He'd done that on occasion when he didn't want her to worry. She knew the pilots and engineers had spent longer than normal hours over at testing this week, because of a design change. Were they going to secretly fly a test before the day was out? It was 4 P.M. Curt said it would be at least two hours before he was home.

Frowning, Becky put her daughter down and went to the kitchen. She knew they were behind schedule, at least, that's what Melody had said in her last phone call. Was Curt lying? Were they going to fly a last-minute test today?

Bending down, Becky opened the liquor cabinet and pulled out the whiskey bottle. Hands shaking, she took down a tumbler from the cupboard. Melody had also said Sam Holt was flying in today from Maryland. That made it even more likely that a test would be flown. But, by who? If she called Ops, they wouldn't tell her who was scheduled in Sam's place. Uneasy, Becky swallowed some of the whiskey. Immediately, as it burned its way down her throat and into her stomach, she began to feel a slight soothing effect on her jangled nerves.

Patty came racing into the kitchen.

"Mommy, Mommy, come and play with me!"

"No, honey, not right now."

Pouting, Patty walked toward the front door. "You said you'd play with me."

Taking another huge gulp, Becky gave in to her daughter. She couldn't stand to see tears in Patty's eyes. "Oh, all right. Come on, we'll play out in the front yard and wait for Daddy to come home." That way, if she saw an *Eagle* take off, she'd know there was a final test before the week drew to a close. The only question would be: who was flying it? Curt or Jack Stang? She knew Sam Holt was supposed to fly in later this evening from Maryland, so only her husband or Stang could possibly fly that test flight.

Standing out on the front porch, Becky's heart began a frantic pound. She saw an F-15 coming in from the east, headed toward the runway. An icy fear hit her, and she clutched her stomach as the gray fighter loomed closer. It was one of the test planes. Mouth dry, she whirled around, stumbling back inside, going to the kitchen. Finding the bottle, Becky poured as the contents sloshed out of the tumbler and onto the counter. She gulped down what was left in the glass. Who was flying? Who was flying?

Leaning heavily on the sink, Becky closed her eyes and tried to shut out the growling sound of the approaching jet. Sweat broke out on her brow, and she was consumed by the thought of Curt dying in a crash. How many minutes she stood there, frozen, Becky had no idea. The alcohol was fogging her brain and taking away some of the fear.

Suddenly, she heard the low, mournful wail of the crash siren begin to shriek out its message across the base: a jet had crashed! It had to be the *Eagle* she saw coming in for a landing! With a cry, the tumbler slipped from between her nerveless fingers, hit the floor, and shattered. Becky sobbed, lurching toward the front door. She flung it open, staring wide-eyed towards Operations in the distance.

There was a huge plume of black smoke rising off the desert floor, toward the end of the runway. She could hear the high-pitched wail of crash truck sirens as they sped toward the site. Because of distance and hangar buildings in the way, Becky couldn't actually see the plane that had gone down. The dreaded column of black smoke rising hundreds of feet into the air was all the evidence she needed.

"Oh, my God, my God," she moaned. There was nothing she could do but wait. The instant the crash siren was heard around the base, the network of wives would wait for calls from their husbands. Every husband knew he must call home instantly to reassure his wife that he wasn't the unlucky pilot who had augered in. In turn, each wife would call the next wife, to tell her who was on the ground, or confirm who was flying at the time. It was a terrible thing to wait. The woman who received no phone calls was the unlucky individual. She would then wait for two officers to drive up, grim faced, and announce that her husband had been killed in a crash.

Twisting around, Becky moved drunkenly toward the phone in the kitchen, grabbing the whiskey bottle. Even now, the radio stations would be contacted, and within seconds, the same message would reach Lancaster, blaring out the tidal wave of bad news. Many wives of pilots lived there, and not on the base. They too would have to wait in a special hell, praying the phone would ring, letting them know their husbands were safe.

Megan was at school when the crash siren went off. The pen in her hand slipped and dropped to the desktop. Megan gave a little cry. Sam was to fly the test this afternoon!

"No . . ." she whispered, "no!" Sam had that flight! Reeling, Megan left her classroom and staggered outside. She saw an ugly cloud rising into the bright blue sky near the end of the runway in the distance. Jerking her gaze upward, she searched for a parachute. There was none! Sam couldn't be dead! He just couldn't be! A huge sob tore from her. In that instant, Megan felt the total love she'd held at bay for Sam, and had tried to ignore for so long. Sam's face wavered in front of her. She loved him! How and when it had happened, Megan had no way of saying. Was he dead? Injured?

Knees shaking, she ran down the hall to the teachers' lounge and reached for the phone. What was the number at Ops? If she could only get through to them! Trying to stop sobbing, Megan found the number and dialed it. A loud busy signal met her ear. She hung up and tried again. Vision blurred by tears, she shakily wiped her eyes. Of course, every pilot at Edwards would be calling his wife to tell her he was safe. She had to persevere, to find out about Sam. The phone was the only way to get information. Dazed, she remembered Becky Merrill's number. Maybe she knew something. Wives of pilots had a grapevine in times of emergency and they inevitably knew who had augered in.

Barely able to dial the number, Megan sat down before she fell down. The phone rang and rang and rang.

"C-curt?"

Megan swallowed hard. "No . . . Becky, this is Megan Roberts—"

"Crash . . . the crash . . ."

"I—I know. Becky, have you heard who it is, yet?"

"Curt . . . it might be Curt . . . no call . . . no call yet . . ."

Megan tried to steady herself, realizing Becky's voice was heavily slurred and very faint. "Becky? Becky, are you okay?" There was silence at the other end of the phone. Licking her lips, she felt a wave of panic hit her. Something was wrong with Becky.

"H-help . . ."

"Oh, my God," Megan breathed. "Hang on, Becky, just hang on. I'll be over there in just a few minutes!" Shock made thinking difficult. Megan got up and turned, her movements jerky and robotlike. She reeled between Sam being dead or injured and Becky's plea for help.

* * *

Megan mounted the wooden steps to the Merrill home on shaky legs. She heard Patty crying somewhere inside the home and jerked open the screen door.

"Becky? It's Megan Roberts," she called. Patty sat on the floor in the hall next to a closed door. Her heart rate picked up and she hurried toward the child.

"Mommy, Mommy . . ."

Megan picked up Patty and held her in her left arm. "It's going to be all right, honey. Shh, it's all right." She tried the door. It opened. Patty stopped crying as the door swung wide.

"Oh, my God . . ." The words were torn from Megan as she stood poised at the entrance to the bedroom. The air reeked of whiskey, and it made her wince visibly. Becky Merrill lay unmoving, stretched out across the bed, unconscious. Her gaze moved from the woman to the dresser. On top of it was a nearly consumed quart of whiskey. Megan tightened her embrace around Patty. She fought the urge to scream.

Whirling around, Megan walked unsteadily down the hall and located Patty's room. She got the child in her room, and shakily put crayons and paper before her.

"Stay here," she quavered, "no matter what happens, stay in your room, Patty." Megan winced as Patty's tearfilled eyes moved to her. She was looking at a replica of herself at Patty's age. Swallowing against a lump that threatened to shut off her breathing, Megan left and went back to Becky.

As she approached the bed, Megan saw an opened prescription bottle on the green carpet. Hand trembling, Megan read the label: Darvon. It was a well-known tranquilizer. Choking against the bile in her throat, Megan tried to ignore the stifling odor that hung in the room. She couldn't control her own escaping emotions.

Megan made sure Becky's head was tilted back so that she could breathe properly. This was like one of those weekly nightmares she had had as a child, and then as a teenager. How many times had she found her own mother like this? Fighting the urge to vomit, Megan grabbed the phone and called the base hospital.

Her mind spun with options. If she said Becky had tried to commit suicide, it would be logged on the hospital records. It would be a black mark against Curt, and his career could be destroyed. Suddenly, Megan didn't care. Becky's life was at stake, and this was no time to skirt the issues, career or no career.

The second phone call she made went to Ops. Megan knew she had to get ahold of Curt. Miraculously, the line was open and an airman answered it.

"This is Megan Roberts. I'm over at Captain Curt Merrill's house. His wife Becky is very ill. I've called an ambulance. Get ahold of him and tell him to get over here. Now!"

"Yes, ma'am. Right away, ma'am!"

The phone dropped from Megan's hand, and she sobbed, holding her hand across her mouth. Forcing herself past her own nightmarish past and reactions, she got up to help Becky.

"Who in the hell hit that crash siren button?" Holt cursed from the Ops desk. He'd just returned from Maryland, landing at 5 P.M., when it had gone off. An oil fire had been deliberately set ablaze near the end of the runway seconds after he'd landed the F-15. Every once in a while unsuspecting fire crews were tested on their response time to a crash. Fires were lit in several oil drums in a firepit specially made to resemble a real crash. The only problem was the crash siren wasn't supposed to be triggered.

"Don't know, sir," the airman at the desk replied, taking his completed flight plan.

Worriedly, Holt walked out to the front of Ops and looked out the wall of glass windows that faced the runways. He saw the lime-green fire trucks screaming down toward the contained fire. It was simply a drill. Turning, he couldn't shake the terrible feeling stalking him.

"Hey, listen to this," the airman said, "the radio over in Lancaster is even announcing there's been a crash. Talk about stupid."

At that moment, Curt Merrill appeared in the hallway, his brow wrinkled.

"Curt," Sam shouted, "better call Becky. It's a false alarm."

"Oh, Christ," Merrill muttered, whirling on his heel and making his way back to Design to make the call.

Sam swore under his breath. That cinched it! Megan would be home by now, in her apartment. Had she heard that announcement? She still thought he was flying a test today because he hadn't been able to call her and tell her he had been in Maryland until today. Damn! Picking up one of the many phones, Holt dialed her residence. No one answered.

The airman behind the desk answered another phone. When he hung up, he had a pained look on his youthful features. "Captain Holt, you'd better go get Captain Merrill. A Megan Roberts just called from his residence. She just found Mrs. Merrill real sick and needs help."

Momentarily stunned, Sam grabbed his duffle bag. He'd just landed and was still in his G-suit. "I'll get him," he rasped, running around the desk and down the hall toward Design. Megan was with Becky? How? Why? And something was wrong with Becky! He swung through the door and Curt was still on the phone.

"I can't believe this," Merrill said angrily, "the line's busy."

Holt tried to steady his breathing. "Curt, Megan Roberts is at your house. Something's wrong with Becky. Come on, let's get over there. She's probably calling an ambulance."

Curt froze, the phone clutched in his hand. "Becky? What's wrong with her?" Merrill went white.

Holt took the phone and put it down in the cradle. "I don't know. Let's go!" His Corvette was parked out in the lot adjacent to Ops. Sam knew Megan had heard about the crash.

Racing out of the doors and down the steps, they quickly made it to his black 'Vette. In moments, they were driving away from Ops and heading for Sharon Drive. Sam knew it was against regulations to wear a G-suit on base except for Ops, but right now, time was of the essence.

Grimly, Sam wondered how the wives of the pilots were taking the stupid crash siren error. It always sent such a wave of fear and lethal dread through the small, tight community.

Agitated, Curt whispered, "What could be wrong with Becky? And why is Megan over there? Jesus Christ," he pressed his hands to the sides of his head.

"Becky! Becky!" Merrill took the stairs two at a time up to the front door of his home. He heard Patty shrilly crying. Jerking open the screen door, and breathing hard, he squinted against the gloomy interior. No lights were on. Patty was sitting on the carpeted floor, crayons and paper in hand, wailing.

"Curt!" Megan cried, running out of the bedroom upon hearing the door open and close. She stared past the pilot, seeing Sam at his shoulder. Relief shattered through her. Sam was alive! Alive! Gulping, Megan cried out, "Come in here. I think Becky took pills and alcohol together, and she's unconscious!"

With a cry, Merrill ran down the hall. He knelt at his wife's side, sweeping her into his arms. Her face was very pale, mouth slack. Fingers shaking, he touched her skin. It was cool to his touch. There was an odor of alcohol on her breath.

"Becky!" he sobbed. "Jesus, Becky! Wake up! Wake up!" Tears blurred his vision as he held her limp, frail body to him.

"Easy," Sam breathed, gripping Merrill's shoulder. "Let's get her up and try to get her to come around."

Megan had picked up Patty, and kept the child away from the bedroom. Fighting back tears, she stood at the screen door, watching for the ambulance.

Hands shaking, Curt, with Holt's help, got Becky off the bed and on her feet. She sagged between them, barely conscious. Curt jerked up his head. He heard the ambulance siren. "Let's get her out to the living room," he gasped, "the ambulance is coming." Brushing Becky's thin blond hair across her unmarred brow, he wondered if this time, he was too late. Too late . . .

Megan's eyes widened as they brought Becky out into the living room. She looked like a limp butterfly with broken wings between the two pilots dressed in their olive-green flight suits. Curt was pale, his eyes dark with fear. To Megan, the scene smacked of military power bracketing a woman who didn't have the kind of strength her man possessed. Becky was just one more casualty of the military world. Just as her mother had been.

Megan shut her eyes and moved onto the porch as the ambulance drove up and screeched to a halt. Her mother . . . vivid, terrifying images slammed into Megan. Pressing Patty's head against her shoulder so the child wouldn't have to witness the paramedics racing up the sidewalk with gurney and bags in hand, Megan shut her eyes. A gamut of emotions tore through her.

Holt came out to the porch once the paramedics took over. He glanced to the left. Megan stood pale, clutching Patty to her. Walking over, he gripped her arm as if to steady her.

"Let's get Patty over to the neighbors," he rasped. "They'll take care of her while we go to the hospital with Curt. He needs our help."

Mutely, Megan agreed, relief spreading through her as Sam kept his hand on her arm. She felt weak, almost faint. Within minutes, Patty was taken care of by a captain's wife who had been watching from her window. As they hurried back to the Merrill house, Holt's arm went around her waist.

"How are you doing?" he asked. Megan's eyes were narrowed with pain, haunted looking. He knew this crisis must have triggered old memories of her own mother.

"N-not very good, but better than Becky."

"Hang tough," he murmured. Holt wanted to protect her from all of this, but knew he couldn't. The need to love her, to tell her of his love for her, was almost torn from him. Instead, Sam tightened his grip around her and pressed her against him.

Megan leaned heavily against him at the white picket fence gate where the ambulance was parked. Becky was strapped to the gurney and being loaded into it, with Curt following close behind.

"We'll follow you," Sam called.

Curt nodded. "Yeah . . . thanks . . ."

"Come on," Sam coaxed to her, "we'll take my Corvette."

Numbly, Megan nodded.

On the way over to the hospital, Sam never let go of Megan's damp, cool hand. Worriedly, he looked over at her from time to time. Her mouth was stretched in a line of pain, her eyes closed.

"I'm sorry this happened. It's the last thing you need to witness," he said, squeezing her hand.

"I felt like I was stepping back in time, Sam," Megan choked out softly, the sting of tears behind her lids. "Becky was my mother. My mother was Becky. I flipped out. I lost it."

"No you didn't. You kept your head and called the ambulance, and then called over to Ops to get Curt. That's not flipping out."

Sniffing, Megan tried to combat the wall of pain exploding through her. "I was so afraid you'd crashed. I remember you said you'd be flying the Friday afternoon flight. When I heard the crash siren . . ." the words died on her lips, and she lifted her lashes, holding Sam's burning gaze. "I thought you'd died." The words were so final, so terribly final.

"I was gone all week, Megan, to Maryland. I tried calling you several times, but we just didn't connect. I landed at 1700, and I think Becky thought my test plane was the one that Curt was possibly flying. I don't know. The fire siren was a mistake," Sam explained. "Some jerk pushed the button by accident. The crash team was on a drill. The smoke you saw was rubber tires burning down at the end and to the left of the runway. They have a fire pit there, and that's where they practice for air crashes. I'm sorry, Red. So damn sorry."

"You could have died," Megan whispered, "you could have died . . ."

Too much was happening too fast. Sam gripped her hand tightly. Was this going to destroy the fragile trust they'd built with one another? Would this scare Megan off? Fear ate at him. "But I didn't. Look, let's get to the hospital and support Curt. I don't know Becky's condition. Later, we can talk. Okay?"

Silently, she agreed. Their talk could wait. "I think Becky's in serious condition," Megan rasped. "I found my mother like that at least half a dozen times. And every time, it was worse than before. Becky could die. My mother died from an overdose of the very same damn tranquilizer. My God . . ."

Taking a deep breath, Sam nodded. "Let's take this crisis one step at a time, Red. We've got each other, that's more than what Curt has right now."

Megan wasn't sure of anything except the widening pain in her heart over the past coupled with the realization that she might have lost Sam. And he was right: Curt needed their help, their support. One thing about the military family, they were there in a crisis. It was one of the many positives about them, and one Megan applauded. Clearing her throat, she gave a jerky nod of her head. "Yes, we'll be there for both of them . . ."

— 14 —

CURT stared miserably across the empty waiting room, uncomfortable in the plastic chair. Megan sat next to him, and Holt paced slowly back and forth out in the hall. Rubbing his face tiredly, he shook his head.

"God, how did this happen?" he uttered softly. "How? Becky seemed happy this morning when I left . . . or at least, I thought she was."

Megan placed her arm across his slumped shoulders. "When I had that teacher's conference with Becky in September, she told me how afraid she was of you flying."

"Her folks live in the mountains of Arkansas. They're pretty basic people, but nice. They really aren't a part of the twentieth century in a lot of ways."

Megan knew many women became enamored with a man's uniform, and they fell for the image he projected. None of them foresaw the terrible days or months of loneliness without him. She'd seen many marriages torn apart by less than Curt testing jets for a living. "You don't have to be from rural Arkansas to have a fear of losing your husband to a plane." Her mother was an ideal example of that. Fear chose no particular economic stratum.

"I guess not," he said tiredly. Fear that Becky was dying dug into his gut and was slowly clawing its way up through him, into his heart, and he kept swallowing, trying to keep it at bay. Closing his eyes, Curt felt the sting of tears against his lids. What was wrong with Becky? If alcohol or drugs hadn't caused her unconscious state, what had? How could he *not* have noticed if something was *that* wrong with Becky?

"Captain Merrill?"

Curt snapped up his head, unashamed of the tears streaking down his cheeks. A woman doctor, a major, stood before him, her hands clasped in front of her. She wore her gray hair in a neat bun at the nape of her neck. The white jacket and pants increased the aura of power surrounding her. "Yes?"

"I'm Dr. Anna Cartwright, and I'm in charge of Becky's case. Your wife is resting well, now. Becky's conscious." She smiled slightly, reaching over and squeezing his shoulder.

"Thank God," Curt choked.

Megan gasped. She saw Sam halt at the door and grin. "Wonderful!" she whispered, gripping Curt's hand. Seeing that the doctor wanted to talk to him further, she got up, offering her the seat. Cartwright nodded her thanks and sat down.

Glancing up at Megan and Sam, she told them, "I'd like to speak to Captain Merrill in private."

"Sure," Sam said, "no problem." He put his arm around Megan's shoulders. "Come on, let's celebrate. We'll get a cup of coffee. Curt, when you can, come down and join us in the cafeteria."

Gratefully, Curt gave them both a wobbly smile, relief that Becky was going to live showering through him. "Sure . . ."

Dr. Cartwright waited until the couple had left. She turned her attention back to the husband. "Your wife tried suicide, Captain. She took an overdose of a tranquilizer along with at least a quart of whiskey. We pumped her stomach and have her on I.V.'s to rebalance her electrolytes. She's out of the woods—this time."

Blinking, Curt gawked at the doctor. "Suicide?" His heart lurched with agony that Becky had attempted it. Guilt strangled him. How much had he to do with her near death?

His mind whirled. Was Cartwright going to make out a report on Becky's condition and notify Colonel Yale? If she did, his career was shot down. Looking at the silver-haired woman, Curt hoped the compassion in her blue eyes was just that.

"I've checked Mrs. Merrill's record. There's no previous history of suicide attempts. At home, has she ever taken a combination of drugs and alcohol, Captain?"

Merrill wanted to cry for Becky, for himself. "I—yes, sometimes she'd have a couple of drinks before I flew a test flight. But nothing like this!"

"Has Becky always drank? Or is this a recent pattern of behavior?"

"She never touched a drop. Not until she married me," he said hollowly. "That was eight years ago."

"I see. Is there a history of alcoholism in Becky's family?"

Rubbing his brow, he answered, "No . . . not that I know of. Doctor, may I see her? She needs me." Curt needed her.

Grimly, Cartwright rose with him. "Of course you can." She gripped his arm before he started to move away. "Captain, I'm *strongly* suggesting you *and* your wife get some counseling. Suicide attempts are a cry for help. I can recommend several fine psychiatrists here at the hospital."

Stung, he stared straight ahead, his jaw tightening. "This was an accident, that's all." Curt didn't want any records floating around on base or from Lancaster showing Becky receiving psychiatric evaluation. She wouldn't want to go anyway, afraid that people would call her crazy.

Gently, Anna said, "People who are in trouble, Captain Merrill, usually don't know what's good for them, or what they really need. I hope you can get her to someone, even if it's a civilian agency off base."

Heat nettled Merrill's cheeks. The doctor wasn't fooled in the least by his defensive attitude. She knew he was balking because he didn't want anything on Becky's medical records that the commanding officer was privy to. "Becky didn't know she wasn't supposed to mix a drink with tranquilizers. She's from a simple way of life. It was just an accident."

Cartwright pursed her lips, but said nothing more. "Becky's in room 105, down at the end of the hall on the right. Don't stay long. She's very tired and emotionally exhausted."

Curt felt shaky as he entered Becky's room. His gaze went to her. How small and fragile she looked in the huge bed, but then, Becky was a bird-size person anyway. The white sheets and the light-blue gown she wore emphasized her waxen features. At first, as he approached, he thought she was asleep.

Holding her hand, Curt noticed there were I.V.'s in both her arms. She would be terribly bruised by them, and that made him ache for her. As he gently caressed her cool, almost cold fingers, he saw her lashes flutter against her cheeks.

"Sparrow?" he whispered, leaning across her. Placing his arm next to her head, Curt kissed her brow.

Dragging her lashes open, Becky stared dazedly up at her husband. "Curt?"

He managed a lame smile, tears burning his eyes. "It's me. Everything's going to be okay, Sparrow." He pressed a kiss to her cheek. Her flesh was frighteningly cool, and it scared him badly. "The doctor said you were out of the woods. All you have to do is rest and get well."

"I'm sorry . . . I didn't mean to be here."

"Sshhh, it's okay." He shut his eyes and rested his head lightly against her brow. "I was so scared, Sparrow. I—I tried to get ahold of you when the crash siren went off. It was a lousy fluke. There was no crash. The firefighting crews were simulating a crash exercise and the smoke you saw was from the tires they were burning."

"Oh, dear . . . ya'll be in trouble with the Design people if ya'll left early."

A sob caught in his throat, and Curt gripped her fingers tightly in his. "No, don't worry about me, Sparrow. It's you I'm worried about." He lifted his head and saw the confusion in her eyes. "The doctor said you took tranquilizers and alcohol. You know better than that. You can't mix those two and get away with it."

With a small sigh, Becky closed her eyes. "I just fell

apart when that crash siren went off. I—I thought you'd died in that crash. I couldn't face it, Curt. I couldn't face ya'll being gone.''

"Honey, listen to me, please,'' and he gave her a small shake, forcing her to open her eyes. "You've *got* to stop this! What about Patty? She was found by Megan Roberts sitting outside your room crying. She was scared to death.''

"Oh, dear . . .''

Merrill mentally kicked himself and watched the darkness come back to Becky's eyes. "Never mind,'' he rushed on, "it's over. Patty's okay and so am I. The important thing is that you get well, Sparrow. God, I love you so much.''

"You're crying.'' Weakly, she lifted her hand and touched his damp cheek. "You never cry . . .''

"I'm crying,'' Curt choked out hoarsely, "because I thought you were dead this afternoon when I got home.''

Tears formed and fell from Becky's eyes. Sniffing, she whispered almost inaudibly, "Please, Curt, quit. Quit flying. I—I can't take it no more . . .'' She lapsed into a deep, troubled sleep.

Gently kissing her damp forehead, Curt made sure she was well covered and left to tell Sam and Megan that Becky was going to be all right. He ran his fingers through his hair as he slowly walked down the hall toward the elevator. Guilt plagued him, and he no longer knew what to do, because Becky wasn't all right.

Sam took Megan home afterward. Her silence ate at him, and he felt such explosive emotions around Megan that it was simply a matter of time until they overwhelmed her. All he could do was hold her hand and be there for her until she was ready to cope with the horror of today.

Megan leaned her head back on the seat and closed her eyes. Right now, she was barely coherent, finally giving in to her raw, bleeding feelings. Her hammering heart wrenched with the terror that she could have lost Sam today. If she could get to her apartment, she would be safe, insulated from a violent world that had already taken so much from her.

At the apartment, Megan opened the door. Sam stood there, watching her gravely. With a one-shouldered shrug, she said softly, "I don't want to be alone right now. Will you . . ."

Guiding her into the apartment, Sam quietly closed the door. "I'll stay as long as you need me, Red."

Just the hushed whisper of the endearment unstrung Megan. Everything in front of her blurred because of the tears jamming into her eyes. Trying valiantly to stem the tide of tears, she wiped them away with the back of her hand. "I—I feel as if someone's tearing me up into pieces inside." She turned, only a few feet separating them.

Holt stood there, poised, eyes narrowed upon her. To Megan, the way he was dressed in the body-hugging G-suit that framed his lower body, and the olive-green flight suit, he looked like a warrior torn out of the pages of a war story. There was agitation on his tense features, the worry in his eyes was reflected in the grim line of his mouth. His name slipped from her lips, and she took a hesitant step forward.

So many impressions assailed Sam as he put his arms around Megan and dragged her against him. He held her tightly, never wanting to let her go. Megan's eyes were huge with anguish. Her skin was so pale that he could see the blue veins beneath her flesh. Her mouth was parted, and pulled into a tortured line of pain. The storm in her eyes was going to break any second now.

"It's okay," he breathed raggedly. "I'm alive and safe. It's okay . . ." All he could do was crush her warm, yielding form against him, and try to convince her he was alive, not dead.

The strong odor of his perspiration struck Megan's nostrils as she leaned heavily against Holt. His voice was urgent, shaking with raw feeling. *Alive*. Sam was alive! She felt the rough creases of his flight suit beneath her damp cheek, smelled his fear, and more than anything, felt his arms, strong and protective around her. His heart was a staccato beat beneath her ear, and he was breathing heavily. *Alive*. His words slowly impinged upon Megan, and blindly, she followed her heart's need because he could have died today.

She slid her hand up across the material of his flight suit, and felt the taut response of muscles across his chest beneath her fingertips. Yes, Sam was real. This was real. They were real. Megan shut her eyes tightly, absorbing every particle of his being into herself. She was shaking like a leaf, and couldn't stop it.

"Hang on," Holt said grimly, picking her up, bringing her into his arms. Turning, he headed down the hall, searched for and found her bedroom. Sam deposited Megan on the dark-blue bedspread that was finished in fine, ivory lace. Sitting down next to her, he bracketed her head with his hands. Every tear that formed in her troubled green eyes tore at him. Helplessly, he caressed her red hair that lay in disarray around her drawn features.

"I'm sorry, sweetheart. It was a stupid mistake that triggered everything this afternoon. Jesus, I'm sorry."

Megan's brow wrinkled. She stared up into Holt's suffering features, his words barely registering upon her shocked senses. Only his touch and the concern burning in his azure eyes were real. Her breath was sporadic, because it hurt to breathe, to feel.

"I—I thought you were dead." Her voice cracked. "I felt as if someone had killed me when I heard that siren go off."

Taking Megan in his arms, Sam held and rocked her. He slowly repeated the same information to her, realizing she was in shock. Wouldn't he be too? Yes. Every second was painful as he witnessed the devastating results the day's events had had on Megan. If ever he needed convincing that she loved him, the proof was in her eyes, in her reactions. With a shake of his head, Holt hadn't wanted it to happen this way.

Gently, he brushed her wrinkled brow and then her tear-dampened cheek with a kiss and tried to convince her he was here, uninjured. "Everything's going to be okay," Holt promised her thickly. The urge to claim her parted lips was too much, and he covered them with his, tasted the bitter salt of her tears, the yielding texture of her mouth, and the inner sweetness that was uniquely Megan.

With a moan, Megan returned his hungry, searching kiss, as his mouth moved in abandon against hers. Sam was alive! He was here, with her, where he belonged. The shock had torn away all her defenses and silenced her suspicious mind. Only her heart, her untrammeled emotions, ruled her now. Nostrils flaring, she caught his male scent, dragging it deep into her lungs, as if breathing life back into her cold, numbed depths.

Megan moved her hands upward, sliding them along the coarse fabric of his flight suit, and touched Sam's face, convincing herself he wasn't a ghost, but so very real, so very warm and human. She couldn't get enough of him, and devoured his kisses, the roughness of his sandpapery face against her cheek heightening her need of him. Nothing mattered except now. They were both alive. Suddenly, life had to be proven to Megan all over again. Finding the zipper to the flight suit, she pulled it downward.

Holt gripped her hand and stared intently into her eyes. "Megan," he rasped unsteadily, "is that what you want?"

His voice, deep and dark, vibrated through her. She held his smoldering eyes that promised so much. Her hand stilled at his waist where the G-suit prevented the zipper from moving any farther. "Yes," she whispered. Megan felt his fingers tighten around hers, and tears welled up in her eyes. "Love me, Sam." It was a plea, a need torn from her heart. Megan was helpless to stop herself, and didn't want to. The man sitting with her, his features taut, was who she wanted. Megan didn't see his uniform, she saw only the man. Humbling herself because she saw him waver on her request, she murmured, "Please?"

Holt released Megan and stood, his gaze never leaving hers. The G-suit chaps came off easily, and he tossed them to one side. He was troubled as he unzipped the rest of his flight suit, shrugged out of it, and allowed it to pool around his feet. Did Megan want to be loved by him for the right reasons or the wrong ones? If she was reacting to the trauma of believing she had lost him, it could destroy what trust he'd built up with Megan. On the other hand, if the news had shocked her into realizing she honestly loved him, then coming together like this would be the most right thing in the world. Which one was it? Pushing the suit aside, he pulled off the dark-green cotton T-shirt, revealing his chest. Next came the socks, and then he stripped out of the cotton briefs.

Megan sat there, staring up at him, and absorbed his very male form through her eyes, her senses. Holt was tightly muscled, his chest broad with dark hair, and it tapered into a hard belly, narrow waist and hips. His thighs were flexed and powerful, knees and calves well proportioned to the rest of him. She saw the question in his eyes as he stood there beneath her appraisal. He made no move to touch her, and allowed her to make the decision, to tell him what she wanted next. There was such raw, primal energy radiating from him, that she felt dizzy with expectancy. He was beautiful, his lines cleanly sculpted, shouting of his inherent maleness. Megan lifted her hands and began to unbutton her pale-gold blouse. She fumbled with them, feeling suddenly inadequate against Holt's strong, potent presence.

"Let me help you," he said, and sat down next to her. The instant his fingers touched hers, she allowed him to finish unbuttoning the blouse. A new yearning careened through Megan as he slid his hands beneath the blouse, barely skimming her flesh, and easing it off her shoulders. As his gaze caressed her breasts, Megan felt them tighten, begging to be touched by him. Fractionally, she leaned toward him, closed her eyes, and silently asked for his contact.

She wasn't disappointed, feeling his hands slide around her breasts, the thin fabric of her lingerie a meaningless barrier between them. A small sigh escaped Megan as she rested her brow against the hard line of his jaw. His fingers outlined and stroked her taut nipples, and a flood of sensations jolted through her.

"You're so beautiful," Holt whispered against her ear, nuzzling the lobe, the silk of her hair tickling his nose and cheek. Sweet God, was she ever. In moments, he released the filmy bra, recapturing her small, lovely breasts. With his tongue, he caressed each one, feeling her soft intake of breath, a wild, fine quiver racing through her. Her lashes swept downward and she grew restless beneath his moist, heated onslaught. The moment spun to a halt, and instinctively he sensed that each touch, each stroke of wet fire suspended them in the present. Their past was forgotten. No future existed.

When Megan's lips brushed his cheek, Holt turned, finding, pressing her mouth against his. Her breathing was chaotic, telegraphing her need and dissolving his control beneath the fever of her request. Megan's urgent demands shattered his good intentions as her hand slid up his chest, entangled in his thick, dark hair, brushed his nipples, and sent a torrent of urgency through him.

In moments, Megan felt her slacks being pulled away from her hips to reveal her long legs. She felt no shyness as Holt joined her on the bed, skimming her torso and her hips as he removed the last of her lingerie. His smile was very male when she leaned upward, claiming a long, drugging kiss from him. His fingers combed through her hair, and gently, he guided her down to the bed and smiled into her eyes.

"I need you," he breathed. "I want you more than anything I've ever wanted." And then, he leaned down, running his tongue across her lower lip, feeling her quiver and then arch up against him. The contact was electric, fiery. Holt released her thick hair, caressed her small shoulders, and captured her breasts, drawing the first nipple into his mouth.

A little cry escaped from Megan as he lavished her with attention. Her world spun around her senses, around his strength as a man, and what they shared together. There was such satisfaction as he groaned when she pressed herself against his hips. The sound reverberated through her, and she felt a part of him on so many other levels already. Slowly, he released the puckered, throbbing nipple, a smile in his eyes. The depth of his worship of her skittered through Megan's scattered senses, telling her that he applauded her equal assertiveness in lovemaking. She smiled back, running her fingers through his short, dark hair, and felt his muscles tense across his back and arms, wherever she touched him.

Nothing had ever seemed so right to her. She saw the smoldering look in his eyes and a small breath caught in her throat as his hand moved downward across her belly. Shimmering rings of fire radiated downwards and Megan grew taut, expectant. His hand eased between her thighs.

"Silk," he murmured against her lips, "you're like sweet, hot silk." She was smooth, warm velvet as he caressed her inner thighs, feeling her small cry as he gently stroked her for the first time. There was such a moistness to welcome him as he lavished her, explored her with loving strokes meant to pleasure her, that it humbled him. Each time he touched her, a little cry burst from her. Sweet, vibrating sounds, a primal music to his senses.

Tiny, rippling warmth burst within her as he continued to caress her intimately. His mouth suckled her other nipple, and the tension tripled throughout her. Fingers digging deeply into his taut shoulder, Megan made a little sound of frustration. She needed to feel him deep within her, to feel captured, loved.

As if sensing her need, Holt rolled over on his back. Her red hair became a crimson pool across his chest as he brought Megan on top of him. The strands were thick and heavy, carrying her spicy scent as he placed his hands on her hips, guiding her as she sat up. There was such joy in her eyes that his heart burst with an unparalleled feeling of happiness. It took his breath away. They were evenly matched to one another, both knowing it, both savoring the moment to come.

"My beautiful red-haired woman," he whispered huskily, guiding her, wanting to feel himself deep within her sweet, molten confines.

Gripping his arms, Megan felt herself being lifted. Her breath caught, and she arched, throat exposed as they made contact. There was such strength and hardness against her soft, womanly moistness. He sheathed deeply into her, taking her, creating wave after wave of motion that unhinged her. His groan reverberated through her. Power met and melded into a cauldron of tempestuous heat and flame. He gripped her hips, and cajoled her to express all of herself within his hands, his body.

Eyes shuttering closed, Megan felt the heat welling up deep within her, so hot and explosive, that she cried out as she gave the gift of herself to him. Seconds later, she felt him stiffen and groan. Her world collided with his, they both shattered, and were reformed again seconds later in the fire of their love. Lightheaded, Megan swayed, completely disoriented, feeling, not thinking.

Holt guided her down on him so that her head lay where his shoulder connected to his neck. Her hair was a molten pool of red across his chest, just as he had always envisioned it, wanted it, dreamed of it. Megan quivered in the aftermath, but it wasn't out of fear, it was out of good lovemaking. A smile touched Sam's mouth. Sweat trickled down his temple as he skimmed his hand cross her damp back and shoulders. The words that begged to be torn from him, *I love you*, remained stuck in his throat.

Instead, as he continued to caress her, worship her firm, loving form, he rasped, "A long time ago, I dreamed of you, long before I'd ever met you." He sighed, feeling her move and lift her head to meet and hold his gaze.

Megan drowned in Sam's smoldering dark-blue eyes. There was such love in them for her that she couldn't speak. Words weren't coming easily, anyway. It was as if loving Sam had erased the shrill voice of doom in her head. If fact, she had no mind, only a rich tapestry of feelings and lingering aftershocks of pleasure after loving him. A soft smile formed on her lips, and she leaned down, her brow resting against his mouth.

Sam kissed her brow, tasted her saltiness, and inhaled her very feminine scent. Lifting his hands, he threaded his fingers through that mass of fiery hair. He watched her soft smile of womanly knowing in her verdant gaze that was partially hidden by her thick lashes. "This dream," he went on in a low voice, "had a red-haired Valkyrie in it. She had your face, your color of hair." Placing a light kiss on the tip of her nose, he added, "But most of all, she had your wild, beautiful green eyes." And then, Holt sobered, growing serious. "I like what I see in them now, Megan. I want that look to always be there, to be shared by us."

With a sigh, she laid her head down on his shoulder, content to feel his arms go around her. "I never remembered my dreams," she admitted wistfully.

"If you had, I would've been in them."

Laughing quietly, Megan nuzzled Sam, kissed his neck and then his jaw. "You're so conceited."

"No, honest."

It was her turn to become serious. "That's something we've always been with one another, hasn't it? Our honesty?"

Gently, Sam placed her next to him, and levered himself up on his elbow, his other hand cradling her flushed cheek. Megan's eyes glowed with such life that he never wanted to forget that look which had been created between them, because of them. "Yes," he said hoarsely, "I'm not sorry this happened, Megan. Only the way it happened."

She nodded, closing her eyes momentarily, the pain of nearly losing him still sharp and hurting in her heart and memory. "I thought I was in a nightmare. I—I couldn't believe you might be dead, Sam."

Tracing her brow, he removed those small wrinkles of pain he shared with her. "I know. I nearly came unglued over at Ops. I was at the desk filing my flight plan when the crash siren started screaming. I found out it was all a drill. A lousy drill."

Megan grimaced. "I wonder how many pilots' wives it affected similarly?"

"All of them," he said grimly. She was warm and soft beside him. Sam admired her long, slim body, an alabaster color against the cobalt blue of the bedspread. "But enough about them. All I was worried about was you. Your reaction."

Megan sought his arms and pressed herself against the length of his body. There, she found sanctuary, safety. He continued to caress her, and kept her fears at bay.

"Talk to me, Red. I can feel you thinking."

"How?" she asked, amazed. It was impossible that he could read her mind. And then, Megan realized that he was a highly trained test pilot, sensitized to even the slightest change of pressure, position, sensing perhaps more than actually seeing her discomfort. "Never mind," she said.

With a sigh, Sam sat up, leaned against the headboard, and brought Megan into his arms. She came without hesitation, and that was reassuring. "How can I 'never mind' when I care about you, your thoughts, and how you feel?" he teased her gently with a smile.

"I don't think you want to hear it. No pilot does."

Sam gave her a small shake. "You're talking to Sam Holt, the man. Remember?"

Megan didn't know whether to believe him or not. If only. . "Loving you was the most right thing I've ever done, Sam. I felt so"—she groped for the right words—"free to be myself, to be all that I can be." Looking up, Megan held his gaze. "Does that make sense?"

"Sure does. I felt the same way. We're good together, sweetheart."

"We're opposites."

With a laugh, Sam said, "Oh?"

"You're the extrovert, I'm the introvert."

"So, we'll counterbalance each other's moods. That's a positive."

"You're able to laugh at life. All I see it as is a responsibility."

Stroking her shoulder, he leaned over, placing a small kiss on it. "I'll teach you how to laugh, and you teach me how to be more responsible toward you."

Touched beyond words, Megan grew quiet. How could this be a line coming from Sam? He sounded so sincere. She was quiet for several minutes, mulling over their other problems.

"I can hear you thinking. Want to share it?" Sam coaxed. He closed his eyes and savored Megan's warmth. There was something so incredibly peaceful about having her with him. It was so right that it hurt.

Megan's throat constricted, but she forced the words out.

"I didn't want to like you, Sam. Somehow, you got to me. I don't know how, you just did. I was getting so tired of fighting you off, telling you to go away when you wouldn't . . . and all the time, I was afraid."

"Of what?"

She shuddered, feeling his arms tighten momentarily around her. "I was afraid of ending up like my mother. Every time my father flew a test flight, she hit the bottle hard. When I'd get up in the morning, she was already roaring drunk. Father wouldn't say anything. He'd just leave early to get away from her tears and yelling. Becky's suicide attempt today brought all those horrible memories back to me."

With a sigh, Sam rested his chin lightly against her shoulder. He wanted to protect her from the anguish in her voice, in the pain she still carried in her heart. "So you got the brunt of your mother's anger over your father leaving without a word?"

"Yes." Miserably, Megan added, "Monday, when you flew, I began feeling shaky and fearful inside. Mother used to describe to me how she felt before Father flew a test." Her voice became thin, inaudible.

"And you felt the exact same way last Monday?" Sam guessed.

To say the words was like admitting she was her mother. Something inside her couldn't do that. "It was awful, Sam," and Megan gripped his hand.

He kissed her fingers and then rested her head against his chest, over his heart. "I had a feeling you were worrying," he confessed. "I tried to call you after the test, but I got hung up in a Design meeting. By the time I could break free, it was 3 P.M., and you'd already left school. And then, I had to take that TDY flight to Maryland. I'm glad I called the school and left you a message on Monday. At least you didn't have to wonder where the hell I was, or what I was doing."

"It wasn't your fault."

"More than anything," Sam told her earnestly, "I don't want you to worry. We have something special Megan, something I *know* can transcend your fears." He saw the doubt in her eyes, not ever wanting to lose her now that she had trusted him enough to give herself to him. "Look, not every wife or girlfriend of a pilot has the fears your mother had. Or that Becky Merrill has. There have got to be ways to cope with this. The other wives do it."

Could love overcome her fear? It hadn't in her mother's case. And Becky had made the ultimate cry for help, the fear too much for her to handle any longer. Megan was unsure about herself. Looking up, she studied Sam's serious features. The ache to tell him that she loved him was real. It was too soon, their relationship, too tenuous. "I think," she said softly, "we have to take what we have one day at a time. If I look at my past, I get afraid because of what happened to my parents. If I look to the future, my imagination runs away with me, and all I see are the negatives, a crash, and," Megan choked, "losing you. I thought I'd lost you today."

"It's not going to be easy," Sam agreed, "but more than anything else, we've got to talk. Communicate. Some of the other pilots I've overheard all say the same thing: talking helps dispel the fear." He wanted so badly for Megan to see and understand his point of view. "What do you think, feel?"

A quiver of a smile fled across her lips. "Sam Holt, you could sell anybody anything, do you realize that?"

"Honey, the only thing I want to sell you on is us. The day I met you, I felt like somebody clobbered me with a baseball bat. You stood out in that crowd, so beautiful, so independent and apart from everyone else." Sam kissed her cheek and relished her velvet softness. "I couldn't get you out of my mind or dreams. I didn't want to."

Giving him a shy look, Megan admitted, "I couldn't get you off my mind, either."

"Was I in your dreams?"

"Yes."

"Want to share them?" He grinned.

Megan laughed fully, throwing her arms around his neck. "Sam Holt, you're such a conceited male animal."

It felt so good to stretch out across the bed and lie at Megan's side. Sam skimmed his hand over her clean-limbed body, savoring her. Megan was responsive, the heated look in her green eyes telling him everything. He wanted to make passionate love with her again, a celebration of their joy. Holt stilled his hunger for a moment longer, his hand coming to rest on her hip.

"One day at a time, with lots of talking, right?"

Megan nodded. "I don't know where this is going, Sam. No promises."

He leaned over, tasting her lower lip with his tongue, and felt her press provocatively against him in response. "No promises, just hard work because we want this, deserve this," he whispered, moving his hand to her breast and cupping it. "But we're going to push the envelope on what we have, sweetheart. That's the only way to find out."

The test pilot term, "push the envelope," vaguely registered on Megan as she responded to his mouth trailing a lingering trail of kisses down her throat to her awaiting breasts that cried for his knowing touch. If a plane stayed within the limits of its flight envelope, it remained stable and flyable. If it went beyond it, the plane became out of control, frequently crashing. There were no guarantees, no promises to their relationship. Just risk, with huge gains and equally huge losses. Megan shut off her mind and centered on Holt's searing touch, if just for a little while.

— 15 —

MEGAN was shaky and raw feeling the next day as she waited for Melody Stang to show up at the Antelope Valley Inn. Sam had slept overnight, leaving around 10 A.M. He was going in to visit Becky at the hospital, and then drop over to see if Curt needed help at the house. A fierce love for Sam welled through Megan as she sat with a Perrier in hand, waiting for Melody to appear.

Sighing, she could do nothing but feel. Last night, a huge barrier had been torn down and taken from her by loving Sam. A part of her knew it had been right and good. This morning, she awoke not being sure at all. Sam had sensed her vulnerable state, and had wisely said nothing unless she wanted to talk about her feelings.

Frowning, Megan took a sip of the Perrier, not tasting it. Too much had happened too quickly. She needed time to assimilate and absorb it all, and he uncannily sensed it. Sam's sensitivity toward her did nothing but unstring more new emotions toward him she'd been hiding from herself.

"There you are," Melody greeted, thanking the hostess and joining Megan.

Forcing herself back to the present, Megan managed a slight smile. "Mrs. Stang."

"Please," she said, taking off her black leather gloves, "call me Melody."

Megan was dressed in a pale-pink dolman-sleeve pullover tunic and a pair of tan tailored pants. It was Saturday, and she wasn't going to dress up for anyone. On the other hand, Melody was elegant in what Megan was sure was a designer suit. Which designer, she didn't know. The dark-gray wool peplum jacket was set off by a jabot blouse of pale-cream silk, and finished off with a sleek, narrow gray skirt. By any standards, Megan thought, Melody dressed the part of a successful officer's wife on the way up the ladder to claim his general's stars.

"Of course, Melody."

She gave her a brittle smile, ordering a manhattan from the waitress, taking no note of Megan's disapproval. "Thank you for meeting me here. It was quite a surprise to see you at George's on Friday night."

Megan smiled to herself. No one called the commanding general of any base by his first name. Especially a captain's wife. How sure Melody must be of Jack's forthcoming major's leaves, and his power on the base. "My father knew General Dalton for twenty years. I more or less grew up in front of his eyes at the different bases he and my father were assigned to."

The drink came, and Melody thanked the waitress. Lifting the tumbler, she took a small sip, and then set it down on the linen tablecloth. "I'm grateful you didn't bring up Scotty's predicament. Thank you."

"I don't believe any child should be used as a lever in any political situation or power play," Megan said tightly.

"How honorable of you, Megan." She laughed. "In our business, politics is the name of the game, isn't it?"

"Unfortunately, it can become that."

"Everyone's fair game. That's the rule."

"Not in my book. Children are a sacred trust. They shouldn't be used like pawns on a board to further someone else's career."

Melody's eyes constricted as she studied her. "You wield considerable power at the base. That surprised me."

"And that's why you're here, isn't it?"

Taking another drink, a longer one this time, Melody nodded. "This is strictly off the record."

Megan smiled, holding her cold gaze. What Melody meant was: none of their conversation had better leak out to anyone else, or Megan would pay a heavy price for that indiscretion. "Any conversation I have with parents about their child is always held in the utmost privacy."

Melody stared hard at her. "You're an Air Force brat. You know how the system works."

"Yes, I do. But I don't like using the system, Mrs. Stang. Only when I'm backed into a corner and my children are at risk, will I use it."

"Like you did last Friday night."

Megan shrugged, tense. "What I did isn't important. All children will win if my program gets pushed through."

"Brad Jamison doesn't like your idea."

Wondering how Melody knew Jamison, she shrugged again. "We've agreed to disagree, that's all."

"You fight for what you want. Your father was legendary for that same trait."

Her lips compressed. "Mrs. Stang, don't ever compare me to my father. His motives were entirely different than mine."

"Still, you have his stubbornness, his grit." She grinned. "I admire that in my enemies."

"And I'm your enemy because I'm insisting that Scotty be tested for hyperactivity?"

Taken aback by Megan's bluntness, Melody looked away for a moment. "I meant what I said: I want our conversation off the record. Will you promise me that?"

Melody's voice was surprisingly husky with emotion. Megan nodded. "You have my promise," she said softly, leaning back against the black leather seat.

Glancing around before she spoke, Melody made sure no one was within earshot. Lowering her voice, she leaned forward. "I'm aware of Scotty's problem, Megan. I've got a degree in child psychology, and I can spot hyperactivity."

Megan met her gaze. "So you agree, Scotty is hyperactive?"

"Yes." Melody frittered with her leather gloves. "I've known it for some time. I've tried to help Scotty, but . . . he's getting worse. I can barely control him at home, so I know what he must be like in your classroom."

Anger sizzled through Megan, and she sat up, inches separating them. "Then why haven't you gotten your son the help he needs?"

Brows knit, Melody refused to hold her furious green eyes. "You wouldn't understand."

"Really?" Megan's voice held disgust. "Let me guess: your husband's going up for early promotion and he doesn't want anything to mar his perfect, flawless fitness report. God help the officer who has a child who's less than perfect, who has a flaw in him or her." She clenched her fist beneath the table. "Don't sit here and tell me *that's* not the reason why you haven't done anything to help your son, Mrs. Stang."

Glaring at her, Melody hissed, "You *know* that's the reason! I came here today to ask you to stop putting in those weekly reports on Scotty. Jack finds out about his promotion in January. If you can just wait until then, I can promise you, I'll take my son to a doctor and get him the drugs he needs."

Eyes hardening, Megan rasped, "No deal, Mrs. Stang. How *dare* you put your husband's career in front of your son's needs! He's a human being, for God's sake! A human! Not a miserable promotion, not a pair of oak leaves on your husband's shoulders."

"Wait until January, Megan."

When Megan spoke, her voice wobbled with fury, with barely withheld personal feelings. Long ago, her father had thrown her and her mother to the wolves, too, in search of his next promotion. She wouldn't allow it to happen to Scotty. "No way."

"You'll be fired for this."

Megan's mouth barely curled. "So far, my union is backing me on the request for Scotty to be tested."

"Jamison will have you fired!"

Getting up, Megan grabbed her purse, her body a line of tension as she looked down at Melody's furious features. "I'll take the risk, Mrs. Stang. At least I have my priorities and values straight: your son is more important to me than he ever was to either of you. What a pitifully sad commentary on you, as parents, and on a system that condones that kind of behavior. Someday, Scotty will recognize it, too."

Getting to her feet, Melody towered a good six inches over Megan. "I don't care for judgmental ingenues straight out of college, either."

"I may be young, Mrs. Stang, but I'm old and wise to the way the military works. I've got more time in grade than you and your husband combined, so don't try and get to me through any more power games. I think you realize General Dalton is on my side."

Jerking on her gloves, Melody warned tautly, "You'll be sorry for this. That's a promise. I'm only asking for two and a half months before Scotty gets the help he needs."

Megan straightened, as if throwing off tension in her shoulders. "I don't compromise on the needs of my children. Not now. Not ever."

Purse under her arm, Melody raised a brow. "Battle lines are drawn, Ms. Roberts. And no quarter will be given."

Megan stood there, watching Melody march imperiously out of the inn. Her breathing was ragged with anger, and she took several gulps, trying to settle down. Thank God Sam didn't know the extent of this.

There was one word Sam wanted to use to characterize Design the next morning. It was *tenterhooks*. Everyone was edgy, grim, and uncommunicative. Lauren was utilizing the bulk of information he'd brought back from Maryland with him, her desk cluttered, civilian design engineers surrounding her like an enthusiastic wolf pack, all adding input.

Things were cooking over at Lauren's desk, and that was good, but it was tense. Real tense, because they were behind schedule.

From his desk, he could see Merrill, who looked pale and shaken, his eyes dark with rings under them. Becky was still in the hospital, under observation. Today, she'd be coming home. Curt had withdrawn, moody and silent, so Sam didn't know what he was thinking—or feeling. In truth, when he looked into his mirror to shave this morning, he had shadows under his eyes, too. Holt tried to concentrate, but it was impossible.

Loving Megan Friday night was the best thing that had ever happened to him. And to her, he reminded himself. He'd remained at her apartment and slept with her that night. Megan had been restless, but at least she slept. Sam hadn't, laying awake in the dim morning hours thinking.

Actually, Holt admitted to himself, it wasn't thinking at all, it was worry coupled with anxiety. He was afraid when Megan woke up this morning, she'd revert back to her former decision, and tell him to walk out of her life forever. Any moment, he could lose her, and he knew it. Everything was tentative with her, like walking on eggshells. Could the love they forged with one another hold them together through the coming days and weeks of stress, of the personal demands each of them wrestled with? God, he felt fragile this morning. And helpless.

"Hey, Holt!" Stang called from his desk, "You got a lady picked out to go to the Christmas ball over at the O Club?"

Sam studied him. What was Stang up to now? "Hadn't even thought about it," he mumbled, pretending to pay attention to the report in front of him. That was a baldfaced lie, of course, because he'd asked Megan to accompany him, and she'd agreed.

"Melody wanted to know what your lady was wearing. Yours too, Merrill. What's Becky got picked out for this mandatory dog and pony show?"

"Don't bother me," Merrill growled.

Undeterred, Jack continued. "Melody's got this lavender Ungaro designer dress, and she didn't want to clash with what everyone else was wearing. You know how women are. Holt, who you taking to the ball, anyway?"

"I didn't say." After Becky's suicide attempt, Sam wondered if Megan would *want* to go to the O Club, back to memories of her father, and his abandonment of her and her mother. There would be a lot of drinking, and he knew Megan hated being around liquor. Still, he *had* to show up for that, date or not. It would make the evening go faster and less painfully with Megan at his side.

Stang slid a glance in Porter's direction, raising his voice a notch. "You know, Holt, there's a hot little number over at the O Club. She's got every single jet jock drooling over her. Her name is Liza Cooper. Now, there's a willing filly."

Sam was about to respond, but Porter's head snapped up. She shoved her chair away from her desk and pinned Stang with a glare. "Captain, I think we've got a hell of a lot more to do in here this morning than gossip, don't you?"

Grinning, Jack went back to work. "Sure thing, Major, sure thing."

With a sigh, Holt took Lauren's directive. She was in no mood to be pushed or pressured. She was under enough strain with the design changes to the engine structure. Making a mental note, Sam decided to buttonhole Curt at noon. Something was eating him up alive. He looked positively ill.

"Hey, buddy, what's going on?" Sam cornered Merrill in the parking lot where he was slowly walking around in deep thought. He noted Curt's hands in his pockets, and the fact that his head was bowed, as if in defeat.

Curt turned, and then frowned. "Sam?"

"You looked like death warmed over in there, and I didn't want to say anything with Stang around." To make sure, Sam glanced toward Ops. No one was within earshot of their conversation, but he wouldn't put it past Stang to invite himself over to eavesdrop.

Running his fingers through his hair, Curt replaced his dark-blue garrison cap. "The day Becky tried . . ." he couldn't bring himself to say *suicide*. Instead he stumbled in a raw voice, "In the hospital room, she said something I'd never thought I'd hear from her," he told Holt, needing to share it with someone.

Frowning, Sam stared over at the jets sitting on the apron. The wind was cool because it was December, but the sun was pleasantly warm. "What'd she say?"

Agitated, Curt leaned against the wire Cyclone fence that divided the parking lot from the runway area. "Becky asked me to quit."

"Quit what?"

"Flying."

Sam's eyes widened. "Flying?"

"Yeah." Curt shook his head. "Christ, Sam, I can't. I mean, it's my life. I love it. My father brags to everybody how I'm a test pilot. I can't let him down."

A strange, unsettled feeling moved through Sam as he stood there, not knowing what to say. "Well . . . what are you going to do?" The choices weren't many. Sam had seen too many marriages break up because the wives refused to live under such pressures. Somehow, he couldn't envision Curt and Becky getting a divorce. They were just too right for one another. And then Sam laughed derisively to himself. He felt Megan and he were right for one another. The road they recently chose to walk together was just as unsafe and littered with land mines as the one Becky and Curt were on.

"What are you going to do?" Holt finally asked, breaking the heavy silence.

"Hell, I don't know. I've tossed and turned every night since then. Couldn't sleep. I mean, what can I do?"

"Do you love Becky?"

Curt lifted his chin and held Holt's gaze. "Yeah, I love her."

How much? The words almost came out, but Sam knew

he wasn't in any position to play devil's advocate. The exact same scenario could be played on him by Megan at *any* time. And if she gave him that choice: quit flying or lose the relationship with her, which would he take? Holt didn't even want to think about it.

"I'm going to try and devote at least an hour a night to Becky and Patty," Curt responded softly. "I think we need quality time together. It means an hour less on study, but somehow, I've got to do it."

"That might help," Sam said. It would play hell on Merrill's testing, because every pilot spent hundreds of hours pouring over computer data, reports, and attending briefings in order to absorb highly technical information that would all come into play when they took up an aircraft for testing. Even an hour less, on a critical manual, might mean the difference between life and death. But then, Sam told himself, the Merrills' marriage was at that juncture, too. Who lived? What died?

"I'm going to do it," Curt said with resolve. "I love her so damn much. She's right: I have been ignoring her and Patty. I haven't meant too, but this project—"

"Has been a sonofabitch."

Merrill managed a pained grimace. "Roger that one." He wrapped his fingers through the fence wire, staring off into the distance, and saw nothing. His voice was low, tense. "I can't lose her, Sam. I can't lose Becky. . ."

Placing his hand on Merrill's tense shoulder, Sam stood there. Words were useless. There were no simple answers. And then, Holt began to tell Curt about Megan and himself. Just being able to share it with someone who understood, took a tremendous load of fear off his shoulders.

Merrill smiled slightly afterward. "I like Megan. But your situation is no more stable than mine."

Nodding, Sam rested his back against the wire. "I'm living one day at a time," he admitted slowly. "It's like carrying around a live grenade: I never know when it's going to go off and kill our relationship."

"You mean if she asks you to make a choice between her and flying?"

"Yes." Across the base, Megan was teaching her class. What was she wearing? He sharply recalled how fragrant her skin had smelled, how soft it was. The thick silk of that fiery red hair spoke of her spirit, her strength. He hoped she remained strong about their relationship.

Merrill sighed. "We're both in a hell of a fix."

"You think Becky will be ready for the Christmas ball?" It was coming up in two weeks and was mandatory that every officer and his wife show up for it—or else.

"I don't know. The doctors will release her today. Becky knows how important it is to make an appearance at it. Are you inviting Megan?"

"Yes, but I don't know if she'll still come." Sam didn't add because of Becky's suicide attempt.

"Well, Becky really likes Megan. And she hates these functions, always feeling ill at ease at them. Maybe, if Megan comes, Becky wouldn't feel so pressured. Could you ask her to come for Becky's sake, if for no other reason?"

Holt got the message. "I'll talk to her tonight about it."

"Christ," Merrill said in a low voice, looking back toward Ops, "if Stang *ever* gets ahold of all this, my career is shot down. I'm sweating out someone getting wind of the fact Becky's been in the base hospital for two days."

With a snort, Holt pushed away from the fence. It was time to get back to Ops. "Worse," he muttered, "is the damage it wold do to Becky. Right now, I don't think she could take that kind of cruel gossip."

"Well," Curt added, slowly walking across the parking lot with him, "let's just get past this damned Christmas ball. One step at a time."

Holt was struck by Merrill's words. Those were the exact ones he and Megan used with one another, a reminder that there were no promises, no "for sures" in life. What a hell of a way to live. But he disliked the other choices even more.

* * *

"Isn't that our cozy group we've been waiting for?" Melody leaned over and whispered to her husband, who looked darkly handsome in his dress officer's uniform. Gala Christmas music was being played by the five-piece Air Force band. The huge, rectangular room at the O Club was crowded with men in their dark-blue and silver dress uniforms, and women in subdued, but tasteful pastel gowns.

Stang lifted his head from the group of majors he was making small talk with. Soon, he'd be one himself, and he wanted to remind them of that. Captain Curt Merrill, his pale wife, and Megan Roberts had just arrived. Becky was clinging to her husband's arm as if she were scared to death. She wore a bright-yellow cocktail dress, the color out of place among the pastels of the group. Worse, it hung on her, fitting poorly. Becky appeared haunted and fearful looking. Megan Roberts hovered protectively at Becky's side, like a maid-in-waiting to her.

"Interesting," he whispered back to Melody. "I'm glad Holt and Porter are TDY in Maryland. It's a shame they had to miss the ball, but this gives us open season on their significant others."

Melody winked, feeling a thrill as they were about to engage their prior Tac and Strat plans from the night before into high gear. Since her meeting with Megan Roberts, the teacher's firing was at a stalemate. Jamison was doing all he could, for a considerable amount of money, to continue putting pressure on from the administration side to have her relieved of teaching duties. Unfortunately, the union was fighting back with a demand that Scotty be tested.

They had agreed to allow the situation to remain a stalemate. Megan couldn't put in any more reports on Scotty until the situation was resolved. It was in their best interests to let it drag through January until Jack got his early promotion. Melody clenched her silk-gloved hand. Then, she would enjoy watching Megan Roberts get booted out on her ear. Absently, she caressed the lavender fabric across her small waist, the most elegantly dressed woman at the ball. Making a smooth exit from the group of majors and their wives, Melody glided toward Megan and the Merrills.

"God, you look gorgeous," Jack said with fervor. Indeed, Melody looked as if she'd walked straight out of *Vogue* magazine. Her black hair was swept upward, fastened with a real diamond barrette, her feathery bangs barely brushing her arched eyebrows. At her throat was a recent birthday gift he'd bought for her from Tiffany's in Los Angeles: a ten-carat diamond pendant. It caught the light, glinting fiercely with fiery color, and drew attention to her classical features.

The Ungaro creation hugged her form to luscious perfection. Full breasts, Melody had informed him archly earlier while they were dressing for the ball, were in fashion again. Those who had them could flaunt them once more. Those who didn't would rush to their plastic surgeon and get silicone implants to keep up with the latest fad. And she had one hell of a pair, the dress design making them tastefully revealing, celebrating her womanliness, Jack thought. Of course, Melody had spent three thousand dollars on the gown, and none of the wives of the officers here could afford that kind of price. She was a knockout, and Jack enjoyed the catty, envious looks from the wives, and the equally lustful looks from the husbands.

Melody smiled beautifully as she approached the group. "Why, Curt, how are you? And Becky, my, you look lovely in your gold gown. And of course, how are you, Megan?" She went down the line, shaking their hands expertly. Megan Roberts wore a stunning silver lamé dress that complemented the striking color of her unruly red hair that spilled across her proud shoulders. Unlike the other women, she wore little makeup, but she didn't need it.

Instinctively, Megan moved slightly in front of Becky, wanting to protect her from Melody. Sam hadn't embellished the truth: Becky wasn't recovering very well. "Good evening, Mrs. Stang," she responded coolly, shaking her gloved hand lightly. All around them, soft music emanated from the band, Christmas decorations hung on the walls of the huge room. Megan wasn't in the Christmas spirit. The O Club held nothing but terrible memories for her. Becky was little more than a frightened rabbit who hated these functions, and Sam wasn't here. She missed him terribly. A week ago, he and Lauren Porter had to fly to Patuxent River to do some last minute research on the redesign of the engine. They were supposed to be home tomorrow morning, December 24. At least their Christmas plans wouldn't be ruined.

"Well, well, well," Jack said, grinning down at Megan, "we finally get to meet Holt's lady again. It's a real pleasure, Megan." He shook her hand.

Megan kept her face neutral. "Thank you, Captain Stang."

"Soon to be Major," Melody reminded all of them, sure that he was going to get early promotion.

"I'm sure," Megan said, caring less. She knew Sam was up for early promotion, just as Curt was.

"Hey," Jack said conspiratorially, leaning forward, "you know Sam and Lauren go back a long ways. I'll bet you're just a little worried about him spending an entire week alone with her in Maryland."

"Lauren is *such* a beautiful woman," Melody added enthusiastically. "Have you ever met her, Megan?"

Megan stared at the couple, her heart thumped hard, underscoring the fact their attack had hit the target. She could barely respond, her voice tight. "No, I've never had the pleasure."

"Too bad, or perhaps it isn't. Lauren was promoted early to major a year ago, and we can see why. She's the head of the Design team on the *Agile Eagle*. Not only is she a brilliant flight engineer, but she's very beautiful and poised. Sam Holt has made no bones about her being his favorite flight engineer over at Testing."

"Easy on the eyes," Jack agreed. "If Sam has to spend a week in Maryland with someone, he really lucked out getting Lauren."

"It's a shame," Melody said, pointing generally to the left of them, "that Major Ryan Malone is all alone tonight. Lauren is supposedly engaged to him, you know."

"I don't know about that, honey. Look who's coming over to him. That's Liza Cooper. What a looker."

Megan watched the entire scene, nauseated. Blond-haired Liza, dressed in a gold-sequined miniskirt that barely hid anything, sidled up to Major Malone. She slid her hand through his arm and smiled winningly up at him.

"My, my," Melody said to Megan, "I wonder if a similar celebration is going on in Maryland right now? You being an Air Force brat and all, you know how promiscuous jet jocks are. Particularly test pilots." Then, she beamed at her husband. "All except for Jack. I feel we're one of the few couples who have found not only true love, but fidelity."

Nerves raw from the unexpected attack, Megan glared at them. "I really don't appreciate the innuendos you've dropped Mrs. Stang."

"Whatever are you talking about?"

Megan zeroed in on Captain Stang. "I despise gossip. Worse, I don't like people who deliberately try and stir up trouble when the individuals they're talking about aren't here to defend themselves."

Jack frowned. "Megan—"

"It's Ms. Roberts, Captain."

Scowling, Jack felt her rage. "We're not gossiping, Ms. Roberts."

"No? Coming over here hinting obliquely that Captain Holt and Major Porter are having an affair in Maryland is pretty gossipy. Not to mention, bold." *And stupid.* Or was it? Megan recalled a number of times that Sam had said he liked working with Lauren. Not only that, his voice always softened when he spoke of her. Was there something between them? Fear ate at her. It was true, single pilots were known to play the field. To them, it was a game, a score card about which to brag to the other pilots. Was Sam capable of that? Suddenly, Megan wasn't sure because she'd never thought about it. Sam seemed loyal to her at all times. Except when he talked in that soft tone of voice about Lauren.

Laughing delightedly, Melody raised her hands. "Ms. Roberts, we implied no such thing. I'm sure you know of your father's exploits. They're still the talk among the single pilots at the O Club. Like father, like daughter? Will

Sam Holt run around on you, like your father ran around on your poor, sick mother?''

Pain shattered through Megan and her voice shook with emotion. ''When Sam lands tomorrow morning, I'm going to be there to ask if what you've implied is true. The only time gossip can do any damage is if there's no communication between the people involved. And Sam and I know that.''

Jack's gaze narrowed on her. ''Now look, Ms. Roberts, you can't prove anything.'' He grinned at Becky and Curt, who were also frowning. Sweat trickled down from beneath his armpits, soaking into his uniform. Sliding his hand beneath Melody's elbow, he nodded to them. ''Have a good time here tonight. Melody and I have to pay our compliments to General Dalton and his wife. If you'll excuse us?''

''Merry Christmas to all of you,'' Melody added sweetly, gliding away.

Megan stood there, her hand on Becky's arm. She could feel Becky trembling. ''It's okay,'' she told both of them. ''This time, they've picked on the wrong person.''

Merrill slid his hand protectively around Becky's waist. ''You stood up to them, Megan. I give you credit, but you've made some enemies.''

Clenching her teeth, Megan glared at the departing Stangs. ''Wrong, they've made an enemy of *me*. I mean it: I'm going to meet Sam and Major Porter at Ops and tell them what happened.''

With a whistle, Curt shook his head. ''Wait until Port finds out. She's going to have Stang's head on a platter.''

''Right where it belongs,'' Megan answered tightly. Worriedly, she returned her attention to Becky. In the last two weeks, she had been slowly recovering, still a mere shadow of herself. Anger toward Curt ballooned, but Megan knew she had no business saying anything. No, the only life she could control was her own, and no one else's. Looking at Becky's somber eyes, her waxen flesh, she wondered if she'd look like that some day if she and Sam remained together. The thought was frightening. Tomorrow morning,

December 24, Sam would be back. And she'd be waiting for him.

Sam's surprise at seeing Megan waiting just inside the glass doors of Ops turned to pure pleasure. As he and Lauren climbed out of their individual cockpits of the T-38 Talon jet trainer, he hungrily sponged in her awaiting figure. She was dressed in a pale-pink angora sweater with a cowl neck, black wool slacks, and a light-tan wool blazer. The ache to move those fiery strands of thick, free hair through his hands was almost physical.

Holt waited for Lauren at the bottom of his ladder, thanking the crew chief. The week spent in Maryland with the Navy design experts had consisted of grueling sixteen-hour sessions. The five-hour coast-to-coast flight had cost him the last of his physical endurance. All Sam wanted was sleep, and more sleep. Savoring the thought that Megan would be in his arms infused him with desire. First, sleep, and then, after awakening, he'd make passionate, welcoming love with Megan.

Lauren took the flight helmet off, her chestnut hair escaping from the gray skull cap all pilots wore beneath it. Shaking her head, she smiled up at Sam. "Let's call it a day, huh?"

"Roger that."

"Is that Megan?" Lauren guessed, as they walked toward Ops in the distance.

"You bet it is."

"Very pretty, Sam. You're serious about her, aren't you?" The wind blew playfully, cool and welcoming.

"She's special," Sam admitted, a sudden catch in his voice, surprised at the emotions following on the heels of his disclosure. As they drew closer, he saw Megan's features were serious and sober, not welcoming as he'd have thought. Automatically, Sam muttered, "Something's wrong."

Lauren took the steps quickly. "Oh?"

"Let's find out." Sam passed her and got to the door first, opening it for Lauren.

Holt smiled at Megan as she came to meet them. There was a line of tension to her mouth, and he frowned. First, he made introductions, realizing Megan had never met Lauren. The two women smiled and shook hands. Fear gnawed at him. Megan's eyes were fraught with something, but he couldn't figure out what.

"Sam, Major Porter, I need to speak to both of you for just a moment." Mouth dry, Megan dove in, repeating what had been said by the Stangs at the Christmas ball the night before. She saw Sam's eyes narrow with fury. The major's reaction was far more volatile.

"That gossiping sonofabitch!" Lauren cursed fiercely under her breath. "I've *had* it with him!"

Eyebrows raised, Sam slid his arm around Megan's shoulders. He wanted to reassure Megan of his love. She lifted her chin, her eyes mirroring gratefulness for his action. "Easy, Port," he cautioned. Only a skeleton crew was on duty over the holidays, but Sam didn't like the prospect of her words floating around to the wrong ears.

Clenching her Nomex flight gloves, Lauren glared around the quiet lounge area. "I don't care, Sam! Stang has tried so hard to keep everyone on edge. This is *my* project, and I'm sick and tired of him trying to undercut my authority and keep my people upset! I'm going to do something about it." She started to leave, but caught herself, and turned on her heel toward Megan.

"Thanks for telling me this, Megan. Ryan and I have some talking to do. You've saved us from a potentially serious rift in our relationship."

"You're welcome, Major."

"Hey, Port."

She turned slowly, her jaw set. "Yes?"

"Have a good Christmas despite this, huh?"

A slight smile dissolved the tightness around her lips. "I'll try. And Merry Christmas to the both of you. See you on the twenty-sixth."

Sam watched Lauren stalk off, and then devoted all his attention to Megan. He didn't want to kiss her in front of the crew, so took her into a side room where reports were written. Closing the doors, he set his duffle bag and flight case on the table.

"Now, it's your turn," he told Megan, and settled his hands on her shoulders. He saw her eyes thaw and grow warm with welcome. With a groan, Sam growled, "I didn't sleep well without you. I had a hell of a time paying attention to the design efforts. All I could think about, dream about, was kissing you, Red. Come here . . ."

It was easy to be drawn into his arms, to lean against his hard male body and feel his mouth capture hers in a heated welcome that drove the cold fear from the pit of her stomach. Megan inhaled his masculine scent, a faint odor of sweat, and felt the sandpapery growth of his beard against her cheek. With a slight moan, she surrendered to his exquisite assault, wrapping her arms around his neck, and gloried in his joy at seeing her once again.

Reluctantly, Sam broke contact and smiled into Megan's lustrous green eyes. The words, *I love you,* were almost torn from him. He swallowed them. It was too much, too soon. If Megan knew how he really felt about her, she'd run. Placing several small kisses on her brow, cheek, and nose, Sam whispered, "I know what it cost you to come here today."

Megan nodded, content to rest her head against his shoulder, the beat of his heart beneath her palm. "I can remember swearing I'd never set foot over here. I hated Ops so much."

"Because you hated what it stood for," Holt guessed.

"Yes, a place that meant more to my father than we did." More of the terror was draining from her, Sam's arm strong and protective around her.

"You came because you wanted to find out if there was any truth to the Stangs' gossip."

Megan looked up. "Sometimes you amaze me with your perception."

Grinning carelessly, Holt brushed another kiss to her brow. "Hey, I'm just being my old test pilot self."

"Humph."

Sam saw the devilry in Megan's eyes, a flood of relief

flowing through him. "I keep telling you I'm different. You keep denying it, but it's the truth." He guided her to the chair and she sat down opposite him. Gripping her hands, which were cold and white, he said softly, "Red, there's no one but you. I promise you that. Ever since I saw you, every other woman pales in comparison beside you." He smiled gently, running his thumbs across the backs of her hands. "Even Lauren. Okay?"

"I feel so stupid, Sam. Last night, when Melody hit me with that, and then dragged my father's name into it, I lost it." She gripped his warm, strong hands, holding his warm blue eyes. "I'm sorry. Am I forgiven?"

He kissed her fingers. "There's nothing to forgive, Red. You did the right thing: you perceived a problem, and you brought it to me to talk about. I told you before: with communication, we can make this work between us. Any doubts now that we've been put to the test?"

Megan shook her head, dread dissolving around her. "No . . . no doubts."

Sam squeezed her hands. Come the twenty-sixth when he saw Stang in Design, he'd set him straight about his wife verbally attacking Megan. It wouldn't happen again.

"Let me complete my flight records, and then we're out of here."

Megan watched as he pulled a pen from the sleeve pocket of his flight suit. The report before him was painfully neat, no ink smudges, no misspellings. Test pilots were graded on such things. "Sam?"

"Hmm?" He kept on writing.

"When you saw me at the doors, what was your first thought?"

Lifting his head, the pen hovering over the report, he returned her thoughtful gaze. "Well, I could say something flip like you couldn't wait to jump my bones because you missed me so much."

"But you won't, will you?" His honesty with her was the crux of everything good between them. Megan had to have his real feelings.

Setting the pen aside, Sam folded his hands above the

report. Brows drawing downward, he said quietly, "At first, I was happy as hell you'd come. I thought you were trying to overcome your fear of this place, of my job. But then, when I got close, I saw your face, and I got afraid, Megan. My first thought and feeling was: My God, you're going to tell me it's all over, that this isn't going to work out between us. I knew you had to go to that Christmas party over at the O Club alone, and I didn't like it. I wanted to be there with you—for you." Taking a deep breath, he added, "I got scared. Real scared. I thought I knew what fear was, but I've never experienced *this* kind of gut-wrenching fear before. And," Sam paused, "I didn't want to come up those stairs. I was too afraid to find out what had you so upset."

Reaching out, Megan slid her fingers between his hands. Her heart mushroomed with such an incredible array of emotions, that all she could do was stare across the table at him. Words choked up in her throat, and she bent her head, trying to get past the lump.

"If," she rasped, "it makes you feel any better, I was afraid, too. Afraid that the Stangs were right. Lauren *is* beautiful. I stood there teetering between the joy of seeing you again and the terror that you had something going with Lauren." Looking around the light-blue room, Megan added, "And you're right: I had to face another barrier of old fear by deciding to come over here."

Sam picked up her hand, placing a kiss on it. "That's just one of many things I like about you: even if you're scared to death, you overcome it." Watching her lips part, and seeing the vulnerability in her eyes, Holt couldn't ever imagine himself with any another woman. "And as for worrying about me straying . . . well, it just isn't going to happen."

"It could, Sam."

He nodded. "Yes. But honey, we can't live our lives on possibilities. We can't be Chicken Little always running around shouting the sky is falling in."

The need to love him, to be in his arms and a part of his sensitiveness, moved gently through Megan. "Funny how we all have our fears, isn't it?"

"Yes. It's *how* we handle them that counts." Sam squeezed her hand and reluctantly released it. "Give me five minutes and we can go home—together."

Leaning back on the dark-blue aluminum chair, Megan waited. Sam looked so tired. Exhausted was a better word. "I want you to come over to my apartment to sleep. I got a tree. We can decorate it tonight after you wake up."

Grinning, Sam asked, "Does that include dinner in the invitation, too?" He loved good home-cooked food.

Megan colored slightly. "Yes. And don't laugh, but I spent all morning making Polish pirogi for you. We'll have them tonight. On Christmas day, we'll have the traditional turkey and dressing."

Delighted, Sam laughed. "God, I don't believe this! Polish food! At last! I really miss my mom's cooking." In that instant, Sam wanted to simply take Megan into his arms and hold her—forever.

— 16 —

THE instant Sam stepped into Megan's apartment, whatever tension he carried, sloughed off him. They had stopped over at his house, and he'd picked up some clean civilian clothes, his robe, and a few toiletry articles because he was staying over for two days. Lifting his nose, he inhaled deeply.

"Pirogi . . ." And then, Sam smiled over at her, and loved her fiercely for her thoughtfulness. "I *never* thought I'd get them again unless I went home for a visit."

"Trust me, while I was trying to make them this morning, I thought about giving up on the project."

Setting his suitcase in the corner of the bedroom, Holt went over to Megan as she opened the bathroom door. Sliding his arm around her, he kissed her tenderly. When Megan's lashes swept upward, he saw happiness in her eyes. "I'm glad you didn't. Look, I'm going to get a quick shower and cr—" he was going to say "crash," but it wasn't a wise choice of words to use around Megan. "I need sleep."

"I know you're exhausted, Sam. When you wake up, we'll have dinner."

He embraced her, running his hands down her small but strong spine. "Thanks for understanding."

"I can remember the times my father would come off

TDY and sleep for fifteen hours straight, get up the next morning and go back to work.''

With a grimace, Sam released her. ''That's not going to happen to us. I've set the clock.'' He glanced at his watch. It was noon. If he got five or six hours under his belt, he'd be decent company for the evening. By Christmas morning, he'd be in good shape. ''I'll get up at 1700.''

Megan stepped away, moving to the door of the bedroom. ''Fine. See you then.''

Nodding, Sam watched as Megan quietly closed the door behind her. He stripped out of his smelly flight suit and let it drop on the carpet. All he wanted was a shower and bed.

The streams of hot water not only cleansed him, but brought him to the edge of drowsiness. Getting out of the shower and wrapping a white towel around his hips, Sam glanced in the steamy mirror. He needed to shave. To hell with it. He needed sleep worse. Holt stumbled out of the bathroom to Megan's canopied Victorian bed.

As he laid down on top of the covers, he groaned, feeling his muscles begin to relax immediately. Rolling on his side, he realized he should have pulled back the covers. Shaping the lace-bordered pillow, he fell into a deep sleep, the clean, fresh scent of lavender in his nostrils. His last thought, if it could even be called that, was that he'd never felt as content as now. It was because of Megan, he was sure. He loved her.

Megan quietly entered her bedroom. Light from the living room filtered in, allowing her to see Sam, who was sleeping soundly. Only an occasional snore broke the silence as she went to the French-door closets and retrieved a light wool blanket. It was 8 P.M., and she knew he'd sleep the rest of the night without awaking—just as her father used to do.

As she approached the bed, her gaze moved appreciatively down across his naked body. Holt was lean and tight, the dark hair on his chest emphasizing his maleness. The white towel that had once been around his waist, had long since fallen away. Until recently, Megan hadn't thought of men as being beautiful, but Sam was. There was a steel-cable strength that ran through his body, his hips narrow, flowing into long, highly developed thighs and calves. Even in sleep, he looked powerful and sleek. As she carefully placed the blanket over him, she felt shaky with need for him. The urge to lean down, to kiss those parted lips that were used to giving orders, was very real.

Instead, Megan gently moved several dried strands of dark hair off his brow. Sam didn't even move, telling her the depth of strain he'd been under the last week. In a perverse way, Megan was glad she knew about the demands put on a test pilot, because it neutralized her worry.

Unable to move away from him, Megan crouched down. The darkness accented Sam's beard, his cheeks hollowed, almost gaunt appearing. Had he lost weight this week? No doubt Sam had been in marathon brain-drain sessions with other design experts. Both he and Lauren Porter had looked exhausted upon their return. Megan's gaze lingered on his features. The shadows beneath his eyes were disappearing, and his brow, that had been furrowed earlier, was smooth. A soft smile pulled at her mouth, and she lightly caressed his stubbled cheek, a fierce feeling of love sweeping through her.

How had Sam become so important to her life? He looked natural lying in her bed, this apartment—as if he'd always belonged here. Straightening, Megan felt so many new and joyous feelings move through her that the fear she felt dissolved. Turning, she left, closing the door quietly behind her.

The pirogi were refrigerated along with the salad, mashed potatoes, and gravy. Megan ate a small tossed salad, had some French bread, and decided to decorate the tree. When Sam awoke on Christmas morning, it would look storybook beautiful. She pulled out the cardboard boxes laden with pretty Victorian ornaments she'd collected over the years. Some had bits of ivory lace and colorful ribbon. Others were carefully crafted wooden ornaments.

Just knowing Sam slept in the next room brought a

wonderful new kind of contentment to Megan. He was with her in spirit, even though he slept. That was a nice kind of feeling—another new one Megan had never experienced. Had her mother had such feelings about her father in the early days of their marriage?

Chewing on her lower lip, Megan continued to decorate the five-foot Scotch pine that sat in the corner of the living room. She remembered that many of her Christmases as a child were sordid affairs. Her mother always pouted, took verbal shots at her father, and he retaliated by going over to the O Club to drink with the single pilots who had nowhere to go during the holidays. How many times had she sat next to the tree with her gifts, watched her father depart in anger, and her mother go back to her room?

"Not this time," she told the tree. No, she and Sam would have a wonderful Christmas—together. Hope moved powerfully through Megan as she placed the delicate, carved angel on top of the tree. The gown was made out of purple velvet and white lace. The wings had been painstakingly crocheted and starched. Megan loved the antique more than any other. Making sure it was stable, Megan stood back, admiring her efforts. Victorian trees would have candles on the limbs, but she didn't carry the tradition that far, in fear of a fire.

Admiring her handiwork, she hummed along with a Christmas tune coming softly from the radio. The few gifts beneath the tree made it look complete. Megan could hardly wait to see Sam's expression when he saw the tree, because he loved the Victorian era as much as she did. It was time to go to bed.

The thought of sleeping with Sam was heated, filled with promise. Perhaps, when Sam awoke tomorrow morning, they would make love together, a special kind of Christmas gift to one another. Her hands trembled slightly as she wrapped his gift, the thought delicious. And then she laughed at herself.

"Megan Roberts, you are going to go to bed, sleep at his side and *not* wake him up. He needs his sleep. Hands off!"

* * *

"No . . . Russ . . . no. . . ."

Megan frowned, awakened from her deep sleep. She lay curved against Sam's back. He muttered once again, and moved restlessly. Sleep gradually left her as his mumbling increased. She felt him jerk beside her, and she moved away, dragging her eyes open. What was wrong with him? Automatically, she reached over, making contact with Sam's shoulder. His flesh was sweaty, muscles hard and strained. What time was it?

Before Megan could roll over and look at the clock on the bed stand, she heard Holt shriek.

"*Eject! Eject!*"

A cry escaped Megan, and she watched in terror as Holt lurched into a sitting position, his gasps punctuating the darkness that surrounded them. Instantly, Megan got to her knees, hesitantly reaching out and touching him.

"Sam, Sam, it's all right, it's all right. You're having a bad dream." He was trembling, and Megan's fear increased. Holt buried his face in his hands with a groan. Glancing over at the clock, she saw it was 3 A.M. "My God, you're soaked with sweat," she murmured worriedly, moving her hand across his taut arm and shoulder. "Sam? Are you okay?"

His heart wouldn't steady in his chest. It felt like someone was pounding a kettle drum inside him. The nightmare still flashed across the lids of his closed eyes. The terrible G-forces were pulling at him, a trap that could kill him. Worst of all, he could hear Russ's scream in his ears. The blackness of the night surrounded them in that cockpit, heightening his terror.

Megan got up, moving around the end of the bed. Sam sat there shaking badly, the blanket pooled around his waist. Alarmed, she turned on a light in the bathroom, came back, and sat down next to him. Gently, she laid one hand on his drawn-up knees, the other on his right arm. A very old, frightening memory surfaced within Megan. She recalled her father had had punishing nightmares for months on end when she was twelve. His voice would caterwaul off the bedroom walls. She remembered waking up in her room, frightened, not knowing why her father was screaming like that.

"Oh, Sam," she whispered, caressing his damp hair, "it's all right. You're safe, do you hear me? Safe." She rested her cheek against his knees, the trembling that gripped him beginning to abate. Softly, she repeated the litany over and over, not knowing what else to do.

Holt felt Megan's touch on his hair, neck, and shoulder. The fear in his gut was going away sooner than it normally did. Lifting his head, he slid his hand forward across her shoulder, the cool, smooth cotton of her gown pulling him back to reality. Megan was real. Megan was here, with him. He released a ragged sigh and watched her lift her head.

"I'm okay," he said thickly.

"You were having a nightmare."

"Yes . . ." He clung to her shadowed features, her green eyes compassionate, the line of her lips mirroring the pain he felt. That unruly red hair of hers was a lovely frame, emphasizing her honest beauty. A compelling need to love Megan, to bury himself into something good and positive, overwhelmed him.

Before Megan could ask him more about the nightmare, she saw the remnants of it leave his haunted eyes. The smoldering look that replaced it sent her heart skittering and made her tremble with anticipation. Sam laid her down beside him.

"You're so beautiful," he uttered softly, running his fingers through her hair. The light was suffused, and revealed the full length of the white cotton gown she wore. It was like her, Sam thought as he released the first satin bow from her shoulder, sliding his hand beneath it. There was something so good and clean about Megan. The second satin bow fell away, and he eased the gown away, revealing her lovely breasts, torso, and hips.

A sigh escaped Megan's lips as she felt him remove the gown from her. The intensity of his gaze, that predator look that excited her, heightened as he caressed her rounded belly. The thought that she wanted to bear his children seared through her. The predator look disappeared from Sam's sweaty features. In it's place was a warmth, a silent invitation that made her lift her arms and slide them around his neck.

She wasn't disappointed as he leaned down, his mouth capturing hers, swift, hot, and sharing. A moan rose in her throat as he cupped her breast and moved his thumb across the hardening nipple. He left her lips, his mouth settling on its peak, and Megan arched against his strong body.

There was an urgency to his hands, mouth, and body. Her world spun crazily, tilted, and she was swept up in his demand to have her quickly. Sensing his urgency, vaguely aware that she represented reality as opposed to the terror of his dream that had mercilessly stalked him, Megan matched his drive, more than ready to receive him, to celebrate her love for him within herself.

The taste of his salty flesh aroused her senses. His breath mingled hotly with her own as he moved on top of her. They were both trembling, and she opened her thighs to receive him. The instant he thrust deeply into her, she gasped, but it was one of surprised pleasure, not discomfort. Her world blended and melted into a cauldron of heat. The rhythm was wild, starving, and frantic. Exalting in his male strength, joined and equaled to her own feminine demands, Megan cried out as the heat deep within her exploded, spreading pleasure throughout her. As she felt the dizziness strike her, it made her feel floating and joyous. Sam groaned, tensing, gripping her hard, and released within her.

Smiling weakly, Megan lay there in the aftermath and savored his weight upon her. He buried his face in her hair, his breath punctuated against her neck and breast. It was several minutes before she could speak. His hand moved in a caress across her cheek, and she turned, kissing it.

"Fantastic," Sam murmured. "You're something else, lady. Something else . . ."

Bereft when Holt moved off her, Megan was content when he brought her into his arms after he rolled over on his back. Megan liked the way their damp bodies molded perfectly to one another. She placed her arm across his chest, her hand coming to rest on his shoulder.

"So are you," she said faintly.

Sam opened his eyes, and stared up at the shadowy canopy above them. Worried, he stroked her shoulder and felt the firm pliancy of her flesh beneath his fingers. "I'm sorry, Megan. I shouldn't have been in such a hell of a hurry."

With a shake of her head, she answered his unspoken question. "I enjoyed it just as much as you did."

"Seven days apart kind of takes the civilized veneer off us, doesn't it?" he commented wryly, satisfied that Megan hadn't been hurt by his urgency. Miraculously, the nightmare wasn't as potent as it usually was in the aftermath of waking. No, Megan's sweet body, her fire, had burned some of it out of him.

Megan lifted herself up on one elbow. Sam's hair was mussed, making him appear boyish. Moving her fingers across his brow, she whispered, "I like what we are together." The smoldering cobalt heat in his eyes made her feel shaky all over again. And when he reached over, placing his hand against her belly, she had to stop herself from speaking. The words, *I love you,* were there, begging to be said.

"I like your belly," Holt admitted huskily, running his hand gently across it. "Soft, rounded, filled with promise." Looking up into her eyes that were lustrous with unshed tears, he wanted to say: "You'd make one hell of a mother. The mother of *our* children. Made out of the love we hold for one another." But he didn't. Instead, Holt gently eased Megan on her back, leaned down and kissed her there. Then, he laid his head on her belly. He wrapped his arms around her long, slender legs, and allowed contentment to wash over him.

"All week," he confided to her quietly, staring off into the darkness, "I thought about you. I'd catch two or three hours of sleep over at the Bachelor Officers' Quarters between design sessions, and I'd dream of you, of being here.''

Megan caressed his hair, a sharp ache centering within her. Sam had the ability to share, to make her a part of his life and world. She managed a laugh. ''I think my children thought I was daydreaming all the time.'' And then, softly, ''I like the fact you can share with me what's in your head, your heart.''

A wry smile crossed his mouth, and he lifted his head, kissing her belly gently. ''Red, you're the most important thing in my life. Why shouldn't I share with you how I feel?''

Old memories swam before her. ''My father never did it with my mother or myself. I—I guess I expected the same of you.'' She felt Sam squeeze her legs in an embrace meant to take away the memories.

''Old ways die hard,'' Holt agreed. ''But as long as we talk, we'll be fine.''

Megan began to feel a delicious drowsiness overtake her. All she wanted to do now was sleep in Sam's arms and look forward to waking up with him in the morning. ''What about that dream that woke you, Sam?''

His mouth twitched. He wouldn't lie to her. ''It's an old nightmare. Nothing to worry about.'' Moving, he got up and came back to her side, and pulled the covers over them. When he saw the concern in Megan's eyes over his explanation, he added, ''There isn't a pilot alive that hasn't ejected and gotten bad dreams about it.''

Convinced, Megan smiled and settled into Sam's awaiting arms, head nestled against his shoulder. He was warm and strong, giving her happiness that she had never known could exist. ''Good night, Sam.''

He kissed her hair, smiling gently. ''I'll see you in the morning, Red.'' *I love you.*

''Well,'' Sam goaded, holding out his gift to Megan, ''go on. Open it.'' He sat next to the tree, crosslegged. A cup of coffee was balanced on one knee. They had just finished a breakfast of bacon, eggs, and toast. For the holiday season, he wore a pair of jeans and a light-blue chamois shirt with the sleeves rolled up to his elbows. The clock on the mantel read 9 A.M. A perfect time to open Christmas gifts in Sam's opinion.

As Megan took the small box wrapped in red foil paper and a gold ribbon, she felt heat in her cheeks. "Oh, Sam, you didn't have to get me anything. I knew you were out of town all last week."

Sipping his coffee, he smiled. "I got this for you a long time before that." How beautiful she was, dressed in the long, dark-green velvet robe, her red hair a vivid contrast, and cheeks flushed the color of a pink rose. When Sam awoke this morning, he knew he had heaven in his arms. Their morning had been nothing but simmering happiness.

Megan sat down opposite him, arranging her voluminous gown so she could cross her legs. "I'm so excited," she confided, tugging at the gold ribbon. "This has been such a wonderful morning." The steamy shower they'd shared together earlier had been exquisite and molten.

Sam leaned forward, kissing her cheek. "I've liked it," he told her huskily. When she lifted her chin and met his gaze, he added, "A lot." *Forever.*

With a nervous laugh, Megan could hardly wait to find out what was inside the box. "I'm like a kid, Sam Holt," she warned him, and tried to be ladylike about removing the wrapping.

"I like Megan Roberts the kid." And then his grin deepened. "Why don't you tear into that thing and rip it open? I can see you hate doing it the slow way."

Her laughter was rich and husky. "How could you possibly know that?"

He matched her joyous laughter with his own. Ruffling her hair playfully, he said, "Ladies with red hair are *always* precocious little girls at heart. Didn't you know that?"

Megan sobered slightly and studied the unopened gift. "No . . . I didn't know that."

Sam slid his finger beneath her chin and forced her to

meet his gaze. "I *like* helping you discover parts of yourself
that have always been there, sweetheart. It's like watching a
rose bloom before me, one beautiful petal at a time."

Shaken, she threw her arms around him. "Oh, Sam . . ."

*I love you, Megan. God, I love you so much I ache
inside.* Kissing her cheek, Sam whispered, "I hope you see
me the same way: that's what a relationship is all about, the
discovery, the sharing. And it never stops. It can last a
lifetime, if you want." Megan pulled away, and he was
afraid he'd said too much. There was confusion in her
forest-green eyes, but the happiness was still there. "My
mom and dad have been married almost forty years. She
said she's still learning something new about my dad every
day." He took a stray curl near her temple and placed it
behind her ear. "Kind of nice, isn't it?"

Touched, Megan nodded, staring at the gift in her hands.
"Your experience, your family, is so different than what
mine was like."

"Thank God," Holt said, meaning it. He cupped her
cheek, absorbing her vulnerability that was a natural part of
her beauty. "If we can trust one another, we can have the
same thing my parents have. It doesn't have to be the other
way. You know that, don't you?"

Compressing her lips, Megan mustered a smile. "I'm
beginning to realize that, Sam."

He sighed and pressed a kiss to her lips to erase the
sadness he heard in her voice. "It's going to take time, but
we've got that. Now, open that package. I've got to see if
you like it or not."

Giggling, Megan tore it apart—just like a child. It felt
good to be spontaneous, to have Sam's belief and support in
her. Pushing the wrapping and ribbon aside, she peeked
inside the white jewelry box. A gasp escaped Megan. A
delicate oval brooch made from jet, a popular stone in the
Victorian era, stared back at her. On the brooch was carved
a great blue heron standing next to a lake. Surrounding the
brooch was an intricate gold filigree. It was breathtaking.

"Well?" Sam goaded, delighted with her reaction, absorbing the surprise and pleasure in her forest-colored eyes.

Fingers trembling, Megan touched the brooch. "T-this is the most beautiful piece of Victorian jewelry I've ever seen!"

"The best news is: it's yours."

Megan stole a look up at him. Never had Sam looked so handsome, his smile male and provocative. It made him look so young and incredibly desirable. "The cost . . ." It was real gold, the carving exquisite, without a flaw.

"You were worth it."

Megan drowned in his tender blue gaze. "Thank you," she whispered.

"You know, you're like that blue heron," Sam said, cradling her hand between his. "On weekends my dad always took us fishing. There's plenty of lakes around Detroit. I was always fascinated with the great blue herons. They were huge: six feet tall with a seven-foot wing spread." Sam smiled fondly. "Actually, they're responsible for getting me to think about flying as a career. They were so graceful and huge in the sky. I spent hours watching them instead of fishing. They gave me a calmness, a kind of internal strength. A heron never gets flustered or out of control. She moves serenely, not causing any disturbance to the water she's wading in." He looked into Megan's eyes. "You're the same for me. You have that same quiet strength that stabilizes me when I'm feeling out of sorts or ready to blow after a bad day."

Touched, Megan squeezed his hand. "I like being compared to the heron."

"Ever see one?"

"No."

It hurt not to say, *When I take you home to meet my family, I'll take you to that lake and we'll sit and watch them for hours—together.* Holt rankled impatiently beneath the strictures he'd placed upon himself for Megan's benefit. But it was necessary. He had to gain her trust in him as a man so that she would overlook his pilot image. That took time. More time than he wanted to give her. "We'll see one together, someday," he said.

Megan reached under the tree for her gift to him. "Here, it's your turn!" Excitedly, she sat there, waiting for him to open it. It was a huge, rectangular box that weighed quite a bit, wrapped in bright red paper with a white velvet ribbon and a sprig of fresh mistletoe.

Delighted, Sam tore into the package. "In case I didn't tell you, I'm a kid when it comes to gifts, too. My mother always liked to save the paper and ribbon for the next time around, but she never got mine."

Holding the brooch in her hands, Megan laughed and watched paper fly right and left. Her heart pounded briefly as Sam settled the box on his lap and lifted the lid. Would he like her gift? She held her breath.

Sam murmured a sound of pleasure as he pulled off the crinkly green tissue paper revealing a set of Victorian hardwood and brass bellows. They were mounted on a brass wheel, to make pumping them easy. "Where did you *ever* get this?" he asked, completely stunned. "I contacted Sotheby's in England trying to get bellows for my fireplace years ago. They *never* had them."

Overjoyed, Megan smiled. "When I got my pair five years ago, which, by the way, isn't as fancy as your pair, I bought a second pair. I knew how rare and hard to find they were."

"Incredible," Sam murmured, running his fingers across the polished, reddish-colored handles.

"That's rosewood."

With a shake of his head, Sam looked over at her. Rosewood was a rare and highly sought-after wood in the antique world. "Hell of a gift, Red. Thanks."

"Not that you needed any more hot air than you already possess as a jet jock," Megan added dryly.

Chuckling, Holt agreed. "We do have that reputation, don't we?" He put the gift aside, reaching over, capturing her in his arms. Megan came without a struggle, flowing into his embrace, head resting against his shoulder. With a sigh, he held her tightly against him. "This is all I really want or need,'' he admitted huskily. She smelled of her spicy perfume fragrance, her skin warm against his mouth as he kissed her brow, cheek, and finally, her awaiting lips that parted eagerly to allow him entrance. No one could have had a better Christmas.

As Megan remained snuggled in his arms, the Christmas music unobtrusive, Holt wondered how Curt and Becky were getting along. He hurt for the family, and hoped that today, of all days, there might be some joy shared among them.

Curt stared out the living room window, hands behind his back, a parade rest stance. Behind him, he could hear Patty's excited voice and Becky's laughter. Turning, Curt studied them. They sat on the floor with four different kinds of colorful clay spread between them on some newspapers. Becky had given the clay to Patty as her Christmas gift.

Becky was dressed in a floor-length cotton dress of pale pink. The red satin ribbon around her waist complemented the color of her cheeks. His heart expanded with love for her when he heard her breathy laughter. She molded a duck out of the clay. His daughter was still in her red bathrobe and little Snoopy slippers, her pale blond hair caught up in a haphazard ponytail.

Struck by the fact that both his wife and daughter looked like two ageless children playing, entertaining themselves, Curt suddenly felt left out. Older. Becky's eyes danced with such life as Patty made her own duck, albeit a poor copy of hers. Becky clapped her hands, reached over, and kissed Patty soundly, rewarding her first effort.

So many firsts, Curt thought, feeling depressed. Becky had already taken Polaroid shots of Patty opening her gifts. All for the album, she'd told Curt excitedly. He'd bought Patty state-of-the-art toys. Toys, the manager of the store in Lancaster had assured him, that Patty would play with for hours. This morning, surrounded with all those modern gifts, Patty had eagerly opened Becky's only gift: the clay. She had been playing with it for the last hour, ignoring all the other gifts.

Rubbing his brow, Merrill turned toward the window, an ache seizing him. It centered in his chest, and he absently rubbed his hand across that area. Becky was far more in touch with what her daughter loved to play with, than him. Patty was already seven years old. He couldn't remember that many special times he'd shared with Patty growing up—because he hadn't been around to be a part of them. Becky always showed him the photos when he got home from flight duty, TDY, or alert status: The first time she uttered her first word. The first time she crawled. He wasn't even here when Patty had taken her first, tottering steps.

Scowling, Curt winced inwardly as their laughter continued to hurt him. It wasn't their fault. Letting his hands drop back to his side, he stood and watched them. Becky was now making up a story about a mama duck who had lost her baby ducks. Patty was enthralled. So was he. There was so much purity and honesty in Becky. Darkly, Curt admitted parts of himself had been sublimated by the Air Force. It stamped unwanted facets of personality out of the pilots and remolded them into something the military wanted, instead.

And his honesty? He said what the Air Force wanted him to say. He behaved as the Air Force demanded. Curt wanted to kneel down and join his wife and daughter. How long had it been since he'd played with clay? He couldn't remember. Becky was completely spontaneous, and so was his daughter. Longing to recapture that elusive, perhaps destroyed part of himself, Merrill sighed.

Of course, not *all* Air Force pilots felt like he did. Or did they? Maybe they did and just never said anything about it. Maybe family life wasn't the main priority in their life, but just a secondary extension of their career aims. Pilots didn't share much of their personal or emotional side with anyone. Not even with their wives. His mind revolved forward and he stared down Sharon Drive. On the corner sat the Stang residence. Their home was gaily decorated for the Christmas season, even though it was 70 degrees and the sun shone brightly across the desert. Did Jack ever feel as if he'd lost something by not being around his family often enough?

"Now, for the greatest gift of all," Melody announced, approaching her husband. Scotty was playing with his new Nintendo video on the television, completely absorbed in his gift. For once, he was sitting still, in one place, for more than five minutes. Melody was grateful. Jack sat in the leather wing chair, several opened gifts around his feet. He looked very appealing to her, dressed in a pair of cream-colored wool slacks, a dark-green cable-knit sweater, and brown loafers.

"Another present?" Jack teased, grinning. Melody wore a brilliant red silk caftan, hand painted with pink, white, and orchid-colored hibiscus. She had taken great pains with her black hair that was coiffed to perfection, and her makeup only emphasized her stunning beauty. The smile on her lips, the joy in her eyes, made him tighten with desire.

"The last and best one," Melody said breathlessly, kneeling in front of him. "Open it. It's your future."

Stymied, Jack carefully opened the small gift, setting the white ribbon and green foil paper aside. Giving her a teasing look, he held the box in his hand. "What do you mean: my future?"

Leaning upward, Melody pressed a quick, hot kiss to his mouth. "Open it and find out, my love."

Excitement thrummed through him as he lifted the lid. His eyes widened. "My major's leaves!"

Clapping her hands with delight, Melody sat back on her heels. "Do you like them? Aren't they beautiful? Oh, Jack, I couldn't wait! I *know* you're going to get promoted in February, and I just wanted to pin them on you now, just to see what you look like with them on!"

Caught up in her enthusiasm, Jack picked up the two gold, round oak leaves. He ran his thumbs across them in a reverent motion. "Nice, aren't they?" There was a wistfulness in his voice.

"*You're* nice. Now, come on, stand up! I want to pin

them on you. I have to get practice doing this, so that in February, when you're standing in front of the entire base for the ceremony, I don't drop one and embarrass both of us."

Grinning, Jack stood, handing her the oak leaves. "What? Pin them on my sweater?"

"Of course! Don't you want to see how they'll look?"

"Sure."

"Ten-hut!"

Stang snapped to attention, just as they had taught him at the Air Force Academy. His broad shoulders were thrown back, rigid and proud. Melody smiled proudly, and delicately pinned the first rank on his left shoulder, and pretended that there was an epaulet there.

"You already look more handsome," she said admiringly, moving to his right shoulder.

"Wench," he teased, remaining at attention.

"There!" Melody stepped back, her hands clasped. "You look splendid! How handsome you'll be, Major Stang." Gripping his hand, she dragged him down the hall to their bedroom. Coaxing him in front of the floor-length mirror, Melody stood proudly beside him. "Look," she breathed, "how *wonderful* you are! Never has there been a major like you, darling."

Jack stared at the gold oak leaves. "They do look good, don't they?"

"Good? They look *great!*"

Turning, he swept Melody into his arms, ready to kiss her laughter-touched lips; Jack hesitated and moved over to the door, closed and locked it.

"Just in case," Jack told her, and crushed Melody against him.

Giggling, Melody lightly touched the leaf on his left shoulder. "I've never made love to a major before . . ."

"No?" Jack gently removed her earring and nibbled on her earlobe. He felt her respond and press herself against him. The fullness of her breasts, firm and ripe, made him go hot with longing.

''No,'' she sighed. Capturing his mouth, Melody kissed him hungrily. ''Love me?''

Hesitating fractionally, Jack nodded. Scotty was completely involved in his computer video. His son would be glued to the set for a little while. They'd make love quickly, with intensity and passion. Grinning, Jack swept his wife up into his arms and carried her to their king-sized bed.

''Now you're going to find out what it's like to be loved by a major,'' he promised her thickly, lying down beside her. Her smile, filled with pride and love, went straight to his pounding heart. Jack had never had such a wonderful Christmas. Ever.

— 17 —

MEGAN girded herself for warfare the day after school began in early January. She'd received a call from Brad Jamison to meet him over at the principal's office for an urgent meeting. With the help of the union, she had pushed to get Scotty Stang tested regardless of Jamison's threat to fire her. Getting out of her car that blustery, cool morning, she walked quickly into the school. The children were due to arrive by bus in about twenty minutes. She saw a number of teachers wandering around in the halls, gearing up for their charges.

Heart pumping with fear, Megan walked down the hall toward the principal's office, the light on inside the office. Jamison was waiting like a wolf for her. She felt like a quarry. Her mind ranged over possibilities. Last month, after Linda Yarnell, the union president, had told her that admin was balking on the Scotty Stang issue, she had placed a call to General Dalton.

There wasn't anywhere on Edwards that Dalton's influence and power didn't touch. Not even a school board. Megan hadn't mentioned the name or the problem she was facing to Dalton. She asked, instead, that if he had time, could he look into the matter—that she needed his guidance and input on it. Megan knew it wasn't wise to point fingers or name names. No, if Dalton decided to get involved, he'd do it.

Rubbing her damp hands against her tan raincoat, Megan slowed as she approached the office. Contacting General Dalton was as risky to her as it might be to admin. If Dalton sided with Jamison and the school board, she would be fired. It was that simple. Playing high stakes politics with the base commander wasn't something to be done every day. In the Air Force, when one officer owed another a favor, it was called a *chip*. The bigger the favor, the bigger the chip. Powerful favors were referred to as blue chips. Megan had called in a blue chip in her father's name to get Dalton to investigate her problem with Jamison. Had Dalton gotten involved? If so, what was his decision? And how was it going to affect her job status?

Brad Jamison was standing behind the counter dressed in a dark pinstripe suit. He scowled as Megan entered the door.

"We've got business to discuss," he growled at her. "Come into my office."

Megan kept her coat on and went around the counter. Jamison was upset. Something had happened. She couldn't read his features to decide whether it was for or against her. Nervously, she swallowed, outwardly showing a calm she didn't feel. Closing the door behind her, she sat down in the leather chair facing his massive oak desk.

Steepling his fingers, Jamison reared back in his chair, studying her for some moments, the silence taut. "I underestimated you, Ms. Roberts."

"Really?"

Jamison grinned slightly. "There's an old axiom: let sleeping dogs lie. I think it applies to you, in this case."

Stymied, Megan sat there. She knew that Jamison was deliberately baiting her.

Scowling, Brad eased forward and took a file folder, sliding it across the desk toward her. "Two things, Ms. Roberts. First of all, your request to have Scotty Stang tested for hyperactivity has been approved. Secondly, I'm approving your outdoor education proposal. The principal will come back with his decision in late January. At that time, you'll be notified.''

Elated, but not daring to show it, Megan took the file and opened it. Jamison seemed subdued, but she now understood why. Obviously, General Dalton had investigated both matters and backed her on them. Jamison was enough of a political animal to know he didn't dare dispute Dalton's decision, putting his own career in possible jeopardy.

"Thank you, Mr. Jamison." According to the file, Scotty Stang was to be tested immediately, and the results of the doctor's diagnosis had to be reported within the next two weeks.

Jamison smiled slightly, appraising her with new respect. "I hope, Ms. Roberts, that in the future, we can work more amicably on any problems you might encounter."

Rising, Megan tucked the file under her arm. She wanted to jump up and down for joy. Soberly, she nodded. "I have every desire to work within the structure of my union and admin if possible, Mr. Jamison."

"I'm glad to hear that."

She could afford to be generous in victory. "Thanks for your help on these matters." Megan turned, jubilant. Scotty Stang would finally get the help he needed. How would the Stangs receive the dictate? Jack worked with Sam. Would he try and take it out on Sam?

The first thing Holt did when he got into Ops was hunt down Jack Stang. He'd taken leave up until the first day of school in early January. Sam hadn't forgotten what Stang had said and done to Megan at the Christmas party, and he was intent on pursuing the matter as soon as possible. He'd purposely arrived early in hopes that the captain would be there. Entering Design, he found Jack at his desk. The place was deserted. Good.

Sauntering over to his desk, Holt said, "We've got some serious matters to discuss, Jack. I'd have done it a lot earlier, but you've been out of town since Christmas."

Lifting his head from his work, Stang reared back in his

chair, a lazy smile on his mouth. "Palm Springs is a nice place to spend the holidays with my family, Holt." Melody's parents had a winter home at the posh resort. "Now, what's on your mind?"

Placing his hands flat on Stang's desk, Holt leaned forward, his voice low and menacing. "The Christmas party I couldn't attend because I was TDY in Maryland at the time. You *ever* mention Megan Roberts's father to her in that tone and fashion again, you'll be answering to me, Stang. You copy that? And I didn't like that fact your wife was hinting that Lauren and I were having an affair, either."

Carelessly, Stang rocked back in his chair, his hands behind his head. "Is that what Megan told you?" He laughed. "That little lady's stretching the truth—"

With a hiss, Holt's hand snaked out. He gripped Stang by the collar of his light-blue shirt, jerking him forward. Their faces were inches apart. "Don't pull that shit on me, Stang. I know you too well." His fingers tightened on the material, and Holt smiled lethally as Stang's eyes went wide. Stang hadn't expected him to get physical. "I believe Megan's version of what went down. There were witnesses to that little tête-à-tête you had with her. Read me loud and clear on this, buddy: I'm on your six about this. I *ever* catch you talking about Megan in a derogatory way again, I'll have your ass. Understand?"

Lips lifting away from his teeth, Jack gripped Holt's wrist. "You sonofabitch, don't you threaten me or my wife!"

Holt had the better leverage. With both hands, he hauled Stang forward, off balance. "Go ahead," he breathed savagely, "take a swing, Stang . . ."

Stang hung across his desk, several items clattering to the floor. He was up for early major. He wasn't going to lose it in a stupid brawl with Holt. And certainly not over Megan Roberts. "Let go," he ordered harshly.

Holt shoved him backward, releasing his hold on Stang. The captain slammed back into his chair, nearly losing his balance. Straightening, Holt stood there, glaring down at him.

"You copy, Stang?"

"I copy," he growled tensely.

Holt turned away and headed back to his desk, breathing unevenly. If anyone had caught them fighting, it would have been bad for their fitness reports, which were coming up soon. Sam didn't care. Defending Megan was a hell of a lot more important than getting his damned major's leaves early. He was going to protect her against people like Stang and his vicious wife.

For nearly an hour, they worked at their separate desks, the silence overwhelming. At 0800, Stang's phone rang.

"Design," he snapped.

"Jack?"

"Melody, what's wrong?" She was upset.

"I—I just got a call from Jamison. Jack, the school *and* union are demanding that Scotty be tested immediately for hyperactivity."

"What?" He jerked a glance in Holt's direction. The pilot glanced up, and then immediately went back to work. "What?" he whispered, keeping his voice low so Holt couldn't hear the conversation. It didn't matter, Holt got up and left Design, leaving him alone.

"Yes. Jamison said Megan Roberts went to General Dalton! Oh, God, Jack, she went to Dalton!"

"That *bitch*!" he cried hoarsely.

"We underestimated her, Jack. She's Colonel Roberts's daughter. She has clout here at Edwards, and she used it against us."

His fingers tightened until the knuckles were white around the phone. "Christ, my major's leaves! My early promotion! What's this going to do to it?"

"There's nothing we can do, Jack. Nothing! Dalton now knows about Scotty's problems. The only thing we can do to salvage ourselves and your standing with him is to get Scotty tested. I've already called Dr. Alphonse Simmons in

Los Angeles. He's agreed to look at Scotty tomorrow morning.''

Furious over his blunder with Megan Roberts, Jack rubbed his brow. "Yeah . . . that's fine. Take him down. Why don't you leave now?''

"I've called my parents, and they're expecting Scotty and me. Jack, I'm sorry.''

"There's nothing we can do now. We're outgunned. All we can do is implement damage control and hope like hell it hasn't affected my status for early promotion.''

"It won't,'' Melody said. "I'm just sick about this, darling. Sick.''

No more than he was. Jack hung up a moment later. He sat at his desk, fuming. His day had gone from bad to worse. Did Holt know about Megan's machinations with the general? The bastard probably did, wanting to be here when Melody got the word. Closing his fist, Stang ached to smash in Holt's face. An entire day stretched ahead of him. In two weeks, Lauren was going to deliver her final decision on the brilliant test idea he'd come up with. If she approved the test results, he still stood in good with Design, and Dalton wouldn't take his early promotion away from him because of Scotty's screw-up.

"I'm afraid,'' Lauren Porter said with regret to the men surrounding the oval table, "that the engine redesign isn't a complete success for short field landings.''

Stang, who had been leaning back in his leather chair, snapped upright, his jaw hanging. "What?''

Porter's eyes narrowed. "I said: the engine redesign isn't the *total* answer, Captain Stang.''

Holt moved uncomfortably in his chair. Weeks earlier Megan had filled him in on her fight to get Scotty Stang tested. The child was diagnosed as hyperactive and was now on drugs to calm him down. When she told him of General Dalton's influence to bring the problem to a swift conclusion, he flinched inwardly, knowing that Stang would be a bear at work. Not only that, but Stang had been barely able to conceal his hatred of him because he was going with Megan.

Holt sat down at one end of the table, a good view of Stang and Lauren, who were only two chairs apart. The mid-January sunlight filtered strongly through the blinds and lent a radiance to the Design meeting room that no one felt.

"But," Jack sputtered indignantly, "I *know* it'll work!" What was going down? Had Dalton's opinion of him, based on his son's need to be on drugs and well-publicized behavior at school affected Lauren's decision? Stang had no doubt that Megan Roberts's interference was partially responsible for the flight engineer's decision. Why else would she do it?

Fingers tightening around the pencil in her right hand, Lauren glared at Stang. "Captain, the flight engineers, both military and civilian," she emphasized, "have given the *Agile Eagle* every possible chance to show it can land consistently at fifteen hundred feet. It doesn't."

Angrily, Stang stood up, shoving the chair away. "Well, I disagree." He began to pace the length of the rectangular room that was littered with charts and blueprints.

Sam tensed, watching Lauren's set features. No one was happy about the situation. Especially Lauren, because it was her project, and it was not only behind schedule, but nothing seemed to work consistently in slowing down the F-15 sufficiently for a short landing sequence.

"Look, Jack," said Roy Holding, McDonnell's civilian chief design engineer on the F-15, "we've tried everything. But when the winds are wrong, the bird can't make the grade. Your idea was a good one, Jack, but it's not the complete answer," he stressed in a mild voice, trying to ease the building tension.

With a snort, Jack threw his hands on his hips and glared at all of them. His hatred soared as he fixed his gaze on Porter. *She* was the other reason why his idea hadn't worked. Grinding his teeth, he snarled, "If certain flight engineers would ease up on the ratios, the *Agile Eagle would* have a ninety-five percentile short landing record. And that's good enough.''

Sam sucked in a breath, watching Lauren. He had to give the major credit: she wasn't flying off the handle like Stang was. But then, Stang's baby had just been shot down. He'd been relying on the engine design to guarantee his major's promotion coming up shortly, and also to get the vaunted B-2 slot.

"Captain, sit down," Lauren ordered in a tight voice.

Jack's nostrils flared, his fingers digging into his hips. The urge to punch her in the face was very real. The snobby bitch! Everyone in Design was watching him. With a muttered curse he stalked back to his chair, jerked it out away from the table, and sat down. Breathing hard, he leaned forward, nailing Porter.

"Major, I strongly disagree with the parameters you've set up for the tests with the new engine design. If you'd ease those restrictions, we'd get a ninety-five percent across the board."

"Put it in writing, Captain," she said in a steely tone, "and I'll take it directly to General Dalton."

Grabbing a pencil, Stang leaned back in his chair, and refused to say anything. That confirmed to him that Dalton was in on this. Seething with fury, Jack wanted to cry out in pure frustration.

Holt slowly released his breath. This confrontation between Stang and Port had been building for a long time. He applauded her control and good judgment. Stang wasn't going to put anything down on a report. If he was wrong about her use of ratios, it could make him look foolish, or worse, possibly stupid. It wouldn't look good on his fitness report, or help him get another choice slot as a test pilot. Lauren was a damn good flight engineer and knew her stuff. She'd tried every conceivable way to give the *Agile Eagle* a chance to land consistently at fifteen hundred feet. Under certain wind conditions, it wouldn't. She refused to put her signature on the design change, approve it, and tell General Dalton that they'd solved the problem when the tests weren't proving it out.

Idly, he'd been drawing on a white pad of paper in front of him on the table. Unconsciously, he'd drawn the nose and canopy section of the F-15. Holt frowned and looked more closely at his doodles. A light flashed in his brain, and he grabbed the pad. His heart started a slow pound, excitement thrumming through him as he studied it.

"Port . . ." he called hesitantly.

"Yes?" Her voice was brittle.

Sam slid the pad down in her direction. "What if we put movable canards on the nose of the F-15? You know, we use them on the B-1 bomber to slow it down enough to keep it out of a stall position for short takeoffs and landings." He leaned forward, hands clasped on the table. "Hell, yes! Our whole problem has been trying *not* to stall the F-15 by raising its nose too high to create that condition. Those canards might prevent the normal stall angle in the bird. It might give us a few degrees upward, automatically slowing it down so we *could* consistently hit the mark."

"You're full of it," Stang ranted, and stood up. "Holt, you're really reaching! Most fighters don't have canards. Just the bombers."

"Sit down, Jack," Lauren snapped. She looked at Holt's drawing, and then glanced over at her civilian counterpart across the table. "Roy?"

The gray-haired engineer shrugged his rounded shoulders. "It's provocative, Lauren."

"Feasible?" she pressed.

With a grimace, Roy rubbed his jaw, thinking. Design grew silent. The kind of silence that was fragile, at a breaking point.

Stang squirmed in his chair. He glowered at Holt in disbelief. "Canards! It won't work," he muttered defiantly. "You might get the F-15 on the mark, but what will it do to the fighter's performance? Are you going to trade air combat superiority for a short landing? Holt, your idea isn't going to make it."

Sam let Stang's acid comments slough off him. "You got any *better* ideas?"

"Dammit," Jack growled, slamming his fist down on the

table, getting everyone's attention, "I *know* that bird can hit the mark at fifteen hundred feet right now! It's winter, and the winds are choppy and multidirectional. We've been testing under difficult circumstances at best. All we need is more testing, more—"

"Captain, you're way out of line," Lauren grated. "The testing is *finished* on the redesigned engine. It was a good idea, but not a complete one. Now, I suggest you either join us in investigating the canard idea, or take a walk and cool down."

Frustration exploded through Jack. He sat there, looking at everyone. Shoving the chair away, he snarled, "I'm going for a cup of coffee."

Holt watched the test pilot stalk out of the room. The tension dissolved after he shut the door more loudly than necessary. With the promotion list due out sometime in the first week in February, Stang was increasingly jumpy. He wanted his major's leaves so bad he could taste them. So did Sam. But would he, or any of them, get early promotion?

"Hey!" an airman called from the door of Design, "the promotion list was just posted out on the bulletin board down the hall."

Holt froze at his desk. It was late Friday afternoon, and he was getting ready to pick Megan up after school. Stang reacted first, striding toward the door. Merrill slowly got up, as if not wanting to see the results. Hands growing damp, Sam forced himself to finish putting the reports he'd read over the weekend into his briefcase.

"Aren't you going to look, Sam?" Lauren inquired from her desk.

He grinned carelessly. "Sooner or later."

"My, what confidence," she teased.

"No . . . not really. More like unadulterated fear I *didn't* make it."

Porter smiled. "You're something else, Holt."

Sam saw Curt getting ready to leave. "Come on, we'll go down together," Sam told him with a smile.

Managing a pained grimace, Merrill picked up his bulging briefcase and put on his garrison cap. "Misery loves company. Yeah, I'm ready to call it a day."

Holt walked out into the hall. There weren't many captains going up for early promotion, so the list was going to be a short one. Up ahead, on the left, he saw six officers craning forward, looking around one another, to see if they'd made it. Sam had been too busy working with Lauren and the civilian design engineers on the canard idea to think about possible promotion.

Holt's walk was slow because he dreaded looking at the list. Without a doubt, Stang had made it. He didn't think Curt would. Himself? It was a real tossup. The crash one month after arriving at Edwards probably signed his death warrant insofar as getting an early promotion. There were two cries of jubilation. Three more officers turned away, sour looks on their faces.

Just as Sam approached, he saw Stang whirl toward them. His face was livid, eyes burning with anger.

"You're the only one that made it of the three of us," he rasped, and deliberately brushed Holt's shoulder as he passed him.

Stunned, Holt jerked to a halt, assimilating Stang's angry statement. Merrill moved around him and checked the list closely.

"Dammit," Curt cursed, clenching his fist. "Dammit to hell." And then, he caught himself, flushed, and offered his hand to Holt. "Congratulations, Sam. You made it first time around."

In shock, Holt gripped Merrill's proffered hand. "Thanks . . ."

"Well, I've got to get home. See you Monday."

Blinking, Sam nodded. "Yeah, Monday." Had he really made early major? Everyone else had left, and he was alone in the hall to look at the paper. Only three names appeared. His was the last one. Shaking his head, he stood there a good five minutes, hardly able to believe his good fortune. It meant a real shot at the B-2 project coming up.

"Congratulations, Sam."

He glanced to his left. Lauren walked up, a set of huge, rolled-up blueprints under one arm and a huge briefcase in the other. She had her work cut out for her this weekend. "You knew?"

"For a long time. I wanted to tell you, but it wouldn't have been fair to the others."

Nodding, Sam understood. "I can't believe it. At least, not yet."

Laughing softly, Lauren murmured, "You will soon enough. All it really means is more responsibility heaped on your shoulders. A chance to screw up sooner, quicker, and better than everyone else if something goes wrong. And your head's the first on the chopping block sooner and on there longer than anyone else's, too. Some reward, huh?"

That was the reality of the situation. "I'll take my chances with it," Holt said, joining her laughter.

Looking significantly both ways, Lauren said in a low voice, "I wish I could have been out here when Stang found out he crashed and burned."

"Jack wasn't very happy."

Lauren pursed her lips. "That's the last time that bastard manipulates my people, and my project. He's like a lethal, subtle poison infecting everyone. He and his wife. I can't demote her, but I can sure as hell tie his hands and contain him. Maybe he'll learn a lesson from this."

Holt said nothing. He knew Lauren had a great deal to do with their fitness report ratings because she was their boss. "Maybe he'll get the message and start squaring his act away."

With a snort, Lauren moved past him. "Don't count on it. I'm sure for the next month he'll pout like a little boy who thinks he's had his favorite toy taken away from him. See you on Monday."

"Right." Sam glanced at the paper one more time, as if to convince himself his promotion was real. Elation leaked through him, and then it became a flood of dizzying joy. He'd really made it! The door to his career as a test pilot had nowhere to go but up—unless he had a crash or some other major screw-up.

Turning, he went back down the hall and headed for the side parking lot. Mind spinning with possibilities, dreams, and happiness, Sam floated down the concrete stairs to the black asphalt. Around him, the air was chilly, in the fifties, and the sky cloudy. Still, the sun shone strongly, but not warmly. Placing his briefcase behind the seat of his Corvette, he climbed in. Some of his elation was tempered by Megan's reaction to his news. He started up the sports car, the engine growling contentedly. What *would* she think? As he guided the car out of the parking lot, his happiness waned, deluged by cold, harsh reality.

Trying to wrestle with his emotions over the promotion, the joy, and the terror, Sam drove more slowly than usual over to the elementary school at the end of the base. Since Christmas, his relationship with Megan had been steadier, more hopeful. They did take it one day at a time. Since his nightmare at her apartment, Sam avoided staying overnight with her, unconsciously wanting to avoid a talk about Russ, or the crash. When they were together, it was great. But every time he left late at night, he saw the confusion and question in Megan's eyes. He was giving her mixed signals, and he knew it. Afraid to tell her about his fear of dying because it might impact the fragile trust he'd established with Megan, Sam felt trapped.

Much of his joy was left behind in a backwash. Megan had been brutally honest with him about everything. He hadn't been. With a grimace, Holt pulled into the school and spotted Megan waiting for him at the front doors. The wind was blowing, her red hair tousled. The tan raincoat hid most of her, but the orange blouse and khaki-colored slacks beneath it did nothing but emphasize how beautiful she was in his eyes.

Holt got out, opening the door for her. They had made a promise not to show their feelings in public for many reasons. Once in the car, driving toward the front gate, Megan leaned and kissed his cheek.

"It's all over base. Did you make early promotion to

major?'' Megan saw his mouth purse slightly. A part of her prayed he hadn't, but another part, did.

"Three of us made it," he said, squeezing her hand gently. "Curt and Stang didn't." Glancing over at her, he worried about her reaction.

"Congratulations."

Sam studied her. Megan's face was clear, her eyes flecked with gold. "You mean that?"

A slight smiled pulled at her mouth. "Why are you concerned about what I think or feel regarding the promotion?"

"Because you're important to me."

She laid her head on the black leather rest. "My father never asked my mother or I if we cared. But then, I'm finding you *do* care. So, what was your reaction when you first saw the list?"

"When I saw my name on it, I got excited, and then I felt like somebody gut-punched me," Sam admitted slowly. At the gate, the Air Police sentry snapped to attention, saluting and waving them through. Once past the gate, he devoted his attention to Megan, his stomach tight with tension.

"Fear?" she prodded.

"I thought the promotion might scare you, or make you run from me."

His brutal honesty affected her deeply. Megan sighed. "The part of me that remembers my past is scared to death, Sam." She leaned over, resting her head on his broad shoulder. "The other part of me is so proud of you. I know what this means: the B-2 assignment, and ongoing testing as soon as the *Agile Eagle* is completed."

Mouth dry, words came hard to Sam. "What are your feelings about that?"

"On some nights, after you've left, I can't sleep."

"Seems to be a part of our lifestyle, doesn't it?"

She heard the anguish in his tone. "There's a lot of things that make up for that, though," Megan added softly, sliding her hand across the olive-green fabric covering his taut thigh. "I like your thoughtfulness toward me, your sensitivity. There aren't many men who can express what they feel and think, and I like sharing that with you."

Some of the tension began to drain from Sam. "Like the nights we make popcorn in the fireplace while I squeeze those bellows to make the flames nice and high?"

Megan laughed. "Yes, all those things, too, darling."

"You're such a kid," Sam teased, genuinely beginning to feel the elation of the promotion because Megan was cautiously optimistic about it.

"Look who's talking."

With a hearty laugh, Sam nodded. "Shot down again." Megan was an incredibly sensitive woman, the passion they shared made from a rich texture woven with love, even if neither of them would admit it to one another. Sam *knew* she must love him, but he didn't know how much or how little. He loved her unequivocally.

Gently, Megan pushed her fears and her apprehension aside. Sam had made major, and he deserved to celebrate his good fortune. "Tonight, I'm taking *you* out to dinner, Major Holt, to celebrate your promotion."

Pleased, Holt slid his arm around her shoulders and crushed her momentarily against him. "You can take me to dinner, but we'll have dessert at my home."

Heat flowed through Megan, sweet and beckoning as she rested against him. Sam's confidence in himself, in their future together, always awed her. At first, there were more days where Megan feared that their relationship would never work or even survive. Now, nearly three months later, Megan had swung to the opposite opinion. There were more days where she felt sure that what they shared, was love, and that it could work if they continued to tend and cultivate it with care. Closing her eyes, she murmured, "I know it's not right, but I'd sure like to have dessert before dinner. What do you think?"

Pleasure sang through Sam. "Anytime I can have you in my arms, in or out of bed, is all I want."

"I love the idea, Major." The thrill of being in Sam's arms, making hungry, passionate love with him, was always wonderful. It wouldn't be a happy night at the Merrill or Stang homes, however. Megan wondered what it was going to be like at the Stang residence tonight. It could hardly be a celebration.

Jack held on to his anguish as he entered his home. Melody met him at the door, obviously hearing that the promotion list had come out. There was anticipation in her eyes, and he felt shamed that he'd failed her—and himself. Dressed in a long-sleeved white silk blouse, burgundy and gold scarf, and black wool pants, she looked stunning. Melody slid her hand around his arm as he closed the door. He was shaking inside, and clenched his fists to stop from screaming, crying, or both.

"The list," Melody said breathlessly, "did you make it?" Melody looked up, her smile disappearing.

"Where's Scotty?" Jack ground out, halting in the middle of the living room to search for his son. What he had to say wasn't meant for his young ears. Further, he didn't want Scotty to see him like this, almost out of control.

Melody hesitated. "Uh, he's still at school. Remember? There was a slide show on the San Diego Zoo, and then the children were going to have dinner at the cafeteria." She glanced at her watch. "He'll be home in an hour."

Some of Jack's control disintegrated, and he closed his eyes. A scream tried to lurch out of his constricted throat. Mired in grief, he heard Melody's stabilizing voice.

"Jack, what is it? My God, you look terrible. The promotion?"

Anguish soared through him as he opened his eyes and looked down at her lovely face. "I—" and he choked. With a helpless shrug, he forced the words out. "The promotion list came out today. I wasn't on it . . ."

Melody's hands flew to her lips, but the cry got past her. She took a step back, her eyes flooding with tears. "Oh, no! Oh, Jack . . ."

Breathing hard, letting the words, the feelings tumble out of him, he rasped, "It was those two bitches, Roberts and Porter. They did me in. I just know it! Christ, if they were men, I'd beat the hell out of them! Roberts zeroed in on our son, making a big deal out of nothing. Porter's had it in for me ever since I was assigned to this project.'' His vision blurred, and he spun around. Tears! Of all the damned things!

With a muffled cry, Melody threw her arms around Jack's neck and held him tightly. ''I'm so sorry, so sorry, honey,'' she cried, tears streaming down her cheeks. ''This has never happened before! You made early lieutenant and captain. There was no *reason* not to get early major!''

Clinging to her, Jack buried his face in her hair, a sob tearing from deep within him. He crushed Melody hard against him and fought the reaction. Test pilots didn't cry. They didn't show emotions. But Melody's softened weeping only spurred the reaction in him. For the next five minutes, Jack surrendered to the need to cry out his frustration and anger.

Tearfully, Melody eased out of his arms and led him to the couch. She brought a box of Kleenex over, setting it between them. Blotting his cheeks with one, she whispered, ''Tell me what happened. Who else made it?''

Miserably, Jack told her everything. Melody's surprise over Holt making it confirmed his own suspicions. Angrily rubbing his face dry of the tears, he muttered, ''Porter has *always* liked Holt! She's always favored him. And the bastard crashed! He crashed! And he still got early promotion. Dammit, I've done everything right, *right*, and I get nothing!''

Gripping his hand, Melody sat there thinking. ''Holt's got one powerful sponsor, then,'' she said quietly.

''Where the hell was mine when this all came down?'' Jack grated. ''I know I've got one. Or did he desert me over this fiasco with Scotty?'' Once a sponsor left, Jack knew he had no one to back his career. It was a dire sign; something he refused to acknowledge—yet.

''Get a copy of your fitness report, Jack. That's the first thing to do. Let's find out if Porter is playing favorites.''

''I know she is,'' he ground out, glaring out across the living room.

''See what she wrote on your report. If it's vague, you

can fight it!'' Her voice rose a notch with hope. ''Honey, we can fight it. Together.''

He held her tear-filled gaze. It hurt to disappoint Melody. ''We've worked so hard for this. I feel like I've let you down.''

Caressing Jack's cheek, Melody shook her head. ''I don't feel let down. I feel like we've been stabbed in the back.''

''By Porter.'' Taking a deep breath, he added, ''She halted testing on my engine redesign idea.''

''*What*?'' Melody stood up, her eyes huge. ''She *what*?''

''Yeah, that's what I said. I had a hell of a fight this afternoon in a Design meeting with her about continued testing, but she said no.'' Jack shook his head. ''And then that bastard Holt came up with a stupid idea about using canards on the nose to give the bird more lift and keep it out of stall position longer.''

Rubbing her brow, Melody began to pace. ''What a horrible day, Jack, a horrible day. We've got to do something to stop it.''

He snorted, his eyes slits. ''Don't worry, I intend to do something about it, Melody. I've got a plan. I'm not letting that bitch stop me! I'm going to prove her and Holt wrong.''

Delighted, Melody sat back down, placing her arm around his shoulders. ''A plan?'' she said hopefully.

''Yes. First, I've got to do my homework. I'll get ahold of Merrill on Sunday morning. Porter sandbagged him too. I'm sure he'll want to throw in with my plan.''

''Jack, give him time to talk to Becky. He's got to be as upset as you are,'' she counseled swiftly. ''While I make us dinner, you fill me in on this plan. Right now, two heads are better than one.''

Leaning wearily against Melody's shoulder, Jack closed his eyes, needing to be held for just a minute. Melody wrapped her arms around him and pressed a small kiss on his brow. ''Okay,'' he uttered tiredly, ''I'll wait. I'll hit him with it Sunday morning.''

Melody gently rocked him in her arms. "I'm sure Becky's overjoyed Curt didn't make major."

Becky heard the front door open and close. She quickly put the lid back on the dumplings she was in the process of making and peeked out the kitchen. Curt looked tired and disappointed. He dropped his briefcase on the couch, along with his dark-blue garrison cap.

"Ya'll look tired," she greeted, walking over to him and giving him a hello kiss.

Curt barely returned the kiss and embraced Becky because he needed her strength. "I didn't make it, Sparrow."

"What?" Becky tilted her head upward. Curt looked as if he'd been kicked in the head, or worse. What had gone on today? "Oh . . . oh, dear, the promotion list!" Her hand tightened on the sleeve of his flight suit.

He couldn't even be angry with her because she'd forgotten. Curt held her startled expression. "I didn't get early promotion. Holt did, but Stang and I didn't."

Relief shattered through Becky, and she murmured, "Lordy." She felt Curt's arms tighten around her, and she embraced him long and hard, realizing how disappointed he was. Resting her head against his chest, she asked softly, "What does this mean?"

Running his hand up and down her small back, Curt sagged. "Bad news for me, Sparrow. When the *Agile Eagle* is completed, I'll probably get orders to test pilot school to be an instructor or"—he swallowed hard—"get put back into a fighter squadron."

Becky stood there, not believing the words she'd prayed to hear for so long. Curt would stop being a test pilot shortly. He'd stop risking his life on a daily basis. When he had flown the F-15 as a fighter pilot, she had been able to cope with that stress far better than this kind. She released the shaky sigh.

"I'm sorry, darlin', I truly am." Becky hoped she didn't sound insincere. She loved Curt too much to do that to him.

Holding her for a long moment, Curt absorbed her small

feminine form. He needed her kind of strength right now, because he felt the world was crumbling around him. "I don't want to go back to just flying. I like testing. I'm good at it. If only they'd give me another chance . . . if only . . ." And then, he asked in anguish, "What's my father going to think? How am I going to face him? The family?"

Becky held her husband tightly, her knuckles white, fingers dug into her palms as she pressed him against herself. She prayed for the opposite: that they'd release him to active duty flying. She didn't care where, just as long as it was away from Edwards, and the threat of him augering in at least once a week.

"If they truly love you, Curt, they'll understand and support ya'll—no matter what your assignment is."

"My father's going to hit the ceiling when I tell him."

"Wait a few days," Becky advised. "You'll feel better and be able to handle his disappointment." Eventually, Becky released him and led him into the kitchen. Curt sat down at the table and she poured him a cup of coffee. Only then did she return to making the dumplings.

Curt sat there, glumly staring off into space, not touching the fragrant coffee. Ordinarily, when he came home, always starved, he looked forward to the smells coming out of the kitchen. He had no appetite tonight.

"I imagine Sam was happy," Becky pointed out, lifting out the dumplings one at a time from the huge pot of boiling water and into a nearby bowl.

"Yeah, he was." Curt grimaced. "I wish there was some way to prove myself, to prove I can fly as good as he and Stang. I know I can. I've just had lousy luck, lousy weather conditions. Damn."

"It's bad luck," she agreed softly. Compressing her lips, Becky smoothed out her blue and white checked cotton apron across her pink slacks. Today, she had worn a red blouse. Red, her mother had always told her, gave one strength. Funny, how she knew to wear it. Becky didn't even want to think how she'd have felt if Curt *had* gotten his major's leaves. That would've meant at least three more years at Edwards, testing.

Gripping the mug of coffee, Curt whispered, "I *can't* go back to a squadron. God, I'll die there, not after having it all. Not after testing. It'll be boring." He got up, wandering into the living room.

Becky craned her neck, unable to leave the dumplings that were at a critical stage of being cooked in the hot water. Worriedly, she prayed there was no way for Curt to stay at Edwards. It could be a matter of weeks, perhaps a month before the *Agile Eagle* testing was completed. She could hold on for that long, she knew. Just a little while longer . . .

— 18 —

"LOOK, dammit," Jack said to Curt, "my plan *can* work!" He glanced at his watch. "It's 0530. Get into your flight suit, and we'll drive down to Ops. Major Porter is out of town for the weekend, but she approved the test."

Curt rubbed his face. He stood in the middle of the living room, still clad in his cotton pajamas. "Jack, you said you got clearance to take the *Agile Eagle* up?"

"Yes!" Jack said impatiently, I need a back seat. You can double as the flight engineer on this test." He thrust a group of papers under his nose. "I worked fourteen hours Saturday devising a new and *better* test. All we've got to do is fly it! You call out the numbers, and I'll put that baby on the fifteen-hundred-foot mark every time." Jack gestured out the window. "Winds aren't calm, either. They're from the direction that gave us so much trouble before. Porter's test demands were too strict. This time," he said, tapping the papers Curt held, "we'll make those test results stick."

Warily, Curt looked over his shoulder. Becky had awakened when Jack had rang the doorbell earlier. The bedroom door was ajar. Had she gone back to sleep, or was she listening? "But will Major Porter *accept* your flight test even if the bird makes the marker?"

"Hell, yes!" Jack rasped violently. "We'll have *proof* that the bird can do it! There's no way she can dispute success. She'll *have* to take our numbers. Then, we can wrap this project up." Gripping Curt by the shoulder, Jack said, "You want your major's leaves early, don't you?"

"Yes."

Throwing his hands on his hips, Jack gave him a triumphant look. "When we come back after *successfully* flying this test I devised, believe me, we can challenge our fitness reports that Porter wrote up on us. We can challenge them and win! Think of it! You'll be a major!"

Curt heard movement behind him. Becky was up. She'd heard. Gripping Jack's shoulder, he motioned him toward the door. "My wife's up. Since you've got authorization to fly, I'll meet you outside in about ten minutes."

Stang grinned. "You won't regret it, Curt." Excitement rose in his voice as he opened the door and stepped outside. "Hurry."

"Yeah." Curt shut the door and turned. Becky stood in the hall, dressed in her pale-yellow chenille robe. Girding himself, he walked up to her. Her face was pale, eyes huge with terror.

"You heard?" he asked, keeping his voice down so his daughter wouldn't awaken.

"Y-yes. Curt, it's Sunday morning! You never fly on Sunday!" Becky's voice was high, off key.

Curt walked into the bedroom. He opened one drawer and drew out a fresh flight suit. "Jack's got authorization, Sparrow." Slipping out of his pajamas, he pulled on a pair of briefs, T-shirt, and then the flight suit, pressing the velcro shut.

"Lordy, Curt," she cried softly, coming around the bed, "you *can't* fly! Not today!"

"Sparrow," he whispered, cradling her shoulders, "it's going to be fine, I promise you. Jack says this is a way to get our major's leaves. He worked all day yesterday outlining a test for the *Eagle* that will place it at the fifteen-hundred-foot mark every time. If we can fly that now, it will get us noticed.''

''No!'' Becky wailed, huge tears forming and streaking down her face. ''No, Curt! Ya'll can't do this! I don't feel good about it!'' and she placed her fist against her stomach.

Frantically, Curt looked toward the door. Time was getting away from him. ''Hush, you'll wake Patty!''

''I don't care!'' Becky sobbed, clutching the front of his flight suit. ''Curt, this isn't good! No one flies a test on a Sunday! I don't believe Stang! I don't think Major Porter knows about it!''

Leaning down, he kissed her wrinkled brow. Gently he disengaged. ''Sparrow, you're upset. Everything will be all right. Trust me. It's only an hour-long flight. I'll be home before you know it.''

''*Curt!*'' she shrieked as he walked toward the door.

Jerking to a halt, he faced her. ''Dammit, Becky, it's going to be okay! Go back to bed!''

Heart pounding so hard that she could barely breathe or speak, Becky fell to the bed. ''Don't go, don't go . . .''

Torn, Curt stood poised at the door, Becky's sobs tearing through him. Flexing his hands into fists, he turned and walked down the hall in long, quick strides. Becky's cries filled his ears. He couldn't stand to hear her cry. Opening the front door, he left.

Becky heard the door shut and reached for the phone. Her hand shook so badly that she had to dial Sam Holt's home number twice before she connected.

The phone rang, and rang, and rang. Holt muttered, pulling his arm from beneath Megan's head, and rolled over on his side. What the hell time was it? 0545. Who was calling this early on a Sunday morning? Fumbling, Sam lifted the receiver.

''Hello . . .''

''Sam, oh, Sam! This is Becky. Somethin' terrible's about to happen!''

Blinking, Sam sat up in bed, the covers falling away,

piling around his waist. The grayness of dawn filtered into the huge bedroom through the pale orchid curtains. Beside him, Megan stirred. "Becky, what's wrong? You're crying." She spoke in short bursts, punctuated with sobs.

Megan forced her eyes open, hearing Sam's lowered voice. As soon as she heard it was Becky, she sat up. Pushing her hair away from her face, Megan could hear Becky's distraught voice coming over the phone.

"Wait," Sam begged. "Let me get this straight: Stang says he's got approval to fly that bird this morning? Lauren's out of town. How could she have signed the flight orders?"

"Ohhh, Sam, I know it sounds fishy! Please, get down to Ops. Stop them! Stop Curt from flying! I feel awful about this!"

"Just a minute, Becky." Sam slid a glance over at Megan. He put his hand across the phone. "Get me a flight suit out of the third drawer on the right?"

Nodding, Megan slipped out of bed, the pale-pink silk gown falling around her ankles. Worried, she listened to the conversation, her heartbeat picking up. Something was wrong. Stang and Curt were involved. She laid the one-piece flight suit on the bed and then went to the bathroom.

"Yes, I'll get down there as soon as I can, Becky, but it's a good half-hour drive to Edwards. Why don't you meet me down at Ops? Yes, take Patty over to a neighbor, and then meet me there. Wait at the front doors, and I can get you a visitor's pass when I arrive. I'll check with the flight scheduling office and see if Stang's telling the truth. Now, calm down. Get ahold of yourself. You aren't going to do anyone any good by staying hysterical."

Megan emerged from the bathroom just as Sam hung up. "What's going on?" she asked huskily, watching him strip out of the drawstring pajama bottoms and climb into his flight suit.

"I don't know," Sam answered grimly, filling her in on the details of the conversation while he dressed. Grabbing a pair of flight boots from the closet, he sat down on the bed. "If I know Stang, he's lied about flight approval clearance.

Curt's swallowed it. If they take that bird up without Lauren's okay, all hell's going to break loose. They'll both be in so much hot water, it'll make their heads spin."

Megan scowled. "And Becky's going to meet you at Ops?"

"Yeah." He quickly shoved on the black socks, and then put on the boots, lacing them up.

"Then I'm coming along."

Sam raised his head, was going to say something, but thought better of it. "Look, I know Ops isn't your favorite place, Red. You don't have to go."

She reached into another drawer where she kept lingerie. "Becky's going to need the support, Sam."

"All right, hurry."

Hands shaking, Megan quickly slipped into a pair of dark-green slacks and a warm, ivory cowl-neck sweater. Running a brush through her thick hair, she slid her feet into a pair of low-heeled shoes. Sam stood at the door, waiting for her. "God, I'm scared, Sam."

"I know, honey." Holding out his hand, she gripped it. Her fingers were damp and cool. "Come on, we've got some driving to do."

As they raced through the house toward the garage, Megan asked in a taut voice, "Do you think you can stop them, Sam?"

"I don't know. They'll be in the air by the time we get there. The test flight won't last more than an hour. I'm going more for Becky's sake, than to try and order them out of the air. This is Lauren's territory to handle, not mine."

Megan felt the reassuring strength of his hand around hers. His words didn't remove the ugly feeling surrounding her. "Hurry," she whispered, "hurry."

Ops was deserted when Holt drove up to the long, yellow stucco building. Becky stood out front, her composure shredded. The dark-blue wool coat made her look frail. Hearing the growl of the *Eagle's* thundering engines, Holt looked up. He immediately recognized the test bird in the dogleg portion of the flight pattern.

"Oh, Sam!" Becky cried, running down the concrete steps toward his car.

Holt climbed out of the Corvette and embraced Becky momentarily. "It's going to be okay," he reassured her. Looking over, he guided her into Megan's awaiting arms.

"Take it easy," Megan begged her, gaze fixed on the fighter. The early Sunday morning air shook and vibrated with the sound of the thundering engines. Mouth dry, Megan felt her own fears vomit up through her. Becky trembled in her arms as she led her into Ops.

Holt opened the door for them, and Megan led her through the entrance. The tiled floors were highly polished, the visitors' lounge filled with plastic chairs facing the floor-to-ceiling windows that looked out across the tarmac and airstrip. Sam went directly to the flight counter, an airman immediately leaping to his feet from behind the desk. First, he'd get them visitor's passes.

"Come on," she entreated Becky gently, "let's go sit down."

"He's gonna crash," Becky moaned, burying her head against Megan's chest, "I know he's gonna crash. Oh, Lordy."

Biting down on her lower lip, Megan got Becky to a chair before she collapsed. Deeply worried, Megan crouched down next to Becky's bent form in the chair and tried to soothe the distraught woman. Glancing up, she saw Holt walking toward them, his face set and grim.

"What did you find out?" Megan quavered. She took the two passes he handed to her.

Sam leaned down, placing a steadying hand on Becky's shoulder. "The flight's not authorized," he said heavily. "I don't know what possessed Stang to pull a stunt like this."

"What can ya'll do?"

"Nothing. Wait until they land, and then I'll report the incident to Major Porter Monday morning."

The brutal, pounding reverberation of the jet landing, and

then taking off again, drowned out their conversation. Agitated, Holt got to his feet. "Stay with Becky," he told Megan, "I'm going to go outside and try to figure out what they're doing."

"No!" Becky cried, struggling to stand, "I'm coming too!"

Megan placed her arm around Becky.

"All right," Holt said. He led them outside to watch the takeoffs and landings. The *Eagle* flashed by, gaining altitude, the air punctuated with her growl. Angry at Stang, disheartened by Curt's willingness or stupidity in going along with him, Holt stood there helplessly, watching the bird rise into the morning air. Both pilots' careers were in jeopardy because of what they'd done. He felt nothing but sadness.

"Next test," Jack demanded tightly, a feeling of exhilaration flooding him. Thus far, the *Agile Eagle* had hit the fifteen-hundred-foot mark five out of five times. The bird felt solid under his hands and booted feet. He listened to Merrill's instructions.

"Wind's are getting erratic," Curt cautioned, looking around. To his surprise, he saw Becky, Sam Holt, and Megan Roberts standing out on the steps of Ops. A lump formed in his throat. Had Becky called Sam and Megan for support? He felt anger at first, and then, shame. What would it do to Becky to watch this test? Make her worse? Better? Curt wasn't sure, a bad taste in his mouth.

"Coming around!" Jack whooped triumphantly. "Get ready to nail that fifteen-hundred mark!" He began to ease the bird from the mandatory twelve-hundred-foot level, coming in for a landing. The winds were tricky, sometimes strong, sometimes nonexistent. Setting flaps and slats at one hundred percent, Stang knew in order to make this set of tests, he had to pull the bird in nose-high, and just this side of stall position.

Merrill began reading out the altitude, feeling the jet quiver. Inwardly, he tensed as Stang pulled the nose extremely high. "Jack," he warned, "you're too high, you're going to stall out—"

At that moment, an unexpected gust of wind struck the *Eagle*. The nose reared upward. The stall warning sounded harshly through the cabin. Merrill tensed. Stang cursed. Hands and feet moving in a blur of speed, Stang tried to stop the jet from falling out of the sky. They were eight hundred feet above the ground. Damn!

The *Eagle* became sluggish, even though the nose was pointed down once again. Stang couldn't get control of the fighter. Merrill cried out, "*Eject, eject, eject!*" The fighter was now at four-hundred feet, falling like a rock toward the earth.

The seconds before Merrill wrapped his gloved hands around the handles of his seat to trip off the ejection sequence, he thought of Becky, and his daughter, Patty. The canopy popped off the *Eagle*, tumbling end over end away from the jet. In the next second, he triggered the seat, and the rockets ignited. It jerked Merrill out of the cockpit. The world spun crazily around him, the powerful thrust of the rockets jamming him savagely down into the seat. Would he be far enough away from the crash site? Would fire envelop him? Burn him alive? Would his parachute open at all? Or would he tumble out of the sky, only to hit the ground and be killed?

Those thoughts ripped through him as the rockets carried him away from the falling jet. Becky! God, he loved her! And Patty! And then, Merrill's entire life, from beginning to end, flashed across his tightly shut eyes.

Becky shrieked, her fists jammed against her mouth as the first seat ejected from the out-of-control aircraft.

Megan's lips parted as she saw the jet flair and tip drunkenly in the air. She clutched Becky to her. Everything was in slow motion, or so it seemed. Holt had given a cry first, a cry of *no*! As the nose of the F-15 suddenly tipped upward they had all watched as the jet began falling belly first toward the runway.

All Megan's fears played out before her widened eyes.

Holt had moved quickly, running back inside, yelling at the airman to alert Crash immediately. He'd pulled open the doors and watched helplessly as the jet continued to fall out of control. The second ejection occurred only seconds before the jet smashed into the ground.

Holt threw his arms around both women, shielding them with his body. Although the crash occurred at the end of the runway, the explosions sent thunderous repercussions across the entire base. Becky clung to him. Megan buried her head against his shoulder, tense and mute.

The jet struck the lip of the runway, bursting into a huge rolling ball of red and orange flame, the fire shooting hundreds of feet in all directions. The explosions that followed boomed savagely across the airstrip, striking Ops, the windows rattling and shaking violently.

Megan lifted her head and watched as the JP-4 fuel spread out like hungry, fiery fingers from the crash. Huge, roiling black clouds laced with red and orange welts of fire vomited upward. To Megan's horror, she saw the second ejection seat begin to tumble toward the ground, the parachute streaming, not opening.

"Sam!" she cried, pointing to it.

Holt stood frozen, watching the second ejection seat tumble slowly, end over end, toward the earth. Nausea overcame him. Chance of the pilot, probably Stang, surviving, was nearly impossible. He'd ejected at four hundred feet. Far too low. The chute wouldn't have time to open properly. Twisting his head to one side, Holt couldn't watch the impact. Megan sobbed and buried herself against his chest.

The forlorn wail of the sirens spread thinly across the airstrip, barely heard above the roar of the fire. Holt looked up as the gargantuan lime-green trucks speeded toward the fiery holocaust, the men covered in hooded, silver asbestos suits.

"Curt..." Becky shrieked, trying to tear loose from Holt's grip.

"No!" he breathed harshly, pulling Becky back against

him. "No, there's nothing we can do, Becky. You have to stay here."

"But," she wailed, "they're out there! Oh, my God! They're out there!"

A quarter of a mile away, Holt thought in anguish. He saw the first ejection seat gently strike the earth, the parachute bringing it to a safe landing. The second ejection seat had struck the earth with full impact, hidden somewhere behind the huge, rolling clouds of greasy black smoke and red tongues of flame. Who had lived? Who had died?

"I want to go to Curt!" Becky sobbed, leaning heavily against Holt.

Tears jammed into Megan's eyes as she kept a grip on Becky's arm. "No," she whispered, "no, we can't do anything. We have to wait . . . wait . . ."

Never had Holt felt so powerless. He had witnessed what the tragedy had taken from Becky, her cries like a child in the middle of a nightmare. Morose, his gaze moved to Megan. Her eyes were dark with pain, mouth compressed, and her cheeks glistening with tears. At that moment, Sam realized the awful toll that flying extracted from the women who loved the pilots.

"Come on," he told them, his voice unsteady, "let's get over to the hospital. The flight surgeon and ambulance will be taking them over there." Every fiber of him wanted to run down the runway and skirt the crash to get to the pilots. Already, the ambulance was close on the heels of the crash trucks. He placed his hands on the women's shoulders and moved them away from the inferno. Tears watered dangerously in Holt's eyes. There was absolutely nothing they could do to help. Only the asbestos-suited firemen could get near the crash, hosing it down with foam. And only after the fire was extinguished could they get close enough to the pilots to find out if they were dead or alive.

Inside, Ops had jumped to life with personnel on weekend duty, running frantically to their emergency crash stations. Holt stopped at the counter.

"Airman, call Captain Stang's wife. Tell her that her

husband's been in a crash and to meet us over at the hospital.''

The airman nodded, shaken. "Y-yes, sir."

Holt took the Merrills' large, roomy car and drove it over to the hospital. Becky sat curled up in the back seat, sobbing quietly. When he looked over at Megan, he slid his hand across her tightly knotted ones in her lap.

"I'm sorry," he croaked.

Taking in a shaky breath, Megan shook her head. "It's not your fault, Sam."

His hand tightened on hers. Fear that she would run, fear that she would leave Edwards after this, haunted Sam. Megan's voice had been shredded with shock and anguish. There was nothing he could do but hope and pray—for all of them. The hospital loomed in front of them, and he speeded up.

Megan remained at Becky's side in the waiting room. They sat on the plastic couch, Becky huddled in her arms. Fortunately, Becky had had the foresight to take Patty next door to be cared for before she went to Ops. At least the little girl was being spared the agony of waiting...wondering. The Emergency Room area swarmed with doctors and nurses who tensely awaited the arrival of the ambulance bearing the two pilots. Her arm around Becky, Megan was numb. Holt paced relentlessly to and from the nurses' station, awaiting the expected arrival of Melody Stang.

Shutting her eyes momentarily, Megan wondered if either pilot had survived the crash. If so, who? She wrestled with very real feelings that it could have been Sam. Right now, she had to be strong for Becky. And for Sam. He was worried about her; she could see it reflected in his shadowed eyes. What she thought about the crash, and the effect it might have on their relationship was probably running through his mind.

E.R. personnel suddenly disappeared from the halls and moved through the doors marked: OFF LIMITS. Becky stopped crying, clinging to Megan, and waited. Hearing muted shouts and calls through the doors, Holt froze in the empty hall. The pilots had arrived—or what was left of them.

what was left of them. Doctor Anna Cartwright had E.R. duty. Dragging in a deep breath, Sam forced himself to move to the visitors' lounge.

He saw Megan's tense features, her eyes huge, revealing all of her feelings. Sam ached for her, for himself. The crash would forever change their relationship. It had to bring back memories of her father's crash and death. And it brought home the fact that he could possibly die the same way. Rubbing his face tiredly, Sam tried to push his personal feelings aside and focus on Becky. If Curt was dead, she was going to need support and help. His gut knotted hard, and tears jammed into his eyes. *Curt dead. God, don't let it be. Don't . . .* Until that moment, Sam had been worried and aware of everyone else's feelings except his own.

The thought that Curt might already be dead, or lying in there dying just a few feet away, shook him to his soul. Curt was like a brother to him. Sam assimilated the possibility that he was dead, grief spilling through him.

Megan saw Sam draw to a halt just outside the lounge. His face had turned ashen, and his mouth stretched in what she was sure was a sob. Sam's reaction made a lasting impact on her. The death of a pilot affected not only the family, but other pilots, too. It was a galvanizing revelation, something she'd not realized before. But now was not the time or place to discuss it.

Melody Stang's entrance into the hospital riveted their attention. Megan saw the woman run up to the nurses' desk, her appearance startling. It was only 0630 in the morning, and Melody wasn't wearing any makeup. Her hair, normally coiffed to perfection, hung in uncombed strands around her shoulders. She had thrown on a gray sweatshirt, jeans, and white sneakers, a far cry from the elegant picture she normally presented to the world. The change was frightening to Megan. No woman was immune to the threat of her husband being killed or injured in a crash—not even poised, unflappable Melody.

Holt went to the desk and gripped Melody's arm.

"They've just arrived," he told her in a low voice, "and

we probably won't know anything for at least an hour. Come and sit down with us.''

Melody hesitated, looking at the head nurse, who nodded somberly. ''I—oh, God, Sam, what happened? What happened?'' Tears ran from her eyes.

Holt told her everything, and when he finished, Melody uttered a small sound. But, she caught herself and straightened, lifting her chin. To Sam, it was an amazing act of courage under the circumstances. Becky was a basket case. Melody seemed to be able to reach down and find some internal courage. She walked without assistance into the visitors' lounge and murmured greetings to the other two women.

Sam sat down with Melody. He offered to get her coffee, but she refused, and sat there tensely. Heaviness cloaked the room. He glanced over at Megan, finding instant peace as he looked into her green eyes. Managing a slight smile, he wanted to tell her just how damn much he loved her, how much she meant to him. And then, Sam wondered if she felt the same thing, or was contemplating running away from Edwards and all the ghosts that had come to rest on her shoulders this morning. Miserably, Sam wouldn't blame her if she did. How many people witnessed a jet augering in? Or the possibility of two people dying in the crash?

His gaze moved to Becky. She was curled up under Megan's arm, head resting on her shoulder, eyes closed. Trying to swallow past the lump in his throat, Sam bowed his head, his hands clasped between his thighs. Now he understood as never before, what the women went through. God, it was hell. Pure hell.

Megan looked up at the wall clock. Only fifteen minutes had passed. She started to speak to Melody, but the woman avoided eye contact. *Brittle* was the word Megan would assign to Melody right now. But weren't they all? Melody internalized her fears and anguish. Becky had externalized them. And her? Hungrily, she absorbed Sam's figure, his head bent, hands clasped, as he stared down at the tiled floor. Sam was safe, alive, and here, unlike the pilots in

E.R. She prayed endlessly, wanting Curt and Jack to be alive, to be able to see their children's faces, and to hold their wives once again.

Becky saw Dr. Anna Cartwright appear first. She unraveled from her hunched position and straightened as the doctor quietly entered the visitors' lounge over an hour later. The woman's face was grim as she approached Becky first.

"Curt?" Her voice cracked as the doctor halted in front of her.

Reaching down, Anna gripped Becky's shoulder. "Your husband is going to be fine," she said. "He's suffered a broken ankle and some back compression, Mrs. Merrill." With a slight smile, she added, "They're taking him to room 110 right now. He's conscious, but I've given him a tranquilizer to halt the effects of shock from the crash. You can see him in about fifteen minutes."

With a little cry, Becky clutched the doctor's hand. "Thank you, Doctor. Oh, thank you!"

"You're welcome." Cartwright turned, moving across the room to Melody. "Mrs. Stang?"

Melody stared up at her and held herself rigid. "Yes, Doctor?"

"Captain Stang is in critical condition."

Holt put his hand on Melody's arm. She paled and began to tremble.

"Critical?" Melody quavered.

"Yes. He's suffered a severe spinal injury, and is unconscious. We're taking more tests right now to find out exactly what's wrong. I'm sorry . . ."

Sam gripped Melody's hand. She sat there staring up at the doctor, and blinked slowly, as if not believing the pronouncement.

"His chute didn't open," Sam told Melody gently. "It was a four-hundred-foot fall."

Dr. Cartwright touched Melody's shoulder. "Mrs. Stang, he's alive. To survive a fall from that altitude is a miracle in itself."

Melody's movements were robotlike. Pulling a handkerchief from her purse, she pressed it against her eyes. Her voice was hoarse. "Yes, of course . . . Jack's unconscious. What does that mean?"

"I don't know yet. We're taking more Xrays."

"Well . . . is he in a coma?"

"It's too early to tell, Mrs. Stang." Anna tried to smile, but failed. "Just as soon as we can, we'll let you see him. The tests are going to take at least another hour."

"Y-yes, I understand. Critical?"

"Yes."

"C-could he . . . I mean . . . die?"

"No one knows. The next twenty-four hours are the most critical."

Frowning, Melody sat there. "I have to call Jack's parents. They must know. A-and my parents. Jack has several aunts and uncles that must be notified."

"Let me help."

Melody turned her head slowly, in a daze.

Megan mustered a slight smile. "I'll help you, Melody. We'll do this together."

"Thank you."

Holt wanted to take Megan into his arms and kiss her, praise her for her courage under the circumstances. Melody was in shock, there was no doubt. He would be, too. Megan didn't have to do this, didn't have to help make those gut-wrenching phone calls. He loved her courage, tears driving into his eyes. Fighting them back, Sam stood.

"Is Scotty with the neighbors?" he asked Melody hoarsely.

"Yes. Could you call Captain Waverly and his wife?"

"Sure," Sam assured her quietly. "I'll make sure they—"

"Don't tell Scotty what happened," Melody ordered, her voice strident.

"Of course not," Sam soothed. Melody was beginning to unravel. He hesitated, torn between staying to help Megan with Melody, or make the phone call.

"Sam?"

He lifted his head, holding Megan's gaze. "Yes?"

"Reassure Scotty that everything's all right. Tell him that

his mother will call him in about an hour. I'll stay with Melody.''

Grateful that Megan was thinking clearly for all of them, Sam turned. As he left the lounge, he saw a nurse come and get Becky to escort her down the hall. Releasing a shaky breath, Sam headed for the telephone located near the nurses' station. At least Curt was going to make it.

Curt raised his head from the pillow when Becky entered the hospital room. He was still feeling lightheaded and dizzy. Part of it was due to the tranquilizer administered to him earlier in E.R., the other part was, he was sure, shock. He tried to smile, but it was impossible, a cut next to his mouth. His helmet visor had shattered on impact, making several small cuts on his face.

''Sparrow?'' He held his hand out toward her. Tears came to Curt's eyes as she walked unsteadily over to his bed. Her eyes were red and swollen. ''I'm okay,'' he whispered, gripping her hand tightly.

Breath coming in gulps, Becky leaned against the bed for support. ''I—I thought you'd died.'' Curt's hair was still damp and pressed against his skull. The multitude of cuts on his face emphasized the close call he'd had with death. There was anxiety in his eyes, his flesh taut and pale as he watched her.

''So had I, Sparrow.'' He opened his arms and pulled her against him. The gesture hurt his back, but he didn't care. His ankle, in a removable cast, was painful, too. But neither equaled the agony in his heart for what his decision had cost Becky.

Collapsing against Curt, Becky lay there, hearing the erratic beat of his heart beneath her ear. ''I—I thought I'd lost you,'' she said, her voice nearly inaudible.

''I'm sorry,'' and he kissed her hair, unable to get enough of her. ''Patty? Does she know what's happened?''

''N-no.''

Shutting his eyes, he whispered, ''Good.'' And then, he said softly, ''I'm quitting flying, Becky.''

She lay very still against him, her eyes opening. Becky

stared at the white wall for several minutes, not believing her ears. It had to be her tortured imagination! Fingers tightening against his light-blue gown, she shuddered.

"Did you hear me?" Curt asked, and stroked her blond hair, something he thought he'd never be able to do again. "I'm going to quit, Becky."

She lifted her head and sat up, her hand never leaving his. "Quit?"

Nodding, Merrill admitted, "When I ejected, I saw my whole life flash before my eyes. I saw you . . . and Patty. I knew I was going to die and—" He compressed his lips, trying to halt the sob that wanted to tear from him. Struggling with the words, he choked out, "In those split seconds before I hit the ground, I knew what was the most important thing in my life." He raised his head and gazed into her tear-filled brown eyes. "You. You and Patty. God, Sparrow, I've been so damned stupid. I wanted to fly at the expense of everything and everyone else. You started drinking to numb yourself. Patty's been uncontrollable and angry. When I ejected, I thought about all of it. Just before I hit the ground, I made a decision that if I walked away from this, I was going to quit. You and Patty are more important to me than my flying."

The words fell against her, but Becky couldn't believe her ears. Reaching out, she touched his tears with her fingertips. "W-what would you do instead?"

"Get a job as an aeronautical engineer with one of the big defense contractors. Probably McDonnell's. It won't be hard to get a job, not for someone with my background and experience."

Swallowing, Becky clung to his somber features. "You'd quit . . . for us?"

Managing a grimace, Curt said, "Yes. My career's washed up anyway. After this last stunt, they'll want me out when my six years is up. I'll save them the trouble and resign. But I want you to understand: I'd quit even if I wasn't in trouble."

Happiness threaded through her numbness and shock. "You wouldn't miss flying?"

"Sure I would." Curt kissed her small hand. "But I'd miss you two a lot more. And if I can quit the Air Force, Becky, you've got to promise me you'll get help for your drinking problem. We've both got to face the truth. Together."

"Yes, oh, yes, honey. I'll do that. I'll get help." She slid her arms around his shoulders, embracing him. "I love ya'll so much, so much . . ."

With a sigh, Curt crushed her against him, never wanting to let her go.

— 19 —

THE next time Dr. Cartwright appeared, Megan was alone with Melody. Sam had taken Becky home and would return shortly. They'd all been able to visit and talk for a few minutes to Curt, who was resting comfortably.

Megan felt Melody stiffen when the doctor approached. Automatically, they both stood, holding one another's hand.

"Doctor?" Melody demanded in a low voice, clutching at the handkerchief in her fingers.

"Your husband is conscious, Mrs. Stang."

"Thank God. What else? What's wrong with Jack?"

"You'd better sit down," Anna warned, motioning to the chair.

"I'll stand."

Megan chewed on her lower lip and read something tragic in Cartwright's expression. Her mind whirled with terrible options, none of them good.

"Very well. Your husband has sustained severe injury to his spinal column. I'm afraid he's paralyzed from the waist down."

Megan gasped, her hand flying to her heart.

Melody's eyes narrowed. "Are you positive?"

Anna nodded. "He doesn't respond to any of the nerve response tests. Further, he's got two herniated discs, and a severe concussion. Right not, he's disoriented and knows he can't move his legs, Mrs. Stang.''

"I must see him, Doctor.''

Hesitating, Anna said, "He's not in very good shape physically or emotionally right now. I'd give him a tranquilizer to neutralize his shock and handle the pain he's in, but I can't for the next forty-eight hours because of his head injury.''

Dragging in a deep breath, Melody asked, "Is he—is he permanently paralyzed? Couldn't this be an acute state and he'll recover from it later?''

"There's nothing acute about a spinal column injury, Mrs. Stang. I wish I could give you more hope, but I can't.''

Melody pulled free of Megan's grasp. "I'll see him now, Doctor.''

"Of course.''

Megan stood there, watching Melody walk toward the hall. Her shoulders were squared once again, head held high. At the door, Melody halted and turned toward Megan.

"Thank you for your help,'' she said, a quaver in her tone.

Megan nodded, not knowing what to say or do. Right now, all she wanted was Sam. The need to be with him, to hear his voice, to share the shock of this tragedy, was overwhelming. Becky was going to drive him over to Ops so he could pick up his Corvette, and then he'd come back here, to the hospital. Alone once again, Megan turned and looked around the empty lounge, numb. She wondered how many cries and tears the walls had absorbed over the years. Too many. Far too many.

Melody steeled herself as much as she could before she entered Jack's room. A nurse hovered over his bed, and was in the process of adjusting one of the I.V.'s in his arm. A quiver zigzagged through her, and she stopped, dizzy. Jack's head was swathed in a white bandage, the left side of his face swollen black and blue, his one eye hidden beneath the bruised flesh. He was mumbling, unable to move anything except his hands. His wrists were tethered with leather cuffs so he couldn't pull out the I.V.'s, or perhaps cause more damage to his spinal column.

"Mrs. Stang, are you all right?" the nurse asked, coming over to her.

Swallowing her nausea, Melody nodded and moved forward. "Yes, I'm fine. Please, could you leave us for a few minutes?"

The nurse hesitated. "I really shouldn't. Your husband is—"

"Five minutes," she rasped unsteadily to the woman.

"Five minutes, Mrs. Stang."

Melody walked to the bed, leaned over, and placed a kiss on her husband's beaded brow. "It's all right, darling, all right," she soothed. "I'm here. I'm here, and everything's going to be fine . . ."

"My legs, my legs," Jack mumbled, moving his head from side to side. "Can't feel my legs . . . eject, eject! Oh, Christ, I'm not gonna make it!" and he strained, as if to protect himself from the oncoming collision with the earth.

A sob caught in Melody's throat. "Shhh, darling, shhh," and she placed a kiss on his mouth, his lips cool beneath hers. Jack quieted, his breathing labored.

"Melody?"

"Here, darling," and she continued to stroke his uninjured cheek. His one eye was red and swollen, a wild look in the depths. "You're safe now, you're at the hospital."

"Legs!" he burst out in a sob. "Jesus, I can't feel my legs! What's going on? What's happened?"

Framing his face, Melody kissed away his tears. They mingled with her own. "Rest, darling. Just rest."

Jack stopped mumbling, quieting beneath her ministrations. His eyes closed, his breathing steadying out.

Gently, Melody crooned to him, a lullaby she sang to Scotty when he woke up from bad dreams. It had been a song her mother had sung to her. It hurt to see Jack strapped into the bed, a tortured, injured animal in a cage. Tears formed and continued to fall, but Melody sang each verse of the song. Right now, Jack was all that mattered, not his career, not the terrible crash that had occurred. He was in a great deal of pain, and she knew she could take some of it away with just her presence.

When the nurse came back in, Melody told her in a quiet voice to get her a chair to sit on, and to have another bed brought into the room. She wouldn't leave Jack's side. Not now. Not ever.

Megan uttered a little cry when Sam appeared at the entrance to the lounge. She got up and felt his arms go around her.

Holt crushed her against him, inhaling the wonderful fragrance that was only Megan. "You smell better than this hospital," he murmured, and captured her lips against his. Kissing her long and tenderly, Holt reluctantly broke contact. Her huge green eyes were rimmed with exhaustion.

"What about Stang?"

"Dr. Cartwright says he's paralyzed from the waist down."

"My God," Sam whispered, cradling her cheek. He worriedly assessed her features. "How's Melody taking it?"

"Like the military trooper she is," Megan answered wearily. "I admire her guts. She stood there and took it on the chin from the doctor, and then marched down the hall as if everything was going to be fine."

Sam inhaled Megan's fragrance, wanting the reminder of life around him, not death and destruction. "Melody is a fighter," he said.

"She's going to need that kind of courage if Jack remains paralyzed."

Agreeing, Holt allowed Megan to rest her head against his shoulder, and felt all the tension she'd held dissolving beneath his hand as he stroked her shoulders and back. "He's lucky to be alive," Sam finally said. "God, that was a long fall."

"I thought he'd die."

"You ready to go home?" The words sounded good to him, and Sam wondered what the end result of the crash would mean for them. Fear ate him up inside.

Megan stepped out of his arms and went to retrieve her

purse from the chair. "Yes. We're both in shock and just don't know it yet."

"I think so. Your house or mine?"

She stood there, absorbing Sam in his flight suit. He looked incredibly handsome, shoulders thrown back, so strong looking when she presently was not. A warmth flooded her, and Megan whispered, "I don't care, just as long as I'm with you."

Sam understood, moved to her side, and drew Megan against him. "I feel the same way," he admitted hoarsely. Inwardly, he was shaky and unsure. The crash had torn through all his carefully made plans. How much trust was left between them, if any? The urge to talk to her at length, explore her, and find out where she was at, was almost tangible.

"Let's go home," Sam coaxed.

Megan watched the white sand of Lake Rosamond flash by them as they drove toward Lancaster. Sam's brow was furrowed, and she knew something was bothering him.

"What will happen Monday when Lauren finds out about the crash?" she asked.

"Plenty," he growled. "Stang took that plane up without authorization, and lost it. Do you know how many millions of dollars we're talking about?"

"Too many for me to fathom. Do you think they might court-martial him?"

"Maybe."

"What about Curt?"

"He's an accessory. I doubt if they'll court-martial him."

"Becky said he was going to resign."

"I know."

Megan looked at his profile, the thinned line of his mouth. "How do you feel about that?"

For me or him? Holt wanted to ask her. He didn't, though. "I think Curt did the right thing for all of them." Would she ask him to quit flying? To give it up for her?

"That means you'll become chief test pilot on the *Agile Eagle* project," Megan said softly.

"Yes."

"When do the canards go on the plane?"

"Two weeks from now if everything goes according to schedule." Sam gave her a strange look, wondering what was going on inside that head of hers. The crash had brought back to life Russ's untimely death. It was a living thing within him, and tore savagely at his confidence. Emotionally, he seesawed between losing Megan and having to face his fear of death.

"And then you'll fly it?"

"Yes."

Megan looked out the window for a long time. She could feel the heaviness between them, the fear and anxiety palpable. So much of it had been caused by the crash. Struggling to keep her fear in the context of what happened, that Sam hadn't been involved, Megan said, "Now I know how a goldfish feels in a small bowl of water."

Sam forced a slight smile and held her hand momentarily. "We both feel that way, Red."

Megan wandered around Sam's huge, sprawling home. It was only 10 A.M., the morning clear with a breeze, the sky a dark blue. She stood on the sun deck, hands resting lightly on the cedar railing, and looked out toward the desert. Although it was only in the sixties, she was warm in the lamb's-wool jacket. Restless, Megan had avoided Sam since they had arrived home. He'd taken a hot shower and changed. She had paced.

The glass door slid open and closed. Megan looked across her shoulder. Sam was now in civilian attire, a blue plaid cowboy shirt, jeans, and his boots. His hair had been recently washed and combed. He looked worse, in her opinion, completely exhausted.

Coming over, Sam stood next to Megan. Afraid of the forthcoming conversation, he didn't say anything for a long time. Finally, he forced out, "Hell of a day, isn't it?"

"Yes, a terrible one." And then Megan cast a glance at him, a warm feeling inside her because of the look in his eyes. "It could have been worse. Both men could have died."

Sam leaned down, resting his elbows on the rail next to her. "Curt's lucky. He'll walk away from this, family intact and a good future in front of him."

"And Jack?"

"I don't know." Sam pursed his lips. "Funny things happen to men when they survive a crash."

"What do you mean?"

"Some guys it doesn't faze, and they go back to flying as if nothing ever happened. Others, it haunts. In Jack's case, he's probably going to have to not only come to terms with the crash, but what his actions cost him in terms of what it's done to him physically."

"He'll probably never walk again."

"A terrible price to pay," Sam agreed softly. Girding himself, he straightened and turned toward Megan. His heart was pumping hard, and he could feel each beat against his ribs. "I'm wondering what kind of price we're going to pay because of the crash. That's what has me scared."

"Price?"

He ran his fingers through her hair, the strands strong and silky. "Yeah, Red, us." His hand stilled against her flushed cheek. "All morning I've been wondering how all of this has affected you, because in turn, it will affect us."

Megan closed her eyes and rested her cheek against his palm. Holt had a quiet kind of courage, the ability to talk about things that most people would fear to broach. "I was scared, Sam. I don't think my mother ever saw a crash. It was as if I lived out her worst nightmare today through my eyes and heart."

Gently, Holt ran his thumb across her cheek, loving each of her freckles. Loving her so much it hurt to breathe. "She instilled you with a fear of crashes. The truth is: your father died in one."

"Probably very similar to the one that happened this morning."

Throat constricted, Sam held her wide, honest green eyes. "So, where does this leave us, Megan?"

Tears swam in her eyes, his face blurring before her. "You think I'm going to ask you to quit like Becky did her husband?"

Tenderly, Sam removed the tears with his thumbs. "The thought crossed my mind," he admitted hoarsely.

"I wouldn't ask that of you, Sam."

"No?"

"No."

"What then?" Every word felt strangled coming from him.

Megan leaned up, placing a warm kiss on the compressed line of his mouth. "Something happened to me out there today," she admitted in a low voice, feeling his arms go around her and cradle her against him.

"Tell me about it."

"I not only got to see how the crash affected the wives, but how it affected you. Sam, you suffered no less than any one of us. Father had always been so cold and callous about these things, I thought every pilot was like him." Her voice cracked. "I was wrong. I saw tears in your eyes there at the hospital. That's when I knew that my father wasn't like everyone else." She caressed his jaw, and met his unsure gaze. "Today, I saw the man, Sam Holt, for the first time. I never saw the uniform you wore. I only saw your actions as a human being." Touching his lips with her fingertips, she quavered, "I love you . . ."

With a groan, Sam held her tightly. "I love you so damn much," he rasped against her hair. "I've loved you since the day I met you, sweetheart." He kissed her hair, temple, and cheek, holding her tear-filled eyes. "I was so afraid of losing you today, afraid that you'd leave Edwards and call off what we had . . ."

A sob caught in Megan's throat, and she framed his face. "What we have is so very special, Sam. I saw that today. I—I think that if we can always talk, always share what makes us angry, fearful, or whatever, we'll be on solid ground with one another."

"Even if I continue to fly?"

Megan nodded hesitantly. "I'm trying to see it as a job

you have. It's hard, because my childhood was controlled by it.''

Sam understood only too well. "But you've been around me long enough to find out that not every pilot lives, eats, and breathes flying or testing like your father did.''

"You love flying, Sam. But unlike my father, you can separate it from the other parts of your life."

"You're the most important part of my life," he told her, holding her gaze. "Did you know that?''

Shaken, Megan whispered, "No, but it feels good to hear that.''

"You've been number one in my heart from the day I met you. Lauren can tell you how often she saw me sitting at my desk, daydreaming. I'd catch myself thinking of you in moments when my focus wasn't engaged on a design problem, or flying. And at night," he leaned over, kissed her cheek, and tasted the salt of her tears, "you made my nightmares seem not so bad.''

Sniffing, Megan wiped her eyes. "Sam, I have a favor to ask of you.''

"Sure.''

"You don't have to do it, if you don't want to.''

Giving her a small shake, he said, "I'd do anything in the world for you, Megan. You've got to know that by now.''

Mustering her courage, she lifted her lashes and held his darkened cobalt gaze. "I—I think I'm ready to go over to the cemetery—today. I'm ready to face my parents . . .''

His heart swelled with pride over her courage. The crash had ripped off a heavy scar that Megan had been trapped behind for so long. "Okay," he said thickly, "let's go.''

Megan stood at the gate of the cemetery. Sam was at her side. On the way out of the house he'd given her a three-day-old bouquet of flowers to put on the graves, if she wanted to. She loved him fiercely for his thoughtfulness. Swallowing hard, Megan knew what she had to do, and it had to be done alone.

The cemetery was small and beautiful, with Arizona sycamore the predominant tree. There were no fancy headstones, only small, square concrete plaques with bronze lettering to indicate the graves. It was warm, and Megan took off her coat, handing it to Sam.

"I-I'll be back," she choked out.

"Take your time, Red."

Blindly turning away, Megan held the small map she'd gotten from the caretaker's office. Her parents were buried together in the northeast corner. The walks were laid out in precise military fashion, red brick that reminded her of spilled blood. Clutching the bouquet of thornless roses, all red, again symbolizing blood in her eyes, Megan began the long walk by herself.

As she approached the two graves, the last two in the row next to the black wrought-iron fence, tears began to flow unchecked from her eyes. She stood in front of them, sobbing. Her mother's grave was first. Megan knelt down in the springy grass and leaned back on her heels. All the memories surrounding her suicide came back. Megan remembered the shock of finding her mother in the bed, dead from an overdose of sleeping pills. Allowing all those terrible, wrenching emotions to come up and consume her, Megan sat there releasing tears she'd never spilled when she was eighteen.

Finally, the storm of weeping abated, and in its place, a miraculous calm inhabited Megan. With shaking hands, she took six of the red roses, now in full bloom, and laid them across her mother's grave.

"Mom? I—I love you. I always did. I think I understand now how you felt, and why you did what you did." Megan wiped her cheek with the back of her sleeve. "Father was wrong to tell you that you'd finally stopped running. I-If he'd given you support, believed in you, maybe things would have been different." She reached down, placing the flat of her hand against the marker. It was warm and dry. "I'm sorry you had no one, Mom. I now know it wasn't my fault that you died. For so long, I blamed myself. I loved you as much as I could, but it wasn't enough. It could never be enough."

Pulling her hand away, Megan managed a broken smile. "Today, I saw what you feared the most, what you hid from. And to tell the truth, Mom, it was *worth* running from. It was a living hell. But as I stood there, holding Becky, I realized Sam was just as shaken as we were. Mom, not all pilots are immune to human fears. Do you know how much that meant to me to discover that? All pilots aren't like Father was. Thank God . . .''

She slowly got to her feet, smiling down at the six roses lying across her mother's grave. ''I've got a lot to work through yet, Mom. And I'm going to come back here and talk to you from time to time.''

Stepping over to her father's grave, Megan knelt down. Tears didn't come, only a sense of grief and loss. ''Father, I'm still angry with you. I can't sit here and say I love you, because you killed whatever I held for you so long ago. Dammit, why didn't you reach out to us? Why couldn't you have helped Mom? Did it take so much from your precious love of flying to do it? *You* helped Mom commit suicide by the very fact you didn't want to get involved!''

Megan looked up through the spreading arms of the sycamore, her lower lip trembling badly. Hurt soared with her pain. ''I've met a man, Father, who *isn't* like you. Sam's taught me that not all pilots are uncaring and distant. He loves his flying, but he loves me more.'' She shook her head, tears spilling from her eyes as she looked down at the mute grave. ''If Sam hadn't persisted, hung in there with me because I thought he was exactly like you, I'd have lost him. God knows, I never gave him any chances to prove he was any different.

''I'm scared, Father. Sometimes, I feel like Mom did when I think about Sam going up on a flight. But a new side of me, one that I'm learning to trust, tells me differently. You never could talk or share anything with either of us, could you? I don't understand why! Did we mean so little to you? Were we so insignificant to what was really important in your life, that we were little more than underfoot?'' Her voice broke, and Megan sat there in grief.

''It's amazing all the fears and perceptions I've taken on for both of you. I'll probably spend the rest of my life sorting them out from the *real* Megan Roberts. I can't forgive you, Father. At least, not yet. Maybe one of these years I can, but not right now. I hope Sam can help me understand you. If anyone can, he will." She laid the roses down on his grave. "I'll be back, Father. There's so much I have to say, have to ask you. Maybe I'll never get the answers I'm searching for, but I'm going to try. You can't be more silent than you were when you were living, so perhaps this is an easier way for both of us."

Rising unsteadily to her feet, Megan brushed the bits of grass off her knees and lower pant legs. A slight breeze caressed her face, and she turned, going back to the walk. Each step away from the graves made her feel lighter, as if years of burdens were dissolving. In the distance, Megan could see Sam standing alone, holding her jacket. As she drew near, she could see the soberness of his features, the concern burning in his eyes. Each step gave her a sense of euphoria she'd never experienced.

Wiping the last of the tears off her face, Megan halted a few feet away from him. Sam offered her a slight smile.

"Have a good talk with them?" he asked quietly, handing her back the jacket.

"Yes." She shrugged. "I'm not so sure going to the graves of your parents and talking at length with them is therapeutic, but I feel better."

Sam slid his arm around Megan's shoulder and lead her out of the cemetery and back toward the Corvette parked beneath the shade of a sycamore. "Doesn't matter what anyone thinks about it, Red. It's right for you."

"That's another thing I love about you, Sam Holt: you revel in my uniqueness, and you don't try and stuff me under some convenient label."

With a grin, he held her upturned face and those green eyes that glowed with hope. "How can you put a redhead under any label? They're very independent, special people."

"No," Megan quavered, pulling him to a halt and throwing her arms around his shoulders, "you're the one who's really special."

Holt held her long and hard, inhaling her fragrance, the

silk of her hair against his cheek. "We're *both* special," he said thickly. "And I love the hell out of you, Red."

"There's just one more hurdle, Sam," she said.

"What's that?"

"When you fly the *Eagle* with the canards. I'm scared to death already."

Shutting his eyes, Sam buried his face in her luxuriant hair. "So am I," he admitted, "So am I." *But for very different reasons.* Somehow, Holt knew he was going to have to find the courage to face the ghost from his past, just as Megan had faced hers. He kissed her cheek and held her more tightly, if that was possible. Did he have the courage to break that final barrier of fear regarding the crash and Russ's death? Did he? His gut knotted hard, the pain soaring up through him. Holt wasn't sure. Today's crash stripped away the last of his bravado. He felt naked, his armor taken from him, with no way to shield or protect himself from the flight.

As Megan eased from his arms, he ached to tell her of the fears that haunted him almost nightly. For two weeks he wouldn't be flying, and then the all-important test with the canards would occur. Not only would he have to overcome his fear of dying during a landing, but also deal with a jet that had a new design feature installed. How would the *Eagle* handle? The chances of stalling it would be real—just as real as it was for Stang today.

As Sam climbed in the car, enmeshed in a turmoil of emotions, he wanted to talk to Megan. But how could he? She was fragile from the crash, from finally making a breakthrough with herself and her parents. No, he couldn't tell her. God knew, Megan had phenomenal strength, but no person should be asked to shoulder burdens like this. Especially not Megan. Their relationship had survived the crash, and Sam was positive it couldn't withstand Megan knowing about his fears, the ghosts that haunted him.

— 20 —

"WELL," Lauren said to Sam, "tomorrow's the big day." She gave him a game smile, lingering at his desk in Design.

"Yeah, I'll be glad to get it over with," he muttered. It was quitting time, and most people had left. The way Lauren was hanging around, Sam knew she wanted to talk to him. Megan got off work in a half-hour, so he had the time.

Shutting the desk drawer and locking it, he reared back in his chair and met her troubled gaze. "What's wrong, Port?"

She ran her finger along the polished surface of his desk. "The last two weeks have been rotten around here," she said finally.

Wasn't that the truth? "It wasn't your fault, Port," he said, referring to the crash. Lauren had been visibly upset when she got back Sunday night and found out what had happened.

Lauren sat down in the chair next to Holt's desk. "I know it's not a black eye on my record, Sam, but I somehow feel responsible. Could I have nipped Stang in the bud instead of letting him play his petty games with all of us?" Rubbing her brow, she frowned. "Right now, I'm really questioning my management skills."

315

"Don't," he warned her grimly. "Somebody like Jack is hard to deal with because what he does is subtle, and you can't collect the kind of proof you need to haul him on the carpet."

"He really paid one hell of a price," Lauren said and glanced up at him. "Paralyzed for life from the waist down."

The thought scared Holt to death. That could happen to him tomorrow morning. What if he couldn't get past that barrier of fear that had been haunting him? What if he couldn't concentrate? Only this time, it would be he and Port in the cockpit. It was bad enough *he* was there, without having her with him. Port was too vital to lose in a lousy crash caused by his inability to handle his fears. Pursing his lips, Sam said nothing, breaking out in a light sweat.

"They've already left, you know," Lauren said.

"The Stangs?"

"Yes. Melody had Jack transferred to a well-known hospital down in Los Angeles yesterday. I guess the moving trucks are coming in today."

"And then another house on Sharon Drive will be empty."

"Waiting for the next test pilot student to move in," she agreed.

"Life goes on, doesn't it?"

"Yes."

"In a way, I'm glad the Air Force didn't put Stang up for court-martial," Sam said. "I think he got the ultimate prison sentence: confined to a wheelchair for the rest of his life."

Lauren snorted softly. "Gossip going around says that Melody's got him a vice-president's job lined up at her father's bank in LA."

"Jack will make out just fine. I miss the hell out of Curt, though."

Sadly, Lauren nodded. "I can't believe it: a week after the crash, Curt resigned."

"And he's already got a job as an aeronautical design

engineer over at McDonnell. Good money with banker's hours to boot." Sam smiled, trying to bolster her flagging spirits. "Come on, Port, we'll be seeing Curt from time to time. They've assigned him to the F-15 project. He'll be in civilian clothes over here, that's all."

"I guess you're right. It's a shame he believed Stang's lie. I know the Air Force wouldn't have let him resign under any other circumstance. He's a fine test pilot—I mean, was."

"Port, he had family problems. Becky wasn't handling his flying very well. For that matter, neither was their daughter, Patty."

"I guess there is life after the Air Force, huh?" Port noted ruefully, slowly getting to her feet. She smoothed the wrinkled flight suit out across her thighs.

Mustering a laugh, Sam stood and put papers into his briefcase. "For thirty-year people like us, Port, there is *no* life after the Air Force."

"Think it's a terminal condition?"

Grinning, Sam shrugged. "Better talk to the family of the person. They're in for thirty years, too."

"I'm just glad Ryan accepts how important my work is to me," Lauren agreed. "How's Megan doing with your new promotion to major and chief test pilot on this project?"

"Coping."

She tilted her head and gave him a probing look. "What does that mean?"

Snapping the briefcase shut, Sam rested his hands on the top of it. "It means we take one day at a time, and do a hell of a lot of talking and discussing my job."

"Good communication eases fear," Lauren said fervently. She checked her watch. "You'd better get going, Sam. I'll see you over here at 0530 and we'll take a ride in that *Eagle* with the canards. I'm excited about it. I think it'll give us the landing requirements we've been looking for."

Fear snapped through Holt, and he forced a cheerful demeanor he didn't feel. "Yeah, we'll take the girl up for a spin tomorrow morning."

She looked up at him, her eyes penetrating. "Sam, you okay?"

"Yeah. Why?"

"I don't know... ever since the crash, you've looked," she groped for the right words, "out of sorts."

Inwardly, Holt winced, but he kept his face neutral. Every night, he'd stay up until 3 A.M. to avoid the nightmare he knew would come. At first, Megan was stymied by his night-owl tactics. Unable to tell her the truth because she was still recovering from her own crisis, Sam told her he was studying hard every night on the canard flight. She believed him. Getting three hours of sleep at night wasn't enough, and he knew it. But what was he going to do? Go to sleep in Megan's arms and wake up screaming?

If he did, Holt knew he'd have to level with Megan, and he didn't want to destroy the delicate balance of their relationship with his admittance. Somehow, he'd fly the damn test. Somehow. Even though, deep down, he'd wanted to simply crawl into Megan's arms and spill out all the ugly fears that inhabited him. Under any other circumstances, he knew Megan had the internal strength to help him carry his loads.

"The crash shook me up," he admitted quietly, knowing he didn't dare speak to Lauren about his fears. She might get cold feet and have him replaced.

"Piece of cake, Holt."

"Yeah... piece of cake."

On the way over to the elementary school to pick up Megan, Holt chewed over his conversation with Lauren. Exhausted, all he wanted to do was go home tonight, lay down on the couch, and sleep. Did he dare? Would the nightmare stalk him if he took an evening nap? If it did, Megan would want to know what was going on. She had been with him once before when it happened, and would quickly put the pieces together. And then, he'd have to explain. Sighing heavily, Holt swung the Corvette into the parking lot, spotting Megan.

His spirits lifted unaccountably. She wore a pretty pink cotton skirt, a white silk blouse, and a fuchsia scarf around her neck. To Sam, she looked more like a young college coed than a teacher. As always, her hair tumbled in abandon around her shoulders, and it triggered the need to run his fingers through that thick cascade. If only he could get past tonight. If only he could successfully fly the test, things would get on an even keel between them.

Holt made a promise to tell Megan the truth as soon as the flight was successful. He didn't like withholding from her. Their relationship was based upon an honesty that was incredibly refreshing, and it drew them even closer to one another. He'd never experienced anything like it before, realizing it was Megan who had triggered the response in him because of her quest to find out who she really was—not what her parents had made her think or believe about herself.

Megan's smile was radiant with welcome, and Holt felt some of the despair lift momentarily from around him. He opened the door and watched as she got into the Corvette. Leaning over, she surprised him with a warm kiss on the mouth.

"Mmmm," Sam murmured. He gripped her shoulder and held her close to sample her smiling mouth one more time. Releasing her, he smiled and said, "Chocolate chip cookies?"

Laughing, Megan shut the door and donned the seat belt. "One of the kids brought in a plate of cookies. She gave me one." Then she opened her purse and drew out a napkin with a cookie in it. "Here, I saved you one."

Touched, Sam promptly put it into his mouth and savored the unexpected dessert. "Thanks," he mumbled, and drove the car away from the curb.

"One isn't going to ruin our dinner," Megan continued, placing her briefcase on the floor next to her feet. Sliding her hand across his shoulders, she asked, "How did your day go?"

The cookie disappeared quickly. "No last-minute glitches. Lauren and I were over at the hangar today double-checking the canards that were put on the nose of the *Eagle*. It looks fine." He prayed he sounded nonchalant, as if it were nothing.

"Well," she said, settling back into the seat, "I'd like to do two things tonight. First, I think we should go visit Becky and Curt since they've settled into their new house in Lancaster. They only live across town, and we owe a housewarming visit."

Sam nodded. "Yeah, I miss Curt at the office. Hell, I miss the whole family." The only reason they hadn't gotten together after the crash was Curt's swift departure from the base, their move into civilian life, and his own brutal schedule now that he was chief test pilot.

"I've already called Becky and asked her if we could just drop over for a minute."

"And?"

"She can hardly wait to see us."

Sam smiled. "So what's the second part of your strategy, Ms. Roberts?"

"I'm planning a special dinner tonight for us."

"Oh?"

"Sure. Why not? A precelebration for a successful and safe flight."

Her care touched Sam deeply. "A kind of good luck charm for tomorrow morning, is that it?" he teased gently.

"You could say that. Every time my father flew a test flight, my mother went into hiding. I'm not going to do that, Sam Holt. Every time there's a flight, we'll have the works: candlelight, Perrier, a wonderful dinner, and dessert."

"What kind of dessert?"

She grinned. "Anything you want, Holt. The sky's the limit."

He slid his hand into hers, relishing her softness, her thoughtfulness. "You're my dessert."

The last two weeks had been heaven in Holt's opinion. Megan had moved into his house for all intents and purposes, although she still kept her apartment. Both of them had agreed that this was a "test run" of their relationship to see if they could live together. With the exception of him not going to bed until 3 A.M. every morning, the time with Megan had been utter bliss.

Megan smiled. "Let's go visit the Merrills."

"Mommy, Mommy!" Patty shrieked, leaping up and down at the front screen door, "they're here! Uncle Sammy and Ms. Roberts are here!"

Becky was sitting with Curt in the kitchen. Curt rose.

"Come on, let's meet them," he said, rising and fitting the crutches under each arm.

Smiling, Becky got up, slowly following him. Curt still had a limp from the crash, but it was getting less and less apparent with every day. As they walked through their newly purchased house, a far more beautiful one with much more room than the one they had rented on Sharon Drive, Becky sighed. Just seeing Curt in a civilian suit of clothes was like a dream. How many times had she pinched herself to see if it was really real: Curt was a civilian, no longer anchored to the whims and wiles of the military.

Becky lifted her hand as Sam and Megan entered the foyer, Patty shrieking with joy. Tears came to her eyes as they drew to a halt, watching their daughter open her arms to their best friend. Holt's laughter was rolling as he lifted Patty into his arms, and gave her a loud kiss on the cheek followed by a huge bearhug with lots of growling, bearlike noises that made Patty squeal with delight.

"Ya'll come in," Becky greeted, pulling Megan forward. "I've got coffee on in the kitchen."

"Thanks, Becky," Megan said, watching Sam tussle with Patty. *He would be wonderful with children.* The thought sent a flood of incredible warmth through her.

Curt shook hands with Sam. "Good to see you again. Come on in."

Megan sat next to Sam at the kitchen table. The change in the household was startling to her. On base, the Merrills' home had been in a constant state of disarray according to Sam. This home was picked up, and immaculately clean. Becky served coffee to everyone and sat down at Megan's elbow. She smiled at her daughter who preferred Sam's lap.

"Can I have some coffee, Uncle Sammy?"

Holt grinned. "Punkin, haven't you heard?"

"What?"

"Coffee will stunt your growth."

Patty made a face and looked over at Becky. "Mommy, is that why you're short?"

Giggling, Becky nodded. "Yes, honey. Mama and Daddy let me start drinkin' coffee when I was real young."

Curt grinned. "It's good to see you both. Sam, I'll be coming over to consult with you across the table next week on the *Agile Eagle* follow-up. Congratulations on your promotion to chief test pilot."

"Thanks, buddy."

"Speaking of good news," Becky said proudly, "I've got a lady therapist by the name of Molly Dodd, and she's helpin' all of us."

Curt reached over, enclosing his wife's small hand on the table. "Molly is a Jungian therapist who has an office over in Palmdale. We all go to see her once a week."

"Obviously," Megan said, "it's helping all of you."

"Lordy, she has to help me understand why I'm codependent, explain why Patty is angry, and help Curt with his nightmares after the crash."

Soberly, Sam nodded. "Those nightmares will hang around for a while." How well he knew. If only his would go away.

Curt stretched out, opening his arms as Patty climbed from Sam's lap into his. "Maybe. I've been finding out that just talking about it has helped a lot, Sam." He cast Becky a warm look filled with undisguised love and pride. "Molly's retraining me to talk to Becky."

Softly, Becky said, "I like talking to you, darling'. I've always wanted to be there for you."

"Pilots have a tendency to keep everything bottled up inside of them," Megan added quietly. She saw them all nod in silent agreement.

Curt gave Sam a significant look. "Take it from me: talking helps."

With a wink at Megan, Sam said, "I'm finding that out, buddy."

"Ya'll don't realize how nice it is to have your man talk about what's troublin' him. Why, we're strong, aren't we Megan?"

"Women *are* stronger than men."

"And two of the prettiest, strongest women we've ever known, right Curt?"

Grinning, Curt nodded. "In our business, strong women are the only ones who can survive what we put them through."

Becky sipped her coffee. "I like what McDonnell puts you through." She turned to Megan. "Ya'll realize Curt gets home at a decent hour and leaves for work at a decent time?"

"Must be nice," Megan said, meaning it.

Curt ruffled Patty's blond hair. "And I have time for her *and* Becky now."

"You've earned this, buddy."

Megan silently agreed. There was such a difference between the Merrills and other Air Force families. It reminded her what the military could do to some men, women, and children who just couldn't deal with the incredible stresses put upon them. Her mother hadn't been able to either. Looking over at Sam, Megan understood that she would have to find that special strength somewhere within herself, because Sam would never leave the Air Force. He was a thirty-year man.

Later, on the way over to Sam's home, Megan was silent. Sam slid his hand across hers and placed a kiss on it. "Are you upset?"

She closed her eyes and smiled, savoring the gentleness of his hand around her own. "No. Happy for the Merrills."

"Becky looks a hundred percent better."

"So does Curt." She barely lifted her lashes, gazing at his strong profile. "Patty was so happy. Do you see how well-mannered she was? When she was in my class, she was such a disruption."

"A kid who was hurting for love and at the time, neither

parent was capable of giving it to her," Sam murmured. He glanced over at Megan. "You suffered through the same thing. Only, it didn't stop."

"I survived, Sam. That's all that counts. And I'm not over it yet, but I'm trying to understand what it did to me and how to break those old patterns and old fears."

"We'll keep doing it together."

Hope mushroomed through her heart. "Yes."

"I'm starved."

Megan laughed. "These serious conversations are just too hard on that stomach of yours, aren't they?" She liked his little-boy grin. It went straight to her heart.

"You're such a great cook," Sam said admiringly. "I like your meals."

"There's no secret to you, Sam Holt. Cook decent food and you'd be happy."

"What's for dinner?"

Groaning, Sam walked over to the couch in the living room. "I can't eat another bite," he protested. Megan was starting to clear the dishes from the dining room table. The dinner had been superb; steaks grilled with Dijon Mustard, baked potatoes, and a Caesar salad. He knew he shouldn't lie down, but the meal had made him drowsy. Against better judgment, Sam propped a pillow under his head and stretched out on the couch.

Megan came in, wiping her hands on the blue apron she wore. "You ate enough for two people," she laughed. "Dessert?"

"Later, sweetheart, I'm done in."

Sitting on the edge of the sofa, Megan threaded his dark hair through her fingers. "You look so tired. It's all those late nights catching up to you, Sam."

"Don't go getting that worried look on your face," he chided, catching her hand and kissing it. "Wake me up in an hour? I just need a little cat nap, and I'll be okay."

With a nod, she drew the purple and blue afghan his mother had knitted for him many years ago over him. "An hour, jet jock." Megan tucked it in around him and saw his eyelids droop shut. "Go to sleep," Megan whispered, leaning over and kissing his furrowed brow. Before she got to her feet, Sam was asleep, his deep, slow breathing punctuated by an occasional snore.

He was driving himself too hard, Megan thought, moving to the kitchen to finish cleaning up the dishes. And she was determined to let him sleep until he woke up on his own. In her opinion, these 3 A.M. mornings spent studying were for the birds.

Megan didn't have the heart to awaken Sam before she went to get her nightly bath. It was 11:30 P.M., and he was sleeping hard on the couch. It was important he get the maximum amount of sleep before the test flight, and she didn't wake him.

A half an hour later, Megan emerged from the bathroom wearing an ivory and lace gown that brushed her bare feet. She had worn it especially for tonight, in keeping with the idea of a celebration. So far, it had kept her fear in check. The lace yoke was Venetian, showing off her neck and collarbone. The material, gossamer silk, shimmered against her as she moved. Brushing out her hair, Megan wandered back into the living room. She had shut off all but one small lamp, the room covered in gloom.

As she approached, Sam began muttering bits and pieces of unintelligible words. He threw up his hands, as if to protect himself from some invisible attacker, the afghan slipping off him. Concerned, Megan quickly drew closer. Sam's face was bathed in a heavy film of sweat, his breathing raspy and hard.

Just as Megan leaned down to touch his shoulder to awaken him from the terror she saw etched on his twisted features, Sam shrieked. The brush dropped from Megan's hand. She leaped back as Holt swung into a sitting position, his eyes dark, unseeing.

"Sam?" Hesitating fractionally, Megan sat down next to him and placed her arm around his hunched shoulders. He was wringing wet.

"Russ?"

"No, Megan." Worriedly, she saw the terror dissolve in his eyes. Gripping his arm, she was alarmed. He was trembling. My God, what was wrong? And then, Megan remembered: it was probably the same nightmare that had struck Sam that night he'd slept over at her apartment. As she held him tightly in her arms, and allowed him to lie against her, she recalled the conversation he'd shared earlier with her about Russ Davis. That was it: the crash that had killed his best friend.

Rapidly, Megan put all the loose ends together. Sam was still breathing raggedly, his arms going around her, holding her tightly. Softly, in a singsong voice, she kept repeating that he was safe, and he was here, with her. It took a good ten minutes before his breathing evened out. Unnerved because his clothing was soaked, Megan tried to keep her fear at bay.

Finally, Holt sat up. He rested his head between his hands, elbows propped on his thighs. Megan's soft hand moved reassuringly up and down his spine, as if to get rid of the tension that still gripped him. Remnants of the crash blipped before his tightly shut eyes, but so did the horror that Megan had caught him having the nightmare again. Inwardly, he was still shaking like a bowl of Jell-O. The test was coming up within hours. Could he fly it? Would he crash and kill himself and Port? What would it do to Megan if that happened?"

"Sam," Megan whispered, resting her head against his shoulder, her arm around him, "It's Russ, isn't it? Let's talk about it. I can handle anything you want to say." Her arm tightened. "Please, talk to me, darling . . ."

Drawing in a ragged breath, Sam rasped, "Dammit, Megan, I *can't—won't* subject you to my problem."

His quavering voice struck her hard. "We love each other, Sam. Our problems belong to us. Your nightmare about Russ dying belongs to me, too."

"You're not ready for it," he said hoarsely, raising his head. He looked into her compassionate eyes. "I didn't mean to fall asleep earlier. Just one more day, and I'd have gotten us past this point . . ."

Megan studied Sam for a long moment, digesting the fervor in his tone. His eyes were filled with anguish and fear. "This isn't going to go away overnight, Sam." Gently, she asked, "How long have you been having this nightmare?"

Something crumpled inside him. He wasn't able to be strong on all fronts. Sam looked away, resting his chin on his clasped hands. "Ever since Russ died."

"How often?"

"Maybe two or three times a week."

Megan hurt for him. "And they come in the early morning. That's why you didn't want to go to sleep until 3 A.M.?"

His mouth had a bitter taste in it. "Christ, Megan, you don't deserve to be dragged into this. You're still recovering from that crash."

She caressed his damp hair. "I don't know what I'd have done without being able to talk to you, Sam, about my problems. Believe me, it was a relief to be able to dump all my feelings into your lap. I think I can handle whatever you have to say."

He twisted his head, drowning in her shadowed features. "What about your parents? You're still going through hell about them, about Edwards."

Megan moved off the couch and sat between his legs, hands resting on his shoulders, and looked up into his exhausted face. "Let me be strong for you now, darling. Trust me enough to listen. I promise, I'm not going to run away from you, or lose what I've recently gained. Let me help you."

Just the tenor of Megan's husky voice tore away the last misgivings he had. Wearily, Sam reached out, placing his hand on her small shoulder. In a low, tortured tone, he told her everything. When he got to the part that scared him the worst, the words tore out of him in a torrent.

"I'm scared to fly again. I'm scared to death. Tomorrow morning, Port's going to be in that cockpit with me. Jesus, what if I take her life, Megan? What if I die? What will it do to you? I can't bear to think about it. How many lives will I ruin?"

Fighting back her tears, Megan cradled his face. Tears were streaming down his bristly cheeks, his eyes mirroring his anguish. "It's all right to be afraid to fly, darling," she whispered, a catch in her voice. "It's natural to feel fear about these things."

Gripping her hand, Sam hung his head, unable to maintain her gaze. "I'm afraid to die." There, the words, the admission was finally out. It was the real reason behind his fear. Sam waited, feeling Megan grow very quiet in his arms. Her hand was warm and comforting against the chills that racked him.

Murmuring his name, Megan got to her knees, and forced Sam to look up at her. Her mouth stretched into a tender smile meant to buoy him. "And I was afraid to live . . . until I met you, and you showed me that I could do it without the fear of the past controlling me." Megan kissed his closed eyes, his cheek, and finally his mouth, seeking to give him her warmth, her life that he'd given back to her.

Her mouth was wet and sweet, and Sam hungrily consumed her innocent offering, unable to get enough of her. Sweeping Megan into his arms, he plundered her lush mouth, taking her warmth, feeling it start to chase away the iciness that had him frozen with fear. Caressing the rounded beauty of her breast, he felt the nipple harden beneath the silk fabric, and new life flowed through him. Moving his hand across her rounded belly, Sam was stunned with the realization that he wanted her to carry his daughters and sons within her loving body. Those powerful realizations further grappled with his fear. He had so much to live for, to hope for, with Megan as a part of his future.

Easing from her mouth, Sam stared down at her in the darkness. Megan's eyes were lustrous with love, her lips swollen from his assault. Moving his tongue across her lower lip, he wanted to ease any pain he'd caused her in the throes of wrestling with his ghosts.

"I want you to get a shower," Megan whispered, "and then come to bed—with me. You won't have any more bad dreams tonight, darling."

Her bravery gave him the courage he needed. With his

fingertips, he traced the outline of her small nose and cheek. Without a word, Sam stood and lifted her off the floor and into his arms. Currently, Megan was strong and he was weak. It felt good to have her arms go around his shoulders, her supple form pressed against his, infusing him with her strength, her love. Tomorrow would come soon enough, and with it, the most important test of his life.

— 21 —

IT was raining when Holt arrived at Ops at 0530 the next morning. Megan had called in sick at the school, to be with him. Shaken by her loyalty toward him, Sam was glad that she was there at his side. Getting her a visitor's badge at the desk, he led her down the hall to Design. Just as Megan had promised, he'd slept deeply. This morning, he felt physically fit. Emotionally? Holt didn't look too closely at the answer and took things one step at a time.

Lauren smiled when they entered Design. "Hi, Megan, Sam."

Megan returned the major's smile. "Hi, Lauren."

"Going to be Sam's cheering section?" she teased.

"This time only," Megan said, and sat down in a chair next to Sam's desk. Worriedly, she watched him. He was paler than usual, and not talkative. A jag of terror moved through her when she saw his hand tremble as he opened the desk drawer. No, Megan told herself, don't overreact. He's scared, but he's handling it.

"Ready to fly, Sam?"

"It could be a better day," he answered Port dryly.

She sighed and frowned. "I know. The weatherman said it's going to start raining shortly. We've really had rotten luck on this project.

"It can only get better, Port." Sam glanced down at

Megan. She looked incredibly beautiful in the ankle-length, dark-blue ballet skirt and a white silk jaquard blouse. The simple gold earrings and choker emphasized her features to perfection. Despite all the pressures surrounding him, Holt felt his body tighten in desire for her. "I'll take you over to the lounge," he told Megan. "You can watch the test from there."

"Fine," Megan said, getting up. She gripped the small black leather purse and hoped she looked relaxed, as if nothing were wrong.

Lauren waved to her. "See you after the test, Megan!"

"Right."

Outside in the hall after the door closed, Megan said, "I'll find my way down to the lounge. I remember where it is. Why don't you go get ready?"

Sam nodded. The hall was empty, so he leaned down and brushed her lips with a kiss. "I'll see you just before I've got to leave," he promised.

Megan stood tensely at the glass-paned windows that looked out across the tarmac and airstrip. Rain was going to fall any minute now, the sky bruised and swollen looking. To her right stood the silent, poised F-15 *Agile Eagle* outfitted with its new canards along the nose.

Pressing her hands against the glass, Megan watched the ground crew moving methodically around the plane. Her heart was doing a slow pound, and she wrestled with her own ghosts, as well as those of Sam. He seemed tentative this morning, drawn taut, as if one wrong word would shatter him. All Megan could do was keep contact with him through a touch, a smile. She prayed it was enough.

Ops came to life around her. The tension was palpable as airmen hurried down the hall, civilian engineers came and went with harried looks on their faces. Phones rang. Buzzers behind the air desk buzzed. The crew outside with the *Eagle* were hurrying around the jet for last moment checks.

"Can you feel it?"

Megan jumped and jerked around. Sam stood just behind her.

He forced a smile he didn't feel, reaching out and

touching her briefly on the shoulder. "Sorry, I didn't mean to startle you, Red."

Giving an inward sigh of relief that he was calling her Red, she took it as a hopeful sign. "I guess I'm jumpier than I thought," Megan admitted. Sam wore the body-hugging G-suit on the lower half of his body. It made her hotly aware of his masculinity, his wonderful ability as a lover. "How are you doing?"

Sam stood at her shoulder and watched the last minute preparations on the *Eagle*. "Okay."

"Honest?"

His eyes crinkled at the corners. "Honest."

She turned, watching the *Eagle* crew. "I've been standing here thinking all kinds of crazy, weird things."

"Me too."

"Scary things. Awful things. What if's. Wonderful things."

The urge to reach out and embrace Megan was almost painful, but Sam stopped himself. Now was not the time or place. She looked pristine and out of place here at Ops. Refreshing. It gave him hope. Looking down, he caught and held her somber green eyes, a hint of a smile pulling at one corner of his mouth. "Want to share them with me tonight?"

Sam's teasing capped her escaping feelings, and she rallied. "Yes." And then, softly, "I'm always in awe of how we give each other strength." Megan fought back the tears. Sam didn't need to see her cry. Not now.

"I am too." He grazed her chin with his thumb. "I love you."

Megan drowned in his devastating smile that held her heart gently in his hands. The words, low and husky, surrounded her. "I love you, too. Be safe, darling . . ."

Fighting the excruciating urge to lean down and kiss her one last time warred with protocol. Holt dropped his hand from her velvety skin. "For both of us, Red. I'll meet you here after the test."

Sam was gone. Megan blinked, wondering if he'd been with her at all, or if it was her fevered imagination. Minutes later, she saw Sam and Lauren climbing the ladder and getting into the *Eagle*. Hope warred with agony. His touch might have been the last she would ever experience. His words might be the last she'd ever hear from his lips.

Pressing her hands against the cool, clammy glass, Megan absorbed the scene, burning it into her memory. After the engines were started on the jet, she saw Sam lift his gloved hand and throw her a thumbs up. It was a sign that everything was going to be fine. Would it be?

"This rain's depressing," Lauren muttered from the rear seat, the F-15 bumping along the concrete, heading for the takeoff point. The clouds had split open minutes after they had gotten in the plane. Puddles were already forming along the concrete surface.

Holt couldn't agree more. He made a concerted effort to stick to business and not allow his emotions to interfere with what had to be done.

"My check list's completed, Sam."

"Roger, Port."

"God, I hope these canards do the trick."

He smiled under his oxygen mask at Lauren's frustration. "Ease off the throttles, Port, they'll work." They *had* to. The *Eagle* felt good under his boots, the engines making the bird quiver. To him, it felt like her pulse, reminding him that she was a living, breathing thing. Most test pilots would have laughed him out of Ops if he confided that to them. That was another thing he wanted to share with Megan: how he felt about planes. Each jet was different, possessing an individual personality and temperament.

Looking up through the plexiglass canopy, the sky was getting darker, which meant more rain. Sliding the clear visor down across his eyes, Sam made sure it was tight against his mask. The red flags on either side of the runway indicated the fifteen-hundred-foot marker. To the left was a truck with civilian design engineers on board. The new test pilot, Captain Chuck Hamilton, was with them. To the right, the videotape machines and people who would man them during the test flight were ready to videotape.

Swinging the *Eagle* around, Sam scowled. Making the last-minuted checks, they were ready. His heart began a rapid pound in his chest as Port called for and received clearance from Edwards tower.

"Ready, ready, now," Lauren said.

"Roger." His gloved left hand wrapped around the throttle, easing them forward. As the F-15 began to howl, the fear rose in him. Last night, just before he'd fallen asleep in Megan's arms, she'd told him how she handled her fear.

"Just let it be there with you. Acknowledge it, but don't fight it. Let it alone, and pretty soon, it will begin to fade away because you're not putting any energy into denying it."

Compressing his lips, Sam pulled his boots off the rudders that also acted as the brakes. The F-15 lunged forward, shaking and growling like a grayhound running full tilt. Well, he was going to take her advice and try it. He didn't have any other options or ways to deal with his fear. All his previous efforts had failed.

The F-15 handled slightly differently with the canards on the nose. Holt was too busy feeling the jet out to pay much attention to anything else. After fifteen minutes, he decided to try a normal landing. Port gave him authorization, and he swung the bird into the landing pattern.

As the lip of the airstrip came up, Sam was wildly aware of the fear sitting in him. Purposefully, he left it alone, concentrating on the lift of the nose, and watched the speed indicator. As the ground came up, Holt broke into a sweat. Blinking, he held the bird steady, keeping the wings level.

"Touchdown!" Lauren announced. "Not bad, Sam. Two thousand feet. How're the canards feeling?"

He lifted the F-15 back off the runway, pulled up slats, flaps, and landing gear. "Good."

"She felt easy at two thousand."

"Roger."

"Want to try fifteen hundred?"

His sweating increased. Fear was his best friend, still there, still twisting his gut, but he refused to fight it. "Roger."

The rain worsened, the clouds gun-metal gray and hanging close to the the one-thousand-foot ceiling where they flew. The winds were changing. All of this impinged on Sam, fed through the stick he held in his right hand and boots that caressed the rudders beneath him. Lining up the F-15, he aimed it at the beginning of the runway.

Russ's face hung before him. Sam blinked away the sweat. They were descending now, four-hundred feet . . . three hundred . . . two . . . The wind sheared unexpectedly across the runway. Instantly, Holt corrected, crabbing the jet sideways to get back on glide path. *Come on,* he told the jet, *steady out. Steady out* . . . Slats and flaps were at one hundred percent. The landing gear was down and locked. Beads of perspiration trickled down the sides of his taut face.

The F-15 was shuddering, growling at being held in check to just this side of stall speed. Holt's grip on the stick tightened. He lifted the nose one degree beyond what it was supposed to be, anticipating the stall warning buzzer. Nothing happened. The plane slowed even more, the lip racing up to meet them.

Down! They were down! Instantly, Holt slammed on the brakes, reversing engine thrust, keeping the bird's nose on the white centerline. His eyes bulged. The red flags were coming up! Then, the bird rolled to a halt, a hundred feet away from the red flags.

"Bingo!" Lauren yelped happily. "Beautiful, Sam! Just beautiful!"

His cramped hand loosened around the stick. Shoving up the visor, he shakily wiped his sweaty face. "Yeah . . . good," he rasped. He'd done it! He'd landed the bird without incident! Miraculously, some of the fear was no longer with him. His stomach was still knotted, but not as painful as before.

"Let's try it again," Lauren urged excitedly.

For the next hour, they made ten landings. And ten times, the *Eagle* remained within the fifteen-hundred-foot requirements. Afterward, Holt took the bird back to the hangar, the rain continuing. Inside the hangar, he shut the jet down, raised the hood, and took a deep breath of air after unsnapping his oxygen mask. His flight suit was soaked with sweat, and he smelled like hell, but he didn't care.

On the concrete floor, Lauren leaped off the last rung of her ladder and came over, throwing her arms around him. "That was fantastic Sam! Fantastic!"

He grinned self-consciously, releasing Lauren. "Thanks, Port."

"I'm so proud of you, Sam. I knew what must be going through your mind about that crash. You did one hell of a job flying today."

Her praise was genuine, and he nodded, tucking the helmet beneath his arm. "How could I disappoint such a beautiful lady?" he teased, feeling the tension begin to dissolve within him.

"Why don't you hop a ride over to Ops and tell your lady that? I'll see you in a little while. I want to check out the canards and brakes to make sure everything's okay."

"Roger." Walking to the dark-blue truck that would take him back to Ops, all Sam wanted was for it to take him to Megan. The driver pulled to a halt in front of the concrete steps of the two-story building, and he made a run up them to get out of the downpour.

Megan stood just inside and watched Sam come through the glass doors, shaking water off his flight suit. She saw the dark patches beneath his arms, and how the suit clung to his lean, tight frame. His hair was plastered against his skull, and she realized the toll on him. When Sam lifted his head, turned toward her, she broke out into a welcoming smile.

Holt didn't care if the whole base was watching. He stepped up to Megan, dropped his helmet on a lounge chair, and swept her into his arms. Crushing her sweet, willowy form against him, he whispered against her fragrant hair, "God, I love you . . ."

Joy shimmered through Megan, the air squeezed out of her lungs, but she didn't care. Whispering his name, she kissed him, feeling the strength, the tenderness of his mouth upon hers. Breathless in the aftermath, Megan clung to him.

"You did it!"

"*We* did it," Sam corrected, grinning.

"How did you feel in the cockpit?"

"Scared as hell."

"And?"

"I just let it be, like you told me to do."

Megan gripped his shoulders, beside herself with joy. "Wonderful, Sam! Just wonderful!"

He led her down the hall, away from all the curious eyes of the enlisted people and officers. Leading her to an unused report room, he ushered her inside it. Megan giggled as he shut the door.

"Am I in trouble now that there's no audience around to watch us kiss?" she teased him. The light in his eyes was a smoldering hue, promising her so much.

Sam leaned negligently against the door and dug into one of the pockets of his flight suit. "Yeah, you're really in trouble now, Red." He located a small envelope and held it out to her.

"I made myself a promise that *if* I landed this bird safely, there was something we were going to talk seriously about. Here, take this."

Stymied, Megan took the small manila envelope that had been painfully and precisely folded many times to fit the pocket of his flight suit. She placed her purse on the table. "What's this?"

"Open it and find out."

Frowning, Megan didn't know whether he was serious or kidding her. There was a white piece of paper inside it. "Sam, what's going on here?"

He gloated, but said nothing, motioning for her to open it up.

Megan finally unfolded the paper. Her brows knitted, and then they flew upward. "*Sam!*"

"Well?"

"Uh . . . this is a marriage license."

He grinned, placing his hands on his hips, and watched her flush. "Sure is. And if you look close enough, Red, our names are on it, too. All we have to do is go get a blood test and sign it. Want to?"

Stunned, Megan stared at it for a long moment. Her

hands shook as she looked up at Sam. That cocky grin shadowed his mouth, giving him an air of arrogance. He wore it well, because Megan knew it was confidence, not pride, that radiated from him.

"Brother," Sam said to no one in particular, "this is the first time I've *ever* seen you speechless. Usually, you've got a retort ready to fire for everything I say."

"Holt, you're such a clown sometimes. Imagine this: you hand me a marriage license!"

He arched his brows. Rummaging around in another pocket, he found a small black velvet box and handed it to her. "Here, does this make you feel happier?"

Megan gave him a wary look and opened the jewelry box. She gasped. Inside was a simple gold ring inlaid with tiny rectangles of emeralds and diamonds in a row. "Oh, Sam!"

"Now what do you have to say?"

"Oh, dear . . ." Tears crowded into Megan's eyes as she picked up the ring and held it in her trembling hands.

Taking pity on her, Sam walked up and settled his hands on Megan's shoulders. "How about, yes? That's all I need to hear."

Sniffing, Megan looked up into his deadpan features. Gone was the teasing. Instead, his eyes were dark with fear and hope. Fear, that she might say no. Hope, that she might say yes. "This-this is so unexpected, Sam."

"Do you like the ring? I wanted emeralds to match the color of your eyes."

"I—beautiful, yes, the ring is breathtaking . . ."

"So are you," and he gently brought her into his embrace, holding her lustrous gaze. "Well? Will you consent to be Mrs. Megan Roberts Holt? Or maybe Megan Holt? Or maybe Ms. Roberts Holt. I really don't care which way you want it, as long as you say yes."

Dissolving into tears of laughter and happiness, Megan rested her head against his shoulder. "Yes, Sam Holt. *Yes!* My God, if I didn't say the word, you'd have badgered it out of me just to marry you!"

Relief, sweet and flowing, swept through Holt as he held Megan against him. "You're right," he agreed with a chuckle. "Did I ever tell you what they called me back in flight school?"

Megan knew every fighter pilot had a nickname, and was frequently called by it, rather than his real name. "No. What?"

"Badger."

She gave him a dirty look. "It figures."

"It fits," Sam warned her. And then, he took the ring and slipped it on her left hand. Proudly, he looked at it and then up at Megan. "What do you think?"

"It's lovely, Sam. I've never seen one like it."

"You won't either. I designed it, and then took it to a jeweler down in Los Angeles to make it." He smiled happily. "A rare ring for a rare lady."

Touched, Megan looked up at him, content to be in his arms. "Our marriage isn't going to be all roses, Holt."

"What one is?"

"I'm still afraid of you being a test pilot."

"And I'm still afraid of dying. Can we be scared together?"

"As long as you and I can talk and share what our feelings are," Megan whispered, "I think we can have a very happy marriage."

Sam sobered. "We'll always talk," he promised her. Running his hand across her hair, he said, "What about kids?"

"At least half a dozen."

"*What?*"

Demurely, Megan looked at him through her lashes. "Too many?"

"My paycheck will never afford that many, sweetheart."

"Two or three, then?"

"I can live with that. How about you?"

She smiled tenderly. "I think we'll make very good parents to however many children we decide to have, darling."

With a groan, Sam said, "Talk about a bunch of little hellions . . . our daughters and sons will have my badgering disposition with *your* red hair!"

Megan threw her arms around his shoulders, languishing

in his hot, melting assault on her lips. In the haze of joy that wove and bound them to one another, Megan looked forward to their life together. Ghosts from their past were in the process of being laid to rest. They had trusted one another enough to share their fears and problems. And because they had, their reward was one another. Megan wanted nothing else. Ever.

GET
LOVESTRUCK!

AND GET STRIKING ROMANCES FROM POPULAR LIBRARY'S BELOVED AUTHORS

Watch for these exciting romances in the months to come:

June 1990
NIGHT FLIGHT by Eileen Nauman

July 1990
BEYOND THE SAVAGE SEA by Jo Ann Wendt

August 1990
THREADS OF DESTINY by Arnette Lamb

September 1990
BY INVITATION ONLY by Catherine Craco

October 1990
PASSION'S CHOICE by Gloria Dale Skinner